True Story

The Deverells, Book One

Jayne Fresina

A TE PUBLISHING SERVICES BOOK

True Story
The Deverells, Book One
Copyright © 2015 by Jayne Fresina

Cover design by K Designs
All cover art and logo copyright © 2015, TE Publishing Services.

ISBN: 1512197432
ISBN-13: 978-1512197433

Olivia Monday, an impoverished widow, has taken a position as "secretary" to an eccentric, scandalous rake - a divorced man with a brood of eight children and at least two gun-shot wounds. For one year, against the advice of her remaining family members, she agrees to live in his remote Cornish castle and put pen to paper on his behalf.

Despite everything she's heard about him, she's unafraid. Olivia welcomes the distraction this unusual post will provide— as well as the large fee— because the alternative of relying on relatives to put a roof over her head is intolerable.

True Deverell has decided it's time to set the record straight. He means to dictate his memoirs to this little widow who, according to the instructions he sent to his solicitor, should merely be plain and have a neat hand. Those are his only requirements. He doesn't want any distractions, has endured his fill of scandal and intends now to leave the "True Story" on paper so that perhaps, one day, people will forgive his mistakes.

But when Mrs. Olivia Monday arrives on his doorstep in her leaky boots and crumpled bonnet, True realizes that perhaps his story isn't over yet.

Jayne Fresina

Chapter One
The Offices of Chalke, Westcott & Chalke.
Three O'clock in the afternoon, Tuesday, March 12, 1832

"Get out of my blasted way," the menacing, deeply disgruntled voice rumbled above her. "What *are* you doing, woman?"

On her knees before him, head down, Olivia Westcott scrambled for the spilled papers that cascaded around his boots when the man bumped into her.

"Some ruse to pick my pockets, eh?" he growled. "Where's your slick-fingered accomplice, or did you think to fleece me by yourself?"

"Sir, I—"

"Good God, must you wretched creatures lie in wait everywhere I turn?"

It was fortunate for this stranger that while assisting in her father's office, Olivia had promised to be on her best behavior. She didn't want to be sent home to embroider yet another ugly fire screen or paint watery, depressing landscapes. So, rather than answer as she would in a Utopia of justice and equality, she bit her tongue, held her temper and said, "Sir, pardon me, but you're standing on the papers."

Great Aunt Jane, always her most indomitable critic, would have been impressed.

Still the towering monolith did not move. His contempt bore down upon her. "Bloody women! Always underfoot."

With one knuckle she nudged her spectacles back up her nose and raised her improved gaze only as far as his knees, where the tip of a riding crop tapped smartly against his mud-splattered breeches. "I

5

Jayne Fresina

wouldn't be underfoot sir, if you hadn't bowled into me."

"You shot out of nowhere. If I didn't have my wits about me, I could have trampled you into the floorboards."

The last sheet was stuck under his heel. "Please move your foot, sir. No! *The other one.*""I suppose you were wandering with your head in the clouds, daydreaming. Relying upon other folk to pay attention."

"I can assure you I was not. *Sir! Your foot!*" Anyone would think he deliberately delayed getting off her paper.

"Butter-fingers, is that not the expression?"

"Better that than Butter-brained." It slipped out on a sly breath before she could restrain herself.

"Tsk, tsk, you know what they say about women with sharp tongues."

"No. Do tell. I am all agog to hear it." Oh dear, now more words came out that shouldn't, linked like scarves pulled from a conjurer's mouth. "And clearly you want to enlighten me."

He replied coolly, "One day they find themselves surrounded by castrated men."

"A tragedy, to be sure. For the men."

At last she pulled the trampled paper free, although it was now decorated with a large, dirty shoe print. Before she could get up off her knees, the man lost his patience and, as if she was nothing more than a puddle in the street, he stepped over her.

"Look where you're going in future, young woman."

She recovered from the indignity just in time to witness his head contact briskly— and most satisfyingly— with the low lintel of the doorway.

"Did the doorframe come out of nowhere too?" she inquired politely.

He stopped with his back to her. "You think that was amusing."

"Well, it does have a certain piquancy, sir." Mimicking his previous tone of condescension, she added, "You know what they say about men who live in glasshouses."

"Yes. They pay a very high window tax." He half turned his head, but not far enough to reveal more than a little cheek and some dark side-whiskers above the tall collar of his greatcoat. No longer quite so terse and angry, his voice warmed with a hint of self-deprecating humor. "And, as I have found, they ought to keep their clothes on unless they have a fancy to exhibit for their neighbors."

He didn't turn to see her blush. In the next moment he was gone and the walls around her seemed to exhale a collective sigh of wanton languor.

"Are you alright, my dear?" Her father had come to find his papers.

"Was that a client of yours?" she asked with as much nonchalance as she could muster.

"That was... a gentleman currently embroiled in a divorce being handled by Mr. Chalke," he replied gravely, taking the documents from her. "Best stay out of his path, Olivia."

"Why?" Her heart was beating too fast, too hard.

"Must you always question, my dear? Now where is the tea?"

She had forgotten it. Vowing to remedy the oversight at once, Olivia waited with her hands meekly behind her back, until her father had retreated inside his office. Then she hurried to the window.

There he was— Mr. Incivility—already down the stairs and emerging into the street. He put on his hat, nodded briskly to the boy who held his horse and tossed the lad some coins. Olivia willed him to look up, so she might see his face, but he didn't.

Glancing at the clock on the mantle, she noted it was just after three. It was a habit of hers to mark the exact time at certain important moments in her life. She stored them all in her brain like ledgers on a dusty shelf. Her stepbrother thought that very odd and mocked her for it, as he did about most things.

But what made this moment so important that it deserved commemoration?

As soon as her father mentioned the man's purpose there she realized who he was. Divorce was rare, almost unheard of, and those few who attempted it became infamous. Anyone who read a newspaper knew *his* name. Consequently, Olivia also knew why her father advised her to stay out of his path. A properly raised young woman of good family should avoid the company of that gentleman. In fact, many people refused to call him a gentleman at all. No one seemed to know where he came from, although there was a general consensus as to where he'd end up.

"Self-made, indeed," she'd once heard Great Aunt Jane exclaim in a huff. "Gentlemen are not *made*. They are born."

Olivia considered that a rather snobbish view, especially coming from a lady who was only a few steps away from debtor's prison for most of her adult life and relied upon the charity of relatives to keep a roof over her head.

She thought back to a conversation several years

ago when that same lady, having remarked upon Olivia's misfortune in losing her mother at such a young age— as if it was a tragedy somehow due to the little girl's own carelessness—went on to criticize her complexion, her lack of social graces and her posture.

"Straighten your spine, girl! You will develop a most unbecoming slouch if my nephew doesn't put you in a backboard immediately. Who will you ever find to marry, child, if you don't improve your posture, take up some feminine pursuits and learn to hold a sensible conversation? What gentleman of any worth would look at such a sulky, sullen, willful creature with a fascination for wicked pranks? You won't be fit for polite society."

This lecture came about because Olivia had sculpted a piece of parsnip to look like a finger, coated the end of it in raspberry jam, and then placed it on the pianoforte keys, to be discovered when the instrument was opened.

"You are a horrid, unseemly child with a dark and devious imagination, Olivia Westcott. I cannot think what will become of you."

To which she replied, "I shall marry Mr. True Deverell, shan't I? People say he's not fit for polite society either. But he's rich as Croesus and I hear he knows his way under a woman's petticoats."

This bold declaration had shocked everyone present into silence. These things — and men— weren't meant for drawing room conversation in mixed company, and the adults were probably wondering where she'd even heard his name. But Olivia was not the sort of girl who listened quietly and contentedly to sweet fairy tales. "Once upon a time" made her want to spit nails. Once upon *what* time? *When*? What on earth did that even mean, for pity's sake? How could anyone take such a feeble, flimsy narrative seriously?

No indeed, Olivia preferred darkly gothic yarns and bloodthirsty horror stories not meant for the ears of little girls. Should that mean eavesdropping at keyholes to get her entertainment, so be it. Even if she didn't fully understand what she heard.

In any case, on that long-ago occasion, the mention of his name had got her sent up to bed immediately, saving her from a very dull evening. As she ascended the stairs, she overheard the adults discussing her.

"One must make allowances for the poor child, growing up motherless."

"Allowances? Where would we be if we made *allowances* for bad behavior? Another sliding of standards! No, no, that girl was impertinent long before she lost her mother, who was herself a stubborn creature with a distressingly romantic view of life and her head in the clouds. What my nephew saw in her I'll never know. A difficult woman."

Was she? Olivia had known her living mother for eight years and, at the time of this conversation, been without her for two, yet already shards of memory were breaking away and leaving her, like pieces of a shattered mirror that glittered brightly as they spun into darkness. She tried holding on to the broken glass even when it hurt her small hands and made her cry, but tears were something she had to hide from her father, who never wept himself and had no patience for those who did. He was, of course, cut from the same cloth as Great Aunt Jane, who placed extreme importance on the immovability of one's upper lip, which should remain as constant as one's temper and the heat of one's blood. A passionate display of any kind was anathema in their family. Surrounded by these strong, rather formidable characters, Olivia struggled to follow their example and keep her real thoughts and feelings to herself. Especially those she secretly nurtured about dangerous men.

By the age of eighteen she thought she had those feelings fairly well under control. Fairly.

Peering down through the window again, she watched Mr. Incivility ride away down the busy thoroughfare. The brim of that tall hat still hid his face, but her gaze followed him until her breath clouded the view.

So there he went. The notorious True Deverell. He who must not be mentioned.

She really couldn't see what all the fuss was about.

A storm in a teacup.

Oops, the tea! Where was her mind today?

Why, where else should a young woman's mind be? On the man her ten year-old self once proclaimed she was going to marry, of course. Whether the poor fellow liked it or not.

With an unladylike snort of laughter at her own foolishness, she turned away from the window.

"A man like that uses women for only one thing," her stepbrother had exclaimed once, when he looked over her shoulder to catch her reading a lascivious piece about Deverell in the newspaper. "But the scoundrel would never look twice at you, Livy, so you are quite safe."

And that, she mused, was precisely where men like True Deverell went wrong, because they didn't see her coming and then they tripped over her. Poor mutton-head, wouldn't know a decent woman if he bumped into her. A fact of which she now had evidence.

True Deverell. Even his name sounded as if it ought to be whispered. It slipped off the tongue like a silky sheet from a bare thigh.

"Olivia," her father called from his office, "The *tea*, if you please! Or must I send for it from China?"

Oops.

It was lucky she could blame her pink face on steam from the teakettle.

Chapter Two

A sniff skyward told him when, or if, he might soon hope to feed. The creak of the farmhouse kitchen door and the clang of a spoon, audible to him from two fields away, turned his direction as sharply as a shepherd's whistle called dogs to heel.

But when the scraps were put out, he waited until the other strays had taken their share before he dove for his, scurrying away with it into the bushes, or the barn, just as they did.

Once, when he lay curled up sick in the hay, an old sheepdog bitch brought him some food, carrying it across the yard in her mouth. Accustomed to his presence as if he was one of her own litter, her mothering instinct was too strong to let him suffer. It was the only act of tenderness he ever knew.

Years later, when someone eventually asked his name, he chose the first that came to mind; the name of the half-blind, sweet old bitch that once fed him— True.

* * * *

London, 1840

There hadn't been time to undress her, nor even exchange more than a few words. But then he was never much of a polite conversationalist.

Not that she would mind, of course. He was not generally wanted for his conversation, but for one of two things: his money or his skills in the bedchamber. He was known to be generous with both, although, in the latter case, he often wondered how the original compared to the fantasy. Women built things up in their minds and saw only what they wanted to see.

13

When they found his tastes a little *too* "uncivilized", and they had their eyes opened to reality, it was then he who was at fault. It was he who broke their hearts and abused them, destroyed their innocence. As if he had proven to them that the Beast never would change for Beauty, a hard truth they could not bear to believe.

"Oh, Mr. Deverell..."

The woman clawed at his back, her body pressed urgently to his, her gasping breaths pummeling his cheek.

But even as her hands wandered, so did his mind.

The first galloping hooves of thunder approached over the rooftops, obscuring her panting pleas. The deep, powerful rumble seemed, to him, like something more than the warning of a storm and tonight his skin reacted to that vibration with more eagerness than it did to the touch of a woman.

A happening beyond a spell of bad weather was coming to change his world, he sensed it. The air was thick with anticipation for more than a brief tryst. Deverell, whose life had been unpredictable as the weather itself, just didn't know what. Yet.

Her hands slipped downward, under his loosened breeches, her fingernails digging hard into his tense buttocks. He groaned. *Ouch, that would leave a mark.* What was it about women that they always wanted to leave their mark on him? He'd had nails scraped across him more times than a carpenter's bench.

Wait...was her name... Violet? Iris? Lily? Something floral, he was almost certain. For now, "Miss Pridemore" would have to do. It was unlikely he would have reason to know her as anything more.

Below his chamber, a masquerade party was at

full clamor. Such events at his London house were legendary for their Bacchanalian quality, and True continued the tradition, despite the mellowing of a once insatiable, impatient appetite for all things wicked. And people came, despite the host's dark reputation— or because of it, in some cases. But frankly, he'd begun to find these parties deadly dull. Too much of a good thing, perhaps? Tonight he'd taken the chance to slip away quietly for some time alone, and when Miss Pridemore came scratching at his door he almost hadn't let her in. Then he decided he needed something to help him sleep, so why not? He wasn't the sort for warm milk and a wooly cap— if he ever resorted to that, they might as well dig his grave.

There were too many distractions tonight, however. Internal *and* external.

Over the woman's head, through his open window, he watched clouds roiling and bubbling, waiting for another brilliant, jagged spike to part the sky. To his eyes, that raw, untamed beauty was far more exciting than the carefully cultivated prettiness of the willing young creature on his bed. It couldn't be helped; his attention was seized by the striking, untamed view above the black silhouette of spires and chimneys.

As a stronger breeze pushed at the curtains, he felt the first drop of rain, like the damp thumbprint of a parson, christening his brow

"Oh, Mr. Deverell," the woman beneath him exclaimed in a louder voice, sensing perhaps that his mind was elsewhere. "What must you think of me?"

"*Think* of you?" He finally looked down at her. Was she blushing? Hard to tell in the dim light of one oil lamp, but the odds were against it. A bashful woman wouldn't come knocking on his door, and one attired in frilly garters beneath layers of costly lace and silk petticoat, meant for them to be seen and appreciated. He'd only seen women dressed this way in Parisian bordellos.

"Being engaged...and yet sneaking into your room. Like this." She ran a fingernail down his bared chest, and trailed it through the dark curls of hair. "I don't know what came over me."

A few years ago he wouldn't have cared that she had a fiancé, anymore than he would care if she had a husband. If a woman grew bored and came seeking him out for a stolen interlude, why disappoint her? Women were created for sport. They existed for man's pleasure.

Except for his own daughter, of course, he thought sharply. Damn.

And there lay the crux of the matter— the reason for these unsettled thoughts.

He was the father of a fifteen year-old girl and constantly reminded of this discomforting fact: where once he was the fox, now he was the farmer.

He suffered a painful pinch in his gut, followed by a rapid deflating. Again he looked down at Miss Pridemore, who must have a father somewhere and who he really shouldn't have let into his room.

It was no good; he had completely lost the desire to proceed.

Abruptly he rolled off the bed and pulled up his breeches. "I'm afraid I must say good evening, madam. It was a mistake to let you into my room tonight. Forgive me, but I'm much too tired and won't be able to entertain you after all."

The pink ribbon of her mouth unraveled downward at the corners. Her eyes looked puzzled. "I...I suppose I ought to call off my engagement now."

"Whatever you think best," he muttered, bemused. "I am the last man in the world to ask about marriage and commitment." Searching in the dim light for his shirt, which had previously been tossed to the carpet, he added, "But since you came after me like a bitch in heat tonight, I'd advise you to carefully consider your motives in marrying. Before you ruin a few innocent lives."

He really thought he was being helpful.

Apparently not.

The silk slipper, hurled at the back of his head, narrowly missed as he ducked at the same moment to retrieve his shirt.

"A bitch in heat?" she exclaimed. "How dare you?!"

"In what other way might your behavior be described?" He saw no insult in it. Dogs, in his opinion, were an improvement on the human race. They knew what they needed to survive and went after it without excuses, procrastination and guilt. Dogs didn't lie.

"As if you did not encourage me!"

"Encourage you? Madam, when you arrived at my door with such clear intentions I thought it only polite to let you in."

Like most women he'd known, however briefly, she preferred another view of the circumstances that got her to his bed. God forbid, she take any responsibility on her own shoulders. "You are a wicked seducer! I don't know how you can look at

17

yourself in the mirror."

He began to wonder if she was an actress. She was certainly performing now.

And then she added, "Attempting to deflower your own son's fiancée!"

"I beg your pardon?"

More rain blew in at his window, but he made no move to close it.

She snatched her slipper from his hand. "That's right, Mr. Deverell. Your own son. What do you suppose Ransom will have to say when I tell him about this?"

Ah. He might have known. History repeating itself — or rather, reversing itself, since it was he who once seduced his own father's fiancée.

This was unfortunate. He wasn't on the best of terms with his eldest, legitimate son and this would certainly put another cat among the pigeons. Ransom was a hot-head, always looking for an excuse to side with his mama, despite the fact that she'd never been the maternal type and used her children as nothing more than weapons and leverage against her former husband at every opportunity.

He cursed under his breath— didn't approve of his offspring at these parties, but some were old enough now to do as they pleased. And they did, taking after him in more ways than he cared to admit.

Ransom, he thought crossly, needed something to make use of his time and intelligence. Both were clearly being wasted. Better amend that at once.

"I didn't see my son downstairs tonight."

"That's the trouble, Mr. Deverell." Her laughter scratched at the air. "He says you never do see him."

"Nor did I hear about any engagement."

"He didn't want to tell you until tomorrow, after the other guests left. For some reason he's afraid of you and had to get up the gumption. So now what are you going to do?" The woman was triumphant, eyes agleam. "What would my silence be worth to you?"

"Silence about what? You came to my door begging to be let in. Fortunately, I retrieved my senses before anything really happened."

"That's my word against yours," she replied, lashes flapping. "Who do you think he'll believe? I'm sure you have some way to ensure my discretion. A pair of diamond earrings, perhaps. Like those they say once belonged to Marie Antoinette— that you demanded back from your wife when she left you. I'd happily take those as your wedding gift to a future daughter-in-law. Or some equal payment."

He watched her calmly as another flare of white lightning ripped across the angry sky and lit her smug face. "I'm not going to pay you a penny, Miss Pridemore. I wouldn't want you to feel like a blackmailing whore."

She squinted very slightly, her lips ruffled with a quick intake of breath.

"It matters not to me, whatever you tell my son," he added, shrugging into his waistcoat. "Firstly, at only nineteen he's too young to marry and, secondly, I'm aware my sons will attract women who want them for all the wrong reasons. My cubs have yet to learn that money is the motivating force for most females. You will, no doubt, be a harsh but necessary lesson for him."

"You really are a rotten bastard!"

"Precisely." He buttoned his waistcoat. "But despite my best efforts to go to my grave a selfish old rake, I still care about my ungrateful litter. Alas, I can't help myself. So if you don't tell him, perhaps I should."

"I doubt he would thank you for the lesson."

He sighed. "I have found fatherhood, on the whole, to be a thankless task."

"Fatherhood?" she spat. "From what he tells me, you don't know the meaning of the word."

"As well as you know the definition of fiancée."

The thwarted Miss Pridemore left in a flurry of perfumed lace and silk, flushed livid and muttering under her breath.

He kicked the door shut after her.

Well, that was no great loss. His son would recover. Deverells were resilient. They had to be.

Foolish woman. Had she simply asked him for money and explained honestly why she needed it, he would have given her some. But if there was one thing he couldn't abide it was vicious deceit, especially when it would hurt one of his litter.

Another rumble of thunder echoed overhead and he smiled, the tension in his shoulders relaxing.

He loved a good thunderstorm. It was said that an old gypsy woman had found him as a babe washed up on a Cornish beach after a shipwreck, during a particularly brutal tempest, so perhaps that was why it affected him. When Nature took its temper out on the land, bending trees with the power of its wrath and cracking a silver whip across the sky, True Deverell felt his blood surge with energy as if he was one with the storm, his body rejuvenated by it, reborn.

Once, at a very grand party he'd attended without an invitation, a gossiping old hag had exclaimed,

"You, sir, will go back to hell the same way you came out of it. And the sooner the better."

Yes, many folk liked to tell him how they thought his end would come— if the hangman's noose or a vengeful victim of his astute card playing didn't get him first. True rather enjoyed the idea of meeting his end during a roll of thunder or a sizzling flare of lightening. In a storm like this one tonight, for instance.

But although he knew the haughty woman at that party had referred to bad weather, he chose to misunderstand her.

"There is every chance you're right, madam," he'd replied. "I'm quite sure that as I came into this life between a woman's thighs, there is every chance I'll leave the same way. I certainly hope so."

Remembering that harpy's shocked, indignant face, his smile broadened. How satisfying it was to get the last word over her sort.

Funny how the upper classes felt they had a right to say anything they wanted to him, while he was supposed to mind his manners, just because he was a foundling. But despite Deverell's harsh beginnings, he was now a man of wealth and power. Society couldn't keep him out. They couldn't ignore him, because he had something they wanted— and yet he didn't need anything from them in return, and that troubled the upper classes. He wasn't one of their "sort" and never would be, but he had a damn good time making his presence felt among them. A stray dog worrying the sheep.

He straightened his cravat, smoothed a hand over his dark hair, and checked his reflection in the tall mirror as another blast of lightning lit the room.

Wind filled the drapes behind his image so that they swelled and lifted, a backdrop of luxurious silken sails.

You are a wicked seducer! I don't know how you can look at yourself in the mirror. Attempting to deflower your own son's fiancée!

Deflower, indeed! He very much doubted there were any petals left to be plucked on that particular bloom.

He laughed and gave his twin in the mirror a cheery wink, which was, of course reciprocated.

That's how I look at myself, young lady, he mused. A man could always be sure of an understanding ally when he looked in the glass. No other soul would ever know him so well, would they?

Unless...perhaps one day, if he wrote his memoirs.

Not that he owed anyone an explanation, but really he ought to tell the whole story. His side. One day, once he felt he'd done all the living, he'd write a book about it. Then finally his children might understand—

Suddenly the door swung open and Ransom stood there with a pistol in one hand, pointed in a manner that left no question of his intent, despite the slightly weaving motion of that tall, lean body.

Thunder bounced and banged across the sky.

"Just couldn't keep it in your breeches could you, father?" Ransom slurred as he stumbled forward and his shoulder hit the doorframe.

There was a flash, a loud crack, and True Deverell had only one thought.

Damn. Should have started his memoirs sooner.

Chapter Three
The Coast of Cornwall
Half past seven in the evening, (an approximation due to
circumstances of travel), Wednesday, August 31st, 1842.

The jagged cliff edge appeared to crumble away
beneath them, and it was a mystery how the horses
found their footing. Venturing to look out through
the carriage window was not for the faint of heart, but
while her traveling companions avoided the thrilling
view on the left side of the vessel, Olivia admired it
bravely, longing for a gulp of that fresh sea air. The
interior of the coach was crowded, stale, and she was
crushed so far into a corner that if the door should
suddenly fly open she would undoubtedly tumble to
her death.

It was not a prospect that worried her unduly.

Certainly there was little left for her on this side
of the divide and if her end came about by catapulting
out of a speeding carriage, the event would have a
satisfyingly dramatic flourish. She pictured the
curiously shaped dent her corpse would make in the
wet sand below. Some mischievous person might
carve a commemorative line into the cliff side.

In this place Olivia Westcott Ollerenshaw Pemberton
Monday finally left a good impression.

A figure suddenly passed into view— a man on
horseback galloping through the rippling waves of the
pretty bay below, scattering a flock of gulls up against
the strawberry sunset. The rider drew level with the
coach and then, in a wild, frothy spray, pulled ahead
with ease, leaving a mess of hoof marks across the
formerly pristine sand.

Of course, any time there was a peaceful scene a

man could be counted upon to spoil it.

While a woman riding alone in such a fashion would be subject to censure, that handsome creature was free to race with the wind and the tide, foam and seaweed flying up his riding boots and sticking to his breeches. He wore no coat, just the white sleeves of his shirt, curving like the sails of a racing frigate. He was hatless, his hair on the longer side, flowing defiantly free in the wind.

Shocking! As prickly old Great Aunt Jane was fond of exclaiming, *Another example of standards slipping. Where shall we all be in twenty years when such liberties are taken with propriety?*

Today Olivia agreed with her. Was the man on such an urgent mission that this state of undress was really necessary? Did he think he was a character in a gothic romance?

She shook her head, tut-tutting softly under her breath. Good thing she didn't have to do *his* laundry, whoever he was.

Despite his wild pace, she was forced to admit that he sat well in the saddle, managing the power of that horse with a firm hand and skilled thighs. Not that she ought to be looking at his thighs or even thinking of their bulging existence. That sort of thing had got her into trouble before, with her first husband— delightfully naughty Captain Ollerenshaw. Poor Freddy. Some would say she should have learned her lesson with Freddy.

"*She's doing it again,*" she could hear her stepbrother exclaim in the distant corridors of her twisted mind. "*Someone ought to stop her.*"

While Olivia was still thinking about not looking at the man on the horse, he lifted slightly from the saddle, showing a glimpse of taut, tidy buttock.

She must have sighed out loud then– or made some sound— for several faces turned to stare at her, their curiosity burning holes through her widow's veil.

Slowly she sank into the corner again, giving up her splendid view. When a heavy-breathing, red-faced gentleman seated opposite continued to stare at her while running a thick tongue over his sparse front teeth, she closed her eyes, escaped into darkness and willed the wheels to spin faster, the horses' hooves to sprout wings.

At last the coach turned right. Crackling and creaking like an old lung, it pulled into the yard of a noisy inn and came to a groaning, depressed halt. To Olivia's intense relief, all the remaining passengers emptied out, leaving the interior to her alone. No one else, it seemed, cared to venture farther along the rocky coastline today, and most of them looked back at her as if she was mad to try it.

But now she had the coach to herself. Heaven! So for those last few miles, back on the cliff road and winding downhill, she made an attempt, finally, at a real nap, only to be bounced savagely awake by a violent jolt just as she found a semi-comfortable spot for her head.

Tipping forward, her bottom almost sliding off the seat, she heard the coachman curse loudly— having no care for the ears of a lady— and then he yelled, "Can't get no further up yon lane. Mrs. be trottin' rest o' way to the Devil's 'Ell on her own hoofs before the tide comes in."

The Cornish accent was thick, but she caught enough of it to understand that this is where she was to be dumped out of the coach and left to her own fate. And yes, she was familiar by now with the name the locals had given to Roscarrock Castle— Devil's Hell. A charming alias full of wholesome, welcoming warmth.

The sunset had turned a sinister shade of blood and ochre, and the sound of the sea— once a distant, lazy sizzle over sand —was now closer, a rhythmic, disgruntled slapping against rock. The tide was coming in and before too long the rocky outcrop on which her destination crouched menacingly would be cut off from the mainland until tomorrow. If she didn't make haste to beat the sea's advance, she could be swept into the water and drowned.

Really, she thought in some bemusement, a man could not get much farther from civilization, or discourage it from visiting quite so effectively.

But Olivia was not afraid of the darkening sky, the encroaching tide, or of walking alone. Or of much at all, she liked to think. If she were, she wouldn't be there now, would she? Certainly enough people had warned her not to go, citing the dangerous reputation of the man who had— by letter and, as far as he knew, entirely sight unseen— engaged her as his secretary.

She opened the carriage door, took her hatbox from under the seat and climbed out while the grumbling coachman untied her trunk.

The remaining stretch of causeway shone damply ahead of her, seawater already pooling on the stone. It was a treacherous path of lumps and bumps leading to the steps that would take her up the side of a craggy island to the grim silhouette of the house.

At least the coachman had got her as far as he could. Olivia thanked him and counted some coins from her purse, laying each one carefully in the palm of his outstretched hand, while she felt his eyes staring at her, hard and disapproving.

"You sure now, Mrs.? T'aint much of a place for a frail bit o' woman like yerself. If yer mind be changed, I can take yer back with me to the town."

Frail bit of woman? Olivia wanted to laugh. She was eight and twenty, had survived three husbands, a jilting fiancé and five wet winters in the same pair of walking-boots so shamefully full of holes that she never dared change in or out of them in the company of others. She may not possess great beauty or a heavy purse, but having never known circumstances that were anything other than reduced, she was adaptable, capable and never balked at a challenge. "No. Thank you. I shall be quite alright."

He looked at her again as if he thought her unhinged. "You do know about yon feller and his wicked ways, since backalong eh?"

"I do indeed." She'd even met him once, ten years ago—well she'd met his large stubborn feet anyway— when he stepped over her in her father's office.

"It ain't put you off?"

"Not at all. I am not afraid of my employer."

"Employer?" The coachman's scowl deepened another few notches. It was not considered genteel and certainly it was rare for a lady of "good" family to earn a living, but Olivia considered this attitude remarkably cavalier, since it assumed that all such ladies would find a man willing to keep them fed and warm— and in fine shoes— until the end of their days. What if she never found a man? Or what if she found several and they kept dying tragically and in

27

near poverty, until she was finally left with nothing but some books, walking boots full of holes and the very small portion left to her by her father? A portion, by the way, that could barely cover the cost of an annual coal supply for a small house. Then, that unfortunate widow would become a burden to relatives, or at the mercy of the parish and sent to the workhouse.

The shadow of miserable Great Aunt Jane Westcott loomed over her in warning, every time she thought of how she might end up if she sat back and let fate take its course.

No, Olivia would make her own future, take her opportunities as they came, and stand on her own two feet. They were not large and they were invariably cold, due to circumstances already mentioned, but they were competent. Like the rest of her.

"You see, I have an advantage over Mr. Deverell," she told the coachman.

"What advantage could you 'ave over that feller, missy?" the old fellow muttered dolefully.

"While I know all about Mr. Deverell's wicked ways," she smiled, folding her widow's veil back over her bonnet, "I'm sure nobody has warned him about *mine*."

Even as she said it, she thought what a good thing it was that Sergeant O'Grady of the London Metropolitan Police wasn't nearby to hear. That fellow already had some dreadful suspicions about her and he quite lacked a sense of humor.

Oops, not Sergeant any longer, she corrected herself; he had recently been promoted to *Inspector* O'Grady, since the formation of the new detective division. He had taken pains to inform her of his advancement.

But despite the title, as her stepbrother pointed out, he was still the same "ill-mannered vulture in cheaply tailored clothes."

Poor Inspector O'Grady. She would miss their little chats.

* * * *

"We weren't expecting you today," the sour-faced butler objected, as if Olivia's windblown arrival was a great inconvenience.

"But the arrangement was for me to come today, was it not?" she said with as much politesse as she could manage after dragging her trunk and hatbox across a wet, slippery causeway, then up a flight of no fewer than ten stone steps.

"No one ever gets here as planned, madam. Not with these roads. They usually get held up at least a day, sometimes a week." His thick, grey-tipped brows lowered and drew close, forming a shape not unlike the wings of a hawk about to swoop down and seize its prey. "Often they never arrive at all. The master has been known to make wagers on whether or not an expected guest will get here in one piece. He finds it most amusing."

There was a time when she would have appreciated the entertainment value of such a sport, it must be said, but Olivia had formed a distaste for gambling since her first husband's demise. "Well, I suppose one must fill the time however one can in such a place as this, but your master will lose if he bets against me. When I say I am going to be somewhere on a certain day, at a certain time, you can rest assured I'll be there in my best hat and coat."

The butler cast a cold, disdainful eye over her damp and sandy bonnet, before his gaze slid downward to the saltwater stain around the hem of her coat.

"The tide came in faster than I could drag my trunk along," she explained.

As she first began climbing the steps to the house, Olivia had paused to wonder whether she truly needed any of the items in that trunk. The temptation to let it fall into the sea was all too powerful as her temper mounted and her arms grew tired. But she'd recovered her determination and managed eventually, with no help from anyone, to mount those steps and haul her luggage along behind her.

Well, at least it wasn't raining, she thought.

She used to love the rain— the sound and smell of it in the morning, and the birds singing afterward, but lately the rain seemed crueler, angrier. It was more of a nuisance than it used to be. Probably because she was getting older.

"The master of the house did receive the messages I sent along my route, did he not?""Yes, madam, he did receive your messages."

"Then he knew—"

"He wondered why you thought he might care, madam."

She stared.

"You weren't any use to him until you got here," the butler added. "*If* you got here. So he really wasn't interested in your messages en route. The odds, he said, were against you."

Olivia wanted to laugh suddenly. To fall to her knees and laugh hysterically until they took her away to Bedlam. Perhaps it was tiredness after her journey, but everything about this venture now seemed so ridiculous she didn't think she could go on. It was, however, only a moment of doubt— like that pause on the steps when she feared the weight of her trunk was too much. Somehow she composed herself.

Do not let this get the better of you, my dear. Do not show that it matters. Whatever you are feeling now, it will pass. Worthy advice from her second husband, elderly Sir Allardyce Pemberton, a firm advocate of keeping up appearances— a fact to which his extensive and colorful wig collection could attest, before it was confiscated by the bailiffs, along with everything else he'd owned.

"But I am here now, aren't I? Despite the odds."

The butler's eyebrows writhed and his lips reluctantly cracked apart. "Apparently. Madam. And in your *best* hat."

She ignored his tone and prompted gently, "So Mr. Deverell might want to know I've arrived."

"Now?" he drew back, looking horrified. "He won't want to see *you* yet. These days, he says, women upset his indigestion after sunset."

Olivia suspected he was trying to frighten her off just like everybody else. Wearily she replied, "Yes, that is when we ladies are at our most dangerous. That, and when we haven't eaten for an extended period. As indeed, I have not."

She waited, but no offer issued forth from those tight lips.

"You do have a bed for me?" she added.

"There's plenty of beds," he snapped. "But none aired."

Having waited again to see if he might come up

with a solution, she finally suggested, "Perhaps while I have something to eat, a bed could be warmed?"

"Dinner was cleared an hour ago at least."

"But there is food in the kitchen? Anything will do. I can cook for myself. I've had nothing all day and although it may not be ladylike to admit it, I'm fair famished."

His lips parted in a tense murmur, as if he feared the words might cost him coin. "Yes. Madam."

Removing her gloves, Olivia looked around at the dark paneling and the shifting shadows of the medieval hall.

Suddenly she realized there was a man standing on the stairs. He'd been there listening all along? Her heartbeat scrambled for balance, like a cat on a rolling barrel. But when the butler raised his oil lamp to point her in the direction of the kitchen, she saw tongues of light lick not only at the tall, still figure, but at a large, gilt frame surrounding it.

Her pulse slowed to a steadier pace. Good heavens, it was only a portrait. Life-size.

As the glow of the butler's oil lamp arched over the picture, it revealed a large gash in the canvas and a dark, blood-red stain, obscuring more than two thirds of the man's face.

"Is that Mr. Deverell?"

"It is," the butler muttered, adding stiffly, "Handiwork of the former mistress of the house."

"She was an artist?"

He sniffed. "No, madam. I refer to the wine stain. And the hole."

"Ah." Something heavy and sharp had gouged the canvas quite severely in the spot where his face should be. "Must have been very satisfying for the lady. I wonder why she didn't take aim at the real Mr. Deverell. She wouldn't be the first, would she?"

The butler cast her another frown. "You'd be wise to keep such remarks and opinions to yourself in this house, madam."

"Yes, I daresay." It was the case in every house in which she'd ever stayed, of course."The master has been greatly maligned by uninformed gossip."

"I'm sure. You must excuse me. When I'm hungry and weary my tongue does tend to run on untended." She could also blame it on the excitement of her journey, for she was a long way from home now, a good distance from anything familiar.

The butler's brows had twisted into a knot midway down his forehead and his nostrils flared so wide she heard wind rushing through them.

Olivia blinked innocently. "I have no doubt Mr. Deverell is the most upright and benevolent of gentlemen. A victim of malicious rumor. A veritable saint."

He eyed her warily in the lamp's glow.

"I won't believe a word said against him," she added. "I too have suffered from vile rumors and unkind speculation, so you may rest assured your master has an ally in me. I only meant that his wife must have been relieved to dispel her pent up anxieties and frustrations on a portrait. We women suffer terrible hysteria at times and for little reason, as you must know. We are flighty, temperamental creatures, are we not? That is why they call us the weaker sex. It's fortunate we have men and corsets to keep us in our place or we might explode into little pieces." She smiled brightly. "Do lead the way to the kitchens, sir."

As she followed the butler, Olivia thought again of the coachman's shocked expression and his concern for her body and soul while in the company of the reprobate Mr. Deverell.

Frail bit of a woman, indeed. A quick snort of laughter shot out of her and ended up speared on the end of the butler's long nose, when he twisted his head around and glared over his shoulder.

"Are you quite well?" he demanded.

"Me? I am riddled with good health. It's the men around me who don't fare so well."

"*Chin up, m'dear*," she heard her first husband Freddy exclaim in his booming voice. "*Always walk with your head high and don't you look down. Don't ever look down.*"

That was how he had walked too, with his chest thrust out, a merry smile on his face for everyone he met. And if, as often happened, he stepped in horse dung because he didn't look where he was going, he'd shout, "Muck means luck, Mrs. Ollerenshaw! See, we're coming into a bit of fortune soon, mark my words."

They never did, of course. No matter how much horse manure he gladly stepped in.

But his irrepressible high spirits had not had enough time— during that brief, twelve-day marriage— to wear out their welcome on her nerves, and since Olivia had never seen Captain Freddy Ollerenshaw downcast, she followed his example, keeping her own insignificant chin well raised.

Chapter Four

"The *secretary* has arrived, sir," Sims intoned with somber apology.

The deep emphasis placed on "secretary" had not escaped True's notice every time it was uttered, but he had no intention of rising to the inquisitive butler's bait. He made it a rule never to explain himself, nor did he feel it necessary to defend his actions.

Besides, if Sims suspected this woman came to Roscarrock for some other, more pleasurable purpose, the butler ought to realize by now — having seen her with his own two eyes— that this was not the case.

"She's here already?" True shoved a mess of papers aside to look at his ledger and check the date— something he never could find these days.

"It is the thirty first, sir."

"Then she's bloody prompt."

"Indeed, sir."

"What did she do, fly here with her own little wings?" he marveled with a low chuckle.

Sims looked sorrowful. "The lady assures me she is always punctual, sir. And I suspect she is, in the same way that indigestion is prompt after bad oysters."

"You took a dislike to her already?"

"I'm not entirely certain what I took. I shall let you see for yourself, sir."

He leaned back in his chair. "I'm intrigued. Where did you put her?"

"Currently she is in the kitchen, and I will prepare a bed in the old nanny's room if that is acceptable, sir. She'll be out of the way there. Unless...

of course... you would prefer a room in your wing? Perhaps, for your purposes, that might be more suitable?"

True smirked, quietly amused by his butler's continuing curiosity about the new arrival's role there. "I'm sure the arrangements you've made will be adequate, Sims. I wouldn't want to put you to any further trouble." He held out his empty brandy glass for a refill, and the butler turned away to reach for the decanter.

But when the old fellow's white-gloved hand picked up the sherry instead of the brandy, True knew his faithful Sims was definitely in a perturbed state of mind. Muttering something low to himself, shaking his grey head, the butler replaced the sherry and hurriedly took up the correct decanter, making the stopper rattle, crystal chinking against crystal and setting True's teeth on edge.

Sims didn't generally do a lot of hurrying and he didn't make mistakes.

The quiet, still evening suddenly took on a new air. The spirits of the house were playful tonight, as they hadn't been for a while. Stirred up, one might call it.

"What's she like then?" True demanded of the butler, his interest piqued.

Sims considered for a moment and then said, "Small, but...sturdy."

"Is that the best you can do?"

The butler poured both the brandy and his words with equal caution. "The woman is much as promised in Mr. Chalke's letter. Mostly."

"Excellent." True had specified that she be plain and have a neat hand.

"She asked to see you, sir, but I told her you would not want her until the morning." Sims had half turned toward the door, but now he hesitated, hovering.

"What else?" True demanded. "Something wrong?"

"I must say, she seems a trifle...opinionated."

"Opinionated?" That certainly wasn't one of his requirements. She'd better not be trouble. He didn't want any distractions while he worked on his memoirs, as he'd explained when he wrote to his solicitor in London, asking him to find a secretary. Of course, he could have hired a man and removed any chance of such distraction. Abraham Chalke, however, had highly recommended this woman— the daughter of an old friend— and sworn to her absolute trustworthiness. At first, True wasn't certain about the idea of a parson's widow. She may be too prudish for the story he had to tell, but Chalke had insisted she was the best he could get, and the only one willing to leave their life behind for six months.

The solicitor had also mentioned Mrs. Monday's difficult financial circumstances, and True was glad the fee would go to somebody who really needed it. Remembering his own humble start in life, he liked to give a hand up whenever he could, to those deserving and in difficulties.

"She boldly expressed her approval of the former wife's retaliation against your portrait in the hall, sir," Sims complained. "The woman also appeared annoyed that you would not see her at once. As if she was entitled to an audience on demand. But I set her straight and she will soon learn her place."

"Very good. Thank you, Sims."

True had not bathed or changed since his ride along the beach at sunset and he was in no fit state to greet a female guest. He hadn't even shaved that day. A properly raised lady would be appalled by the sight of his scruffy cheek, untucked shirt and grimy riding breeches.

But when the butler left the library, True was seized by a sudden idea. Perhaps it was the fault of Sims' strange behavior and those mischievous spirits he felt in the air, but he was very eager to get a look at the new woman in his house, this "opinionated" parson's widow from the tame, leafy lanes of peaceful Chiswick.

Time for a bit of fun. It was overdue, actually.

He removed his corduroy riding jacket, rolled up his sleeves, ruffled his hair into an even worse state, and went in search of his new employee.

The old dear would be shocked regularly anyway, he mused, once he began dictating his colorful life story. True wasn't about to begin being bashful and polite. May as well toss her in at the deep end and start as he meant to go on. If she sank, he'd bundle her off back to Chiswick tomorrow. If she swam, then he'd know she was right for the post.

* * * *

Olivia had put together a small plate of cold food for herself and sat at the kitchen table alone to eat by the light of the fire and a solitary oil lamp.

"Jameson, the handyman, will be in shortly, as soon as he's carried your trunk up to the room," the butler had muttered. "Be advised that he only takes orders from myself or Mr. Deverell directly. He's not here to do your bidding. And you'll have to unpack your own trunk. There are no maids about the place. Don't expect to be pampered. Until recently Mr. Deverell spent most of his time in London, so this house has never been fully staffed."

"Worry not, for I have no such expectation. I've never been pampered in my life and at my age I sincerely doubt anyone is going to start for me. Thank goodness."

He'd left her alone then, after another stern glance and a stiff jerk of his head.

The only sign of a cook was the food left in the pantry, but perhaps they only came to the island during daylight hours and did not care to be stuck here when the tide was in. Understandably. She could guess this house was not a place one stayed in for long, unless one had a great desire for isolation. Or the need to hide away like a hunted criminal, as Inspector O'Grady would no doubt point out. She frowned at her plate, as he crept into her thoughts again. That odious fellow was like a bulldog with a juicy bone and if he expected Olivia to sit around waiting while he tried to build a case against her, he was very much mistaken.

Assessing her surroundings with a quick eye, it occurred to her that there was no evidence of children about the place, although Deverell was the father of six— seven, if the rumors involving paternity of the mute boy he'd adopted several years ago were ever confirmed. She'd heard that his former wife now resided in Edinburgh, although the lady had enjoyed a separate life away from her husband for a long time before they were finally divorced.

It was a terrible scandal, of course. Slow and

expensive to achieve, divorce was seldom attempted. Women had no choice in the matter; they had no legal identity separate from their husbands, and so if any suit was brought it had to be initiated by the man. Olivia had some knowledge of the complications involved, since her father was once a principal partner in the law firm of Chalke, Westcott and Chalke. She had taken great interest in her father's work and helped him with correspondence when his eyes were very bad and his hand trembled too much to hold a pen. With Olivia at his side, he had worked up to the very day he died. Therefore she knew a vast deal about the law, including the difficulties of divorce, which was a costly enterprise— and not merely in the financial sense. It also ruined the reputation of everyone it touched.

If they had a reputation worth saving in the first place, which True Deverell did not.

"Livy, you wretched thing," her stepbrother, Christopher, had exclaimed, "you cannot consider living under the same roof as a man like that for six months. What will folk think?"

She had replied, "I must go where I am needed. Besides all his children will be there and, no doubt, many other people too. He is a busy man with a very full life." And, as she might have reminded her stepbrother in his own words, True Deverell would never look twice at a girl like her, so she ought to be safe.

"But you are needed *here*," he'd argued.

"I'm quite sure you can manage without me." After all, sometimes he didn't even know she was in the same room.

"You are only just out of full mourning. Again.

Your reputation—"

"Considering what happens to most other men in my life," she pointed out, "Mr. Deverell has more cause to distrust my company than I do to fear his."

On his way out to a fitting with a fashionable tailor whose services he couldn't really afford, Christopher did not stay to worry long about his thrice-widowed stepsister's reputation. "It is impossible to quarrel with such a headstrong woman. I might as soon blow into the wind. You have chosen to enter a den of iniquity, Livy. Since Chalke is aiding and abetting you in this improper, foolhardy idea, for reasons known only to him, I suppose I must tell everyone that you've gone into the country to recuperate from some illness."

She couldn't imagine who this "everyone" might be, for she sincerely doubted she'd be much missed. Besides, she had tried the ideas and pursuits considered proper for a young lady and look what happened. Good men died.

Now she sat alone in the large kitchen of Roscarrock Castle— the den of supposed iniquity— and realized she couldn't hear another soul anywhere in the house. So much for all those other people she'd expected to find surrounding her new employer. From the surly butler's description, it seemed as if the notorious fellow had become something of a recluse living on this island.

She thought how desperate Mr. Deverell's wife must have been to get away, since she allowed her husband to accuse her of adultery and thereby risked the whole of grand society snubbing her for the remainder of her days. And while that lady had theoretically chewed her own elegant foot off to escape, she, Olivia Monday, had put herself voluntarily into this eccentric fellow's company.

Mad as a March hare– she had to be, just as her stepbrother had proclaimed.

Glancing upward to the shining rows of copper pots and fragrant bunches of dried herbs hanging overhead, she muttered wryly to herself, "I don't suppose the fashionable Lady Charlotte ever spent much time in this kitchen." Of course, as the daughter of an earl, Mr. Deverell's wife kept her title when she eloped to marry her commoner husband. Indeed, that title and her famous beauty were just about the only things she *had* kept when she married, since her outraged father couldn't take them away from her.

While Olivia pondered the odd, impulsive choices women— herself included— sometimes made when selecting their future mate, a tall, untidy fellow lurched into the kitchen, holding an oil lamp in one hand and a riding crop in the other, apparently prepared to chase off intruders.

He stopped sharply when he saw her. With eyes of a brilliant metallic shade that Olivia had never before observed on a human being, he stared fiercely across the kitchen. His big hand swung the lamp up high with what she considered reckless disregard for fire safety. "There you are then, woman," he snapped. "Talking to yourself, eh? I see you sniffed out the food already."

Must be another servant, according to his attire and generally scruffy appearance. Ah, yes, the handyman about whom she'd been warned. She could see he must be very "handy" indeed, for the size of him almost filled the doorframe and the sleeves of his shirt were rolled back, revealing broad, strong forearms.

"Mr. Jameson?" She got up to be polite, even though manners appeared entirely absent in that house. "Mrs. Olivia Monday. Pleased to make your acquaintance."

He glowered at her, every bit as angry, disappointed and appalled, as if she'd just spat at him and slapped his face. Perhaps, having heard about the dead men she left in her wake, he'd expected a ravishing woman reminiscent of Nell Gwynn, complete with a magnificent bosom and cherry red lips. He wouldn't be the first man to be disappointed at the sight of her face and she had no idea what Mr. Chalke had told these people about her.

"I was enjoying a light supper before I went up to bed," she said. "Don't mind me. I won't bother anybody. I daresay, after a little while you'll forget I'm even here. Most people do." Olivia sat to finish her meal. "As you see I don't take up much room, I only require feeding when hungry, and let me assure you the butler has already informed me that I won't be pampered here. Although why he thought that announcement necessary in light of the delightfully warm welcome I've received, I really cannot say."

The man set his oil lamp beside hers on the table, making a wider arc of amber light over the two of them. "*Delightfully warm welcome?*" he repeated, the words falling like hefty lead weights. "What did you expect, woman? Trumpet fanfare? Hope you're not the precious sort who needs attention all the time. The master just got rid of the last bit o' skirt we had here, so why he wants another about the place so soon is beyond me."

"Pardon me... bit of skirt?"

"He doesn't keep any for long these days. The wenches soon wear out their welcome. Then he pats them smartly on the backside and sends them on their way. But they always cause trouble for the master while they're here warming his bed. I was hoping we'd have some relief for a while after the last hussy."

Olivia felt her temperature rising, the ache in her head quickly multiplying. "I am not anybody's *hussy*, Mr. Jameson."

"What other purpose could you have here? You're a woman, aren't you?"

Oh, that was the way it would be, was it? Splendid. Apparently all Deverell's servants were strangers to simple courtesy.

She looked up at him as he stood with that riding crop in his hands, scowling fit to scare crows from the seedbed. He needed a good dousing with soapy water, a hairbrush and a razor, she thought. Perhaps a flea dip too. He might have been half way to handsome if he bothered. Probably just as well then that he didn't. That was all the world needed, another attractive man who thought women existed for only one use.

Do not let this get the better of you, my dear. Do not show that it matters. Whatever you are feeling now, it will pass.

Chin up, Mrs. Ollerenshaw!

Her job here was to keep out of trouble and write, not to let herself be distracted by her temper, or her wayward imagination with its tendency to lean on the dark and naughty side.

With this in mind, she swallowed her anger and said as calmly as she could, "Yes, Mr. Jameson, I am indeed a woman, as you shrewdly pointed out. But oddly enough, I am not here to warm anybody's bed but my own. I hope that's not too confusing a concept for you."

The handyman scratched his rumpled head. "I don't know what the master will make o' that. He says there's only one thing women are any use for."

"Perhaps I'd better go to my bed now then, before I feel the urge to find your master and give him a piece of my mind. I am rather tired and unfortunately that makes me short of temper and long of tongue."

His lips twitched, then disappeared from view as he rubbed his nose with the back of one large hand. "What piece of your dainty little mind did you think to give the master? Women don't generally have much to spare."

There went the ability to hold back her anger. "The piece that objects to being left on the mainland as the tide comes in, to manage my own trunk across the causeway and up some steep steps. And don't be misled by my size, I'm far from dainty, but even I struggled." She paused, drew a quick breath and stole a sullen glance at his exposed forearms. "I'm sure the cumbersome burden of my trunk would have been nothing to you, but perhaps it amuses your master to see a woman almost tip off balance and into the sea."

"If he knew you were coming, he would have sent someone out to help."

"Oh, he *knew* I was coming."

The handyman rubbed his nose again and his eyes narrowed. Olivia got the sense he was hiding a chuckle. "I don't think he knew *you* were coming."

"What, pray tell, does that mean?"

Jameson grabbed a chair and dropped heavily to the seat facing her, hands slammed down so hard on the table they made the lamps shake. "Don't get your drawers all twisted up, woman. I know who you are and why you're here. I was just rattlin' your cage."

"If you knew that, why—"

"You're a widow, so they tell me."

She eyed him warily, beginning to understand how a mouse felt when trapped in the paws of a playful tomcat. "I am."

He'd stretched his legs out under the table, so she was obliged to slide her feet away beneath her chair. The riding crop now rested on the table between them, a boundary line she was glad to observe.

"Thought you'd be older," he snapped.

She moved her hands into her lap, pressing the palms together.

"You were supposed to be a great deal older," he added, scowling at her across the width of the table.

"Oh?"

"I pictured a stout-boned lady with white hair, spectacles and seven chins."

Olivia's desire to remain stoic was now challenged by her sense of humor. "Well, I do have spectacles for reading and I keep my spare chins with the luggage. About the white hair there's not much I can do. However, if everything I hear of your master is true, perhaps that will be amended before my residency here is complete."

Jameson's gaze searched her thoroughly, taking it all in. Although still now, his presence felt restless, impatient, overflowing with too much vigor. He seemed to fill the kitchen, his dark shadow a great bulk that stretched up the wall and across the ceiling, but she refused to be intimidated. He might be large, pounce about like a tiger, and have a habit of staring rudely, but if this "handyman" also meant to scare her off, he'd be just as disappointed as the butler.

"Think you can manage the master, do you?"

"I am certain of it."

"I hope you're not squeamish."

She laughed acerbically at that. "Squeamish? Mr. Jameson, I see you have a low opinion of women in general. But you may rest assured, there is nothing that frightens me, nothing to which I cannot turn my hand, and no beast too contrary for me to handle."

This was not hollow boasting. When her last husband, William Monday, had decided to keep pigs, she had not raised a single protest, even though the task of feeding and cleaning them out soon fell solely to her— as she'd suspected it would— because he found himself much too busy, and the dirt too pungent.

And that was not all. When a tree had to be chopped down it was Olivia who tackled it with an axe to save William's back and his coin, because the local woodcutter charged more than her husband would pay for the service which "anybody could do for themselves", and she found his inevitable need to bargain far too humiliating.

She'd dug an entire vegetable garden without help, chased pushy tradesmen off the doorstep armed with nothing more than an apple corer, faced bill collectors without the slightest tremor— or ability to pay them, and had removed wasps nests by herself. Subsequently tending to her own stings later.

So no, she was not *squeamish.*

Jameson— poor, misguided fellow— had no inkling of what he was up against.

His gaze now filled with little flames, reflecting the firelight and the glow of the lamps. Deep lines carved into his skin shot outward from the corner of his eyes like sunrays. "At least you're plain," he muttered. "That's one thing they got right."

She drew her toes even further back under her chair and sat straighter. "Your master hired me to be useful, not an ornament."

"Are you sure? Doesn't sound like him."

"Never underestimate a plain woman, Mr. Jameson. I am at peaceful liberty to do a great deal more thinking about the world, and I never have to worry about the arrangement of my face while doing so."

He squinted at her, scratching his chin with a rather long and disturbingly lively set of fingers. "You'd better be damned useful. I hope, for your sake, you don't disappoint the master."

"He will have no cause to complain. I'm a hard worker, diligent and efficient."

"But the master can be a difficult man. Hard to please. Demanding. Can fly off into rages if he doesn't get his own way. Haven't you heard the things they say about Deverell?"

"I've heard plenty. None of it tries my courage, only my willing suspension of disbelief."

His lips couldn't seem to decide whether they should turn up or down. "Sims was right, you are a mouthy wench."

"Sims? Is that the butler's name? He didn't introduce himself."

"I daresay he thought it wouldn't be worth the trouble." He leaned across the table toward her. "Decided you probably wouldn't stay long, but would turn your frilly little tail and flee as soon as the tide goes out again."

"Mr. Jameson, there is nothing *frilly* about me. Have you naught else to do but sit here being tiresome?"

Abruptly he brought his palm flat down on the table, making another loud bang that echoed through her bones and was felt in the very balls of her feet. "Come then. Let's get on with it."

Thinking he meant to show her to her room, Olivia got up again.

But he remained in his seat. "Did they tell you about the tradition of Roscarrock?"

"What tradition?"

His eyes narrowed. "A Jameson has worked here, keeping the place standing since it was built. I'm the last of the line, a lucky mascot of sorts. But I have to be kept happy or else a dreadful fate will befall the residents of the castle."

Olivia wondered where this was heading and had the distinct feeling it wouldn't be good for her.

"When a new woman sets foot on the island she has to give Jameson a kiss." He sighed, flexing his shoulders. "It's tradition."

She promptly took her seat again. "Such nonsense."

The cocksure fool grinned, his eyes gleaming wickedly. "In the olden days it was more than a kiss that got sacrificed to a Jameson to keep bad luck at bay. Good thing for you, we've moved on with the times, eh?"

Olivia decided to finish her supper, as if he and his suggestive remarks could not be heard. Sadly that was easier thought than done.

"Tell you what, woman, you and I will wager how long you stay, before you've had enough of this place and our odd ways and run back to Chiswick."

"No, thank you. I don't gamble."

His fingers flexed upon the table before her. Grit had formed in the creases of his knuckles— sand, perhaps, for she already felt how it got into and under everything here. Black hair crisscrossed his forearms, very masculine, making her wonder how it would feel to be caught in his embrace. How thick his wrist seemed, powerful. She imagined his pulse throbbing, full of vitality.

In the olden days it was more than a kiss that got sacrificed to a Jameson to keep bad luck at bay.

The kitchen was warm and so was she. Getting warmer by the minute, her temperature increasing with the speed of her heart's beat.

But Olivia Westcott Ollerenshaw Pemberton Monday was not afraid of anything. Least of all a man who clearly had the wrong idea about her. *Handy man*, indeed!

As if those two words had any business being put together.

Chapter Five

"You don't gamble, eh?" Then what was she doing there with *him*? True was amused and intrigued. "Think I might win?"

"I know you won't."

How stiffly she sat, and how clipped and sharp her voice. Weary hollows were evident under her eyes, but she didn't sag, didn't even rest her arms on the table. "Then what do you have to lose, Mrs. Monday?"

"I told you, I do not gamble. Nor would I take money from a fellow who is, in all likelihood, in need of coin to feed his wife and children."

He laughed. "Trying to find out if I have a wife at home?"

Her eyes glittered with icicles of righteous anger. "I merely—"

"I'll save you the trouble and tell you now. I don't have a wife."

Her gaze skimmed his shoulders and then she stared at the table, apparently studying the wood grain. The tiny pearls hanging from her ears trembled indignantly. They were her only jewelry; the only decorative touch to her apparel. She wore no bows, frills or fancy lace. He'd never seen such a miserable gown. The color hovered in some purgatory between raincloud and ditchwater, and it looked as if the pieces of it were cut to a pattern of indifference, then stitched with resentment.

"But don't get any ideas and start eyeing me up for yourself," he teased. "The master doesn't encourage romance between staff."

"Nothing could be further from my intentions."

51

He leaned back and burped. "Because I've had enough petticoat to last me a lifetime and I'm not looking for more."

She winced. "Really? So many women and not one of them taught you any manners."

"Too busy enjoying my other talents, weren't they." He winked.

"Clearly those talents do not involve a razor and comb."

"I don't believe in gilding the lily." He smirked, rubbing the stubble of his chin and relishing her expression of polite dismay. "Any woman who tries to keep me clean shaven and fragrant, like a dandy, must not know how to appreciate a real man."

"And any fellow who abandons all good manners for fear it might somehow make him less of a man, must not know how to appreciate a real lady."

"I see we're going to have friction between us, you and me."

Her eyes widened.

"Best be careful we don't cause a spark of fire," he added.

"Fortunately we are surrounded by water. I'm confident any wayward sparks can be doused efficiently."

No wonder Sims had been unable to describe her. She was a curiosity. Accustomed to less complicated women whose motivations were usually as blatantly displayed as their bosom, True was utterly baffled by this briskly no-nonsense widow who had bizarrely, and knowingly, put herself in his way. Despite her unexpected youth, she was every bit as stern as he would expect of a parson's wife. But the haughty expression and starched manners didn't fit her any better than that ugly gown, the sleeves of which were too big for her wrists.

This woman, he decided, was a fibber— trying to persuade him that she was something she wasn't. Perhaps even trying to persuade herself too.

Her hair was brown, divided by a center part and swept back into a tightly braided lump at the nape of her neck. No ringlets, nothing to soften her face, except those tiny pearl earbobs. The bonnet set beside her on the table was a simple, old-fashioned straw poke with a wide brim and a pewter ribbon. The style of hat that hid a lady's face completely from the side and reminded True of a horse wearing blinkers. Her version even included a black widow's veil, just to be doubly sure she was well hidden.

"So you think you can put the master in his place, eh? Make him behave himself? A sad little thing like you?"

"I didn't come here to be Mr. Deverell's nanny."

"It's a natural instinct in females. Makes 'em think they can change a man, once they get their infernal fingernails dug into 'im."

"I keep my fingernails well trimmed and always to myself."

"That'll be a change for the master then," he muttered drily.

Her lips were very tightly pressed together, her jaw set firm with the determined mien of one who expected argument. And would cling to her side of it until blood was drawn.

"You seem tense, woman. Unduly cross."

"I have endured a long and tiring journey, which involved changing coaches many times. You'll have to forgive me if I'm not bright as a daisy."

"Should have come at least part of the distance by railway. 'Tis faster and cheaper."

"Cheaper?" Her shoulders became even more rigid, as if bone might soon poke through the material. Even her lips paled. "Money is not a concern." Her spine was ramrod straight, her expression defensive. "And as for the railway, I would never venture onto that wicked, modern contraption."

"It is quite safe. There are just as many accidents with coaches as there are with steam trains, but because the railway is still a novelty, we hear those tragedies reported the loudest. It's progress, Mrs. Monday. No need to fear it."

"I am not *afraid* of steam engines," she exclaimed scornfully. "Nevertheless, *if* I must travel, I shall continue to go by traditional methods, tried and trusted. Not something that relies upon fire and rude eruptions of explosive steam to get me from one part of the country to another in a cacophony of vulgar noise."

Laughter sputtered out of him. Of course, she wasn't afraid; she wanted him to believe she merely objected to the noise, the soot and the speed. "Well then, you must do as you wish."

"Thank you, Mr. Jameson. I shall. How relieved I am to have *your* approval."

True rubbed a finger along his bottom lip, watching her thoughtfully. "If money is no concern, why would a young lady like yourself travel so far from your home to work for an old rogue like Deverell?"

"I hardly think that's any business of yours, Mr. Jameson. So, if you don't mind, I'll keep my reasons to myself."

Well, whatever she said, he knew she needed the coin. Chalke had told him about her financial situation. But was this post really her only option? He'd expected an elderly lady with a hint of desperation about her edges. There was nothing desperate about Mrs. Monday apart from her clothing. She acted as if she did *him* a favor by taking the post, not vice versa.

As the owner and creator of London's finest gentleman's club, and a man who had made his fortune from understanding the stimulus of risk, True Deverell had seen a great many gamblers throw in their all to 'play deep', unable to walk away from a chance. But while he was adept at reading a customer's thoughts and motives, his mind easily calculating the odds against them, in the case of Mrs. Monday he suddenly hadn't a clue.

Before either of them could speak again someone entered the kitchen behind him and her gaze shifted upward, over his head.

"Mr. Deverell, sir, I just brought in the lobster pots and tied up the boat. Looks like a chill fog is coming in over the sea tonight. I lit the beacon early, sir."

"Ah, thank you, Jim," he said, stretching back in the creaky wooden chair, still watching the woman across the table. "Yes, the weather has definitely turned today and I think we've seen the last of the summer."

Mrs. Monday blinked, just once, and then she pinned him again with her steady regard. Her lips parted a little, allowing the escape of one crisp, frosty huff.

He bounced upright, scraping chair legs loudly

across the stone floor. "Jim, this is my new secretary, Mrs. Monday. She's come to help me write my memoirs."

"Aye, sir. I just carried the lady's trunk upstairs to the old nanny's room."

"Excellent. We must take very good care of her. She seems to think she's not welcome, and we can't have that, can we? This, Mrs. Monday, is Jim Jameson, the handiest man on the island. Far more use than me, as you will no doubt agree."

Jim tugged off his cap. "Pleased you've come, Mrs. It's time we had a lady about the place again. There's been no woman here since..." he screwed up his face, struggling to recall, "well...since the young miss went orf to her mother."

"Quite." True turned to look at his new secretary. "Since my ingrate daughter upped and left me there's been no reason to keep a female on the permanent staff. You will find us a rough-edged, uncivilized bunch, Mrs. Monday."

She stood, pushing her chair back and muttering under her breath, "*Really?*"

True scratched his chin where she was making his stubble itch. He was quite sure she caused the irritation. Perhaps it was her perfume. Although very faint, it had stealthily crept into his notice while they talked. He began to get the sense they'd met before, but he couldn't think where. It was rare for him to forget a face. "I'll show you to your room now."

"If you give me directions and a lamp, I'll find my own way. *Sir.*"

"You will not. I'll lead the way."

"But I'd much rather—"

"I insist."

From the tightening of her lips, she was not accustomed to relying on anybody to show her anything.

"I hope you're not going to be difficult, Mrs. Monday," he added smoothly.

She glared.

"I expect my employees to do as they're told." He gestured at the door with one sweep of his riding crop. "It's a small island. No room for contention and disobedience."

"I've never been contentious in my life," she muttered— an unmitigated lie as he knew already. And as she further proved in the next moment.

On her way to the kitchen door she stopped in front of his handyman and said curtly, "I understand this is tradition, Mr. Jameson," before leaning forward and planting a kiss on the fellow's weathered cheek. "For luck."

The poor man, staring bewildered, tipped backward like a wooden skittle at the village fete, but somehow kept his balance.

Having performed this little display, she arched a defiant eyebrow in True's direction and then marched out of the kitchen, leaving a slender drift of that insidious perfume in her wake.

Jameson's eyes had glazed over. "Well, I never...."

"Do close your mouth, Jim, before something flies into it." True hurried after the truculent woman to stop her wreaking further havoc.

Aha, there she was, moving across the hall, as if she didn't think she needed a lamp or his direction.

He overtook her with his long stride. "I must give you a tour of the house, Madam. Sims usually obliges the guests with his—"

"Surely that can wait until tomorrow?"

Holding the lamp high, he studied her frayed expression. "I'll take pity and give you the shortened version then. Sims is the history enthusiast and he usually gives the tours, but I'll try my best in his absence."

She closed her lips in that grim line again. The woman must be wondering what she'd got herself into, he mused. Made two of them.

"Roscarrock Castle was built in fifteen...something or other... by the third Earl of...something or other. The fellow didn't live in it for long as he lost his head to the temper of Good Queen Bess and then the property passed to the crown. It was left empty for many years. No one fancied the isolation, it seems. The place is rumored haunted by the headless earl, so if you hear steps up and down the gallery late at night, best not look out to see who it is."

He bounded ahead of her up the stairs. When he looked back, she was poised with one hand still resting on the newel post while she examined his shattered portrait. Her face was very white as it caught the curved edge of lamplight.

"I hope you're not frightened by ghosts, Mrs. Monday."

"Good heavens, no. I'm on their side. Who would possibly pass up the chance to get a little spirited vengeance on those who once plagued them?"

He laughed. "Is that a warning for me?"

She did not respond to that, too preoccupied by the painting. "Why have you not restored the portrait?" she asked, gesturing to where the image of his face should be.

"It stands there as a reminder never to marry again."

Having considered this for a moment, she said, "And no one can say how young you looked then, or remark upon the silver strands creeping along your temples now. Your vanity is safe."

"For your information, madam, I grew into my looks. I was not as handsome then as I am now."

"Well, I'll have to take your word for that, shan't I? Precisely my point."

Amused, he cleared his throat and moved on, taking the stairs three at a time in his usual fashion. Only when he reached the landing and found her still some way below, negotiating the steps in semi-darkness, did he suppose that he should have taken a slower pace to provide her with more light.

But she managed, skirt lifted with one hand.

He raised his lamp higher and saw that she wore some wretched old boots indeed. Suddenly he realized she was looking up at him and must have seen his puzzled glance at her feet. Her cheeks turned dusky pink, and she hastily dropped the hem of her skirt.

Clearing his throat, he continued, "The castle was eventually occupied again and passed down through a Cornish family, although the last inhabitant before me was accused of smuggling and deliberately luring ships into the cliffs to claim whatever bounty they carried. Thus, he met his end on the gallows. His son never wanted to live here and—"

"You won the place from him in a game of cards," she interrupted. "Yes, so I read." After a pause she added, with cutting deliberation, "Considering the gloomy history of the house, it would seem very few generations failed to keep the custom of kissing a Jameson."

"Exactly! See what happens when superstition is scoffed at, Mrs. Monday? And you thought I made it up." He heard a dismissive huff. "I suppose you believe I won this island by dishonest methods," he added.

She raised her shoulders in a stiff shrug and looked bored.

"Cheating, Mrs. Monday, is not necessary when one has a natural genius for numbers."

"Indeed?"

"A careful calculation of the odds alone can ensure the house eventually triumphs, every time. One must merely have the capacity to hold numbers up here." He tapped knuckles to his forehead.

"*Fascinating.*"

"But while working for me you'll learn the whole story of how I earned my fortune. *If* you decide to stay and we don't frighten you off."

"I agreed to six months and so for half a year I shall stay." Her voice was very firm, decisive. "I never go back on my word. And I never change my mind."

Well, we'll see, he thought. Women, in his experience, were changeable as the weather.

As True led his new employee down the passage, he noted dust on the console table and cobwebs on the paneling. Would have a word with Sims.

He opened the door to the old nanny's room and saw that a fire had been lit. At least Sims had seen to that, so he must not have despised the new arrival too severely. It was a sparsely furnished room though, a bit grim. "Here we are, Mrs. Monday. There are spare candles in the box on the mantle. I hope you'll find it comfortable tonight."

She walked into the room, her gaze quickly assessing the place. "I'm sure I'll manage." Then she looked at him again. "I daresay it amused you to make a fool of me just now, sir, pretending to be Jameson." Her head tilted to one side and a flicker of candlelight caught on the soft luster of her pearl earbobs, drawing his attention to them again.

Interesting that she wore no other jewelry— not even a wedding ring. He knew, thanks to his instinct for probability, that those earrings were handed down, not bought specifically for her. The woman's complexion was not suited to pearls so no man who knew anything about jewelry would buy her pearls. Diamonds or sapphires would suit her better. That meant the pearls had belonged to a close relative and were passed down to her. But since she apparently disdained ornament, Mrs. Monday must wear them only for sentimental reasons.

Therefore, although she seemed intent on denying it, this woman did possess some feminine tenderness after all. One soft spot. Somewhere under her armor.

Uh oh, her lips were still moving. Better pay attention.

"I was warned that you enjoy practical jokes, Mr. Deverell, so I should have been prepared. But I hope you got that mischief out of your veins tonight. I would not want anything to prevent us working efficiently together from now on."

He studied her thoughtfully, wondering again what she was doing there. And why she thought she had any authority to chastise her employer. This was not at all what he'd expected when he sent his request off to Abraham Chalke. It wouldn't do, of course. She was too young, too argumentative, too disruptive— upsetting the staff. Poor Jameson probably still stood in the kitchen with his mouth open, and Sims pouted in a corner somewhere, licking whatever wound she'd given him with her sharp words.

She couldn't stay. He must think of his staff's sanity and the smooth running of his household.

And he wasn't looking for more trouble from a dratted woman. He'd had more than his share in that regard.

Looking up at the ceiling, he pretended to consider. "Hmm. Have I got the mischief out of my veins? *Have I?*" After a moment he looked down at her again and sighed. "Too early to tell. Sleep well, Mrs. Monday. In the morning we'll discuss this matter."

"The matter of your unacceptable behavior, sir?"

"No, madam. The matter of yours."

With that he left her, closing the door and walking away with his lamp, loudly whistling the Sailor's Hornpipe. A jaunty tune that she, her pitiful boots and battered trunk had, for some reason, brought to his mind.

Chapter Six

Roscarrock Castle, Cornwall
Early morning (Time regretfully uncertain)
Thursday, September 1st, 1842.

Upon waking Olivia went directly to her window, eager to examine the view in daylight, but there was not much more visible now than there had been in the dark of night. Swaddled jealously in a thick cloud of fog that rolled off the sea, Roscarrock Castle appeared to float in a world of opaque nothingness. The chilled silence was broken only by a distant low rumble as unseen waves collided with rock. And by the steady beat of her heart, thumping reassuringly in her ears.

Well, here she was. She had arrived in one piece, despite Mr. Deverell's "odds" against her, and there was considerable satisfaction to be felt in this achievement, especially for a woman who had never been far outside Chiswick.

She went to the chair where she had hung her coat last night and felt in the pocket for her father's old fob watch, even though it had stopped working at some point during her journey. Forlorn, she opened the engraved case anyway and stared at the still hands. The timepiece had never let her down until now. The winding mechanism appeared to be stuck.

Snapping the case shut again, Olivia took a deep breath. She'd manage without it. She must. A fog-bound, time-abandoned, drafty old castle inhabited by an eccentric gambler was easy to bear when compared to the only other option of remaining in Chiswick, to watch her stepbrother, Christopher, marry Miss

Lucinda Braithwaite.

Yes, Lucinda was primarily ornamental, whined like a kettle left on the fire too long, and would probably prove expensive to keep, but if that was the wife he thought would make him content, it was none of her business. Olivia had known three husbands— married each one in opposition to her stepbrother's opinion— and just because she wasn't capable of keeping any of them alive, that was no reason not to want better fortune for Christopher. He could be very smug and had the uncanny ability to keep his boots well-polished in all weathers, but it was hardly his fault that all the puddles lurked in wait for her.

Putting that thought to rest, and with it any temptation toward uncharitable feelings, she opened her scuffed trunk at the foot of the bed. Too tired last night to tackle the job, she'd left her unpacking until morning, draping her coat, gown and stockings over a chair to dry, and sleeping in her petticoats. The devil only knew what a crumpled mess her carefully packed garments and belongings would be in now after so many days of rough travel.

Fortunately the first item she encountered was her old woolen shawl. She quickly threw it around her shoulders in a warm hug, holding it to her face just to inhale a breath of familiar scent. How could she have considered letting her luggage fall into the sea yesterday? That proved how tired she must have been.

She thought over her conversation with Mr. Deverell last night. Not a very good start. But Olivia would never have said many of those things to her employer, had she known who he was when he entered the kitchen. Today, well rested from her journey, she must keep her opinions and thoughts to herself, not let him goad her into any sort of debate.

One by one she rediscovered her old gowns from inside the trunk, shook them out and laid them in a thin, neat pile on the bed. Fortunately, she'd never been able to afford servants, so she'd sewn all her garments in a way that meant she could dress and undress herself. That would be useful now, since there was no maid at Roscarrock Castle either. Olivia's gowns possessed no troublesome out-of-reach hooks, so she was entirely self-sufficient. As for her hair, she'd never been one to try new styles. A simple braided bun was quite enough for her, could be managed easily with her own pair of hands and didn't even require any heart-breaking consultation with a mirror.

Reaching further into her trunk she recovered the small, framed silhouette of her last husband, where it was nestled protectively in the soft, worn velvet of her best evening gown. The need to keep his picture safe from damage was the only reason why she packed that particular gown, for she certainly didn't expect to wear it here. But poor, dear William deserved to be kept safe in the folds of her best gown. Theirs might not have been a passionate love match— his greatest devotion was to his faith— but it was a practical union that saved them both from loneliness and helped steer Olivia onto a better path, away from the wayward direction in which her bad temper and sinful imagination might otherwise take her.

After a first brief marriage embarked upon in lust, and a second short union initiated by her pride and wrath, a penitent life with William Monday had probably saved her soul. Or, at least, it was on its way to saving her, until sudden death took him too from her side, and then Olivia was forced to find another purpose. She certainly couldn't risk getting married again.

What would William make of her coming here and taking this position?

Why, he would say she must go where she could be most useful, of course! That was her kindly William, always so wise and never a thought for his own comfort.

On the other hand..."If you take that position so far away in Cornwall you won't be here for my wedding," her stepbrother had protested. "Who will make certain everything is done correctly and on time? Lucinda has no mother to look after all those little things, and we were relying upon you to sort it out." That was her stepbrother Christopher— full of his own immediate needs and never able to understand hers. Always hard-done-by in his own mind.

It would surely do her stepbrother good to learn how to do all those "little things" for his new bride himself. Alas, Olivia could quite imagine the pretty couple slowly starving as they lay in bed waiting for someone to feed them. Like baby birds in a nest with their beaks wide open.

"That young man is dreadfully spoiled," William used to say. "It seems his mama did him no service while she was alive, adoring and coddling him as she did. And now you are in danger of doing the same because of this partiality which allows you to willingly overlook his faults. He is not your responsibility, my dear, and one day he must stand on his own two feet."

Yes, standing on one's own two feet was very important.

She gave the glass of William's silhouette a quick huff and rubbed it with a corner of her shawl. Perfect, not a smear! Rising from her knees she went to the mantle, wiped a spot clean in the dust, and placed him there with reverence. Now he could watch over her in his calm, steady, knowing way.

Beside him she placed the painting her stepbrother gave her several years ago. Well, he didn't exactly give it to her. She'd found him throwing it out, so when she said she liked it he told her she could keep it.

"You never did have any refined taste," he'd said with a sigh.

Christopher had been raised to appreciate the finer things in life, even though he couldn't afford them. He liked nothing until he'd been assured it was fashionable or expensive. Olivia's more impulsive, instinctual, mostly unfashionable tastes irritated him.

When their parents married, Olivia was sixteen, her new stepbrother a year older. Christopher was very close to his mama, but she died within a year of the wedding, and then Olivia took on the role of listening, sympathetic ear. She spent much of her time looking after Christopher. Most often, however, she was of no more importance to her handsome stepbrother than a chair against which he was accustomed to stubbing his toe. An old, out-dated piece of furniture in need of restoration, but reliable when there was a shortage of seating.

Once, as her father and Christopher played chess and Olivia read a book nearby, she heard her stepbrother exhale a sharp expletive of disgust at losing. When her father reprimanded the young man for using such a word in the presence of a lady, he'd looked over, smiled pleasantly, and said, "Well, goodness, it's only Livy. I thought you meant someone else had come in." Then he turned back to the game.

She had, several times, overheard him lamenting that she would, one day, become his "burden" —even calculating how many years she might live, how much she would cost him in food and board. "One doesn't like to be morbid, but one must think of these things," he had said to her father. "It is not likely she will marry, is it?"

Why not? Because, in addition to her lack of dowry, dark sense of humor, unfashionable features, refusal to dance, and reticence to speak much in company, Olivia had once committed the greatest social faux pas anyone within fifty miles had ever heard about.

Sent against her will to be "looked at" as a potential governess for the daughters of Lady Arabella Frost, and finding herself surrounded by a cluster of haughty society ladies who were plainly trying not to laugh at her old, ill-fitting frock, Olivia took the last rout cake from a three-tiered china serving platter and calmly stuffed her face with it, much to the silent but very obvious indignation of those present.

As she had said to her father, "Someone was going to eat it. Why shouldn't it be me?"

Needless to say, she was not engaged as a governess. One might think the incident too small and insignificant to make many ripples for long, but in the close-knit circle of that society they apparently had little else to talk about. The incident was never forgotten, nor forgiven. Wherever she went, she was The Girl Who Ate The Last Cake.

But then Olivia met boisterous and lusty Captain Frederick Ollerenshaw, who accidentally stumbled into her at a ball and lost half the contents of his stomach on her gown. Her sensible, helpful composure in these circumstances won fun-loving Freddy's blurry-eyed gratitude, and she impulsively seized the chance of making herself indispensable to someone new.

Her father was markedly relieved he'd found someone to take her off his hands, and although he did not much care for the Captain, when Olivia convinced him she'd be happy he did not stand in her way.

"Are you in the position to provide for a wife, yet?" her father had inquired of Freddy— a fellow notorious for more open-hearted generosity than acumen. "How will you support my daughter?"

"With a little light pressure under the elbow while crossing the street, I suppose," replied Freddy, punctuating his answer with a genial gust of laughter.

For the few days of their marriage, Freddy was very enjoyable company, wonderfully uplifting for a girl's spirits. Unfortunately, Freddy was also uplifting to many other young ladies' spirits too. That was the trouble with attractive, merry gentlemen like Captain Ollerenshaw. They never could stop being so generous with their merriment.

When Freddy was killed, while foolishly racing an unstable phaeton for a wager of fifty pounds, Christopher immediately sprung up at her side to say,

"Perhaps you have got that out of your veins now, Livy, and you see the error of an impulsive choice."

But she missed Freddy, despite his faults and the little time they'd had together. At night it was very hard to go to one's bed alone after enjoying the pleasures to which he'd introduced her. Admitting this to her stepbrother, of course, was out of the question.

Next came her engagement to Arthur Pemberton, an earnest young man whose palms were always damp with sweat and who never seemed capable of looking her in the eye. It was a shock to Olivia that he ever got around to proposing, but somehow he did. She thought this marriage would at least last longer than a few days and that her husband's anxious, timid eye would not feel compelled to follow every pretty girl that passed.

Sadly, Arthur's nervous disposition prevented him from making it to the altar. He left his aging bachelor uncle, Sir Allardyce Pemberton, to make his apologies on the very day of the intended nuptials, and before the flowers could droop, Olivia was married to Allardyce instead. Looking back on her mood that day she realized her temper and pride had got the better of her. She could not bear to go home defeated again, to hear once more Christopher's snide remarks. Rather than let herself be gossiped about as a woman humiliated and jilted at the altar, and feeling rather mutinous that day, she'd rashly accepted another offer. After all, the last thing she wanted was anybody's pity.

Christopher had sneered, "If you're going to make a habit of this, you should at least marry for money. Old Allardyce hasn't a bean, you know."

"There is more to life than money," she'd replied, at which her stepbrother shook his head, lips grimly pursed.

Within six months she was widowed again, when Allardyce choked on a fishbone in his pie at the local tavern.

Now a woman considered unlucky and, as Christopher said, "used goods", she might have sunk under a lace cap and retired into a corner. Fortunately, however, William Monday, the reserved, contemplative parson who often came to Sunday dinner at her father's house, saved Olivia from this dolorous end by quietly stepping in and proposing a marriage arrangement.

"She's doing it again," Christopher complained loudly. "Someone ought to stop her."

But this union was different. There was no physical attraction, as there had been with Freddy, and there was no pride to be saved, as in the case of her marriage to Allardyce. William Monday was a steady man, extremely frugal and patient, keen to help her find a purpose in life. His good example would help cleanse Olivia of those wicked impulses that did her absolutely no good in the past.

If she served William with humility and became a good wife, she thought, it might break this string of bad fortune. So, as William Monday's companion, she managed the small, damp parsonage, visited his parishioners, darned his bed socks and made his tea. That marriage also allowed her to stay close enough to her father that she could still help him with his work as needed. It was a comfortable solution.

But only for a little less than five years.

Now both her papa and William were gone and it

was time to take a step into the unknown. If she stayed in Chiswick there appeared to be only one choice and she could not bear it.

"As soon as Lucinda and I are settled," Christopher had said to her, "you can have a room in my house. We'll find somewhere to put you, and Lucinda will need assistance with our children as they come along. You will be of great help to her. *Old Aunt Livy* our children shall call you. They'll keep you so busy that you'll never miss not having any of your own."

My house. Ha! Christopher lived in the house that her father had left to them both equally, but despite William's advice Olivia had not asked her stepbrother to buy her out. It felt too awkward and unnecessary. She knew that if Christopher ever sold the house, then she would get her half of the profits. There was no hurry yet, was there? She really did not think he would cheat her out of her share, whatever William had said.

But when it came to the idea of living there as unofficial nanny to her stepbrother's anticipated offspring...that was a prospect too dire to be considered. Instead, she had grasped at the first alternative to come her way.

Working for the notorious True Deverell would provide her with enough funds that relying on relatives— or finding another husband— for a roof over her head would not be necessary. No, she would not become another Great Aunt Jane, taken in by family out of pity but never really welcomed, and always causing her hosts to roll their eyes behind her back.

Deverell's generosity would be her way out of all

that, and he could certainly spare a few coins. He was the richest self-made man in England, so rumor had it. She'd read that he once won a hundred thousand pounds in a single, twenty four-hour game of hazard.

One hundred thousand pounds.

The possession of so much money must lead a person into all manner of mischief, so it was a jolly good thing it would never be hers to worry about. Olivia certainly didn't need any more temptation.

She'd heard a rumor that her employer was American, although she had detected no accent of any kind.

At last, after all these years of speculation, she knew what he looked like.

A wolf. A steely-eyed wild beast. With manners and scruples to match.

Olivia wrapped her shawl tighter around her body and gave dear William's picture a hasty nod and a smile. With his reassuring presence looking over her from the mantle she felt better already. Even the stifling curls of fog against her window did not bother her unduly now. So what if she could not go walking outside? Adventurous walks over rocky terrain were not very ladylike in any case. As William would remind her, such rambles—whenever she'd indulged in one without due caution— made her hair become unruly and brought too much livid color to her cheeks, as well as a disturbing spark to her eyes, something perilously close to suggesting an utter lapse of decorum was at hand.

"It is no surprise your boots are in disrepair, my dear," he would say.

Dear William was quite right, of course. She must make certain the rest of her did not end up in the same state as her boots. Thanks to him, she was no longer the Girl Who Ate The Last Cake. She was composed, efficient, held her temper — under some very trying circumstances of late—and had impeccable manners.

Most importantly, she had finally learned to keep her thoughts and feelings on the inside, safely hidden.

True Deverell's wicked ways would not lure them out of her.

Chapter Seven

"But my brother Justify was allowed to join the Naval Academy when he was only fourteen. Nobody stopped him when he went off to Portsmouth. I am two years older than that now and what have I done with my life, but slave over books and listen to dreary lectures?"

"Justify never possessed your capacity for study. The Navy was a good choice for him, and he has done well with it. Your talents are different. I do not see the Navy in your future, Damon."

The young man would not sit still but got up again and paced around the chair. Watching his son, True thought how time flew. It seemed like only yesterday when Damon, at two years of age, sat on his knee and sobbed over the death of his mama.

Never one to keep his children in the dark when it came to life's ups and downs, True had told both Damon and his elder brother of their mother's passing as soon as it happened. He did not use flowery words, but told them straight and then all he could do was offer his arms while they cried. Mercifully her illness was short and she had not suffered too much. True saw to it that his mistress had the best doctor and medicines available. Right to the end, he'd stayed by her sickbed, despite the animosity it caused with his wife.

"We did everything we could for your mama," he'd told the two boys, "but it was her time to go. As it is time for us all eventually."

"Has she gone to heaven, papa?" Justify, then three years old, had said.

That was the only time he lied to them, for he

did not know if he believed in heaven and hell, but what did one say to boys so young? The responsibility of children had taught him that one could not always say the first thing that came to mind. So he replied, "Yes. Your mama has gone to heaven."

"Then we'll see her again."

"As long as you behave. There are good odds that you will."

The idea of heaven had its uses, of course. It had served as a warning and a threat for thousands of years, so why shouldn't he use it too?

Unfortunately, all True's sons were too old for that now. They were not fearful of much with which he could threaten them.

Damon had just arrived at his most rebellious stage, questioning everything about life and his place in it. Having been through this already with three elder boys and a daughter— who was, in many ways, a greater challenge than his sons— True was not terribly troubled. All children, so he'd learned, tried their boundaries occasionally, even the quiet ones. Even those who used to sit on his knee and cling to him with sticky fingers as if he was their savior.

"Perhaps I'll go without your permission," Damon exclaimed, jaw pushed out, eyes fierce, those once sticky fingers tapping the chair back upon which they hovered with all the flighty tension of sparrow's feet. "I could. I could do that."

But he knew his son was too clever to make such an impulsive mistake. Damon would think it through and this idea of the Navy would pass. Aware that the quickest way to get his stubborn son to that point of reason was to let him find his own way to it, he said, "Of course you could. You must do as you see fit and suffer the outcome later, as we all do when we make mistakes. Maturity is not only about being free to make your own choices, but to face the consequences too. No one else can face them for you, so they should not make the decisions for you either."

His son's frown deepened. He had wanted a fight, no doubt. "Then, if I refuse to go back to school, you'll do nothing?"

"What would you like me to do, Damon? Should I wrestle you to the ground, bind you in ropes and keep you in the attic until this fancy passes?" He smiled, hoping to hide his impatience with this conversation. "Then you can blame me. Then you have another excuse to be angry at me. If you'd like that, it can be arranged. I believe there is room up there among all the other lost souls in rattling chains, held prisoner by my foul temper. Or else you'll just have to make your own decision and then have only yourself to blame for how it all turns out."

His son's eyes narrowed, his jaw jutted out.

"If I were you," True added, "I'd return to Eton and finish my education." His son had no idea how much he would have given for such an opportunity himself as a boy, but everything *he* learned was self-taught. Well, almost everything. Alas, while he wanted all these chances for his offspring, they did not appreciate it. "In another year, if you are still averse to Oxford or Cambridge—"

"I shall be."

"Then we'll address the possibilities at that time. I ask simply that you think a little longer on the matter. But, naturally, that is only what I would wish for you to do. As you keep pointing out, you are old enough to choose for yourself. I must stand aside."

It was clear that Justify's successful advance through the naval ranks had caused this jolt to his younger brother's prideful spirit. True's children all had that urge to be noticed, to distinguish themselves in some way from the pack.

Damon fidgeted with the cuffs of his jacket. His very stance— heels apart, toes tapping— seethed with irritation.

"You are young," True added. "It may not feel like it now, but there is so much life ahead of you. Time enough to go out into the world and make your mark. But you must be well prepared for it. Whatever successes your brothers have found— whatever adventures they have had— remember they were once sixteen too and restless as you are now. You will find your purpose, just as they have."

Perhaps he should explain to the boy that he had hopes of Damon one day taking over the helm at Deverell's, but no doubt that would sound very dull to a sixteen year-old. At that age True was working a fishing boat and contemplating a life of piracy, having narrowly escaped a swing from the hangman's noose. He'd had nothing to his name back then but reckless courage and a quick mind for numbers. He could never have imagined where he'd end up, presiding over London's most notorious and successful gentleman's club, which he hoped to hand over to his ungrateful brood.

Currently it was Ransom, his eldest legitimate son, who was being groomed to take over at Deverell's. But True felt something special in Damon. Was it because the boy used to be so close, so full of unconditional admiration for his father? Ransom, on the other hand, still strongly favored his mama and thought her the wounded party. She must have whispered plenty of her lies into the boy's ear over the years, and prodded at him with her cruel knives of jealousy, so it wasn't Ransom's fault he was confused.

True didn't even blame his son for the bullet which, two years ago, chipped the bone of his right shoulder.

"Accidents will happen," he'd amiably exclaimed to the Justice of the Peace.

Fortunately that "accident" had put a stop to Ransom's engagement with Miss Pridemore, who would have caused the boy endless pain. True was happy to sacrifice more than a bit of shoulder to keep his son out of trouble. It only gave him a little stiffness from time to time, the odd twinge if he'd been sitting still for a while and then moved suddenly. Fortunately, since he wasn't a man who spent a great deal of time sitting still, his shoulder rarely had a chance to seize up.

But really, he mused, none of his boys understood the lengths he would go to protect them. As for his daughter, she may as well be from another planet, or France. That was why he felt it necessary to get his memoirs down for posterity.

"So the choice, dear boy, is yours," he said to Damon. "But remember, once made it cannot be undone. You will then be trapped. I suggest you give the idea more than a few hours to ferment, but beyond that I cannot make you do anything. I wouldn't dare try."

With one final groan of frustration, the young man turned sharply, strode to the door and jerked it open.

* * * *

Olivia stumbled, swaying back on her worn heels.

The young man stared in surprise, one hand on the door handle. He bore some resemblance to his father, but his face was softer, more spoiled, as yet unmarked by life and experience.

"Sir!" he exclaimed, "There's a stray, odd-looking female skulking about in the hall."

She hastily gathered her wits. "I was not skulking." Scrambling for an explanation, she added, "I was looking for...anybody." Since there had been no other sign of life when she came downstairs, Olivia went searching and followed the sound of raised male voices to this door.

Her new employer suddenly appeared beside the younger man, leaping into view— with considerable vitality for that hour of the morning. His eyes raked over her and then flared brightly, as if they were matches and she a piece of flint. "Ah, Mrs. Monday. Finally you rise. May I introduce my son. Damon, this is Mrs. Olivia Monday, a parson's widow from Chiswick, and my new secretary."

The young man scowled. "What on earth do you want with a female secretary?" His tone oozed suspicion as he looked Olivia up and down again.

"I'm dictating my memoirs, dear boy."

"*Memoirs?*"

"What else would I want her for? Look at that pinched face, ready to disapprove. Hardly ornamental, is she? Not to be confused with a chorus girl from the Drury Lane Theatre."

"Your memoirs," his son repeated yet again.

"Quite so. I am writing my life story so that

when I am dead I shall leave behind me the True gospel, by which you may lead your life. After all, when I am swept up by the Grim Reaper, who will there be left to guide you with wisdom? Even I —fine male specimen that I am—cannot live forever."

Damon gave his father another skeptical glance and then swept by Olivia with a low grunt, "Something to look forward to then."

The boy strode away down the hall with no further word to his father, who now left the door open, suggesting he expected her to enter. If she waited for a polite invitation, Olivia supposed her limbs might grow cobwebs, so she followed him into the room.

"I feel your gaze burning holes in my back," he muttered. "Your faun-like eyes hold a particularly intense quality, Mrs. Monday. You have questions to ask?"

"No, sir. None." She would watch her tongue today. However he behaved this morning, she would not comment on it. Who did she think she was—Great Aunt Jane? It was none of her business what he did or said or thought. As long as he paid her.

He swung around and propped the seat of his riding breeches against the front of his desk, arms and ankles crossed. "Your lips, madam, are so tightly stitched together, I fear they have something to withhold, but I would rather you keep nothing inside. A woman's thoughts, when not allowed air, are like thorns buried in the skin. They become infected if they are not plucked out the moment they stick there. So we shall be honest and straightforward with each other, Mrs. Monday, if you please."

"Shall we?" *Ha! After the way he deceived her last*

night? She held her tongue, but only just.

"You will never get anything from me but the truth, however unpalatable. But then, I am a man. I don't have the deceitful tendencies common in the female sex."

She remained silent, knowing full well he wanted to prod her into an argument again. He reminded her of one of those very large dogs with too much energy— the sort that left muddy paw prints on a lady's gown and occasionally knocked her down with his cheeky enthusiasm. A dog whose undisciplined behavior was usually dismissed airily by its owner as "high spirits".

"What did you think of my son, Mrs. Monday? Too handsome for his own good, eh?"

Her answer was a tight, "Yes." For anyone's good, she suspected.

"You saw the family resemblance. People do say he takes after me the most of all my cubs."

"I'm afraid so." Oh, dear, she couldn't stop herself. Under no circumstances should she let this friction between their personalities become one of those sparks he'd warned her about, but there she was again, being scornful, when a simple "Yes" would have been sufficient.

"We have not impressed the parson's widow with our Deverell charm, I see. You disapprove of us."

Olivia's fingers began to hurt in their tense knot.

"Hmph. I suppose I should be glad of that," he added. "Wouldn't want you trying to seduce me, panting after me with your tongue hanging out."

"I didn't think that was one of the requirements of my position here." *Why the devil couldn't she stay silent?*

He laughed lazily. "So what do you think of me?

Go on, Mrs. Monday, describe me— as I seem through your large eyes —in three words."

"I'd rather not." She'd said enough already, more than she'd meant to.

"Can't you think of any?" he challenged. "Don't disappoint me today by suddenly being shy with your opinions."

Olivia struggled for a moment, searching for words that were honest but wouldn't get her into trouble. "Large...loud... lively."

"*Lively?*"

"Restless." The word that came to mind was 'potent', but that could mean too many other things and he would define it in some way to embarrass her, no doubt.

"Why was your plain little face so shocked just now?" he demanded. "No doubt you think my son disrespectful and you wonder why I would allow it."

Had her expression been so obvious? "If you knew that, why ask me?"

He walked around his desk to his chair. "Damon is sixteen. I don't waste my breath on correcting the inevitable." Pausing a moment, he gave her an odd look for which she had no apt description. Then he added, "Of course, you're not long out of that age yourself."

She almost laughed. "I am eight and twenty, Mr. Deverell."

"Really? I would never have guessed. I suppose it's because you're so small and nondescript."

"And I certainly never spoke in such a tone to my father, at any age."

He stared at her for a moment, then cleared his throat and ran fingers through his hair. "So I am a bad parent." She caught a slight smirk play over his lips as he dropped into his chair and swung his booted feet up on the desk. "I thought I'd get that particular criticism out of those terse lips eventually."

Olivia hastily replied, "I know nothing of being a parent. I am here only to write for you."

She'd never seen a man sit with his boots up on a desk before. Not even Freddy Ollerenshaw would do that, although he didn't own a desk to put his heels on anyway.

Such a pose was something one might expect from a naughty child but not a grown man of forty-four. *If* that was Deverell's age. No one seemed to know for sure, not even Mr. Chalke. He did have a scattering of silver sprigs about his temple and a few weathered lines scored into his face, but nothing else seemed to fit a man of his purported age. This morning he had shaved, adding to the inappropriately youthful appearance.

When he used his riding crop to scratch down inside one boot, Olivia didn't know where to look. The casual impropriety of the gesture seemed quite unconscious on his part, as if no one had ever troubled him with what was, or was not, the "done thing".

"I've seen you before somewhere, woman," he muttered suddenly.

"Yes."

"Where on earth would I have seen you? I don't usually forget a face."

"Well, it *was* a long time ago. And to be frank, I don't believe you saw my face. I didn't see yours either."

At once his gaze re-established that playful

twinkle. "Now, I am intrigued. What parts of me did you see?"

She felt the urge to laugh, but held it strictly down. "Mostly your big feet. When I was eighteen, I often assisted at my father's office. You tripped over me there one day when you had an appointment with Mr. Chalke."

"I did?"

"You trampled some important papers, stepped over me, and never apologized."

"Ah. How much do you want?" He reached into his desk as if to hand over some bank notes or gold sovereigns there and then.

"What can you mean, sir?"

"I know how women hold bloody grudges. I suppose you've let that fester away for years and now you came here to make me pay. So how much does a lady charge for the inconvenience of being stepped over?"

She couldn't tell whether he was serious, or merely teasing her again.

"I don't do well with apologies," he added. "So I'd take the money, if I was you."

"Sir, I had entirely forgotten the incident until now."

Just after three o'clock in the afternoon, Tuesday, March 12th, in the year 1832.

He wore a long, midnight blue coat, beautifully made; buff colored gloves, grimy at the finger tips; and top boots of very rich looking leather. He had smelled of tobacco, brandy and spice. Of adventure, and daring, and everything forbidden. For those few moments her heart, like an over-wound pocket watch, had stopped...

Olivia bit her lip, turned away and stared out of

the nearest window. A pointless exercise since there was nothing to see but that colorless cloud of fog. And, of course, his reflection. She was unable to escape the man. Again, Olivia thought of last night in the kitchen, when he let her mistake him for the handyman Jameson, and she had been struck by the overwhelming strength of his presence. Like the first time they collided with each other, she felt a connection, which was quite ridiculous in light of who he was.

She wished it *had* been possible to forget their first encounter, but now fate— in the bent and wizened shape of Mr. Chalke— had brought them together a second time. It was a jolly good thing Great Aunt Jane was no longer alive.

"You are a girl with a dark and devious imagination, Olivia Westcott. I cannot think what will become of you."

"I shall marry Mr. True Deverell, shan't I? People say he's not fit for polite society either..."

"I see something through my window amuses you, Mrs. Monday."

She straightened her lips. "Your son returns to school today, sir?" she asked, changing the subject.

"Yes." He sighed gustily. "The brat could do very well there if he only applied himself more to his studies. But he thinks he can do without school. Arrogant chit."

"He seems very...confident. I'm sure you and your wife are proud."

Behind her, Deverell exhaled a taut huff. "He's not one of my wife's litter. Damon is the younger of my two sons by a mistress, Emma Gibson. When she died I brought both boys to live with me."

"Oh." Only a man with Deverell's excessive

86

wealth and audacity would launch his illegitimate children into the world without even trying to mask the truth, without shame or apology for not marrying their mother.

She turned away from the window and faced him boldly. "It is a curious name— Damon. I do not think I ever heard it before."

"Greek. Loyal friend to Pythias, for whom he was ready to sacrifice himself."

"You are a student of Greek mythology, Mr. Deverell?"

He smiled at her, head tipped back against the leather chair. "I am a student of life, Mrs. Monday."

"Life?"

"Stories. I love people's stories. Don't you?"

His smile was pleasantly crooked. Olivia could see how some might find it alluring. Even infectious. "I never really considered—"

"For instance, *yours*, Mrs. Monday." His eyes simmered, like cool winter sunlight on ripples of icy water. "I would wager it's most interesting."

"Why?"

"A young, sensible woman like you, abandoning respectability to put yourself under my roof. What could have driven you here to me? What secrets lurk behind those big, round eyes of yours?"

"Oh, my story is very dull." She touched the back of her neck where a small curl of hair had begun to tickle. Her skin seemed more awake than usual, feeling and reacting to every tiny draft, any little contact.

"Well, let's see...*Olivia*," he muttered thoughtfully. "I like unusual names. I made sure to give all my children names that were uncommon, unexpected."

He paused. "The name Olivia was first coined by Shakespeare, you know. Your parents must have enjoyed the playwright's work."

"Perhaps." Not likely her father, she thought; he always kept his nose buried in work and never read anything for entertainment. Her mother, however, possessed a more sentimental soul. Her parents' marriage had been a love match, so Olivia was told— her maternal grandmother had been so angered by it that she'd cut her daughter out of her will and refused to see her again. But despite the romance of all that, Olivia's parents never showed much affection in front of her. It wouldn't be proper, of course, and it would embarrass her father. Love was signified by a gentle pat on the hand or the shoulder, and never in front of company.

She walked away from the window and stood before Deverell's desk, trying not to see his boots and long, firm thighs stretched out. He smelled of leather, hay, sea water and wet sand. Had he been out riding already? She waited for him to invite her to sit, but no such offer was forthcoming. He continued to stare at her in a quietly amused way, now tapping the riding crop on the outside of his boot.

Before he could ask her another question, she said brightly, "Damon is your youngest child?"

"No. Rush is fourteen and the last of Lady Charlotte's litter." To her relief, he finally swung his feet down to the carpet where they should be. "There is also Bryn, my adopted son who also just turned fourteen. They are both at school together in Exeter. I thought it best not to send all my boys to the same schools, but those two are inseparable. You will meet them in the term holidays." He paused. "Should you

88

stay, of course."

Olivia refused to reassure him, yet again, that she honored her commitments. Instead she said, "And there is only one daughter?"

"Yes." He looked away, staring at the bookcase. "Bloody women."

She took a breath and plowed bravely forward. "Shall we get started, Mr. Deverell? My term of employment has begun already, and we haven't written a word."

His gaze snapped back to her. "We can't begin work until we know each other, Mrs. Monday."

"Know each other?"

"We need to...sniff one another out."

She did not. Like. The sound. Of that.

"Would you agree to embark on a long, intimate journey with someone about whom you knew nothing?" he added, making his face solemn in an utterly unconvincing way.

"I'm not sure what sort of intimate journey you—"

"The journey of my life story, Mrs. Monday. I will be confessing all my deepest, darkest sins to you, commending my secrets to your hands. But how do I know I can trust you, since you keep hiding your fingers from me?"

She gasped. "I do not."

He pointed with the riding crop to where she kept her hands tightly clasped in a knot before her. "Show me."

Olivia slowly unwound her fingers and slyly wiped her palms on her skirt before she turned them for his examination. He leaned forward, his gaze sternly perusing her hands.

"I am adept at the art of palmistry, you know," he warned.

"I do not believe in that nonsense."

"Then you needn't be worried. Keep your hands still, woman, and let me study the lines."

"They *are* still."

"You're waving them about all over the place." He used this as an excuse to grab her left hand, and Olivia felt her pulse quicken. His grip was very strong, crushing her fingers.

She tried— she really tried. But it was no good. Unable to bear his scrutiny, which felt twice as fierce as Inspector O'Grady's, she pulled her fingers away from his grip and put both hands behind her back.

"Mrs. Monday, you are being truculent again."

"I am not, sir," she exclaimed breathlessly. "I gave you long enough to study them. They are quite innocent and capable."

"Hmm. The former, I have yet to ascertain. The latter I will agree with, although *what* exactly they are capable of remains to be seen." He grinned in that lopsided way. "I confess I can't wait to discover it for myself."

He was testing her, she sensed. Trying his boundaries.

"You had better behave, sir, or you just might find out."

She knew she should never have said it, but there it was. He drew out the worst in her, it seemed.

Rather than be put off by this remark, his eyes gleamed polished silver. "Shall I be spanked and sent to a corner?"

"If that's necessary, sir."

"You'd have to catch me first. I'm very fast."

Olivia arched an eyebrow. Perhaps, despite his love of tales, he'd never heard the fable of the tortoise and the hare.

"But only when I don't want to be caught," he added slyly.

"I'll bear that in mind then, sir."

He fell back into his chair, making it creak loudly. "Shakespeare's Olivia, if I recall correctly, declares herself in mourning for seven years— until she falls stupidly in love with Cesario, simply because he has a habit of saying exactly what he thinks, not coating his words with honey for the lady."

"Oh?"

"But it turns out that Cesario is a woman living in disguise as a man. So there is a lesson for you, Mrs. Monday."

"Never to fall in love with a woman dressed as a man?"

He laughed. "Or...first impressions can be misleading. People are not always what they appear to be, or... what they want you to believe."

Olivia suddenly felt as if he had somehow stripped her naked with the sharp edge of his steel-grey gaze.

It was, by no means, as unpleasant a sensation as it should be, but every pore on her body felt the wicked caress of that blade, whispering over the surface of her skin.

Chapter Eight

There were few things worse than an itch one couldn't scratch. This particular itch was moving around his limbs like an adventurous flea, but he sensed it was not caused by a tiny insect. He was fine, not a disturbance anywhere on his person, before *she* came in.

He eyed Mrs. Monday cautiously, wondering what part of her might be causing this reaction. She wore another day gown of dreary grey. It could be the same as she wore yesterday, for there was nothing distinctive about this one; it was equally dismal, a shade only slightly lighter than wet mud.

He imagined how she would look in blue. It would bring out the rich brown of her eyes, which were actually quite pretty, he supposed. When they weren't being scornful.

This morning she remained a mystery, gripping her secrets with determined fingers, but he would trick them out of her hands somehow.

Still young enough to remarry and not completely unattractive in daylight— well, it would help if she unpursed her lips and loosened her poor hair from its tightly-wound, unforgiving knot— she'd severely endangered her reputation by agreeing to live under his roof for half a year. That would lessen her chances of finding another suitor. Did she understand the consequences? She must; she clearly was not stupid.

Yes, now that he was over the shock of finding her in his kitchen last night— a woman quite different to what he had expected— he could admit she was not so very plain.

Damn that drunken sot, Abraham Chalke, for sending such an unsuitable woman. Fellow must once again be downing four bottles of Madeira daily.

Since Mrs. Monday had enjoyed a full night's sleep, he ought to send her packing and put her on the next coach back to civilization for her own good. She may as well go safely back inland with his son today. He could give her the money he'd promised, even slip a little extra into her trunk for the inconvenience. When she wasn't looking, of course, because she was clearly the self-suffering, dignified sort who wouldn't take charity, and then he—

"I'll need paper," she said suddenly.

"Paper?"

"To write. As your secretary. The position for which you hired me, sir."

Apparently she thought she was staying and saw no issue with this chafing of their personalities. Now would be the time to tell her to pack her trunk, but instead he said, "Paper? Really?"

"To write."

"Ah."

"And ink."

"Ink? Good lord."

She exhaled a soft sigh. "And a pen, sir."

"Did you not bring these strange, otherworldly materials with you, Mrs. Monday?"

"No. I assumed—"

"This is why women should not venture into employment outside the home. They're not thinkers. I suppose you packed your frilly petticoats and hair brushes, but entirely forgot the tools of the trade for which you were hired."

The woman unclenched her lips to exclaim, "I

have some personal writing materials, which might be used until you can provide me with others."

"Sakes no, Mrs. Monday! I would not purloin your personal things for my own use."

"Then what do you suggest—?"

He pointed with his riding crop, and she looked over her shoulder to the small painted bureau by the wall. "I believe you'll find everything you need within it."

She glared at him, her slender brows drawn together like two pulled stitches. "Would it not have been simpler to tell me that from the start?"

"But not nearly so much fun."

Sims appeared in the open doorway, looking annoyed. "Breakfast is finally served, sir."

True leapt to his feet. "Aha! Very good. I'm famished. What about you, Mrs. Monday? Of course, you stayed under the covers enjoying my hospitality like a lazy slug-a-bed this morning, until long after the lark had gone about his business. You have had no chance to work up an appetite yet, I suppose."

She hesitated, half way between his desk and the bureau, her countenance trying to stay vexed with him, but the lure of food on the horizon apparently caused her quite a challenge. The creature certainly looked in need of a good meal before he sent her back to Chiswick. If he told her now that her services weren't required she'd probably go off — alone and in a prim huff —to the mainland, looking for the next mail coach. Who knew when she'd have the opportunity to eat well again? No, he wouldn't let her run off unescorted or unfed. Or unpaid.

With winter coming the woman needed a new pair of walking boots. No doubt, many more things besides.

He directed the point of his riding crop toward the door. "Let us make haste before my greedy calf devours it all. He must be ravenous since we delayed breakfast to wait for you."

"For me?"

"Of course. While you lay snoring snugly abed, the inhabitants of the house tip-toed about for fear of waking you. Sims was instructed to hold breakfast until you finally came down, and as you can see it has made him most irritated. So, to the dining room, if you please."

With those "innocent and capable" fingers she clung to the pleats of her dull skirt. "But I should eat in the kitchen...surely."

"Why? Do you have some dreadful habit you don't want me to see? Wooden teeth to take out before you eat?"

"I meant that I am a member of the staff, Mr. Deverell. Not family."

"I do not stand on ceremony here at Roscarrock. This is my kingdom, and we live by my rules." He smirked. "Or lack of them."

Again she hesitated, fingers restlessly rearranging and smoothing down the world's ugliest frock.

Too hungry himself to wait any longer, he said, "Remember, Mrs. Monday, there is no room for contention on this island. When I make a command it must be followed. Should I steer you onward with the crop?" He swung his arm toward the door again. "*Cush, cush,* as they call to herd the cows. Did I just hear your dignified insides let out a rumble, madam?"

Her eyes flared. She took a deep, noisy breath and, with her head held high, she followed Sims out of the room.

* * * *

Damon Deverell was already seated at the table and he looked only faintly surprised to see her there. He did, however, stand when she came in, which showed he had acquired *some* manners from somewhere.

"Fog's lifting, father," the boy muttered, dropping back to his seat and stuffing another slice of ham into his mouth. A slice which slid down so speedily it did not impede his speech at all. "So the coach shouldn't be held up. You'll be rid of me before noon."

"Excellent. You can take—" His father caught Olivia's eye and after a short pause continued, "some of Mrs. B's seed cake back with you. She told me yesterday that she was making one for you, spoiling you as usual."

The two men were soon involved in a conversation as if she was not there. Apparently Damon had damaged a curricle belonging to one of the masters at his school. His father, rather than reprimand the boy, muttered, "I'll send you back with some money to recompense the fellow. Enough so he can cease his whining and buy himself a half-dozen blasted curricles."

After that, they spoke of horses and the sport of racing, soon completely losing Olivia in that jargon.

She slyly perused his son's face and marked all the similarities between the two men. Both were dark in coloring— apart from the very slight advance of silver visible at the father's temples. Both had sharp features that gave them a very distinctive profile. Theirs were the sort of faces one saw at museum exhibits— tough, merciless, awe-inspiring Roman Generals carved for posterity in marble. They were both loud, and had a habit of speaking before the other had finished a sentence. She suspected that neither really listened to the other, each too determined to get their own point across.

Damon is the younger of my two sons by a mistress, Emma Gibson.

What must it be like, she wondered, to grow up knowing one was illegitimate? Not only that, but to be raised in such a family where one's father — who was occasionally shot at—made a fortune from gambling, and where a scandalous divorce was procured at great cost, played out in all the papers. It could not have felt very stable and secure for the boy. Olivia knew, from her own experiences, that everyone needed stability, every soul searched for that elusive somewhere to belong.

"Why did you take this post, Mrs. Monday?" the young man abruptly demanded.

She hastily dragged her mind back to the present. "It was recommended to me by a gentleman who worked with my father. In a solicitor's office."

"It is unusual for a woman of your class to take employment, is it not? What happened to your husband?"

It would be futile, no doubt, to wait for his father's intervention. Deverell had already made some attempt himself to dig out her reasons for being there, so he would hardly prevent his son's bold interrogation. Olivia set her coffee cup down. "My last husband died over a year ago. Once I was out of full mourning I did not wish to continue being a burden on my relatives and when this opportunity arose, I took it."

"Your last husband? There was more than one?"

Inside Olivia a small groan erupted and was quenched. "Yes. I have been married three times."

"And all are dead?"

Still his father made no attempt to halt the questioning. In fact, he looked at her with even keener curiosity than his son.

"Yes."

"Were they very old?"

"Not particularly. The deaths were all accidental."

"Forgive me, Mrs. Monday, but you do not act in the manner expected of a grieving widow," Inspector O'Grady of the London Metropolitan Police had remarked when he found her cleaning mashed potato from the hall tiles.

"I was not aware I had an expectation to fulfill. Do tell me how I am supposed to act and I shall, of course, try to comply." And she scrubbed harder at those tiles, grinding her teeth.

"I have not seen you shed a tear, madam."

"If you knew me, Inspector, you would know I'm not the kind of woman to melt in a paroxysm of tears unless I'm chopping onions."

Her father had never cried. It was not the done thing in her family. One simply took the blows and carried on.

"Crikey," young Damon exclaimed, finally pausing his greedy consumption of ham.

She picked up her coffee again, ignoring the sickness that suddenly twisted inside at the memory of William Monday's puffy, ashen face staring up from the murky green water of the lake into which he'd fallen when the old wooden footbridge broke under him. The Coroner's theory was that the weeds became tangled around his vestments and dragged his body under. At such an early hour no one else had been passing, no one heard his cries for help.

Inspector O'Grady of the London Metropolitan Police— as he always introduced himself, no matter how many times he paid a visit—could not believe it happened that way, and neither could Lord Frost, the local magistrate, who had called O'Grady in to investigate the death. They both seemed convinced that Olivia had some part in her husband's demise.

"A young woman with three husbands buried," O'Grady had muttered, "seems more than a coincidence, don't you think, madam?"

To which she had replied, "Perhaps, when I married them, I should have asked for a guarantee of life expectancy. Men just don't last the way they used to."

Inspector O'Grady of the London Metropolitan Police was not amused.

Neither man at the breakfast table said how sorry they were or gave Olivia any of the usual platitudes. She found it something of a relief.

"How long were you married?" her youthful interrogator continued.

"Twelve days the first time. Three months the second. Almost five years the last time."

"And you have no children?"

"No. None."

"How did you manage that? Didn't you want any?"

At last his father intervened. "That's enough, Damon!"

"I was merely trying to understand why a respectable woman would risk her reputation by coming here to work for you and wondering why there was no one with the sense to stop her, not even a child to keep her at home and out of your way."

"Well, don't be such a damnably nosy brat. It's none of your business. Now, apologize to Mrs. Monday for distressing her. She's a proper lady. I know you haven't had much experience of those, Damon— none of us have— but now she's here this is your chance to learn how not to make a fool of yourself. She knows it's too late for me, but your clay isn't dry yet."

The boy's face flushed scarlet and he snapped out a sullen, "I am sorry, madam. Do forgive me."

Olivia nodded. "That's quite alright."

"No, it isn't. Don't let him off that easily! It's not his place to ask you impertinent, personal questions." Deverell gave her a sly grin. "Those are for me to ask."

Tense silence fell over the table. She watched the young man buttering his toast with vicious slashes of a knife blade.

Clearing her throat she said, "As a matter of fact, I would have liked children, Master Damon. But God did not see fit to bless me with any."

The boy's gaze flashed across at her with something like surprise and gratitude. He fidgeted in his seat and stole a sideways glance at his father. "Hmph. Odd, isn't it, how some people who want children can't have any, while others have a surfeit that they didn't want and don't know what to do with."

Her employer opened his lips to speak, but

Olivia beat him to it. "God works in mysterious ways. He knows what is better for us, even if we don't know it for ourselves. Perhaps God saw that Mr. Deverell needed so many children."

"For what purpose?" the boy exclaimed.

"Oh, to keep him busy and teach him patience, perhaps. Make him look where he's going."

The man at the end of the table exclaimed, "And you needed no lesson in the eyes of the almighty, eh, Mrs. Monday? No such occupation to keep you out of trouble?"

"Certainly not. I've always been perfect. Never put a foot wrong."

She caught True Deverell's eye and saw an odd flicker of something she'd never seen in anyone's regard when they looked at her. Whatever it was, it kept him from replying and he quickly hid his lips behind the rim of a coffee cup.

It left her feeling slightly breathless.

* * * *

God works in mysterious ways, eh? He'd heard that before. Did that account for what happened to her three husbands too? How did she explain those deaths being the providential work of her benevolent, all-knowing god? Now, perhaps, was not a good time to ask. She seemed in a better mood this morning and he'd prefer to keep her that way. Let his son ask the questions and take the blame.

She was certainly entertaining Damon. It was a while since they'd had a woman about the place, as Jameson had observed.

He scowled, pushing a piece of ham around his

101

plate. What was he going to do with this woman who was so unlike the one he'd asked for? Sending Mrs. Monday back to Chiswick would mean having to find another secretary willing to put up with him, and it took Chalke over a year to find this one. Irksome.

His thoughts were soon torn away from that dilemma, however, by the arrival of a letter. Sims carried it to him on a silver tray, announcing solemnly, "Mrs. Blewett brought this over with her this morning, sir, from the farm."

It was unusual for important letters not to be carried across by his first-born illegitimate son, Storm, who managed the mainland farm belonging to Roscarrock Castle. Unless the letter contained something that Storm knew would put his father in a rage, then he wisely avoided handling the missive himself and sent it over via the cook, who divided her time between farm and castle— and who couldn't read a word, so she was blissfully ignorant of anything such a note might contain.

A sense of unease immediately settled over True as he reached for the sealed letter. When he recognized his former wife's handwriting the sick feeling in his gut multiplied. Storm would have recognized it too, and a letter from that woman could only ever contain bad news.

"Well, I'll be off father," Damon was saying. "It was a pleasure to meet you, Mrs. Monday. I do hope your stay here with my father won't be too trying. Do not believe a word he tells you, for he enjoys tall tales."

Preoccupied by the letter in his hand, True mumbled a goodbye and waved his son off with a mechanical reminder to behave himself and write if he needed more money. He was vaguely aware of his secretary rising to bid the boy a safe journey.

Meanwhile, he stared at the words slanted viciously across the paper, their spiteful news no doubt bringing great glee to the woman who had written them. One by one he absorbed those syllables and all the vitriol they contained. Like poison it writhed and burned in his stomach.

He looked up to find Sims still waiting beside him, tray tucked under one arm. "Sir, shall I—"

"Yes, clear the breakfast things, will you?" True bounced to his feet, crumpling the letter and forcing it down into the pocket of his riding jacket. "I must go at once to the farm and tend to some business."

On his way out of the room, he found Mrs. Monday underfoot, looking up at him expectantly.

She was still here? Of course she was. He hadn't yet decided what to do about her, had he?

"When can we begin work? You are already paying me, sir." Apparently this little fact bothered her greatly.

"Mrs. Monday, you have a day off today. There, you see, I might not possess any gentlemanly manners, but I am a benevolent employer. You did not expect that, eh?" He put his hands on her shoulders and turned her toward the door. "Do go and enjoy your day off, Mrs. Monday. *Cush, cush.*" Probably shouldn't have put his hands on her. The woman almost leapt out of her skin, but she said nothing.

Besides "probably shouldn't" had never stopped him before.

Hopefully she would take some time today to think about what she'd done by coming here. She

103

appeared to be a woman of wit, intelligence and surprising good sense. Perhaps, when he returned, she'd be packed and ready to leave. Then he wouldn't have to tell her to go, because he was finding it unduly difficult to get the words right.

Tripped over her once, did he? Didn't sound like him. He wasn't in the least clumsy. The part about failing to apologize did sound typical, though.

He'd have to make that up to her somehow, before she left.

Three husbands dead, eh? He was right then. Drab-drawers did have an interesting story of her own.

Chapter Nine

"Writing his memoirs indeed," the cook exclaimed. "Who would want to read that filth? I never took to books and reading. Why would he put the evidence of his sins down on paper?"

"He says he's writing it for his children, Mrs. Blewett. He believes the truth would be a service to them."

"Pah! That lot aren't waiting for any service from Mr. Deverell other than a share of his handsome fortune, mark my words. They're all greedy fledglings. Except for Master Storm Deverell. He's a good lad, and the only one I've got time for."

Olivia said nothing about the making of that seed cake for Master Damon, which suggested the cook's opinion of *him* was not so wholly bad as she made out. Indeed, Damon had departed the house that morning with a large hamper filled with Mrs. Blewett's baked goods— enough to feed not only him, but also all the other boys at school. It had required both Damon and Jameson to carry it.

"It's the master's fault for not raising 'em with a firmer hand," Mrs. Blewett added. "He looks around sometimes as if he doesn't know how he came by so many children, as if they just followed him home like confused ducklings. Throws money at 'em and hopes for the best."

Yes, she had already witnessed his propensity to use money as a cure-all. "Perhaps he's writing the memoirs for himself too. I suppose he wants to get things off his chest. Make his confession, so to speak."

"Not dying, is he?"

"Not that I'm aware of." He certainly looked healthy enough, she thought with a cross sigh. It made her job much harder, while he had too much energy to dash about all over the place and couldn't be pinned down at that desk.

"He's got *too much* life in 'im, if you ask me. Flitting about all over the place from sun up to sun down, as if his arse is afire." Mrs. Blewett laughed heartily at her own crude remark and then again when she saw Olivia's expression. It seemed as if laughter was never far from the cook's lips, and when she dissolved completely into the jolly, raucous noise her whole body trembled with the motion. "That wicked feller will outlive us all, to be sure, no matter how many times they shoot at him."

"Have you worked here long?" Olivia inquired.

"I came here as cook the first time his wife left him. Twenty years ago, it must be now." She shook her head. "Twenty years at least. Time flies, as they say. I worked at the farm over on the mainland, you see, and when Lady Charlotte decided to run off back to London, she took the chef with her— some fancy fellow from the continent. Mr. Deverell asked me to come and fill in here and that's what I've done ever since. He doesn't care for fussy cooking," she explained with pride. "Likes my plain, hearty honest fare."

"The *first* time his wife left?" Clearly she had come back again, since some of his children were born less than twenty years ago.

"Oh, there were many such times. The lady was gone more than she was home. Always came back though, when she ran out of money. The screaming fights those two had could be heard on the mainland if it was a still night. But no, that was the first time she left *properly*— the first time she packed more than one trunk and was gone for a lengthy spell."

"Is that when she damaged the portrait in the hall? The one above the stairs?"

"Aye." The cook lowered her voice and leaned closer. "His fine lady wife found out, you see, that the master paid to send his first bastard child— young Master Storm— to school and that he arranged a monthly stipend for the boy's mother too. Lady Charlotte was furious, claimed he paid more attention to the bastard than he did to his legitimate son, Ransom. The master replied that young Storm was just as much his responsibility as her own child."

"I see."

"She wanted to take her child with her when she left, but the master refused to let her have him. Called her an unfit mother. That's when she threw the crystal wine decanter at his portrait."

"Ah."

"Storm Deverell now runs the home farm on the mainland for his father. He was always a hard worker. Not spoiled like the others. Has his head on straight. He ought to be married by now and a father himself— there's many a local girl had her eye on him— but he avoids all talk of matrimony and uses the farm as his excuse. Says it takes up all his energy. Mind you, he still has time to chase after a pretty face when he fancies it. Quite a charmer he is. Trouble for the ladies, just like his father."

Olivia, warming her hands by the fire, thought that someone ought to speak up on behalf of the betrayed wife in all this. "It must have been hard for Lady Charlotte, to know of her husband's infidelity.

For it to be so public."

"Well, Storm was born *before* the marriage to Lady Charlotte. Mr. Deverell weren't much more than a boy himself — only just fifteen or sixteen, so 'tis said—when he fathered the lad by a gamekeeper's daughter out Truro way. Mr. Deverell didn't know about the babe until years later, after he were wed. His wife wanted the child and its mother out of her life, but the master said that since she'd married him for his money, she could take all that came along with him and not just the luxuries."

The cook's story was cut off sharply when Sims entered the kitchen. "I trust you have plenty of work to keep you busy, Mrs. Blewett? If not, I'm sure more can be arranged."

"Just having a friendly word with this young lady."

"And now perhaps you can complete some tasks more pressing."

Olivia hurriedly got up from her chair by the fire. "Is there anything I can do? I am at rather a loose end this morning, since Mr. Deverell took himself off to the mainland."

"*You?*" The butler glowered down his superior nose at her. "No, there is nothing you can do, but wait for the master to return, and try not to get under our feet in the meantime."

"Well then, since the fog has lifted slightly, I'll venture outside, Mr. Sims, and get myself acclimated. Mr. Jameson might have work for me there if I can find him."

"I would not advise it. The fog still lingers around parts of the island and you are unfamiliar with the territory," he muttered. "The master would be most displeased if he returns to find you damaged in some way, or lost over the edge. It would be a great inconvenience."

She chuckled dourly. "Yes, I would hate to *inconvenience* Mr. Deverell by getting swept out to sea. Well, if he spends a lot of time away I shall have to ask him to leave me tasks. I don't care to be idle."

Both cook and butler gave her odd looks and exchanged an even odder one between them. "I fail to see what he might give you to do when he is not here," Sims proclaimed in a deeply disgusted tone. "You sole purpose is to amuse him."

"*Amuse* him?"

The cook winked. "You mean, she's to write the master's *memoirs*."

It occurred to Olivia that her role in that house was being misinterpreted. "That is exactly what I am here for," she exclaimed. "I am a secretary."

"Of course you are," Mrs. Blewett rolled her pastry out with considerable force. "If that's what they're calling it these days."

She spun around to confront Sims, who surely knew the real reason for her employment there and was probably just being his usual uncooperative self, but the butler had already gone out again. The cook began to hum loudly as she worked, bouncing and tapping her toes against the stone floor. Olivia decided to sort this out with Deverell as soon as he returned. Better let him deal with his own servants. It wasn't her place.

Apparently she faced several challenges in her new job already. One of her most trying missions there would be keeping her slippery employer focused— rather like corralling an escaped seed ox.

Another would be persuading the other staff of her chaste purpose in the house. From what she had already seen of Deverell, he would likely take mischievous delight in their mistaken assumptions.

Young Master Damon had warned her, "He will tell you all manner of nonsense. That he was left by a mermaid on the sand. That he can read the history of an object just by holding it. That he once fought a dragon...the tales are endless. The sort of thing only a child can believe. I'm sure you won't be fooled by any of them, Mrs. Monday."

He was right, of course, she would not be fooled. Even as a child she'd never enjoyed fairytales— only those of a decidedly midnight pallor.

As she left the kitchen to explore the house, Mrs. Blewett called out merrily, "Now don't go kissing Jameson again. The poor fellow still hasn't recovered from last night and the master won't want his handyman indisposed."

Oh dear! She really must apologize to poor Mr. Jameson, and explain herself when she saw him again today.

Such a menace she was to men, and yet she'd only ever tried to be useful.

* * * *

"Father," Storm greeted him with the usual sunny smile. "I thought you'd be by today, checking on the harvest."

The boy— yes, True still thought of his eldest son as a "boy" in many ways— must have been up since dawn. He looked tired, but happy. Evidence of how much his son enjoyed working the land. Storm

was not the sort to want town life, fine clothes and
Society parties. He lived plainly, had a good head on
his shoulders and a warm heart in his sturdy chest.
How could a father not be proud?

True's wife had despised his eldest child and
made no effort to hide it. From the moment she
learned of his existence she set out to destroy the
poor boy. It was the only thing, apart from her
appearance, into which his wife ever put any effort.

"I fail to understand why you must pay for that
bastard's education," she had exclaimed. "Let him and
his slattern mother manage their own affairs. I
thought she was married to a blacksmith now."

"She was, Charlotte, but he has passed away.
Since Storm is my child, he is my responsibility in any
case."

"To send him money is tantamount to stealing
from your legitimate child."

"If we are to discuss thievery, dear, should we
not raise the matter of your cousin Horace?" She had
begged him to hire Horace— a complete and utter
wastrel— soon after their marriage, but he'd been
caught stealing money from the club and had to be let
go. "If Storm and his mother receive stipends from
the Deverell coffers at least it is with my knowledge
and consent. Unlike the unsanctioned allowance that
managed to find its way regularly into your cousin's
pockets until it was discovered. But then, your family
has never been known for honesty has it, Charlotte?"

"How dare you compare my cousin to that slut
and her bastard?"

"Quite. It was wrong of me. It is an insult to my
eldest son and his mother."

Charlotte had thus declared her intention to

leave. True didn't stop her, but when he asked what she meant to do about her own baby, she was adamant that she didn't want the boy with her. "Why would I want your offspring hanging on me?" she'd exclaimed, her eyes overflowing with volcanic spite. "A reminder of the worst mistake I ever made!"

"He is your child too, Charlotte," he'd reminded her.

"Do you think I don't know it? That I don't know how bearing your son has ruined my looks? As if that is not bad enough, now you force me to leave all my friends in London and live in this dreadful place, isolated from Society for six months of the year? And why? For you to be near that wretched little bastard of yours and his whore of a mother."

"I thought it would do you good to leave London for a while." There were many things and people in Town that were bad for his wife, but she couldn't stay away from them.

"So I could become even more dowdy and unfashionable? No, you can keep that needy brat of yours. You deal with its tantrums and that surly, pudding-faced nurse-maid. I'm going back to my life!"

Charlotte had no maternal instincts. Selfish to the bone, her thoughts were always for herself. She only complained about his illegitimate son taking attention away from her child, because she was thinking about the money. That's all her children ever meant to her; they were conduits to True's fortune and as such they would keep her in luxury for the rest of her life. Or so she thought.

"If you leave the boy, Charlotte, you can forget about coming back here again. You can forget about me sending you any allowance. Go back to London and your friends and we'll live separate lives. If you prefer their society so much, let them take care of you. But you'll get nothing more from me. Not a damn penny."

The wine decanter hit his portrait soon after. It would have hit him had she possessed better aim in her soused condition.

Storm was too young then to understand the animosity caused by his existence. It didn't take long, though, for his eyes to be opened. Growing up, the boy was victimized by Charlotte's spiteful rancor more than once, but he bore it stoically. Perhaps that annoyed her even more, True mused. Storm didn't fly into rages like his father; his mild manners he clearly got from his mother. If anything he avoided confrontation.

Just as he avoided carrying post to his father when he guessed it brought bad tidings.

True took the crumpled ball of Charlotte's latest letter from his pocket. "Did you know about this?" he demanded. "My daughter has always shared her troubles with you rather than me. You must have known something was afoot."

"Something? Like what, father?" Storm couldn't lie to save his life. His eyes were very blue and in pain anytime he thought he might disappoint. It made True think suddenly of Mrs. Monday's eyes and the similar light within them— muted in her case, but just like a pup ready to flinch.

"Raven, it seems, is to be married. And I must be the last to know."

His son groaned, set down the pitchfork and shrugged into a worn leather jerkin. "Raven wrote to me that her mother had introduced her to some rich fellow in silk breeches. But in all honesty father, I can't keep the names all straight in my head. One in-bred aristocratic dandy sounds much the same as another to me. Besides, I didn't think she took any of 'em seriously. You know how Raven is, she likes to have her fun."

Oh yes, he knew his daughter. Sadly. Raven was more intent on rebellion, in many ways, than his sons. Her mother made a great fuss of her because she was the only girl, but it was all empty affection— all for show. And revenge against him, of course.

His former wife had wanted a large, extravagant "coming out" ball for Raven in London, but True would have to pay the bill and he declared his daughter too immature, too deeply under her mother's influence.

"What's the quote from that book you like so much?" he'd said to Raven. "*Until you can prove to me that you've spent ten minutes of any day in a rational manner...*"

It may not have been an exact quote, but it was close.

After that his daughter fled up to Edinburgh in a mighty sulk, anxious to be consoled by her mother. Since then Charlotte had been parading their daughter about like a piece of meat on a butcher's wagon, trying to catch the deepest pockets in Scotland. Now, according to this letter, an engagement had been settled upon. Without True's permission, or even consultation.

Storm confessed. "I would have told you before, father, if I thought anything would come of it. But I never thought Raven would agree to anybody her mother picked. Doesn't seem like her at all." The two

114

men walked together into the barn, and Storm poured two tankards of cider from a barrel that stood just inside the door. "I thought she'd get beyond this stage by now and be back here to make it up with you."

True laughed harshly. It spat out of him before he could take his first swig. "That girl will never come back for my forgiveness. She's stubborn— like all my sons— but with the added trait of feminine irrationality. It's a wretched combination. Worse still, she's been under her mother's influence ever since I told her I would not pay for that damned ball this past spring."

He'd refused because he knew Charlotte's so-called friends would attend merely to gawk at his daughter, as if she was a public curiosity. The vultures waited for Raven Deverell to make one mistake— they looked for fault. But no, her mother did not care about Raven being an exhibit. Charlotte wanted a gaudy performance with herself in the midst of it. Now she'd managed this engagement to some oily cretin. And True would be expected to pay for the wedding, or else he would, once again, be the enemy in his daughter's eyes. Apparently, he was the one who thwarted all her chances for happiness. That was the accusation Raven had shouted at him before she ran off to her mother.

"Well, this engagement may not last, father. These things often come to a natural end," Storm said placidly. "Raven may be wild, but she's not a fool. She's probably gone into this engagement just to get your attention again."

True shook his head. He knew that this was his former wife wielding influence over their daughter by constantly rubbing on the fact that they were the only two women in a family of men. And both supposedly injured by True.

If he did not give Raven his permission to marry it would push her a further step closer to her mother and away from him. It would be another tug of war, with no victor except Charlotte.

"Don't you see the injustice though, father?" his son teased gently now. "You want me wed and the sooner the better, but you'd hang on to Raven until she was gray rather than lose her to a husband."

"Girls are different," True replied gloomily.

"That is certainly what I've found," Storm sputtered into his cider. "It's not hard to spot the differences. And I'm grateful for 'em. As, I believe, you are too, father. At least, in the past you have been, although it's a while since I've heard of you keeping female company up at Roscarrock. You ought to have a woman up there to keep you in a better mood."

Reminded of his new employee, True looked thoughtfully at his son. "Come over and dine with me soon."

"The harvest will keep me busy, father. But I'll come over when I can."

"Good. I'll look forward to seeing you. Oh..." he cast a quick eye over Storm's tattered clothing, "..and neaten yourself up a bit."

"What the devil for? Not entertaining royalty are you, father?" Storm laughed, blue eyes shining. He got those eyes from his mother, True thought, remembering sweet Louisa the gamekeeper's daughter who once, so long ago, initiated him into the pleasures of "tupping" as she called it, on a warm haystack. Smiling Lusty Lou. Gone a few years now, but not forgotten.

"Just...dress tidy, son. I've let things slide a bit of late. Ought to make an effort once in a while at dinner, or I'll get out of practice, shan't I?"

Storm looked quizzical, but shrugged again and poured them both another tankard of cider.

* * * *

When Deverell still had not returned by early evening, Olivia decided to wash her hair. This was a sizeable undertaking, because her hair was very long and thick, and took hours to dry, but surely there was time. It seemed unlikely her employer would return for dinner— Mrs. Blewett informed her that the master often stayed overnight at the farm if they were busy with harvest—so she heated some water by the kitchen fire and carried it into the scullery, to wash her hair in private. After that, Olivia planned to sit by the hearth in her room and read a book.

However, while waiting for her hair to dry, her thoughts returned constantly to the master of the house. She finally gave up trying to read when her eyes had tracked five times over the same sentence, and then she closed her book and stared into the sputtering flames.

It occurred to her now that the man she saw riding along the beach from her carriage window yesterday was, in fact, True Deverell. How strong and powerful he had looked, wild and free, but also in control. Olivia could only imagine the state her hair and clothes would be in if she rode like that.

Deverell, of course, had no one waiting at home to disapprove. He did as he pleased without deference

117

to a single soul.

From everything she knew about him before she arrived at Roscarrock, she was prepared to find a man who was irritating, frustrating, arrogant and not very pleasant. In truth, he was a little of all those things, but so much more beyond. She couldn't quite get him straight in her mind.

Without his energy the house felt...empty. The skeleton staff waited for his return, of course. But even the walls and floorboards seemed to sigh with impatience to feel him there again. Olivia was not accustomed to men with a great deal of vitality. Well, not since Freddy, whose energy was mostly misdirected and came in sudden spurts between long periods of sleep. Rather like the damp fireworks display she once saw over the river in Chiswick.

What Deverell had, she supposed, some would call "charisma".

A sudden shiver stroked her skin, like the swift brush of a goose feather quill. Must be a draft from somewhere, although the fire was crackling cheerily, the flames sturdy and tall.

With a brisk huff she reopened her book and made a sixth attempt to start the next Chapter, but her mind simply could not concentrate. True Deverell crept back into her thoughts. In fact, he galloped across her page on his horse, splashing through the printed letters and knocking them asunder.

She should not think of him in any terms beyond the professional. He was her employer. He was also deliberately naughty, very aware of all that he did, and quite bereft of good manners. Not to mention the divorced father of seven children—not all of them legitimate— and owner of the most notorious gaming den in London.

Despite all that, the one thing bothering her most about him was that he had the gall to accuse her of being afraid of steam engines. As if she was ever afraid of anything! The railway was simply a passing caprice for men like him, who always had to be in a hurry to get anywhere and thought that because something was new and fashionable it must be better. She was quite sure rail travel was a trend that would never catch on.

A loud rap at her door dragged Olivia abruptly out of her thoughts.

"Yes? What is it?"

Sims shouted crossly through the wood panels, "Mr. Deverell desires your presence at once. In his library."

She scrambled to her feet. "But I...my hair is wet."

"I'm sure he won't care, madam."

Whatever time was it? She'd heard nothing to suggest the master of the house had returned. It was black as pitch outside.

Blood rushed through her veins so fast it made her dizzy. She stopped, drew a deep breath and steadied herself.

Chin up, Mrs. Ollerenshaw!

As long as one was in control of one's emotions and nerves, one was in control of life.

If she pretended everything was quite normal, it would be.

Charisma. Pah! William Monday certainly would not approve of charisma. Neither would Great Aunt Jane.

Chapter Ten

True waited by the fire in his library. Hoping to clear his head of all but sensible ideas, he'd taken a ride along the sands before coming back to the island. He wasn't sure yet whether it had worked— whether the sunset exercise had helped make his decision about sending her home, or letting her stay.

When she entered the room he turned to look at her, and in that moment he knew his answer. "Mrs. Monday. I hope I did not disturb you?"

"Disturb me?" She swallowed, one hand to the throat of her ugly grey gown. "Of course not."

"Good." He nodded. "I have decided to begin my memoirs now."

There went his chance to send her away. It was done. She was staying.

"Oh." He could almost hear her mind exclaiming, *At this hour?* She blinked, tried to resettle her expression. Alas for her, he'd caught the split second when she let down her blank guard.

He'd seen other things too, before that.

"What have you done to your hair?" he asked, as if he didn't already know and hadn't, quite by chance, spied upon her in the scullery.

"I washed it, sir." She raised a hand to the oddly tilting mess and made an attempt to hoist it further upright. "I thought...I was not expecting you back this evening."

He stared at her for a moment, picturing how she had looked earlier with all that hair down. If he was a gentleman he'd feel guilty about spying on her, but since he was True Deverell he felt fortunate. Very fortunate.

Arriving back at the house he had meant to enter through the scullery, as he usually did when his riding boots were full of wet sand. But through the crooked diamonds of the leaded window he had unexpectedly found his new secretary, in the dusky light, and aided by one flickering candle flame, washing her long hair.

Her back was to him, her arms bare, and he'd quickly realized she must have lowered the bodice of her gown to save it from the soapy water. Beneath she wore a corset over a sleeveless linen and lace chemise.

His quickened breath tickled the ivy that climbed the stone wall. His eyes greedily devoured every detail. The slender neck and fine slope of her ivory shoulders, the gently curved arms reaching up like angel's wings, the seemingly endless lengths of dark hair falling in a slow, luxurious tumble. The swaying line of her corseted torso, down to the narrow waist. The dip between her shoulders, just below the nape of her neck, where a drop of water trickled down, a slivery tear that he wanted to—

"Sir?" she said.

He snapped back to the present, remembering why she was there. "You had better come here by the fire, Mrs. Monday. I can't afford to have my secretary becoming ill with a cold before we've even started, can I?"

Slowly, cautiously she approached his roaring fire.

"Sit," he demanded, pointing at the hearthrug.

Her eyes glistened in the firelight. "Pardon me, Mr. Deverell, but I am not a dog."

"I meant for you to be close to the fire." When he moved aside, she looked relieved at the sight of a small table and writing box set out for her before an old settee. "May we begin, Mrs. Monday? Haven't you delayed me long enough?"

Moving swiftly forward now, lips pursed, she sat where he pointed and cast her eyes over the writing materials he'd set there. She tidied them with quick hands, arranging the goose quills in a neat row beside the pot of ink. As she swept by him, True had caught a fragrant wave of rose water. It tempted him to touch her damp hair, to coil the loose strand around his finger. But he resisted, turned his back and strode to the other side of the fireplace, where he moved a velvet-covered ottoman close to the fender with one booted foot and lowered himself to the seat.

Well, he had called her down to his library at this hour. Better get on with job at hand.

Stop thinking of her shoulders. Of her neck. Of her bare arms.

All he could see of those angelic wings now were her hands and slender wrists. Good. He ought to be able to concentrate if she didn't distract him too much.

He watched her preparing the sheets of paper and then the nib of a goose quill in the ink. Her movements were very precise, very neat.

"You must stop me," he muttered. "If I go too fast."

"I'm sure I'll manage." She had just hooked a pair of spectacles over her small ears. Now, eyes down, she waited.

True cleared his throat. "I was born," he began, and then stopped.

She looked up.

"I was found," he corrected, "on the sand near

Truro in the midst of a violent storm."

"Found?"

"Yes. I was left there by a mermaid."

The scratching of her pen paused.

"You doubt me, Mrs. Monday?"

A slight frown creased her brow. "I'm surprised it wasn't the pixies. Are there not many of them in Cornwall?"

He stared at her lips, but she kept them firm, no hint of a smirk. "It was a mermaid," he assured her sternly. "Which explains my fondness for the sea and my affinity with the creatures in it."

"I see. And what year was this?"

"How would I know?"

"You do not know when you were born?"

"You sound incredulous, Mrs. Monday. But how could I know?"

"Someone, surely, must know."

"No one who cares to admit it."

She shuttered her expression behind a sweep of lashes and looked down at the paper again. "Well...What is your first memory, sir?"

"Running amid the sheep."

"Running? You must have a memory before that."

So he told her about the hands that found him on the sands. They were big, rough fingers with yellowed nails. The beachcomber must have been hunting for washed-up treasure on that bleak night of violent wind and rain. He recalled how she smelled of damp earth and wood smoke, and how she sang to herself. How dark and stuffy the sack was in which she put him. What she meant to do with a baby, who knew? The others, when they found him, forced her to leave him behind, because they didn't need another mouth to feed.

He told his secretary about the fields that became his hunting ground after that, of the food and clothing he stole, and of the farmer he watched warily from a distance — a man who tried, in vain, to capture him.

"I thought he would try to train me as he did the other dogs, so I kept my distance for a long time." He watched as she tapped her goose nib on the inkpot. "The farmer eventually gave up chasing me off his land and put me to work instead. He taught me how to wield a hammer and nails when I was barely big enough to hold them."

"So he took you in?"

"Not exactly. My place on his farm was like that of a stray cat, kept around to chase mice out of the barn. As long as I made myself useful I was welcome to the scraps they threw out, but I wasn't a pet. I wasn't domesticated. I learned not to get underfoot."

"Did you try to find your family? Your father?"

He stood and paced to the window, opening it for some cool air. "I didn't need anyone. I looked after myself."

"Yes, but he might have—"

"I learned early on that I must take what I wanted or starve. Rules and laws were for men who knew when their next meal would come, not for me. I lived with the animals of the farm. I belonged there, raised among them and by them."

When he glanced back at her again, she sat with her head bent over the little table, her hand moving steadily between inkpot and page, his words forming neat lines across the paper. A wet strand of hair had fallen loose down the side of her face, but she did not pause to fix it. The only thing she adjusted —her spectacles— were swiftly nudged back up to the bridge of her nose by one knuckle. He noted the bent wire that didn't quite fit and caused them to keep slipping forward. No one had bothered to fix them for her, but he, surely, was not the first person to notice the problem.

"Has my beginning as an unwanted stray softened your impression of me, Mrs. Monday?"

"I was thinking how little you've changed. Still a boy who refuses to follow rules."

"I am not the only one with a mutinous soul, am I?"

"Your meaning, sir?"

"Surely, for you, taking this post is an act of rebellion against your very proper upbringing. You decided to break some rules yourself."

She shook her head and another damp lock drooped against her cheek, reminding him of the candlelit scene in his scullery. A woman's bared neck and shoulders had never seemed so naughty, so forbidden to his eyes.

"Or perhaps you came here, simply so you might put me to rights, tell me how wicked I am, and get your long overdue apology for once being stepped over."

She stared, eyes wide through the round lenses of her spectacles.

"Or were you looking for adventure, Mrs. Monday? Were you bored with the oh-so polite gentlemen of Chiswick and decided to throw in your lot with an uncivilized beast, just for the thrill?"

Now her face was tense. "I needed employment.

To be busy and useful. One should go where one is needed. Find a purpose."

Naturally she would not mention the money. It wouldn't be proper. Yesterday she was affronted when he dared suggest her in need of funds. Did she imagine he wouldn't notice her tired old boots and that dreadfully depressed, out-dated bonnet? Well, he was considerably more observant than the other men in her life must have been, for he knew she was hiding something. More than a very fine set of shoulders.

"Shall we proceed?" she asked calmly, pen poised over the paper.

Feeling overheated, he removed his jacket and tossed it over the back of the small settee. Another thing he shouldn't do in the presence of a lady, but True never listened to "shouldn't" and he wasn't about to start just for this strange creature.

He continued, "One day I was caught poaching on the squire's estate. He wanted me swinging from a gibbet and out of his sight for good. The very knowledge of my presence was galling to him."

"Why?"

True paused. "There were rumors." He took a breath. She was watching him intently, waiting with patience. "Some suggested that I was not the orphan of a shipwreck, but that the squire's son had fathered me and abandoned my young, unwed mother, causing her to leave me on the sands that night. Of course, the squire could not bear that idea. *Me*— the feral boy who could barely speak in any recognizable language? He did not want that shameful blot on the family escutcheon."

"I see."

He lifted one shoulder in a lazy shrug. "I never believed it any more than he did, but despite his son's denial, he wanted rid of me and of the rumors. It was said his son had violently forced himself on one of the very young dairy maids. None of it could be proven. The girl— if she existed—had run off, too afraid to come forward and accuse him. That left only my presence to point a finger. Better, therefore, if I be dead."

After a pause, she said, "You must have been afraid to be friendless and all alone in the world."

"No. Not fearful. Angry. Yes, I remember fury as a driving force in my youth, spurring me on."

She nodded. "And it drove you to success."

"Against the odds." He walked around her chair, breathing in more of her fragrance. It was subtle, but pleasing. "Do you think, in common with most, that because I was base born I should have stayed down in life?"

"Not at all, sir. Some great men in history were lowborn. Cardinal Wolsey was a butcher's son and Thomas Cromwell the child of a blacksmith, to name only the first two that come to mind."

"You flatter me." He laughed, tugging on one ear. "My achievements are not so great as theirs. I am not a man of books and no king will ever consult with me."

Her eyes blinked, the pupils expanding as his shadow fell over her. "You should not undervalue your success, sir. You have done far more with much less, than many men in this world who sit back and make no effort."

Disquieted by her solemn, earnest gaze, he put his hands behind his back and proceeded to walk around the settee again, reversing his direction. "In any case, I escaped my fate on the gallows and fled England on a fishing boat. But I swore vengeance on the family that had wanted me hanged. I would get it too, in time." He finally lowered his seat to the velvet ottoman again, boots stretched out before the fire. "The unfortunate thing about vengeance... it has a habit of turning on the man who yields it and slapping him hard in the face. But we shall come to that."

Mrs. Monday set her quill aside to let the nib dry and picked up another. "So you went to sea. What then?"

"I took every lowly, menial job I could find. Anything to make coin. I discovered then my talent for figures and calculations. I could keep great sums in my head, you see, even as a boy. When I found it earned me coin I practiced often, sharpened the skill. I made a study of gamblers and the risks they took, and I saw how they were drawn in by only the slenderest chance of a win. I traveled abroad, began to accumulate winnings at a rate that soon made me unwelcome and kept me moving from town to town. After five years — and my first bullet wound—I returned to England with a good-sized fortune." He smiled. "Many would call it rotten gains, Mrs. Monday."

"Only those who are envious of your success. There is never a person quite so self-righteous and noble as one who can't afford to be anything else."

He laughed, more relaxed with her than he had felt for a long time in anybody's presence. Yes. Underneath those dull garments she was not all forbidding, sharp edges.

The amber-tinted image of this woman standing in his scullery, arms above her head, returned again like a flame struck into being, flaring and stretching. The deep curve of her waist, waiting for his hand upon it, the sensuous line of her neck, traced by a dribble of water that caught the light and sparkled lustily.

For one breathless moment he had longed for her to turn and see him there.

What would she have done? What would he have done? Usually he knew. With this woman he wasn't sure.

Chapter Eleven

You will wonder why this young man, with all his limbs intact, didn't go to be a soldier and fight Napoleon. Well, this boy did not feel great allegiance to any king or country— or even to the human race.

He had spent his youth kicked from pillar to post, no one wanting him about for long. The only thing he fought for was his own survival.

But he was young then, of course, and youth is selfish. He knew no loyalty to his fellow men. For the longest time he was all alone in the world, and glad of it.

A man travels faster when he is lighter and has no burdens to weigh him down.

"I heard once that you were American," she said, her pen still scratching away at the paper.

He leapt to his feet again and returned to the window, although it was dark out, not even a moon to trace the outline of distant waves. Distracted by his thoughts, True saw nothing anyway. "Yes," he muttered, "I heard that too. I spent time there as a young man, so that must be where the rumor started. I sailed from Ireland, landed in New York and enjoyed eight months in the company of a very generous, very wealthy, older lady who helped me discover more talents than I knew I had. She took me under her wing, sought to give me something of a gentlemanly veneer."

"How fortunate that you found a benefactress."

True strode back across the room to where she sat, looking over her shoulder as she wrote. "I was lucky, yes. She taught me a great deal. In bed and out of it."

Her fingers tightened around her pen and he heard a startled intake of breath. He smirked, feeling playful.

"Shall I show you some of the things she showed me?" Not waiting for an invitation, he dropped to the cushion beside her on the little settee. "She taught me one of the most sensitive spots on a woman's body."

"I don't think I—"

With great care he touched his finger to the back of her neck and drew a circle on her skin, just below the coils of damp hair that escaped her hasty knot. Did she tremble or was that just a draft touching her pearl earbobs?

He ran his fingertip down the side of her neck to the grey collar of her gown.

"It was all very pleasant until my lady friend in New York began to consider me her pet. Wanted to put a collar round this throat of mine. When I proved resistant to some of her more...fervent...methods of training, she did not like me so much."

"Oh." A fat splodge of ink spoiled the paper and he thought he heard just the hint of a swallowed curse.

"But our parting was amicable. We had both received benefit from our companionship, and she repaid me very well for the time I spent in her company."

She dipped her pen in the ink again.

"After that I went south, rode a paddle-steamer along the Mississippi river to gamble. That was the first time someone shot at me. A bitter loser with a large pistol and very bad aim. I dove overboard." He chuckled. "But I out swam an alligator that night in the dark. I can only conclude the beast had already eaten well that day, was feeling fat and couldn't be bothered to race after me."

When he looked at his secretary she had removed her spectacles to clean the lenses with a kerchief.

"You don't believe I claimed victory over an alligator, do you?"

"Oh, I can believe it. More likely than the dragon you once fought, according to Damon."

He sank from the settee to the floor by her feet, stretching his legs out, his upper arms resting on the cushion behind him. "Yes, I had to adapt the story for the boys when they were young. And it looked like a dragon to me in that dark, swampy river, with bullets flying over my head." He smiled up at her. "Occasionally I like to embellish just a little. Makes it more exciting."

"I doubt you need to embellish anything, sir," she muttered wryly.

After a pause while he waited for her to finish cleaning her spectacles, he continued, "I was a curious young man in those days, wanted to try everything once. It often... cured me...." She had just wet her lips with the tip of his tongue. *What was he saying? Oh, yes.* "Cured me of the desire to do so a second time. What about you?"

"Me?" She looked startled.

"Yes, you." He grabbed the spectacles from her hand and held them out of her reach, wanting her answer before he would give them back.

"Yes, I was curious, sir. But when I asked questions it had a tendency to irritate people. I didn't have the opportunity to try things for myself the way you did. I had to rely on books, or answers. When anybody felt obliged to give me any, which wasn't very often."

He thought that very sad. Couldn't imagine not being able to do whatever he wanted, to feel and taste for himself.

"Of course," he said softly, "when I *wasn't* cured of the urge by trying something once, it was likely to become my new addiction." True looked at her lips and saw that she'd dampened them again with the tip of her tongue. "And then I couldn't get enough of ...of it. Whatever it was."

"I have noted the tendency to overindulge." A little smile wandered across her mouth as if it was lost there.

The fire crackled and coughed. He thought how pleasant it was to have her quiet, gentle company.

"I would always answer your questions, Mrs. Monday," he said suddenly, "if you wish to ask me any."

She looked at him warily.

"I will tell you anything you want to know," he added brightly. "Don't hesitate to ask."

After thinking for a moment she said, "What if you don't know the answer?"

He grinned. "I'll make it up, of course."

"Well, thank you for the offer," she replied, her tone cautious and hand outstretched, waiting for the return of her spectacles.

She had not, he noticed, offered to let him ask her anything in return.

"Shall we get on?" she said firmly.

True held her spectacles up to his face and peered through them. Hmmm. Interesting. "By the time I returned to England I had shot up several good

133

inches and grown into my breeches. I bought new clothes and a fine carriage, found a name and set myself up as a gentleman of means, gambling in London, Brighton and Bath. I made a study of every titled young man and every inheritance in the country, so I knew where the pickings were rich, and where they were not so well guarded."

"And I suppose it was not only gentlemen who were taken in." She snatched her spectacles from his hand and quickly put them back on her own face.

"Quite. There were ladies just as eager to wager their baubles. And more."

She shook her head very slightly and then pretended it was because of another inkblot and a faulty nib.

"You, of course," he muttered, amused, "would never have been tempted to misbehave with me, the way they were. You are too shrewd."

"I am."

"You never enjoyed a moment of illicit pleasure?"

Still looking down, she hid her face from his perusal. "Pleasure does not have to be illicit, sir."

"Oh, I don't know." He chuckled. "I've found some of the best of pleasures seem to be on the forbidden list."

No response.

So he continued, "So many foolish young men ready to wager their fortunes, desperate for entertainment. They ventured into the seediest of gaming hells, where instantly they must be at some unease and on their guard. What they needed, I saw, was a more refined establishment. A gentleman's club that did not hide away in a side street like a dirty secret. A place where they would feel in control, on their own ground. It must be exclusive, with fine dining, chandeliers, a French chef and polite staff in livery— where the gaming was almost by coincidence."

"Which gave you the idea to open Deverell's."

"Yes, I opened the club on St. James Street in London the same year I returned to England." He stared into the fire. "I enticed those bored young aristocrats, and soldiers on leave, looking for excitement. I pampered them in the plush environment of Deverell's. I spent every evening there and the rattle of dice in the box became as regular to me as the rhythm of my pulse." He smiled, thinking back to those early days of success, how he could smell the money as it walked through his door. "There, one evening, I came face to face again with the man once rumored to be my father, the old squire's son. He didn't recognize me, of course, but I never forget a face. With him was his fiancée, a beautiful young woman draped in a great many gaudy jewels. Lady Charlotte Rothsey, daughter of a Scottish nobleman."

His secretary paused to fill her pen. When she was ready again, he proceeded.

"Women were not permitted in the club, but he brought her with him even so, to show her off I presume. I had the immense pleasure of tossing them both out."

"How humiliating for the lady."

He laughed. "Ha! Not Charlotte. She has no sense of shame. She loved the attention. In any case, that was how I encountered my future wife, while she was engaged to the man who might have been my father. You will be shocked by that, eh?"

Her mouth tightened, but she did not reply.

True rested his arms across his parted thighs, hands clasped together. "My reputation did not warn her off. I told her I wasn't safe to be around. Never had been and never would be. I warned her that I was not the sort to fall in love. I'm not made that way. Even so, she pursued me. If anything, my reluctance made her more determined." He stood quickly, resuming a restless circle around the room. "Why do women always assume they can change a man?"

"So Lady Charlotte seduced *you*," his secretary muttered drily. "It was not your fault."

"I do not say she was solely to blame. I saw a way to get my vengeance on the family who would once have put a noose around my neck. I decided to steal her away from under that man's nose, just because I could. Then I would take her in every possible way and leave nothing for him to enjoy. Oh yes, my plan was villainous.

Alas, one night in a woman's bed can have consequences for a lifetime, especially when she has a scheme of her own. When she is just as lacking in scruples as the man who meant to use her in his game of vengeance." He paused. "Do I go too fast, Mrs. Monday?"

Her cheeks flushed, she belatedly shook her head.

"Do I speak of matters that embarrass you?" he demanded.

"I'm sure I'll get accustomed to it." She looked up, eyes wary. "You do not mean to describe it in detail, surely?"

"It?"

136

"The act itself."

"The act itself?

She pressed her lips shut and glared.

He laughed. "Fucking, Mrs. Monday. I believe that is the word you seek. And no, I do not mean to describe the fucking in great detail, inch by inch."

"Thank goodness," she muttered, breathing hard.

"Wouldn't want you getting all overwrought and agitated under your petticoats, would I?"

She shot him a piercing glare, much like a bullet and better aimed than those usually headed his way. "I don't get *agitated*, sir. I'm a lady."

"Is that so?" He tried to keep a solemn face. "I've a lot to learn about proper ladies."

"So it would seem," came her tart reply.

"Really, Mrs. Monday, you'll have to make allowances for me."

"Allowances? Where would we all be if we made allowances for bad behavior?"

"I don't know where for certain." He smiled. "But we'd all be having a bloody good time with not a damnable care in the world."

Was that the hint of a smile? Perhaps, but she hid it well. As if she'd had a lot of practice.

What the devil was she up to in his house, playing the meek and proper lady? And wearing spectacles made of plain glass, behind which she tried to disguise herself as harmless?

Chapter Twelve

So it began.

As he told her his story, Olivia felt herself drawn in. He was interesting in ways he should not be, and the fascination she felt at ten years old when reading about him in the newspaper had not diminished when she met him in person. When she got to know him as a real being, not just a dark, shadowy legend.

Now she heard, first hand, all his wickedest secrets and he held very little back to spare her blushes.

Deverell had an aversion, it seemed, to working in daylight. He found other things requiring his attention until dusk settled over the sky. Then he called for her, and, closeted away with him every evening, the curtains drawn, she became his confidant, his confessional.

Also, much to her despair, she sensed she had become his amusement too. Subject to his wicked teasing, she could do nothing but hold her chin up and bear it, thinking all the while of that handsome fee he promised to pay her.

During the day she tried to make herself useful around the house. Mrs. Blewett, surprised at first to find a willing helpmate, agreed to let her assist with the cooking and was vastly amused when Olivia readily conceded, "I have never been very good at it, just enthusiastic."

"Didn't your mama teach you, then?"

"No. She died when I was eight. We had a girl from the charity school a few days a week, but she wasn't terribly friendly and had no time for me. I was instructed to stay away from the kitchen when she was there. At other times, papa had to make do with my efforts."

The cook turned out to be a patient tutor and was pleased to show Olivia a few skills with pastry and sauces.

When Deverell came in from his ride one morning and found the two women laughing together, Olivia covered in flour, he demanded to know what they were up to— as if they might be plotting to put poison in his pie. Apparently he wasn't accustomed to much female jollity in his house.

"Mrs. Blewett is teaching me to make pate feuilletage," Olivia said proudly.

He eyed her messy pinafore. "Sounds painful."

"Puff pastry, as decent folk call it," the cook explained.

"And hopefully it won't be painful to eat," Olivia added. She was very warm from the heat of the kitchen and knew her face was probably an unappealing mess of scarlet blotches and perspiration, but Deverell was staring at her in an odd way.

"Where is it then?" he demanded.

"It's baking. It's not ready yet." She hastily moved in front of the oven, hands behind her back.

"Hmm." His gaze narrowed. "I can't wait to sample your delights, Mrs. Monday."

"Well, you'll have to wait, won't you?" Mrs. Blewett exclaimed, chuckling. "Unless you want to burn that cheeky mouth of yours."

He looked affronted. "Mrs. B, it's not like you to be so insubordinate. I hope my new secretary isn't rubbing off on you. She does have an uncommonly sharp tongue, as I know already to my cost. I fear she will be a bad influence on my staff."

Both women stayed silent. Olivia was not sure if he meant it, or if he was jesting again. She had yet to learn all the subtleties of his expression.

He turned to leave the kitchen, but fired one last arrow over his shoulder, "And Mrs. Monday, be sure to wash that flour off your face before you come to me later, or I shall be tempted to deal with you as a cat does with a kitten."

The cook giggled at that, but Olivia did not. She was left to picture him licking her face and it was all too clear a vision in her imagination. Knowing his improper habits, it was also entirely too possible.

Unfortunately the pastry did not rise at all as it should have done. Even Mrs. Blewett was dumbfounded. They put it out for the birds and when Deverell later asked for it, Olivia explained that he would have to wait a little longer still.

"My first attempt was... lacking somewhat," she muttered, "but I shall persevere."

"I'm glad to hear you don't give up, Mrs. Monday."

"Certainly not. Nothing is ever too hopeless."

He gave her another of those strange looks and she raised a nervous hand to her hair, just to be sure it was every bit as tidy as it should be.

* * * *

One evening, while they worked late into the night, the butler appeared with a large tray of supper.

"Ah, splendid, Sims. Thank you." Deverell took the tray and set it down on the ottoman. "I thought we might enjoy a late repast in the manner of a casual picnic tonight, Mrs. Monday. Food helps the brain cells, so I'm told."

She looked doubtfully at the overloaded tray, spectacles clasped in one hand.

"Don't be timid," he added, once Sims had left the room, "Dig in at the trough. I shall. In my world, Mrs. Monday, if you don't eat when the opportunity arises you might be the one that gets eaten."

It would have been unthinkable in Chiswick. Occasionally she'd sat up late to help her father with work, or to assist her last husband with a listening ear when he composed a particularly important sermon, but never had she sat on the floor and eaten a picnic by the fire. With a man who seemed to think— and celebrate the fact— that he'd been raised by farmyard beasts.

She must not be misled by the easy informality with which Mr. Deverell treated her. He had hired her for one purpose only and liking him at all was not necessary.

"Try this," he said, cutting her a large slice of pie and passing it to her with his own fingers, as if it was the most natural thing in the world for a man to do. "Mrs. Blewett makes an excellent pork pie. I would wager you've never tasted anything like it. Ah, but I forgot - you don't wager." He held it out for her lips, but Olivia carefully took the slice in her own hand before she tried a timid bite. "Well?" he demanded impatiently, eyes gleaming in the firelight, jaw thrust forward as if daring her to criticize his cook's endeavors.

I wish he would tie his cravat, she thought anxiously. It hung loose tonight and his waistcoat had a few buttons undone. Just a few. She hadn't counted how many.

Three. Three were undone, actually.

It was a black silk waistcoat decorated with raised gold thread. Not too fancy a pattern, but very rich and quite beautiful when one saw it at close range. He wore it with casual disregard, however, treating it the same as he did the simpler, stained and worn corduroy waistcoat in which she often saw him.

"Well?" he repeated. "How is it?"

"Good," she replied, finally remembering the pie.

"*Good?*" He sat back, forearms resting on his parted knees, long fingers hooked together between them. "That's it? That's the best you can do?"

"I...I like it."

"Good lord, don't overdo it! The superlatives are killing me."

"It's very well seasoned," she added, hiding a chuckle at his frustration.

"It's the best pork pie you've ever tasted. Say it. I demand that you say it!" From the look on his face anyone would think no one had ever failed to be intimidated by him before.

"Well...I would hesitate to make such a sweeping statement. I've tasted many good—"

"You're remarkably hard to please, woman," he exclaimed gruffly.

"I did say it was nice."

"Nice? *Nice?*" He snorted. "Is that what passes for praise in Chiswick?"

"Mr. Deverell, it is possible to be pleased with something and not feel the need to leap up and down, shouting it from the rooftops. I told you, I like it."

"I suppose I must be satisfied with that then." A lock of dark hair fell over his brow, making him look somewhat like a crestfallen puppy, much to her further amusement. How easily he changed from fierce, surly beast to a naughty boy at whom one *should* be cross. As he swept that stray wave of hair back with the fingers of one hand she felt a shiver run down her spine. It was almost as if he had stroked her with that impatient hand.

She took another bite and stared into the fire, glumly thinking of what William Monday would have to say about all this. His advice was silent this evening and Deverell's presence dominated her thoughts. Even when they *weren't* in the same room. When they were, it was like being intoxicated— as she was once when she drank too much sherry before Sunday luncheon and then couldn't stop giggling at the Brussel sprouts.

Olivia could well imagine how young Deverell had swept through the halls of his infamous club as an ambitious, vital, mysteriously handsome figure, and secured the attention of Lady Charlotte Rothsey. As well as many other women, and men too. *He* could not be ignored or pushed away into a corner. If he took the last rout cake, no one would dare reprimand him.

"I can assure you it's the best pork pie in the county," he grumbled. "Mrs. Blewett has won awards at the county fair. I'm surprised she has not told you, but perhaps you spend your time in the kitchen prying for information about me."

"I beg your pardon?"

"I wondered what could possess you to spend so much time in my kitchen, when it's not part of your duties here. But Sims told me he caught you on the very first day, prying for information about me. You were, weren't you? And that's why you spend your time with Mrs. B, listening to gossip."

She wiped her fingers on a napkin and watched him pour two glasses of wine. "I was making conversation with Mrs. Blewett on the first morning, and since then I've been trying to help her, although I'm afraid I've been more hindrance than anything. And I'm not interested in gossip."

"Of course you are. You're a woman. But if you want to know something, ask me in future."

When he passed her one of the very full glasses, she mumbled, "I really shouldn't ...this late at night." Not that she had any idea what the time was. That fact was almost as unsettling as his proximity.

"But you will. I insist."

"You cannot insist that a person drink wine."

"Yes I can. My rules, remember? And I'm paying you well to be an obedient subject on my island." He frowned. "Don't fret. I don't plan to get you inebriated and senseless. You need a steady hand to write."

With a deep sigh she took the glass. "While we are on the subject of my role here, sir, I would appreciate it greatly if you could assure your staff that I was engaged as your secretary only. There seems to be a general assumption that I am here to serve you in some other capacity, and they won't listen to me."

"Some other ...capacity?" His eyes twinkled at her.

"I believe you know what I mean, sir."

He muttered gruffly, "Well, that's your fault. And Chalke's. If he had sent me someone closer to what I expected there wouldn't be any misunderstanding about your purpose here. No one would suspect us of anything like that, if you were different."

"What precisely about me would lead anyone to think I could be your ...your..."

"Mistress?"

She took a hasty sip of wine. "I would imagine I'm the last woman in the world that could be confused with that."

"Hmm. On the surface, you don't look like my usual company, I'll grant you that." He tilted his head, considering her through narrowed eyes. "There is something impish about you though."

"*Impish*?" A little wine spilled over the rim of her glass and wet her fingers.

"Naughty. Something you're trying to hide."

She huffed. "I am exactly what you see. What could I have to hide?"

"I know not, Mrs. Monday." A slow smile made him intolerably handsome suddenly. "But I will find out. I'm very good at uncovering ladies' secrets."

Oh, she had no doubt of that. "You don't know an Inspector O'Grady of the London Metropolitan Police by chance, do you?" she asked wryly.

"No. Why?"

She shook her head.

"Now try another bite of pie with some pickle," he exclaimed, swiftly diverting the subject. "Perhaps you found it too dry before." He was already cutting another slice for her. "And you look hungry."

"Mr. Deverell, no one has ever been quite so solicitous of my appetite."

"Damn shame. They should have been. Perhaps you'd have a bit more bloom to your cheeks."

Had he just moved even closer to her across the carpet? Olivia glanced sideways toward the sanctity of the chair and little writing table, which were several feet from where she now knelt. Her skin prickled with tension, as if it expected to feel his scandalous touch. "Shouldn't we get on with the work, Mr. Deverell?"

"Plenty of time for that. A man's got to eat, keep his strength up. Woman too."

The way he said the word "woman" was quite fierce— like a pinch or a bite.

"Give me your spectacles," he demanded suddenly.

"Why?"

He held out his hand, palm up. "Do not question your employer, madam."

Tentatively she passed the spectacles to him and watched as he began to press the wire about with his fingers.

"There!" He reached over and put them on her face, his fingertips skimming her ears. "That's better. I'm surprised no one did that for you before."

The fit *was* much improved. No sliding or pinching. "Thank...thank you, sir." She had meant to do that herself, but whenever she had them on her face there was always something much more important to be done. And once she took them off again, she forgot about it. Then they were often sat or stepped upon, or lost.

Deverell was studying her intently, with a knowing look. Olivia quickly removed the mended spectacles and set them aside.

Perhaps she was too close to the fire, which would account for her heightened temperature, so she slid back a little and felt a lock of hair tumble down her cheek as the sudden motion disturbed a pin. She wanted to fix it, but it felt improper to fuss with her hair in his presence. Was it *more* improper to leave her hair in disarray?

Did "improper" really count anymore at this stage, since she was seated on the floor with him? At some point good manners, as dictated by proper society, probably became moot.

He dug a silver spoon deep into the little dish of pickle and dropped a generous dollop onto the newly cut slice of pork pie. It was done hurriedly, but even as some pickle fell to the tray, he still spooned more onto the slice. Did the man do nothing by halves? He was all about excess it seemed. From one thing to the other he veered, his moods inconsistent and unpredictable. But always moving quickly.

"I learned recently that my daughter is getting married, Mrs. Monday," he muttered, his conversation flying off in yet another new direction. Olivia felt dizzy trying to keep up with him. "What do you think of that?"

"I would think it good news, sir."

"Why?"

"It is surely every young lady's hope to be married, and the desire of every father to see his daughter well married."

"Is that what your father wanted?"

"Yes, of course." She knew her father had once worried she would never marry. She'd seen the fear in his eyes, but only in a rare, unguarded moment. And that was all her fault, because she once made the mistake of telling him she hoped to marry for love. It was a foolish thing for a plain, clumsy girl with a very meager dowry to say. A girl who sought out dark corners, too reserved and bookish to catch anybody's eye. Her father— poor fellow— hadn't known what to reply, although his expression had safely discouraged her from mentioning it ever again out loud.

Looking at Deverell, she read anger in his face and something else too. Hurt. "What did you expect for *your* daughter, sir?"

"That she'd stay here to look after me in my dotage," he snapped.

"I'm sure that's not what you wanted." Olivia couldn't imagine this man wanting anyone to nurse him in old age. When he went to his maker it would be sudden and dramatic, she thought. He was unlikely to let his body fail in a lingering, weakening illness.

"My daughter is too young yet, only seventeen, and this man I haven't even met— chosen by her mother, no doubt..."

Olivia waited, but he left his sentence unfinished, as if that should be enough explanation. Eventually she said, "There are many reasons for a woman to marry. I don't know your daughter, sir, but I cannot think she would make such a commitment without good reason. I'm sure she has intelligence enough to know that her future happiness and contentment are at stake. Hers. No one else's."

His head came up again, his eyes fixed upon her face. "Why did you marry your parson, then?"

"Because he promised me a secure home and he was kind. Always very... kind."

"And?"

"Isn't that enough?"

He raised his eyebrows. "Save me," he muttered under his breath.

"You have some objection, sir, to kindness?"

"I'd be distinctly disappointed, if I died tragically

and my clever, witty young widow found it a challenge to describe me by any other word than *kind*."

"I don't suppose you'll need to worry about that."

He laughed pleasantly. "Indeed. My own impression of marriage has been very different to yours. My wife will have many more colorful words to describe me."

Chapter Thirteen

Wait. Had he just called her clever and witty? It happened so fast, she couldn't be sure. Olivia stared at the strong column of his throat as he tipped his head back and tossed a grape into his laughing mouth. He'd thrown those words at her in just the same way— casually— as if they barely mattered and were a mere morsel. As if she must have heard their like many times before.

She had let him lead her into a conversation that was becoming dangerously intimate. The worst thing she could have done. Although she knew they'd taken a wrong turn, Olivia could not stop her worn boots from venturing down that dangerous path.

"Why did you marry your wife then, sir?"

* * * *

"Lady Charlotte Rothsey announced that she was with child," he replied. "So I married her. Does it surprise you that I did the honorable thing, Mrs. Monday? Even after the dishonorable way in which our affair began? After all, I could have let her marry her fiancé."

"But I suppose you wanted your child to know you, because you did not know your own father."

"Yes." True took a steadying breath. "Unfortunately, after the wedding it turned out there was no child. Charlotte had resorted to a desperate deceit. I know not— still to this day— why she wanted the marriage so badly. She had suitors with more to give, titled, respectable men with estates. But she chose to cast her net for me instead."

Mrs. Monday watched him unblinking, eyes wide and so receptive he felt he could tell her anything. Anything. No woman had ever paid attention the way she did. Usually they were too busy thinking about something else, anxious about their appearance, or what he had to give them.

She had not drunk any of her wine except for a sip. Instead she set her glass down as if it was a precious relic entrusted to her care. "Perhaps Lady Charlotte was in love."

"Hmph. Charlotte has never *loved* anyone as much as herself."

Her gaze had not left him. "And you claim you are not capable of love yourself?"

"The word is thrown about with little care, overused and cheapened by tawdry sentiment. It is nothing deeper than a word penned in haste on a lacy valentine. Just as fragile and worthless."

"Although you have never felt it, that does not mean love cannot exist, or bring happiness to others."

"Did you love your husbands then?" he demanded. "All three of the unlucky fellows?"

"Of course."

She answered that too quickly, he thought, and without the slightest warmth of memory on her face. Another ripple of annoyance stirred his blood. She'd called the parson "kind" for pity's sake. *Kind.* Just as Mrs. Blewett's delectable, unequalled pork pie was simply "nice".

"What makes you think you loved them? How did it feel?"

"I ... felt useful."

"Useful?" he repeated, astonished.

"I am not here, sir, to talk about me."

"But I should know something about the woman to whom I'm giving food and board for so many months. Especially since I was deceived about your age. If you don't tell me the truth about your husbands I might imagine all manner of wickedness hidden in your past." He squinted at her, noting the slightly heightened color in her face. It was no good; he couldn't resist. "I must know all about you. Every little thing." True reached over and moved the loosened lock of hair from her cheek, tucking it behind her ear. When his fingertips brushed her skin he felt the heat. It shot through his body and started a low, heavy pulse, a needy hum deep inside. "You must be running away from someone... an illicit lover perhaps? Something has chased you away from your safe, familiar comforts and brought you here. To me."

"Clearly you have a good imagination," she replied, hastily reaching for her glass again and spilling wine on her skirt. "After all, you believe in mermaids."

He released that stray curl of hair. "And you do not."

"No."

Now he knew how her skin felt, he wanted to know how it tasted too. True licked his lips, impatience making his mouth water. "But you *do* believe in that thing called love, madam? Three times you've believed in it. Odd. Still, you *are* a female— if Chalke hasn't lied about that too— and I daresay you have the same weaknesses that plague the sex in general. You just keep yours hidden under that cheerlessly grey suit of armor."

She set her glass down again without sipping

from it, looking confused and then staring in despair at the stain on her skirt.

Before she could grab her napkin, he seized his chance, took her hand and brought the wine-dampened fingers to his mouth. There was a moment when she tensed, tried to tug her hand away, but he pulled back, insistent. Her eyes widened. "Mr. Deverell—"

True licked the wine from her fingers.

He heard the breath catch in her throat, saw her pearl earbobs tremble. She closed her eyes, but they fluttered open again almost immediately when he drew her fingers further into his mouth and sucked.

The taste was every bit as sweet and enticing as he'd anticipated.

"Sir!" she gasped on a rushed breath. "Please..."

He released her fingers. "Yes?"

She stared, eyes huge, lips parted and damp. In that moment he expected a slapped cheek. At the very least.

Ignoring his actions as if they never happened, she said, "Perhaps Lady Charlotte married you for rebellion then. Her family could not have approved her choice."

"That was a part of it, to be sure." He studied her face, more curious now than ever about his odd little secretary and her determination to pretend certain things hadn't happened.

Or were not about to happen.

Blood raced through his veins as desire mounted. Another lock of hair had fallen to her shoulder, but she made no move to pin it up again.

He slammed his own glass down and refilled it to over-flowing, splashing blood red wine on the tray.

After a moment he resumed his story, voice tight. "So, as you see, by the time I discovered my wife's lie—that she was not expecting a child— we were married. She'd got what she wanted. At least, what she thought she wanted. In the meantime, I discovered that I had fathered a son by a woman I knew years before."

Mrs. Monday was preoccupied folding her napkin into a neat square, the corners carefully aligned, the linen smoothed out. She seemed tied up in her own thoughts, not listening to him. Odds were she was thinking of her husbands now. He didn't like that; he preferred to have all her attention.

True leaned closer toward her, pressing one hand flat to the carpet. "My first child had been conceived, so I learned, just before I fled England on that fishing boat. A gamekeeper's daughter who once, most generously, taught me all she knew about a certain sport, bore my first child while I was abroad. She named him Storm. The boy was already five years of age when I discovered his existence. Once I knew, I provided him with anything he needed, of course. I thought it best for Charlotte not to know."

"But your wife found out."

"Not for another three years. I kept Storm out of her way. I knew by then of her vicious temper and did not want the boy to suffer."

She nodded slowly, opening her napkin, turning the square and then refolding it. "Although you say you cannot love— that you're incapable— it's clear you have affection for your children."

"In the case of one's litter there is a natural instinct to feed and protect, a bond that cannot be broken. Or should not be." He thought grimly of his own father, and, of course, his wife.

"The fondness you show for *all* your children does you credit, sir."

"Sakes! Praise at last from your lips, madam. I thought I was already declared to be a bad parent."

"Those were your words, sir. Not mine." Her lashes fluttered upward and True was drawn forward again into the clear, shining depths of her gaze. *How young she looked suddenly.*

Bloody hell. She was supposed to be plain and completely uninteresting. The last thing he needed was a new complication in his life, some new fancy.

Then *she* came along with that steady gaze, heart-shaped face, and brave, uplifted, little chin.

He'd always had a soft spot for the scrappers. An affinity, he supposed.

He quickly turned his head away from the surprisingly strong pull of her gaze and continued his story.

"For the first year of marriage we tried to make the best of it. Charlotte did become pregnant after all, and I was busy at Deverell's. We both had much to distract us. There was no need to spend a vast amount of time together. Her father may not have approved her choice and threatened to disown her, but once the first child was on its way he had to give his blessing, finally."

The woman beside him was still, listening without interruption, but now eyeing the plate of plump, late strawberries from the home farm greenhouse.

"Of course, it was a union made out of deception, Mrs. Monday, and we both suffered for it. I soon saw through my wife's physical beauty to the

155

ugliness within, and she found my lifestyle distasteful, decidedly unromantic. Not what she'd expected. Somehow, despite my warnings, Charlotte had thought to change me. But eventually she realized that I was, in fact, just as I'd told her, an untrainable stray. She found me rough and coarse." He paused, glancing slyly again at his secretary. "In bed and out of it."

She didn't take her gaze from the plate of strawberries.

"But by then she could not go back to her father and admit she was wrong. For my money and her pride, she stayed."

Mrs. Monday finally moved her focus from the strawberries to his face. "You both made that choice, sir. You both stayed."

"As I told you, I married her because she claimed to be carrying my child. A falsehood, as it turned out."

"And yet there were other children to follow. Several."

"It is the natural result of fucking, madam. Your god made it that way."

Her lips parted and closed again.

"What else should I do with the woman who is my wife? Go on, Mrs. Monday, tell me. I insist! Why else would a couple wed but to create children?"

A frown line appeared between her brows, and two hot poppies of color blossomed high on her cheeks. "You did not have to indulge. It is possible to have a marriage without...that."

"I disagree. When a man and woman are thrust together by vows, and they both have urges, what else should they do?"

Her cheeks reddened further. "Practice restraint,

156

sir."

"Restraint?" he sputtered.

"Read a book. Take up chess or...or bird-watching."

He chuckled. "Is that what your husbands did, madam? Perhaps you encouraged those other hobbies to keep them out of your bed. I've heard some women have a distaste for it. Even when it's gentle and tender."

"Once again, sir, we are not supposed to be discussing my life."

"Humor me." He swayed closer to her, wondering how far he could venture with his curiosity. Of course, he knew she needed the fee he was paying her. And True loved chancing his luck when the odds were against him; it kept his soul fed. "I've been told I'm too forward, too direct in my approach when I meet a woman I want. But I never had anyone to teach me manners, so you must forgive my candid curiosity. I've always wondered how the well-bred manage it. For example, how does a *kindly* parson approach relations with his dutiful young wife, without shocking her? Does he ask politely, or wait for her to put her embroidery down and give him a sign? Did you plan by rote, once a month? Surely it was at least once a month. Or did he forfeit his rights entirely out of *kindness*."

"Sir! This conversation is improper."

"You began this, Olivia."

"Indeed I did not!" Oh, indeed she did. Just a single flicker of her lashes brought out the mischief in him and once he began he couldn't stop.

"Madam, you suggested I should not have bedded my own wife as often as I did. When I was completely within my marital rights to do so."

She bit her lip and looked again at the plate of strawberries on the tray.

"Tell me, woman. How would your parson approach the matter of fucking when he was in the mood? I must know! I demand that you tell me."

"Sir, I know this way of teasing me amuses you, but I will not —"

He took a strawberry from the tray and offered it to her. She wanted it in her own hand, but he, holding the stalk, pressed the other end toward her lips. "Honesty, Mrs. Monday, if you please. I am telling you my life story. The least you could do is answer my questions about your own. There is no one here but you and I. How did the kindly parson tell his wife that he wanted—"

"Well, what would *you* say?" she exclaimed crossly.

"I would say..." he paused and ran the strawberry across her lower lip, "Come to bed with me, Olivia."

Her eyes darkened as the pupils enlarged. How long and thick her lashes were. He hadn't noticed until he got this close.

He cleared his throat. "No doubt you were a maiden the first time you married."

"Of course." Her voice was very soft and low, barely above a whisper.

"Did you enjoy relations with your first husband? Honesty!"

Although he thought she would not answer, apparently she was still intent on proving herself fearless. Up went the chin as her eyes flashed boldly. "I did."

"It was *nice*, was it?"

She rolled her lips together, held them tight a moment and then they snapped apart to exclaim, "Yes, I suppose so."

Her mouth looked very pink and full suddenly. Enticing. Had she just wet her lips with the tip of her tongue, anticipating the taste of the sweet fruit?

"These strawberries were harvested from a surprising late crop in the greenhouses," he muttered, his voice hoarse. "There won't be any more this—"

Suddenly, he saw a flash of little white teeth and then the strawberry was gone. All that remained was the green stalk. He was surprised she left his fingers intact.

She chewed slowly, a small bulge in one cheek, eyes gleaming with salty amusement.

Suddenly it occurred to him that she might have been sent there by one of his many enemies. He'd felt instantly that she was not what she pretended to be. This grey-clad widow with three dead men to her name already could be a Trojan horse. It wouldn't be the first time a bitter enemy tried to send him to his maker. Death by Olivia Monday, however, was a novel approach.

"Now it is my turn to ask you a question, sir."

"Is it?" Who made that rule, he wondered. But, being mesmerized by her lips at that moment, he let her get away with it.

"So although you had no love for your wife," she said quietly, firmly, "indeed, you say you are not equipped to love... you still took advantage of her, as if she was your property?"

Frustrated, he exclaimed, "I, like any red-blooded man, require the company of a lover from time to time. If I have one who has bound herself to me by

159

vows and laws, why would I not take my ease? The need to mate is just as instinctive as the need to defend and feed one's cubs. If I no longer felt such a need, I would know I was dead."

"And according to you, this was done with no tender or fond feelings for your wife, no softness in your heart? It was mechanical?"

"She expected to be serviced. If I didn't, I would not be keeping to our marital vows."

"Gracious! And you dare make sport of me for calling my husband *kind?*"

"So we have both endured marriages that were incomplete, unfulfilling. At least I only made the mistake once."

"I think, sir, we have—"

Unable to resist a moment longer, he grabbed her chin, held her face firm, and kissed her on those berry-stained lips.

Chapter Fourteen

It must be the fault of her dreadful curiosity, which refused to sit in a corner and be quiet. Instead it wanted to go wandering, even in worn boots, over this rocky, unpredictable terrain known as True Deverell.

His lips were so savage, so determined. His long fingers held her face and he deepened the kiss, leaning into her, his tongue tangling with hers.

The kiss— she called it that, even though it was like no other kiss she'd ever experienced— lasted too long, and then, somehow, she found the strength to pull away.

He breathed heavily, his eyes dark, his hair and his cravat now in even greater disarray she noted. Surely she had not done that with her own hands? She looked down at them now, checking for signs of misbehavior. Her fingers were curled into fists, hiding from her. Guilty.

"Forgive me," he muttered. "I should not have done that."

Something twisted painfully inside her. "No."

But his supposed penitence was brief. He moved close again, pushing the tray aside, spilling their supper to the floor. She saw it coming, had plenty of time to escape, but she did nothing.

The second kiss lingered even longer. His fingers pillaged more pins from her hair, while his lips took possession of her mouth as if they had some primal right. He was forceful, wicked. Everything people said of him. True Deverell, the legendary lover with dark, dangerous passions— a man that well-raised women only dare whisper about— was kissing her, his hands

161

exploring, his strength overpowering.

She fell back to the carpet and he followed her down, his body covering hers. His firm, determined lips caressed her chin, her throat. Olivia thought she might pass out, but not with helpless fear. With the sheer desire for more.

His hand stole its way upward from her waist, over her bodice, touching her through her gown and not in a gentle caress. Demanding, forceful, devoid of gentlemanly restraint. His teeth nipped the side of her neck. She thought it was by accident until it happened again.

He had led her off down a rocky path and the descent was steep, treacherous. Her heart raced with exhilaration.

She exclaimed in a rush of breath, "This is no way to write your memoirs."

Husky laughter blew warm against the side of her neck and he held her wrists tightly, drawing them up over her head. "I'll write them on you. Inside you."

"We can't." She did not care to be another of his conquests and he had told her plainly what he thought of women.

But he kissed her again and she let him devour her as if she had no choice. As if she was a passive woman without a brain. As if she'd been waiting ten years for this. Ten years at least.

In his hands she became a creature of lust. It raced through her veins, melted parts of her body, stole her anxious breath and replaced it with something that sparkled and sang and laughed. As if she had been frozen, stuck, and now her river flowed again.

Yes, she wanted him to feast upon her. Yes. At

last.

And then, suddenly, he stopped. He still lay over her, his lips barely an inch from hers, his fingers gripping her wrists firmly. "Now describe that," he murmured. "Was that *nice*? Can the pert little widow think of a better adjective now? Perhaps I've inspired her."

She stared up at him, trying to get air back in her lungs with his weight over her, crushing her to the carpet. "I ought to knee you in the unmentionables, sir."

"Oh, do. I dare you." He chuckled and she felt it moving through his chest. And elsewhere too, his manhood hard and moving against her thigh. When she writhed and struggled under him it grew further. His voice turned husky, his eyes at the point where heat turns to smoke. "But we both know that's not what you really want to do."

She tasted the residue of wine and strawberries on her lips. But she also tasted him. Mostly him. Too much of him. Yet also not enough.

"I daresay you'll pack your trunk and leave now, eh?" he muttered.

"Are you trying to frighten me away again?"

"Perhaps." But his hands still held her wrists tightly, not about to let her go anywhere.

"If you truly have a wager against me staying, you may as well concede defeat, sir. Your methods won't work on me." As she'd told him, she did not go back on her word and she did not give in. She also needed the money, not that she would ever admit that.

She lay still now, growing accustomed to his weight upon her, his warmth.

When she looked up into his eyes they were

molten steel. "What if I cannot guarantee this will never happen again? As I said to you, I am not dead, madam. I have urges, needs. The odds are —"

"Against *you*. Not me."

He squinted and she felt his fingers finally loosen their grip on her throbbing wrists. "What do you mean by that, woman?"

As he rolled onto his side, she sat up, briskly brushing at the front of her gown. "You don't want me here because *you're* afraid."

"Of what?" he scoffed, resting on one elbow.

"Of a woman who is not impressed by you. I will neither fall at your feet in breathless adoration nor be shocked into running away. So you don't know what to do with me."

"You may be unusual, Olivia..." His eyes gleamed with a sultry light, unearthly and terribly magnetic. "But I suppose you're all the same once the clothes come off."

"That's something you'll never find out, isn't it?"

"Do I hear a wager in your voice, woman?"

"I've told you before, I don't gamble. Do pay attention. And if you think those kisses did anything to me, you are mistaken." Carefully she got to her feet. "I should go to my bed, sir. My eyes are strained. I am tired. It is very late. I can be of no more use to you tonight." With that halting series of excuses Olivia turned to leave the library, but then paused and glanced back at him again. "You ought to write to your daughter, sir, if you are concerned about her marrying in error. Tell her you will meet this man she's chosen. You may not believe in love because you've never known it, but perhaps she has found something you did not."

"She's still a bloody child."

"Precisely, sir. And you're the adult. Well...", she swept his sprawling form with a haughty gaze, "you are meant to be."

With that, having said much more than she should yet again, Olivia left him to finish the supper alone.

Fortunately a lit oil lamp sat on the hall table and she used that to guide her steps to bed.

She paused on the stairs to glance up at his eerie, faceless portrait.

I, like any red-blooded man, require the company of a lover from time to time.

Present tense, she noted. And at his age too—supposed age. Hadn't he done enough damage?

* * * *

She tasted better even than Mrs. Blewett's pork pie. Just as well she took herself off, claiming eye strain, or he might have gone back for another taste.

Eye strain.

She was a mere eight and twenty, for pity's sake. How much eye strain could she have? And he knew, already, that she wore those spectacles just to hide behind, make herself less accessible. Perhaps she even thought they made her invisible. It reminded him a little of a child, who thought that if they hid behind a fence post then you couldn't find them.

True tipped onto his back across the carpet and stretched, crossing his arms behind his head. His body was far too aroused, aching with desire. He knew he'd best stay there a while, because if he got up he would be tempted to chase her down. This, he thought, is what becomes of a man who survives too long without a feminine playmate— he begins to fantasize about seducing the most unlikely woman he can find. Setting himself a challenge.

When he touched her that night he felt the need churning through her like a ferocious waterfall. It was almost enough to sweep him away. He imagined taking her roughly— in a field somewhere, under the wide-open sky, the fresh, sweet scent of blossom filling the air. Green stains from the newly mown grass brightening her dull gown.

In a fight she would probably give as good as she got, he mused.

Yes, she was a scrapper alright, and she was so bloody polite about it, he couldn't help laughing out loud suddenly.

* * * *

The boy stood very still in the water and waited. He knew the fish would come; he just had to be patient. He'd learned that the hard way, of course, suffering many hungry days with no fish caught because he was too clumsy.

But if he waited, those slippery bodies would come close enough. Then he could scoop them up and toss them onto the grassy bank behind him. He had to be quick. And he was now.

He counted in his head, memorizing the twisting pattern of their dance in the stream, knowing when another would be within reach. To any casual observer the fish moved about in a random manner, but he had studied them long enough to find a rhythm. There was a rhythm to most things in life.

And he had time. Nothing but time and hunger.

One day, he promised himself, he would no longer feel

hunger. And time would be something that troubled other men. They would wait for him, while he did as he pleased.

Sunlight dappled the surface of the water, dazzled his eyes, forced him to squint. The water was warm around his knees, lapping gently. The fragrance of summer swept and soared around him. The earth was alive and singing.

A wasp landed on his arm, but he kept his still pose. The insect crawled along, tickling his skin. If he moved now to swat it away, the fish would know he was there.

Here came his prey now, slithering through the water, tail flicking, mouth gulping. Sun flashed along its silvery body, beautiful and sleek. His mouth watered.

Chapter Fifteen

Morning sun trickled lazily into her chamber like rich, sweet honey from a spoon. For a long moment she lay there, letting the light squeeze under her slowly upward-drifting eyelashes, finding it hard to believe she'd ever managed to fall asleep after the strange events of the previous evening. But she had. Slept well too. Deeply. As if she had nothing to trouble her conscience. As if she had not let that man — her employer, for pity's sake—kiss her and nibble on her skin. She touched her neck, ran her fingertips over the place where his teeth had skimmed her flesh.

Olivia could see she'd have to lay down some rules now, even if her employer had an aversion to them.

Finally dressed, her hair braided in its usual knot, she went downstairs and found the house quiet again. His library was empty, no fire yet lit in the hearth, her writing materials left exactly where she'd discarded them last night. Even the supper tray and the remnants of their "picnic" remained on the ottoman. Her gaze drifted over the carpet and found the torn green stalk of a strawberry discarded there next to a wine stain.

She licked her lips, tasting again his kiss.

He needn't think she was a woman to be taken in and played with like all the others, to be abandoned as the mood took him. He was restless, needed too much of everything, all the time. Could probably never be sated. Must be exhausting company for the women in his life.

Outside the tall windows, sunlight danced on the water and gulls floated dreamily above, ready to swoop down and claim fish for their breakfast. The sea was placid today, the air calm, and the surprising mildness of the weather soon lured her outside. Surely even William couldn't forbid a walk for pleasure on such a morning. God's beauty should be appreciated, should it not?

In her mind, William had opened his mouth to issue a warning about her boots, but really he should trust her by now to know where she was going. Olivia was responsible for her own decisions and standing on her own two feet. He ought to approve.

She quickly tied on her bonnet and strolled out to explore the island farther than she had yet gone. Shielding her eyes from the sun's glare with one gloved hand, she took in the wild beauty of her surroundings— all very different to the orderly rose gardens and sculpted privet hedges of Chiswick.

The far mainland was a stretch of steep granite cliff side with dewy green above and a tawny strip of beach below. There was not a solitary human figure in sight, only the birds out to feed, picking among the seaweed for shattered crab shells. The island of Roscarrock itself was rocky, a terrain littered with treacherous lumps and sudden sheer dips. But Olivia ventured to the very edge, taking a great bold breath of fresh sea air.

A warm, gentle breeze carried the pleasing scent of rosemary to her nose and she looked around to find the source. It must grow somewhere in a rocky nook of the house wall. There she recognized catmint, a cloud of silvery leaves and lavender blue flowers peeping out of the stone. Hardy verbena and merrily nodding daisies had a presence in the rocky garden too, finding any spot to blossom. Bordering the edge of a downward tracking path, she found thick, strappy leaves of a plant she did not recognize and clumps of rosa rugosa, its blossoms now shed to let plump, ruby rose hips flourish with the new season.

Although it was all very wild and unruly compared to her usual surroundings, it was undeniably beautiful. Raw, but breathtaking in a way her last husband would not have approved. William always took steady breaths, was a firm believer in one's bad intentions being directly aligned with the amount of air one's lungs used, and considered activity that broke his usual rhythm to be anything from a mild nuisance to utterly hazardous to his health. Whenever he caught a glimpse of Olivia's boots— clear evidence of over-stimulation and an excessive use of breath— his eyes were heavy with sadness and disappointment.

As she stood on the tip of the island and surveyed the glimmering sea, her eyes suddenly found a dark blot among the waves. Without her spectacles she had to squint, trying to give the blob a shape, but it moved and changed as she watched. Finally she realized it was someone swimming in the sea. A man.

In the next instant she knew who it must be. Who else would go out so far in water that must be chilly, despite the sun? The current was surely strong out there, but he swam easily and then disappeared beneath the surface.

Olivia waited anxiously for his safe reappearance, but when it came he was much closer to the island. Her pulse thumped recklessly. His broad shoulders were touched by sunlight as he flexed them, bringing his hands up over his head. Then he dived forward again. With a jolt she realized Deverell was naked.

Utterly and completely naked as the day he was born.

He was... splendidly beautiful. There, would that be a strong enough adjective for the dratted man? Surely he would like that.

"She's doing it again. Someone ought to stop her."

The rocks under her feet shifted. A few pebbles rolled away and dropped, bouncing and rattling until, with a splat, they landed in the water below. Olivia hastily backed away up the path, her heart pounding.

She sincerely hoped he wouldn't see her watching.

The solution, naturally, would be to stop looking.

There he was again. For a man of his size he was graceful in the water.

Perhaps his mother really was a mermaid, she mused. How long he held his breath beneath the surface! Olivia had never swum in her life. Although she'd heard of ladies occasionally entering the sea with the aid of discreet bathing machines rolled into the water from the sand, it was nothing she'd ever had a fancy to try.

She was very warm, she realized, removing her glove and raising one hand to her brow.

There was Deverell again, diving in and out, quite at home in the water.

Suddenly he flicked his head around and raised his hand to wave.

Olivia hastily turned and reached to pluck some catmint, as if she hadn't been looking at him at all. Then she embarked upon a hurried scramble back toward the house, but she moved so fast that she slipped on more loose pebbles, got one inside her boot, and wrenched her ankle. Her boots were in such a poor state that they gave her no stability and they were not well equipped for this terrain. She should have known better, should have listened to William whispering in her head. Her last husband was always so wise.

Apart from his insistence on crossing that rickety old bridge every morning on his way to church, just to save himself a few steps around the lake...that was not so wise, was it? Not on the last day of his life.

Although it was unfair of her to think that— she shook her head irritably as she scrambled back up the hill. How could he have known what would happen? Poor William. That narrow path around the lake could add as much as half an hour to the distance from the parsonage, especially on a morning when the ground was muddy, and William sensibly preferred to keep his footwear and garments clean. While Olivia would have chosen the walk around the lake and even, when she was alone, stopped to feed the ducks, William always wanted to get to his church and pray as soon as possible, not to be out "rambling and wasting breath". So he used the ancient bridge to take a short cut across the lake.

Stumbling and limping through the wild garden, angry at the world in general and with that stone grinding against her big toe inside her boot, Olivia thought back over the events of William's last day. It was not a memory she liked to visit often, but she needed something to take her mind off the naked man in the water somewhere behind her. What better way to keep herself from the temptation of looking out there again?

"When did you last speak to your husband, madam?" Sergeant O'Grady — as he was called before his promotion—had asked.

She let her mind return to that rainy morning, the last time she saw William alive, when she had watched him take his umbrella from the stand by the door and put on his hat. The same as he did every day.

But on that morning...

"Do be careful, William," she'd said, getting a sudden precognition of something amiss that day. It was April the seventh, 1841, half past seven on Wednesday morning. She knew the time, of course, because she had looked at the long case clock in the passage. Habit.

Her husband was probably puzzled by the tension in her voice. "I am going to the church, my dear. As I do every day."

"Yes, I know. But do take care. A chill just came over me."

"A chill? Then you had best go and stand by the fire."

"I meant that I had a terrible sense of foreboding. As if someone walked over my grave."

"You know I do not approve of such expressions, Olivia. I thought we were in agreement on that score."

She had merely bowed her head in silent acceptance and gripped her hands behind her back.

"Now, I shall return for luncheon at precisely the hour of noon," he had added. "Please be sure the potatoes are properly boiled this time, my dear. They gave me the most terrible indigestion on Monday." At the memory of that discomfort his face crumpled wearily, the lines sagging and folding in like the pleats of a heavy curtain.

"Yes, William." Olivia was deeply contrite about the almost-raw potatoes she had accidentally served him a few days before, after an unexpected visit from Christopher had distracted her from the duty of cooking lunch.

As William passed out into the grey daylight, she'd thought about rushing down the passage and pressing a kiss to his cheek, but she knew he would think that quite unnecessary.

When noon came the potatoes were crumbling apart, as they were overdone. To make them edible, Olivia had mashed them up with butter. She was just carrying them through to the dining room, when the verger came to tell her the terrible news. Her first thought was that at least William would not know how she'd failed again to cook the potatoes correctly— she could not bear to be caught in the frown of his disappointment. Then, as the realization of what had happened sank in fully, she lost her grip on the tureen of unhappy potatoes, letting them fall to the flagged stone floor of the passage.

Once she got around to cleaning up the mess later, the potato had hardened and stuck to the stone. She almost wore out her knees scrubbing it clean again. No one had offered to clean it for her, although they all came to pay their dutiful visits to the new widow and, in so doing, had to step over the mess.

In that moment she had thought to herself, *No one would miss me if I wasn't here.* She was just as invisible to the people left in her life as that dried, mashed potato.

"Why did you feel something would happen to your husband that day, madam?" O'Grady had asked, frowning.

She could give no answer. Perhaps it was because

she had lost two other husbands before William? Was she beginning to recognize a pattern of signs? That much tragedy must leave some sort of mark on a person, she supposed.

"Is that blood on your gown, madam?"

"Yes." Olivia had looked down at the little red splatter on her muslin. "I cut my finger while peeling the potatoes."

The sergeant had then asked her about the pigs they kept. "The neighbors tell me you are quite adept at the slaughtering, Mrs. Monday."

"Well, someone has to do it," she replied sharply, her defenses quickly raised. Didn't mean she enjoyed it. In fact, it brought her out in a cold sweat whenever she knew the time approached, but once again William refused to pay for that service too. She might have added that she was also the person who chopped down trees, dug gardens and chased away bill collectors, because her husband was not capable. But the sergeant didn't want to hear about that.

In any case, she was a person who went on with life, not letting anything distract her from the tasks that must be done— the routine of existence.

Routine was very important. Had William not needed to remind her about the potatoes on that weeping April morning, he might have left the house a few moments earlier and dodged the fateful moment when a rotted section of the footbridge gave way.

Sullen, she sat on a flat rock to unlace her boot and shake out the intrusive pebble. Deverell, meanwhile, must have swum to the island with speed, for she heard him already splashing at the base of the steps, then grunting as he heaved his body out of the water. She looked around desperately. Had he brought no clothes out with him? There must be something laid nearby on the rocks. But no. There were no garments discarded. He would surely not approach her naked? Surely not. Not even him.

She heard heavy breathing as he began his ascent. Of course, she realized in horror, he must think she'd dashed back into the house. He would not expect to find her sitting there with one boot off. Lingering. He might think she did it deliberately.

"Mr. Deverell," she called out, "I have sprained my ankle. Please do not come any closer until I am out of your way."

There was a low curse and then his face emerged between two, permanently wind-bent branches. "You rise early today, Olivia. I wasn't expecting you about for another few hours at least."

Was it early? She had no idea, although the tide was not yet out, which should have given her a clue she realized. Water dripped from his black hair and his eyelashes. This morning his eyes were startling, the color of the moon on a clear night, and full of mischief. She dare not look too long. "How am I supposed to know the time when you have no clocks in the house?" she demanded crossly. "I am quite at a loss!" And she was too. But in many other ways, in addition to timekeeping.

"Perhaps you might lend me your bonnet?" he suggested.

"My bonnet?"

"To help preserve my modesty. Or some of it. If you would be so kind."

Ah. She untied her ribbons and held the straw hat out to him with as steady a hand as she could manage, carefully averting her gaze.

He took it.

"When I woke the sun seemed high," she explained. "Had I known you were out here—"

"No need for excuses, Olivia. Your curiosity about my naked body is perfectly understandable. You're not the first to sprain something trying to catch sight of my superb masculinity."

"I was not—" She heard his low chuckle and realized he was mocking her. Again. "You really ought to have a clock in the house."

"But I like keeping visitors in confusion and myself in a state of timelessness."

"Of course you do," she muttered.

He feigned comical concern, "Are you ill? You're perspiring in a very unladylike manner."

She took a handkerchief from her coat pocket and fanned her face, looking away from the difficult male. "It is warmer today and I think I've had too much exercise."

"You were moving somewhat speedily upward *and* backward. I'm not surprised you twisted an ankle."

"I'll be quite alright. Please go on into the house." She closed her eyes tightly, expecting to hear more rustling.

But suddenly Olivia was swept off her perch and caught up in a strong pair of arms.

She opened her eyes. "What are you doing, sir?"

"You can't walk on that ankle, can you, woman?"

"I can manage!"

"And it will swell up like an unsightly balloon. I have to look at these ankles of yours and I command that you keep them shapely."

"You shouldn't be looking at my ankles," she grumbled. "Put me down on my own two feet."

"Tsk tsk. What sort of gentleman would I be to make you limp back to the house in pain?"

"I didn't think it mattered to you, sir."

"Your ankle? Why would the fate of your sad little ankles not matter?"

"I referred to being a gentleman. Last night you warned me that you could make no promises about your behavior."

"Ah. I can't honestly say it *does* matter to me. But I know it matters to you. So I shall *try* to be good."

Olivia had nothing to say to that. The idea of anything that mattered to her being important to a man like him— or to anyone—was very odd. And if this was his version of trying to be "good" she feared there was no hope, but to say so would be discouraging.

He carried her through the untamed, rocky garden, and she tried to forget the fact that he was naked with only her bonnet tied around his groin.

"Did you sleep well, Olivia?"

"Yes. Thank you."

"I did not. I spent a wakeful night after you left me so abruptly."

"I'm sorry. That is unfortunate, sir." She watched a bead of seawater make its steady course down the side of his neck. "I slept very comfortably."

"I don't suppose you thought about me," he pressed.

"No. Good heavens, why ever would I?"

He scowled, gripping her tighter to his chest.

"I do hope my bonnet doesn't slip," she muttered. "Are the ribbons holding it up sufficiently?"

She dare not look for herself, but she knew they were not terribly long ribbons and badly frayed.

"Ribbons aren't necessary to hold it up," he replied stiffly. "Not at this moment."

"Oh."

"And unless you want us to go off into the realms of the improper conversation again, I suggest you leave it at that, Olivia."

She turned her face so that he wouldn't see her smile. He shouldn't call her by that name. But it was too fine a day to worry about any of that.

She didn't think she would ever be able to put on her bonnet again without remembering this strange moment. Including his boast about not needing the ribbons tied to hold it up.

Crikey, as his son Damon would say.

Olivia's gaze skipped across his damp, wide shoulders and she saw a scar where someone had stitched his skin together over a wound. No doubt there would be other scars, if she looked further. Quite a few people had taken aim at him, according to the rumors, and she had begun to understand why. He was the most infuriating man she'd ever known and firing a bullet at him might be the only way to keep him still.

"I expected to find your trunk packed and waiting in my hall this morning, Mrs. Monday, after my terrible faux pas last night."

Aha! So he *had* meant to chase her off.

"Mr. Deverell, I am not afraid of you, or what you might do to me, any more than I am afraid of steam engines. I have been telling you that I am fearless since the first night. Hopefully you can believe it now and stop testing me."

179

He laughed and she felt it rumbling through his chest. "I suppose I'm just a lot of inconvenient, rude noise and vulgar puffs of steam, eh?"

"Precisely."

"You really didn't think of me last night?"

Aha, he threw that question at her again on the sly, probably hoping to catch her off guard. "I did not," she lied swiftly and pertly.

"How did the kindly parson tell his wife that he wanted—"

"Well, what would you say?"

"I would say...Come to bed with me, Olivia."

She had fallen asleep with those words playing through her mind, tickling her on the inside. Of course, she had asked what would he say to his own wife, not what would he say to her. Deliberately and mischievously he had misinterpreted.

"I ought to drop you over the edge of this island," he grumbled. "Why am I carrying you without even the promise of a thank you?"

"Something about trying to be a gentleman. Not that I believed a word of it."

They rounded a corner of the stone wall and abruptly collided with a man coming from the other direction. The jolt caused Olivia to grab hold of his shoulders on instinct. Deverell almost dropped her, but in the next moment had gripped her even tighter against his bare chest.

"Storm!"

"Father." Sun shone down on a head of tarnished gold hair. A pair of deep blue eyes in a tanned face closed in on Olivia with a great deal of surprise and amusement. "I hope I'm not disturbing anything. Looks as if you have your hands full."

Chapter Sixteen

"I heard a rumor," his son exclaimed, grinning broadly. "Had to see for myself, didn't I?"

"Mrs. Blewett, I suppose."

"You know how she is. Couldn't wait to tell me about the extraordinary new woman in your life."

"Extraordinary?"

"Well, *odd and funny* were the words Mrs. B used. When I saw you with the lady in question I was obliged to reinterpret her description."

True knotted the belt of his robe, snatched up a towel and briskly rubbed his wet hair. "Mrs. Monday is not a new woman in my life."

"She looks like a woman. Smells like one too."

"She's a secretary. It's perfectly innocent."

Storm spun Mrs. Monday's bonnet around by the frayed ribbons, his bemused gaze assessing the debris from last night's supper. "Of course it is. No one can possibly think otherwise. At least the lady had *her* clothes on."

"She twisted her ankle."

"No need to explain. These things happen."

True swiped at his son with the towel to move him aside and walked around his desk. "Glad as I am that you accepted my invitation, it was for dinner, not breakfast."

"Thought I'd come and spend more time with my father, didn't I? After all, I never know when you'll be off back to London again."

"I plan to stay a while at Roscarrock this time." He wrapped the towel around his neck, gathered up the wine glasses in one hand and pulled the bell chord for Sims with the other. "Ransom is doing well

181

enough managing Deverell's, and I can oversee things from here. I've decided to write my memoirs, which is why I hired a secretary to help. So you can erase from your mind all suspicions about her." True set the glasses down on the untidy tray. He took a deep breath and straightened up. "She's a respectable parson's widow in reduced circumstances— which you must not mention— and she doesn't suffer fools gladly." He smiled ruefully. "Not the sort of woman for me at all. So I'll thank you not to embarrass her by suggesting there is anything like that between us."

He'd made up his mind that morning to try a little better and behave himself. Last night he'd gone too far. As he'd said to Damon, they weren't accustomed to the company of women like her. It showed. Unfortunately his actions had probably proven everything she'd ever heard about him.

But then she twisted her ankle and he couldn't let her limp into the house, could he? Jameson was still out fishing and Sims would never manage to carry her. So what else could be done with her? Putting clothes on first hadn't occurred to him until it was too late. She did have a habit of making him forget the best of intentions.

Storm's eyes narrowed as he watched his father trying to tidy the room. Finally he ceased twirling Mrs. Monday's bonnet by the ribbons and remarked, "It's not like you, father, to suddenly become all proper. Or to worry about embarrassing a lady. What's she done to you?"

"Actually, I rather thought she might make a splendid mate for you, son. A decent woman. Well-bred, but not too fancy. She's about your age and could keep you in line. Wouldn't take any of your nonsense."

There, that would redirect the teasing. She was all wrong for *him* anyway. He would ruin her reputation and shatter her wide-eyed belief in "love".

"Me? You got her for me?" Storm laughed loudly.

True tossed the remnants of last night's supper so violently onto the tray that he chipped the edge of a plate. Damn. Never mind, plenty more plates in the kitchen. "I didn't *get* her for you," he glanced anxiously at the door, hoping she wasn't sneaking about on the other side of it again. Just in case, he lowered his voice. "She's not a toy or a puppy! It was quite by accident that Chalke sent her here instead of the older, plainer woman I asked for. But since she arrived, I was thinking she might be just the woman for you."

His son folded his arms, Olivia's bonnet ribbons dangling from one fist. "Why would you think that, father?"

"Because she's polite, well-mannered, quiet, but knows her own mind. Won't let you get away with any nonsense. She's clever, amusing, hard-working, sweet. A bit stubborn, like you."

"You know all that about her already?"

He knew more than that, he mused. She *thought* she was fearless. She was understanding and tolerant of impertinent children, holding her own when questioned by them. She was determined, liked her food, had fidgeting fingers when nervous, and— despite assorted husbands— she had never before been properly kissed.

True decided he'd let his son discover all that himself. Except for the last thing, which,

183

unfortunately, he took care of last night, while he was not in his right mind and suffering from an old cockerel's wounded vanity.

"Men like us don't find her kind around very often. They don't grow on trees," he said with a deep sigh. "I suggest you sweep her up while she's here. If you know what's good for you."

"You're making me exceedingly curious about this woman, father."

"That's the idea, son." He forced a grin. "Now let me introduce you to her properly."

* * * *

"Does he swim... like that... all the time?" Olivia sat in the kitchen with her foot up on a chair and a cold compress wrapped around her aching ankle. "I wish I'd been apprised of the fact."

"The master takes a daily constitutional very early, whether he swims or goes out riding. He believes it keeps him in good health," Mrs. Blewett explained. "I didn't think to warn you that he swims in nature's own. He told me you're a late riser by habit, so I didn't think it mattered."

Exasperated by this lie he'd apparently spread about her being a lazy, sleepy-headed woman, she cried, "Late riser? I was late the first morning as I was tired from my journey and nobody saw fit to rouse me. I can assure you that I am generally up with the lark and prompt when it is required. In future I would like to be warned about what I might see if I venture outside."

"No need to take on! Besides you've seen it all before surely."

"I beg your pardon?"

The cook skimmed over that. "I'm sure it's no skin off my nose when you get up. Now you sit still before that ankle swells up like bread dough."

She poured Olivia a much needed cup of sugary tea for "shock", but really it was not so much shock, as it was amazement and awe that a man could swim so quickly and powerfully like that in the sea, then haul himself up a steep incline, and finally carry her as if she weighed no more than a bunch of flowers— and all while he was barely out of breath. As he carried her against his chest she'd felt his heartbeat and it was remarkably unperturbed. None of her husbands would have managed so much exertion in one morning. Freddy was never up before noon, and Allardyce saved his energy for escaping bill collectors. William, of course, had his troublesome bad back to consider, as well as the desire to keep a steady rhythm of breath.

"The master keeps himself trim and lean as a good steak," said Mrs. Blewett. "I daresay the ladies are grateful."

Olivia hoped her frown would be enough to discourage the woman from that subject. It did not.

"There's always plenty about. Before you came, he often had Jameson row 'em over at night from the mainland. Two or three at a time on some nights. But I must say you seem different to the usual fare."

"That's because I am *not* his usual 'fare'," she exclaimed.

The cook rambled on without listening, as usual. "I thought he'd slow down at his age, but there's no sign of it. Now, here you are, a bit of a girl, to keep him on his toes. I daresay you'll keep him well

185

exercised too, eh?" She erupted into more chuckles that shook her entire body. "If not, he'll be sending Jameson in the boat for a half dozen hussies again. My, you do look a bit peaky, young lady. Grey as a ghost! I'll make you some kippers. I don't suppose you've had any breakfast yet. Keep your foot up. Leave it to me."

Olivia sighed in frustration and snatched up her teacup and saucer. She began to appreciate what her stepbrother and father must have suffered when trying to make *her* see sense.

She had just taken a sip of tea when Deverell and his son appeared in the kitchen.

"Mrs. Monday, I trust your ankle is being well tended, or should I send for a physician?"

"It's only a sprain, sir," she assured him. "No need for a doctor."

"I'll decide that," he muttered, quickly hunkering down beside her, removing the compress and grabbing her ankle before she could protest. It was desperately improper, but once again she was forced to put the gesture in line with all his other improprieties, from which it was difficult to identify the worst offense. When Deverell's hands made contact with her foot and ankle there was only a stocking between his flesh and hers. Thus she was silenced.

How strong his hands were, how masterful his long fingers as they examined the hapless end of her limb, pressing and stroking to feel the bones within. Olivia dare not look up, but it was just as difficult watching his sun-tanned fingers holding her foot as it was to pretend it didn't happen.

With those same fingers he had skillfully mended

her spectacles. The first person ever to bother. A simple kindness she had not expected from a man like him.

Now he meant to fix her body the same way.

There was no clock in the kitchen, nothing to help mark the occasion.

Finally came his assessment. "It is not broken. But rest, please, and don't get up." He stood, those powerful hands flexing at his sides, and then added, "I suppose I should introduce my son properly. It was a trifle inconvenient to do so before." When she looked up, his gaze darted sideways, avoiding her own, and he scratched the back of his damp head in an oddly sheepish fashion.

Guilty, she thought at once. But of what this time?

The other man bowed, smiling broadly and showing off strong white teeth. "Mrs. Monday, I have the honor of returning your bonnet." He passed it to her. "I am delighted to make your acquaintance. My father speaks very highly of you."

She frowned. "He does?"

"Oh yes, cannot stop singing your praises."

"I can't imagine why. He's hardly put me to work yet."

"My father has a tendency to make up his mind about people very quickly. He says it's instinct."

She shot a glance at Deverell, who had walked away to discuss something with Mrs. Blewett. He wore an ankle-length robe in rich emerald velvet with a tall quilted collar. Naked beneath it, undoubtedly. His hair was still wet, wildly rumpled. His eyelashes held tiny prisms of light where they too were damp from his early morning swim. He could be the same

187

age as his son, she thought. Indeed, younger. She knew of no men his age so active and bursting with vitality. In fact she knew no men younger who could keep up with him.

Her heartbeat had gone from a lame nag's near halt to racehorse gallop.

Rowing hussies over from the mainland under cover of darkness, according to Mrs. Blewett. Half a dozen at a time! He was impossible. A glutton in everything he did.

"I hope you won't find life here too isolated, Mrs. Monday."

Olivia forced her attention back to Storm Deverell. "Oh, I'm not the sort that needs to be surrounded by people and activity. I'm rather an introvert."

"But when the weather is bad this island really is cut off from the rest of the world. You will find it eerie when the fog comes in so thick you can no longer see the shore."

"I have my work to keep me occupied. And plenty of books with me to read." She smiled. "As an only child up until the age of sixteen, I'm very good at entertaining myself."

The man's eyes were very blue and friendly as he studied her carefully for a moment. His face was sun-browned, his expression open and interested. She recognized his father in the line of the jaw and the sharp angle of that Roman nose, but where True Deverell's coloring reminded her of winter's stark beauty, Storm's gold-tinted aura was all harmless summer. The richest, warmest part of the season just before the wheat was harvested, when the sun rose early and the dusty days seemed to linger forever. She would have thought him very handsome, if she hadn't seen his father first. But Storm Deverell's sunlight had been eclipsed for her before they even met.

"If you decide you need company, or my father gets too much for you, I can be found on the home farm. I never stray far from it, and the company of a pretty lady is always welcome. Send a note with Mrs. Blewett any time, and Jameson can bring you over for dinner."

"Thank you. That's very kind." *Pretty lady*, indeed. How easily he threw those silly words out. Like his father saying she was witty and clever, as if she ought to be accustomed to hearing flattery of that kind—even in jest.

"The farmhouse is nothing fancy," he continued, "but I can put on a good spread if I know to expect visitors. For you, Mrs. Monday, I'll even wash my hands and wear a clean shirt." His smile broadened, a mischievous twinkle sparking in his eyes. Oh yes, that was familiar to her too now as a Deverell trait.

"How lucky for me," she replied wryly. "But I'd hate for you to go to so much trouble."

"I'll be on my best behavior. You won't know this yet, but I am, in fact, the best of the litter. I don't bite and scratch and hiss like the others."

"That's useful to know."

"And I never lose my temper. Patient as Job, that's me. Read the Bible every night by my fire, and bathe all over once a week, whether I need it or no."

"I am impressed."

"So when you get tired of my father's antics, you come over to the farm for dinner. I'll light the best candles for you."

"Shall we read Bible verses together?"

He hesitated, his eyes simmered. "If you wish, Mrs. Monday. We'll see how the mood takes us."

She had to laugh then as he attempted an innocent countenance. Those blue eyes must have helped him out of sticky situations many times, for they gave him the look of a pious choir boy. Oh, yes, she could quite see how Storm Deverell charmed the local young ladies, just as the cook had warned her. His father would have been the same at that age. Still was now, for pity's sake— scattering her heartbeat all over the place. Carrying her so easily. Teasing her. Kissing her. Assaulting her poor, innocent bonnet with his manly parts. Fixing her bent spectacles.

"Mrs. Monday?"

What had he said? Storm was waiting for a reply of some sort and she was utterly lost.

"You will come to the farm one evening and I'll entertain you," he reminded her.

"But I would not like to get underfoot. Are you not always busy at the farm? I hear it uses up all your energy and doesn't leave time for courting the local girls."

Now his gaze shifted slyly toward Mrs. Blewett and his father who were still in deep conversation, and he whispered, "Well, I can always make an exception for a very special lady."

"There has never been a *special* lady?"

"Not until now." He looked at her again, thoughtful, his voice lowered. "Not like you. The way that you are."

"The way that I am?"

His sun-kissed brows rose. "I would have thought it was obvious."

"I'm afraid not. I'm a very ordinary person, quite

unexceptional."

"Yes." He paused, rubbed his lower lip in a gesture identical to one she'd seen his father use. "We Deverells don't know much about ordinary people. So we're curious. Can't help ourselves." Storm lowered his voice again. "I knew you were different to his usual company the moment I heard my father worrying that I might say something to offend you. He doesn't generally give a damn what any woman thinks."

Olivia realized she'd been pulling at the already frayed ends of her bonnet ribbons, making them look even worse. She quickly knitted her fingers together to keep them still. "He needn't concern himself. I'm simply a secretary and in a few months I'll be gone."

"That's if I don't sweep you off your feet in the meantime, Mrs. Monday." Storm gave her another wide smile that seemed to be lit from within. Like the power of a sun god. "My father is very keen for me to make a good impression, and we Deverells love a challenge. Something...different."

"Actually I'm very capable on my own two feet. Very steady. Not likely to get swept off them."

He pointed to her ankle. "Until today, eh?" When he saw her expression, he assured her gravely, "Fret not Mrs. Monday, you are far from the first woman to fall foul of my father."

"It was an accident."

"That's what they all say."

* * * *

The visit from his son provided her slippery employer with yet another reason to delay their work.

"May as well go out for a ride," he exclaimed merrily. "It would be a shame to waste an unexpectedly fine day— perhaps one of the last this year— by sitting indoors."

Why couldn't it be *his* ankle that got twisted, she thought peevishly. It might have kept him at his desk that day.

Deverell turned to the cook. "Now, you make certain, Mrs. Blewett, that my secretary stays off that dainty ankle. Don't let her go wandering about the place. It seems she's a trifle accident prone, but I can't have her lame and we must send her back to Chiswick in one piece at the end of six months. Extra precautions are required while we have custody of her delicate person."

Olivia glowered at him.

He sighed. "Is a man never free of responsibilities?"

His son gave her another funny, jerky little bow, which made her think he must have learned the gesture from pictures in an instructional flip-book, but never tried it himself. Then he kissed her hand and exclaimed that he hoped to see her again very soon. With that, father and son left the kitchen, shouting loudly back and forth in a manner she could only assume was the usual method of communication in their family. Among the men at least.

She wondered if her employer meant to go riding in the same state as he went swimming that day, and it was some relief when he came back two minutes later to collect his riding breeches from the drying rack beside the fire. As he leaned over to grab the clothes, his dressing gown gaped open at the chest and she glimpsed that dark, damp hair against which he had held her half an hour ago. Perhaps she'd left a little of her perfume on him.

"Remember," he winked at her, "don't go off having any adventures without me. I shall need you when I return. The *moment* I return. Keep yourself in readiness to fulfill my needs, madam."

"Where else would I go?"

For just a moment he seemed serious. "One day you might run away."

"Not until the task for which you engaged me is complete," she said.

His eyes narrowed. "You haven't changed your mind then."

"Mr. Deverell, I never change my mind."

"I'm not too much for you?"

Oh lord, how did one answer that? She thought for a moment and he waited, watching her mouth. Finally she replied, "As long as I am not too much for *you*, sir."

His lip quirked. "I'm sure I can tolerate your saintliness for a few more months."

"Then we should both come out of this unscathed."

His eyes glittered down at her. "Unfortunately."

Again, when he left her, she thought she heard the walls sigh gently. Or did the sound come from inside her?

"Well, they'll be out for the rest of the day," said Mrs. Blewett, shaking her head and smiling indulgently, as if they were nothing more than two schoolboys playing truant, "and come back ravenous for my cheese scones, I daresay."

"I think I'll go up to my room and fetch a book." Olivia looked around for a makeshift crutch and saw a besom broom leaning by the wall. Reaching for it, she added, "Don't worry about me, Mrs. Blewett, I'll—"

"You will not, young lady! Like the master said, you stay off that ankle." The cook swiftly moved the broom away, very prim. "He charged me with the responsibility of looking after you and so I shall."

Even Jameson, who entered the kitchen shortly after, had evidently been warned to keep her busy while Deverell was out, for he pulled up a chair, took off his cap, and over several cups of tea, regaled her with a series of tales about shipwrecks and smugglers of "backalong" days. He promised later— once her ankle was better— to show her the beacon at the top of the tower, which was lit each night for the good of passing vessels whose Captains might otherwise venture too close to the shore.

"But you keep that foot up today, young woman," Jameson exclaimed, his big face creased in gentle concern. "The master needs you in full health and one piece. You're not to go off wandering without him, he says. We're to look after you like fine china. Woe betide any of us if some part of you gets broke while he's out."

It was almost comical. Her father had never made such a ruckus over one of his daughter's injuries. Her mother had been the same, caring in a quiet way, but reserved and always dignified. In Olivia's family it wasn't fitting to overindulge in one's illnesses or to be extravagant with sympathy for trifling little wounds— or even death. They would not coddle a twisted ankle any more than they would walk about the house in a state of undress. And they certainly wouldn't talk about private matters between a husband and wife.

True Deverell didn't understand dignity, boundaries or taboo subjects. He rode right over them. Another reason why she shouldn't find him at all likeable.

But it was too late.

Chapter Seventeen

The boy ran in the meadow where the grass was almost as tall as he. There he could hide when the farmer was in a temper, or when the gamekeeper was after the "stray menace" for lifting from the traps before he could get to them. But he ran there too simply because he loved the soft stroke of the grass, the scent released by the wild herbs crushed under his feet, the gleam of the sun catching on feathery, floating seeds. And he liked to lay among the tall strands, on his back, and watch the clouds sail by, unhurried, slowly turning into new shapes as they passed.

After it had rained, large, glossy drops hung among the blades of grass, perched on daisy petals and nestled in the buttercups, waiting for the tip of his tongue to find them, as if he was a bee seeking out nectar. It was better tasting water than the slightly rusty kind he drank from the trough in the yard or the rain barrel beside the barn. He considered those fresh, new-fallen rain drops his personal treasure.

In later years, as a grown man, whenever he saw diamonds or pearls hanging from the ears of a lady, he felt the same enchantment. It brought back to him those happy moments from his childhood. There had not been many of those. Perhaps that was why they mattered so. The little things were what counted most. The things no one else noticed, but he found.

* * * *

True slowly grew accustomed to the secretary's small, pale face hovering at his elbow, waiting impatiently to work on another Chapter of his memoirs. He expected it to be a vast annoyance, worse than a tailor's pin stuck in his backside, but he was wrong.

Yes, she had her irritating points: the way she managed to nibble her food without spilling a blasted crumb; the tiny sips she took, nursing a single glass of wine for hours; the unrelenting dreariness of all her gowns; the tense way she tightened her mouth from time to time, deliberately denying him the pleasure of seeing her smile. The speed with which she moved her hands away from his, even when his intentions were perfectly harmless.

She made him a new ledger— one without any blots, doodles, torn pages and violent scratching-outs. One that tried to make him stick to a proper schedule, as if he was a bloody mail coach. If he wasn't careful, the woman would organize him right into a coffin. But he could barely remember any longer what it had been like without Olivia Monday hanging about like a good conscience, shadowing him around the house, reminding him to do things he had deliberately tried to forget.

Storm visited for dinner, often calling in at other times of the day too, as if he hoped he might take the two of them by surprise again. But True was careful after the incident with the twisted ankle. From then on he warned her if he meant to go swimming the next day. When Storm pointed out that his father was making unusual efforts to be polite around the woman, he dismissed that remark with a careless shrug. She was one little woman and only under his care for six months. How hard could it be to behave himself that long? Besides, he wasn't always good. A man had to have some relief and stretch in the paddock once in a while, so occasionally he couldn't resist making a comment to see her rather stunning eyes widen in scandalized shock.

That novelty did not fade over time. Neither did the pleasure of teasing her. If anything, it increased.

When his son took Mrs. B into Truro on market day, True suggested Olivia go too in case there was anything she needed to purchase. He meant to slip a few coins into her reticule when she wasn't looking.

"I do not need anything, sir," she said, looking puzzled when he mentioned a trip to the mainland. "Unless there is some purpose I can fulfill for you in town?"

"No, no. I thought you might want to buy a few lengths of some...pretty material."

"Why would I do that?"

He scratched his temple. "You could make a new frock. Something...not the color of a puddle."

Instantly her hackles went up. Shoulders back, head high, she exclaimed, "What, pray tell, is wrong with this gown? You have something against my clothes?"

Yes, he wanted to say, *you're wearing some.* He longed to see her bare arms again, as he did by accident on the first evening. But to suggest that would most certainly earn him one of her scowls. Besides, he was thinking of her for his son, not for himself. So he must be content replying, "Don't you have anything less...melancholy?"

"Mr. Deverell, I am still in half mourning."

Oddly enough it hadn't occurred to him. He tended to be thinking too much lately about what was under her gown, rather than why she was wearing it."Surely you've done your duty for the dead. Time to get on with the living. You'll marry again one day, won't you? You're still young."

Her eyes suddenly looked anxious, but she did

not reply.

He cleared his throat. "I know my son Storm is fond of the color blue. You could get yourself some good silk at the market."

"Silk? There is nothing more impractical. What use would *I* have for silk?"

Frustrated, he gave up. "Do as you will, woman. You can wear a bloody hessian sack for all I care."

His secretary did go to the market that day, and he did slip money into her embroidered purse, but if she bought new material he heard nothing about it. She returned with a brighter color in her face that day and a bit of a smile on her wary lips, so it must have done her good to get out, in any case.

When she tried to return the money he feigned ignorance of how it came to be in her purse.

"Mr. Deverell, I wasn't born yesterday," she said.

"Mrs. Monday, I am well aware of that fact and neither of us are getting any younger. Now can we get on with the work for which you were hired, or must we discuss the contents of your ugly purse for another tiresome hour?"

Most evenings they spent working on his story until late. True went back over his childhood as a feral stray, picking over it for anecdotes, his memory prompted by her questions and encouraged by the intrigued spark that warmed her eyes from time to time.

His mind was freshest at night. In the mornings he was too active to sit for long, his blood pumping with the need to be out and about. This clearly frustrated his secretary, who preferred to work at an earlier hour of the day, but he liked to have her company as the dark night closed in and the heavy drapes were drawn to keep the chill out. Sitting with her by his library fire was something he began to look forward to all day. A far cry from his previous nighttime adventures and preferences.

He watched her closely for signs of interest in his eldest son. But although she was always pleasant to Storm and conversed easily, her countenance never gave anything away, never showed any special attraction. She might have been just as interested in *him*.

On the morning she injured her ankle, and while she was confined to the kitchen talking to Jameson, True had taken the sly opportunity to peep into her bed chamber. He hadn't meant to do it, but after dressing to ride, his feet took him down the corridor toward her door. He told himself he wanted to check for dust on the console table again— to ensure Sims had done something about it.

Then he could not resist opening her door to look inside. Why shouldn't he? She was his damned employee and he was paying her very well. Besides, with a twisted ankle she wasn't able to follow him about, so she need never know he was curious.

As the door opened, a faint wave of her perfume wafted under his nose, reminding him of the pleasant burden he'd carried into the house that morning. Her bed was neatly made, the curtains open to let sunlight spill across the worn carpet, highlighting all the shabby threads and bare patches. She had placed two pictures on the mantle— one a small, oval silhouette, the other a framed, amateurish painting of a sinister-looking cottage with an obsessively neat garden hedge and blobs of garish color growing up the walls.

Some books sat upon her bedside table beside

the lamp. Her battered trunk rested at the foot of the narrow bed, her initials O.W.O. P. M. scratched into the side. The first two letters were larger, the others all different sizes.

Apart from these few items there was little reflection of the new occupant's personality, but True didn't need many clues.

There were two candles in holders on the mantle, but although both wicks were blackened, only one was burned down a few inches. The other must have been extinguished soon after he left her there on the night of her arrival. No other candles from the box had been put into use yet, so she was certainly using them sparingly. The hearth was swept clean, not a sign of stray ash; the bed cover straightened to leave not a single crease. The books by her bed were neatly stacked and a man's pocket watch— the case engraved with G.W.— sat atop the towering pile. A non-working watch, he discovered when he opened it.

The room looked rather sparse, he thought. Should have made more effort for her. She deserved better.

Then his son called impatiently from the hall below and he could explore no further. He simply laid the purple flower of catmint on her pillow— the stalk she'd picked and left on the rock earlier— and closed the door.

* * * *

Deverell shocked her one evening at dinner by saying quite suddenly, "I will ask Sims to move you to a better room in the family wing. It was Lady Charlotte's and has more modern decoration."

201

After a startled pause, she replied, "I am happy where I am, sir. I would rather not be moved now I am settled."

"In the old nanny's room? That was only a temporary arrangement. No, no, it is drafty and the furnishings are sparse. I should have moved you before now, especially with winter on the way."

"Sir," she assured him firmly, "I could not be comfortable in your wife's room."

"Why not? She seldom used it herself, so you needn't feel awkward. You will find it far more comfortable."

Olivia remained adamant and would not move. The nanny's old room was far more typical of accommodation to which she was accustomed.

He scowled at her in frustration. "I can have the door sealed off to my dressing room, if that would make the idea more palatable to you."

It had not even occurred to her that there would be anything to connect the two rooms, but of course, if they were made for a man and his wife, then there would be a passage of some sort to allow private access between them. She stared. "I shall assume, sir, that this was another of your teasing jests and we will say no more about me moving rooms. I can only imagine what the other staff would make of it."

"There's only Jameson and Sims here at night and they know where their loyalties lie. No reason for them to tell anyone about your sleeping arrangements."

"Even so, it wouldn't be...proper."

"Fine. As you wish. Sacrifice your comfort for a little senseless propriety." He snorted. "I suppose the temptation of my proximity would be too much for you, eh?"

"No, sir, but I would have imagined *my* proximity might make things difficult for you," and then she felt her face grow hot as she realized how that sounded, "should you wish to entertain...in the evenings...in private. That is all."

"Entertain?"

"In your chamber."

"I am puzzled, Olivia. Who would I entertain, in private, in my chamber of an evening? What can you be suggesting? Surely nothing vulgar. I'm surprised at you for letting such wickedness fester in your very proper mind."

"It was just a thought, sir. You did mention to me that you are a red-blooded male in need of lovers occasionally. And you are not dead yet, as you pointed out then too."

His gaze, reaching for her between the tall candelabra, was hard and unblinking. "Indeed, I am not dead. Despite a few swift-aimed bullets and other projectiles. Although no one has yet tried to assassinate me with their sharp tongue. Is that why you're here?"

She sighed heftily. "It is best that I stay where I am to avoid any uncomfortable encounters with your female guests in the passage. That is all I was trying to say, sir. I like to be where I am. Out of the way."

He leaned his elbows on the table and picked at his teeth with a slender piece of bone. "But you don't wander about at night, surely?"

"No." Although she sometimes slept lightly, especially when her thoughts were full of him, as they were all too often of late.

"Well, perhaps you are right. I wouldn't want to

keep you awake with my *entertainments* and female guests. Of which you must have heard there are legions of trollops."

"I make no judgments, sir. What you do is no concern of mine."

"But all that...banging about, swinging from the chandeliers and screaming in ecstasy...wouldn't do for the ears of a parson's widow from Chiswick."

The reply shot out of her before she could stop her tongue. "It couldn't be very good for you either, at your age."

His eyes flared like shooting stars. With one savage stab of his fork he speared a boiled potato — without looking at it—as if the hapless vegetable was his arch nemesis. "I keep myself agile and limber. As you know. Certainly never had any complaints."

She touched a napkin to her lips and looked away with studied indifference.

"Should you ever change your mind about your sleeping arrangements," he added, "and feel desirous of a little excitement, you know where to find me."

But she wouldn't know *when*, she mused, thinking of the odd hours he kept. Did the man ever sleep?

"Something troubles you, Mrs. Monday?"

"I was just wondering if you pester your bedmates for compliments, the same way that you do for Mrs. Blewett's pork pie."

He snorted. "Never needed to."

No, she was sure he wouldn't. Impossible man.

"Know what ails you, Mrs. Monday?" he exclaimed suddenly, holding the speared potato aloft on the tines of his fork and pretending to examine it.

"I wasn't aware of anything ailing me." *Apart from you*, she thought.

"Your hair is too tight. You ought to wear it looser. Or down."

"Down? That wouldn't be proper for a woman of my age. It would look ridiculous."

"No one need see it but me. And I won't tell." He thrust the potato into his mouth and spoke as he chewed. "As long as you bribe me not to give you away."

"I have nothing to bribe you with."

He cast her a sinister, sideways glance. "Oh, yes you have."

If only it was that simple. "You should not speak with your mouth full. Don't you remember what you told Damon? That this is your chance to learn how to behave, not to make a fool of yourself around a proper lady?"

"I remember that I said it was *his* chance. It's too late for me. My clay is dried in the grotesque form you see before you."

"Is that the excuse you always use?"

"Yes. Why not?" Stuffing another potato into his mouth, he laughed at her through those unearthly eyes.

"If it's all the same to you, I'll keep my hair in the style I've always worn it, Mr. Deverell."

"Suit yourself," he muttered, reaching for the wine decanter that Sims had left beside his plate before he withdrew, "I've got a good imagination and that'll have to tide me over." He licked his lips. "I shall imagine how it curls and ripples like a waterfall. All the way to the cheeks of your behind."

Olivia hastily resumed her own dinner, not wanting to read his teasing gaze any longer.

And then he set the decanter back without

pouring from it and he shook his head, "Perhaps it is just as well you sleep well away from me. For both our sakes."

Chapter Eighteen

Autumn settled in on Roscarrock island, leaves abandoned the trees and birds gathered to fly south, but they still had not progressed far with Deverell's story. Olivia lay awake at night to think about the abandoned little boy who grew up wild. It was a sad tale, but he did not see it that way. He spoke of his poverty and hunger as if they were old friends. Almost as if he missed them now that he no longer knew either.

He claimed he wasn't afraid when growing up without friends or family, but he must have been, surely. Sometimes a person felt the need to say they were not fearful. As if words would make it so. Olivia knew all about that.

Deverell constantly pried for her opinion, wanting to know what she was thinking, what she felt. But she remained guarded. He was a man with less than flattering opinions about women, and she had been trained to keep her feelings tucked out of sight. So they circled each other — she being wary, and he bemused, curious.

Since he preferred to work in the evenings, Olivia had to give up her usual routine to accommodate his odd hours. Going to her bed so late made it harder to get up early, of course, but she refused to let him call her a slug-a-bed again. If he did not need much sleep, then neither should she.

When Storm Deverell took her over to Truro for market day, she found him good company. He patiently tolerated Mrs. Blewett's chattering gossip all the way there and back with a kindly smile and the occasional, "You don't say" or "He never did!" He dealt with every trader at the market in a pleasant but no-nonsense way, making it clear that he would treat everyone the same, always be fair and never be cheated. Olivia saw many similarities to his father, but Storm did not possess the same unpredictability. He was more content, much less restless.

He may have been safer to spend time with, but he did not make her skin sizzle.

There was only one person with whom Storm Deverell shared cross words that day— an unshaven, dark-haired young man they encountered in the marketplace. Olivia did not know what their angry discussion was about, but she did hear Storm exclaim under his breath,

"Bloody Restaricks. They're all the same. Horse-thieves, cheats and smugglers."

Mrs. Blewett explained later that the Restarick family lived just over the valley from Storm's farmhouse. They had feuded with the Deverells over land ownership and polluted streams for at least a decade.

"Young Joss Restarick just buried his father and took over as the man o' the family," the cook added. "He's got twice the gunpowder and a much shorter fuse. It'll be trouble for the Deverells, you mark my words."

The subject of their conversation had looked over at Olivia and sneered openly before turning his back.

Mrs. Blewett whispered. "They're a bad lot, them Restaricks."

Even worse than Deverells? she wondered, amused by the cook's blind loyalty.

But Joss Restarick was not the only soul to stare

at Olivia that day in Truro. She caught the tail end of many inquisitive glances thrown her way.

"Father doesn't generally keep company with respectable young women," Storm explained. "Don't mind them. They can't help wondering."

"But Mrs. Blewett is respectable."

"You're not Mrs. Blewett, are you," he replied with a meaningful look that swept her like a flare of sunlight.

She began to wish she *was* that lady and thus apparently immune from all this speculation.

When she discovered her reticule suddenly much fuller than it should be, Olivia knew someone had added to it. Both men denied it when she confronted them, but only Storm was convincing. His blue eyes did not hold the power to deceive even partially.

"I expect my father wanted you to buy something for yourself," he said. "He likes to give people money."

"He did mention something about me buying material for a new gown." She was still mystified by that. Surely he had many other things to worry about other than what *she* wore.

"Well, there you are then." He shrugged. "He has probably grown tired of seeing you in that old thing. He always says a woman should take pride in her figure and not hide it."

A woman's figure, indeed! As if it mattered what she looked like. As if he should even be aware of her figure. Just because he was paying her a wage, he seemed to think that gave him rights to take ownership in everything about her, from her ankles to her hair.

Olivia tried to give the money back but her

employer refused to take it, swearing it wasn't his. She would have put it back in his desk drawer, if he didn't keep it locked and the blasted key hidden on his person. When she left the money inside his ledger, she found it back in her reticule the next day, with no hint of how he'd returned it behind her back.

* * * *

When the harvest was safely in, Storm Deverell held a party in celebration at his farmhouse on the mainland. Olivia did not really want to go; she was never very fond of large, boisterous parties and she would have preferred a quiet night in with her books. But her employer insisted she attend.

"Put your books and your spectacles away for an evening. And put a bow in your hair, or something," he said, waving a hand airily in the direction of her head.

"A bow? Now, it's a bow? What sort of woman do you think I am? I'm not five."

"I've seen women wearing bows— women who were most definitely *not* five. All manner of bows in all sorts of places."

"Bows are not my province. Mercifully, they never shall be. I'll leave them to you, sir."

Now he tried on a vexed expression, meaning to mask his amusement. "Pah! Have it your way, woman. I don't know why I bother."

"Nor do I. So please don't."

But she did bind her hair a little looser that evening and picked out her least grey gown— which was more of an orangey brown. For a moment she was tempted to put on her best frock, but she didn't

210

want to make it look as if his criticism bothered her.

Watching her employer that evening, she admired how he moved through the crowd with ease, just as informal with his field laborers as he had been with her. However, there was something about him— that strange, inexplicable air — that kept folk at a respectful distance. He could not be mistaken for one of them, even if he tried to blend in and act as if he felt at home there. He stood out like a black sheep amid a flock of white. Or a wolf among them, she thought, remembering her first impression of the man. His pacing restlessness kept him apart, not to mention his sheer male beauty.

It must be just the same for him when he walked into a group of blue bloods and aristocrats at his club. The man who had named himself True Deverell wouldn't belong among them either. He was one of a kind. Had to be. There couldn't possibly be another like him anywhere.

"Mrs. Monday, you are not dancing," he said, when he drew near to the bench where she sat watching. He wore all black this evening, except for his shirt. It looked very smart, made him appear even taller.

"You are observant, sir. I am indeed not dancing."

"My son has asked you twice, he tells me." He sat beside her.

"He has."

"And you refused. Mrs. Monday, I command that you dance with my son."

"Is everything in life that simple for you?" she exclaimed. "You command and it is done?"

"Usually. It was until you came along and refused

211

to be cowed by my magnificence."

She had to smile at that. "Yes, I'm sure I was quite a shock. But there you see your son enjoying a jig with another young lady. He looks very content, so I don't believe my refusal has injured his confidence. He is much in demand as a partner and only asked me to be polite. Now that he has done his duty by asking, his conscience is served." For a fleeting moment she wondered if her employer would ask her to dance too. Would he think she hinted? Her heart thumped uncertainly, breaking its gentle canter.

But no, she was safe. He had not danced all evening, despite the wistful glances of several pretty women of all ages. Dancing was clearly one form of exercise in which he did not partake. She was feeling rather relieved about it, which was selfish of her. Just because she didn't care to dance, didn't mean the other ladies present shouldn't have the pleasure of his company for a reel.

From the side of his mouth, he whispered, "All work and no play, Mrs. Monday? You know what they say about—"

"I didn't come here to play. You did not engage me for that."

"Good lord, woman," he laughed, "are you sure you're only eight and twenty?"

Olivia kept her face stern, in case anyone was watching them together. His hands rested on his knees, only inches from her.

"What do you do for amusement?" he demanded.

The image came to mind of that parsnip finger placed upon the pianoforte keys in a puddle of jam. She shook it off. "I read."

"For pity's sake," he muttered.

"What, pray tell, is wrong with that? You said yourself that you enjoy stories, sir."

"I do. But I enjoy many other things besides. I don't limit myself."

"So I've noticed."

"Mrs. Monday, that tone of censure will get you into trouble with your employer one day. He does not care to be chastised by a woman more than ten years his junior."

It was not the first time he'd admonished her, but rather than deal out any punishment for her "disrespect" he continued being exceedingly generous. Olivia had begun to wonder exactly what she would have to do in order to win a sincerely cross word from the man.

"I believe, young lady, that every soul needs to play once in a while. There is a child inside all of us. Except you. It seems you were born with the wisdom and maturity of Old Father Time. "

"Some folk are mature for their age, while some folk never grow up at all. Some don't want to."

"I suppose by the latter you mean me."

She glanced sideways. "If the shoe fits..."

"Ah! That reminds me. We really must do something about those terrible old boots of yours. Is that why you are reluctant to dance? Can't have you twisting your ankle again, can we?"

Hastily she drew her feet under the bench. "My footwear is perfectly adequate. And no concern of yours, sir."

He swayed closer, his breath warming her ear, the sweet scent of cider tickling her nose. "Since you came to my island and put yourself in my hands, everything about you, Mrs. Monday, became my concern. Everything. From your doe eyes to your cold toes. And all the delectable delights that come between. If you set aside your fears and put yourself into my hands, I could look after you as you should always have been looked after. Other men may have been remiss. I would not be."

Olivia found herself unable to respond without her voice betraying her unsettled pulse. Then, after another moment he added, "If you are mature for your age— so wise and sensible— while I am unable to grow up, you do realize that makes us a perfect partnership?"

She concluded that he must have drunk too much scrumpy cider. There was an excess flowing that evening.

"A working partnership, of course," he added, straightening up, squaring his shoulders. "You didn't think I meant anything else, I hope, madam."

"Certainly not."

"Because, my son Storm is very...much more suited."

She stole another quick glance and saw him frowning into the distance. Eventually he stood and walked away, leaving Olivia to get her heartbeat under stricter control.

It was becoming more difficult to repair her defenses after every conversation. He had laid siege to her. Each time he made a concerted effort he succeeded in breaching her borders a little more and yet he seemed not to know why he was doing it. He advanced and then retreated.

Olivia wondered if this was his usual habit— if he was amusing himself at the expense of her blushes— or whether he meant the things he said.

No indeed, there was no one else like him in the world. Thank goodness! One was quite enough.

* * * *

She wrote to let Christopher know she had arrived at Roscarrock in good health, and to reassure him that she did not regret her decision. There was hardly anything she wanted to tell him about Deverell— even fewer things she *could* tell him— so she filled the paper with inanities about the weather, and local flora and fauna. She also made polite inquiries about Chiswick and, of course, Lucinda. As she read it through before sealing her letter, Olivia realized it was a very dull, dutiful essay. Its dryness might cause Christopher to suspect her of hiding something, therefore she added a hasty line at the bottom to tell him how only his paint brushes could do the scenery here much credit. There, that was better. More like her old self.

He was probably still angry with her for leaving. Christopher could be very ill-tempered when things did not go his way. Fortunately, Mr. Chalke had arranged for her to travel immediately, the same day she told Christopher of her plans, which meant there was really nothing he could do but stifle his fury. It cut down on the unpleasant scene she might otherwise have faced.

Although she had dismissed her stepbrother's concern with her usual defense of dry humor, she understood that he worried not only for her reputation, but about how her actions reflected upon him, since he was now the one remaining male relative in her life. She was sorry if it caused him any pain, but it would pass; he had hurt her feelings many times and yet never seemed to know it and she concluded this was because he never suffered deeply himself, never let anything sink in below his well-maintained surface. He was lucky.

Could there have been anything more behind his anger at losing her? Sometimes, she let herself imagine that he had finally begun to appreciate her worth. A gratifying idea, but not likely.

Well, it was done now. She had taken herself out of the way. It was for the best. Christopher must learn to look after himself, and his needy bride, without her.

Burden, indeed. But he'd got it quite the wrong way round.

Chapter Nineteen

"What do you plan to do when you leave me, Mrs. Monday?" Deverell asked her one evening. "Shall you go back to Chiswick happily?"

"Why would I not?"

"Living here with me, you might form a thirst for adventure and the wilder side of life. You might be a plant who, having stretched its roots, grows too big for its pot."

"Perhaps I shall find another position, similar to this." She hadn't thought of it until he asked. "Mr. Chalke will help me, I'm sure." Yes, she liked the idea of keeping busy with interesting work, using her mind.

Trouble was, *here* at Roscarrock there was much more than the job itself that she found enjoyable.

She looked at the man across the desk. His head was bowed while he read over another Chapter and scribbled a comment in the margin.

"Think you can put other men in order too, just like me, eh?" he muttered, not looking up.

"Yes. I believe I can do a great service to disorganized, distracted gentlemen all over the country."

He dropped his pen and there was a pause while he examined his knuckles. Then he said abruptly, "If you find yourself in no haste to go home, I could extend *our* agreement beyond the six months and take you to London with me."

"For what purpose?"

Finally he looked up. "You could help me there."

"Doing what?"

217

"This and that."

"Please be specific, Mr. Deverell. Do you mean at the club?"

He scratched his cheek. "I'm not really sure what I mean, Mrs. Monday." A naughty gleam had come into his eyes, even though he tried to hide it by looking down at the papers on his desk again. "You do bring me a feeling of serenity which could be most useful...wherever I go. With you in charge I can't go wrong, can I?" The corner of his lip turned up.

"Oh, am I in charge now?" The idea amused her greatly.

"I think I'm in danger of letting you be," he replied gruffly, gesturing at his tidy desk. "I could easily let you get away with...all manner of crimes."

Olivia counted her neat row of goose quills and tried to calm the rush of light-headedness that swept her so hard it almost lifted her out of her chair. "I can stay with you only half a year, sir. As we agreed." To remain any longer than that in Deverell's employ would make her into a creature too dependent on him, and the whole purpose of this exercise was to give herself a measure of independence from all men.

Then he said, "Perhaps my son Storm will persuade you to stay in Cornwall, if I cannot entice you."

"Why...why would he do that? He didn't mention needing a secretary."

"He may have another purpose for you."

"Such as?"

"Not for me to say," he muttered. "He's old enough to speak for himself." Then he added slyly, "I know how you like to be *useful.*"

Olivia rubbed furiously at an ink stain on her

palm. "I hope I have been useful to you, sir."

"In your own inimitable, damnably annoying way— and despite all my attempts to distract you— yes."

"I suppose that's something then." She was far more pleased by it than she could allow him to see.

After another pause, he said, "You hint that we should negotiate a new salary, I suppose? To reflect your hard work at all hours of the night, above and beyond the terms of service."

"That is not what I—"

"Now that you've wormed your way in and made yourself almost indispensable to me, you want to raise your fee. How much would you charge for the occasional smile?"

Very well, she would go along with his teasing. "It depends what you mean by occasional."

"Shall we say, one a day? I imagine your smiles are costly. Like your kisses. I don't want to ruin myself."

Naturally, he thought money was the answer to everything. Would buy him anything. "I'm sorry, sir. My smiles cannot be bought."

"It's a good thing I can afford the parts of you I have now at my disposal," he grumbled, scribbling messily across the paper to correct something she wrote, his letters tangling with hers. "I suppose I must be satisfied with that."

She stared at his hand, watching as he drew a thick line of ink through another sentence. "I'd rather not talk of finances, sir." The teasing had ventured too far again off the cleared path.

"Ah. One should not mention finances to a lady. I forgot. Does Chalke handle all your affairs?"

"Yes. He is a good family friend. Before my father died he asked Mr. Chalke to look after me."

"Then he did not trust your kindly parson to do so? You were married to him by then, were you not?"

"My father trusted William, of course. But he had known Mr. Chalke for longer, and there can be no harm in two caretakers."

"Seems excessively cautious to me. Especially for a woman who says she is fearless, not in the least delicate and dainty, and who seems capable of looking after herself." Deverell glanced at her across his desk. "Perhaps your papa had a suspicion that Kindly Parson Monday would meet an untimely end as the other husbands did."

"Perhaps. Nothing is certain in life." She didn't want to talk about that again. Her employer often edged the conversation around to William. By doing so he had made her think harder about that last morning. Of William putting on his hat and grasping for his umbrella from the stand by the front door, of the cold grey light falling through the arched fanlight, the moist air clinging to everything like a very fine shroud of damp lace.

That sensation she'd felt of something being...off. If only she knew why such an awful chill had come over her on that last morning, before—

Quite suddenly, Deverell reached across the desk toward her face. Olivia froze, startled. The tip of his finger stilled the little pearl hanging from her ear. He kept it there a moment, his eyes narrowed. Did he look at her lips? She could no longer tell what held his attention.

"Your mother gave these to you," he said.

Her pulse skipped. "She did."

"You didn't keep much of hers when she died, because you're not sentimental. But these you held on to."

"How could you know that?"

Slowly he smiled. "I have my ways." His finger swept along her jaw to her chin and then pressed lightly to her parted lips, before leaving her and returning to its work on the manuscript.

Olivia's mouth felt too dry to swallow. She couldn't speak. His son Damon had warned her that True Deverell claimed to read the history of an object just by holding it. Did that mean he knew her history now too? Would he know what a naughty child she'd been and how hard she'd worked to amend her ways since then?

"Good lord, look at the panic on your face! Fret not, woman. It was an educated guess based on the probabilities. Not witchcraft. Sadly." He stretched and put both hands behind his head, leaning back against the dimpled leather of his chair. "But if you dare tell anyone that, I'll have to punish you."

"I see." The moment of anxiety passed. "So it's not a secret you mean to divulge in your memoirs."

"Certainly not. A man has to have some mystery. You are privileged, Olivia, to be entrusted with that particular secret. I don't know what came over me, but I had to tell you. I fear you hold a key capable of undoing my very soul."

She put her chin up, determined to ignore the wicked sensation he left coursing through her body. "Shall I be sacked if I tell your secret?"

"No," he replied smoothly. "But I shan't let you leave my service. Ever. You will belong to me. Entirely to me for the rest of your life."

She took as deep a breath as she could manage.
"That *would* be a punishment."

Yes, she was getting used to him now. It was
teasing. Merely teasing. And Olivia was learning how
to tease him in return.

* * * *

He knew he had to stop doing that— looking for
excuses to touch her— but he didn't want to stop. In
all likelihood he *couldn't* stop.

That night, unable to sleep, he took a lantern and
strode through the corridors to her room in the far
wing, where he stood outside her door.

There was no sound within, but he saw a little
flicker of light under the door. She must be reading.

True sat on the hall carpet, his back against her
bedchamber door, the lantern beside him. He closed
his eyes and pictured her by the fire, turning the pages
of her book. A calm and quieting presence. She didn't
demand that he talk, and she didn't sulk when he was
silent. Olivia did not require constant attention to
reassure her. She was very self-sufficient, which made
him wonder why she had married three times. It
could not have been for money, evidently, as there
was none.

He remained there for some time, arguing with
the need to knock upon her door. Just to talk to her a
while longer. Or to sit and look at her. That was all he
wanted— her company.

Pah, who was he trying to fool?

He wanted much, much more from her than
that. He wanted to possess her completely, inside and
out. He wanted to understand her, and that was a
desire he'd never before felt for a woman.

Chapter Twenty

One day Sims came to show him a letter she had written.

"I thought you might wish to see this before the Blewett woman carries it to the mainland with the post. I noticed it left on the dresser in the kitchen, sir."

True studied the address written in Olivia's neat hand. "Christopher Chesterfield, esq? Who might that be?"

"I do not know, sir. She has made no mention of a young man. A relative perhaps?"

He was curious. And annoyed.

Sims added slyly, "I know you don't approve of the female staff having *followers*, sir."

No, he bloody-well didn't approve.

A man she hadn't mentioned, but who was special enough to receive her one and only letter. Yet a man who had not been able to stop her from taking this post.

The address was written with her usual steady hand, but there were more curlicues and sweeping tails than he had seen when she wrote for him. Clearly then, it was written with extra special care.

No one ever wrote that way to *him*.

True tossed the letter back to Sims' tray with a terse flick of the wrist. It almost spun right off the polished silver and over the other side, but the butler managed to hold on to it, flipping the sealed missive like a pancake.

"Yes, I see. Thank you, Sims. Diligent as ever."

"Shall I send it with the other correspondence of the house, sir?"

He ground his teeth, glaring at the marks on his desk blotter. "Yes." He managed a tight smile. "Let me know when she receives a reply."

"Certainly, sir."

That afternoon, torrential rain kept him confined to the house. His secretary took advantage of the weather and soon they were at work together in his library. For once it was still light out when they began, but it was a gloomy day, the rain making the clouds heavy, blurring the line between sea and sky.

When he felt cheated out of a day like this, True often became short-tempered over little things. As winter ambled closer into his view, shortening the hours of daylight, a general moroseness settled over him, made him want to hibernate until spring.

He sank in the chair, his heels up on one corner of the desk, chin on his chest, fingers restlessly sending little balls of paper across the room via a slingshot he'd once confiscated from his daughter.

"You seem out of sorts today, Mr. Deverell," his secretary observed coolly. "I was hoping we might advance further with your story."

"I'm not in the mood."

"So I see." She turned to watch another paper ball fly into the far corner, bouncing off a framed map of the Empire. "Perhaps I should make myself useful elsewhere until you are ready to work."

"No. You'll damn well sit there." He glowered across the desk. "Where else could you be of use? I'm paying you, aren't I? So sit there and do as you're told."

"Excuse me for asking, sir, but did you get out of the wrong side of the bed today?"

No, he wanted to shout at her, *I got out of the wrong*

bed. "Damnable rain."

"Yes." She sighed heavily. "I know what you mean. I'm not fond of it myself these days." Her lashes swept downward, secretive again.

He got up and paced around his chair, trying to lift his mood out of this dark place. "I don't like to be trapped indoors," he growled. Why was he explaining himself to her? Perhaps she really did hold the key to unlock his soul.

Another wave of rain hit the window like steel-tipped arrowheads. Behind him she was silent, waiting patiently. All innocence, of course.

Finally he turned to face her again. "I hear you wrote a letter, Mrs. Monday. "

Nothing. She was reading, her head bent forward, eyes hidden.

"I hope you spoke well of me in this letter, and did not feel obliged to tell your lady friend how ill I treat you, keeping you up late, making you drink wine and sprain your ankle."

She looked up, nudging her spectacles back onto her nose with one finger in that gesture now familiar to him. "Why would I tell anyone such a thing?"

He dropped back into his chair. "You might regret coming here and start spilling your troubles to a sympathetic friend, exaggerating. The way *women* do to each other."

"You do not treat me ill at all, Mr. Deverell."

Equivocation! Twice! Aha. Since she wouldn't know he'd seen the address, he'd given her a chance to confess that she wrote to a man, not a woman. Yet she skipped over it.

True aimed another paper missile across the library and it landed in the fronds of a potted plant. "I don't, eh?"

"Not at all. You treat me with prodigious care."

He was somewhat mollified by that. But,
still...."In what way, pray tell? I hope I haven't been
spoiling you."

A real smile at last. Just a little one, shyly formed,
rather ashamed of itself and half hidden by streaks of
shadow from the rain. "I meant, sir, that you take
good care of my appetite especially. I want for
nothing. I am certainly not overworked. In all
honesty, I wish you would give me more to do."

He dropped the slingshot and tapped the edge of
his desk with four fingers, drumming them in a fast
tattoo, mimicking the sound of rain hitting the
window. "Hmm. What else? What else do I do for
you?" True liked hearing her talk of these things she
appreciated, he realized. Felt rather chuffed that he
pleased her. It wasn't an easy thing to do, as he knew
already, and on such a bleak day as this any good
news was welcome.

"My room is more than adequate, warm and
comfortable. Jameson brings up a fresh scuttle of coal
every evening so I never run out." Her clear eyes
widened, shining through the glass of her spectacles.
"And I have two candles, in addition to a oil lamp for
my own use at night, which allows me to read as long
as I choose in bed."

Apparently she didn't need much to be
impressed, he mused.

The rain made lines of gray light flicker
diagonally across her face. She could be a ghost sitting
there, watching him, fading in and out, elusive. He
wanted to put his hands on her, to be sure she was
still there. Suddenly the thought of her leaving his

226

house was intolerable. He curled his fingers, cracked the bones.

"The offer of my former wife's room is still open," he muttered. "There you could have even greater comfort than a few extra candles and some coal."

"I'm afraid anything more would be too grand for me. I wouldn't know what to do with myself in that much luxury."

He scowled. "Well, if you catch cold in that drafty wing this winter, don't blame me." Truth was, he didn't like having her so far off in another side of the castle. She was all alone down there, writing letters to other men. And it *was* drafty. The old nanny used to complain about it all the time.

Olivia showed him the empty inkpot. "We've run out. I made it last as long as I could."

"There's more in the bureau. Take whatever you need. No need to skimp."

Most women he'd known loved to be pampered. This one was so painfully frugal anyone would think she feared an extra bite of cake, or a softer pillow would lead her straight to hell.

If only Storm pulled up his breeches, polished his boots and finally got around to pursuing her properly, she would stay there and True wouldn't have to worry about where she went next or what sort of trouble she might encounter. Or whether she would one day contract a deathly influenza from this foolish insistence on drafty accommodation.

But Storm evidently needed more time to win her over— and encouragement, which this prim secretary wasn't giving. Her politeness, in fact, was more deadly than her sharp tongue. At least when the

latter came out of hiding one knew a soft spot had
been touched.

Unfortunately, he liked touching those soft spots
too much himself.

"Have you given any further thought to staying
in my employ a while longer, Olivia?"

She opened the bureau. "Must we talk of this
again? I cannot stay more than six months as we
arranged."

"Why? You haven't any plans." He felt his
frustration mounting again, as he thought of that
letter.

"But you can't even say why you would want me
to stay," she exclaimed. "Why would I agree when I
don't know what my duties might be? Your memoirs
will be finished by then."

He grumbled, "I may decide they're not over yet.
I may have more living to do, after all."

She said nothing, busy searching in the bureau
for more ink.

Through narrowed eyes he pictured her without
that awful gown, her naked body beneath his,
lightning decorating his bedchamber in pulsing silver
lines, sweat gleaming on his skin, her perfume
surrounding him.

In bed he would conquer her. He would write his
memoirs inside her, just as he once suggested.

Too hot and uncomfortable suddenly, he shifted
in his chair and picked up his letter opener, tapping it
rapidly on the desk.

Damn her. He hadn't felt like this about a
woman in...appalled, he stabbed the silver letter
opener into the blotter. Ever. He had not *ever* felt this
way about a female. It was confusing, befuddling,

humbling. In danger of making him into a fool.

Even now he was a few breaths from storming across the room and sweeping her over his shoulder, when all she'd done was tuck a loosened wave of hair behind her ear.

"So," he cleared his throat, "who is this special friend to whom you wrote your one and only letter since coming here?"

He waited for yet more cunning evasion, but this time she replied, "Christopher Chesterfield is my stepbrother. His mama married my father when I was sixteen. I'm quite sure you read the address, so I don't know why you asked."

A stepbrother. He stopped drumming on his desk. Well, that was good news, wasn't it? For Storm. No prior claim to get in Storm's way. There could be no romantic connection between stepsiblings.

It *was* his son's future happiness he was thinking of, when he first saw that neatly addressed letter. There could be no other reason for his concern.

So he'd had a moment of madness, imagining how he might keep her for himself. That was probably due to the fact that he hadn't had a woman in his bed for quite some time. It was nothing. He would amend that soon; he didn't really know why it had taken him so long. His shoulder wasn't causing him as much trouble now and he really ought to get back in the saddle, so to speak.

Oh, for the love of ... would she stop fiddling with that lock of hair?

He took a deep breath and adjusted himself again. "Christopher, eh? Married?"

She hesitated. "Not yet. Soon to be."

"Hasn't been as unlucky with spouses as you

then."

"No... he is favored with better fortune."

Hmmm. What did that pause mean? He took a deep breath and resumed tapping his fingers, this time with better rhythm. The Sailor's Hornpipe again.

"Sounds like the rain isn't letting up," he exclaimed jauntily.

Across the room his secretary had suddenly frozen. The ink bottle slipped from her fingers and fell to the carpet. Luckily the impact was not enough to break the glass. Her face had gone pale. She stared at the bureau for a moment, as if she saw something else there entirely.

"What's the matter now, woman?"

She didn't answer. Olivia was staring at the wall.

Worried, he got up and walked around the desk. Were those tears in her eyes? He couldn't tell. Could be the shimmer of reflected raindrops, he supposed.

It had better not be tears.

* * * *

Deverell didn't possess an umbrella. Mrs. Blewett had commented on it that morning when the rain started.

"The master says umbrellas are for dandies afraid of getting wet," the cook had chuckled while brushing her steak and kidney pie with beaten egg. "He says he can manage without one."

"Naturally," Olivia had replied.

But the rain today was joined by high winds, so an umbrella would not have been any use to him, even if he had one.

She had thought nothing more about it until

now. However, it must have lurked in the deep recesses of her mind, waiting to pounce out on her again. For suddenly, as she stood at the writing bureau that afternoon with rainy shadows flicking around the walls, Olivia was transported back to another time and place. She saw, once again, the image of William standing by the parsonage front door, reaching into the umbrella stand. He kept a plain black umbrella with a chipped and scratched wooden handle. Not in the least decorative, but serviceable— like everything he owned.

Yet, on that fateful day there was a gleam of silver as he swept the umbrella out of the stand and prepared briskly to go about his business. And suddenly Olivia realized it was not his umbrella William took that morning; it was Christopher's expensive umbrella with the silver swan-neck handle. She remembered admiring it when her stepbrother surprised her with a visit just a few days before. The umbrella handle even had feathers carved into it and eyes of polished jet. He must have left it there by accident and taken William's umbrella instead when he walked out of the house. Perhaps Christopher was just as distracted on the day of his visit as she had been, when she failed to get the potatoes cooked in time for William's luncheon.

She closed her eyes, picturing the ornate, curved silver head of that umbrella.

In the grief of everything that happened after, she had completely forgotten.

So her husband took the wrong umbrella. *That* must be what had struck her as out of place on that day! William was a creature of routine, and any tiny diversion from it was enough to be noticeable.

She exhaled in a rush, her fingers squeezing tightly around the reclaimed ink bottle. Well, that could explain the odd feeling that had lurked within her on the morning he died. A small drop that upset the surface and made a bigger ripple as rings spread and overlapped.

Thank goodness she knew now what had caused that awful sensation. It was a relief to find a perfectly reasonable explanation. She had never been able to explain it to Inspector O'Grady when he questioned her. All she knew was that something had struck her as wrong that day before William left the house.

But how foolish she'd been not to tell her husband that Christopher came to visit two days before while he was out. There was no need for her to hide the fact. Even though William didn't like her stepbrother he would never prevent her from seeing a relative. She should have told William at once, but instead she'd put it off, and the longer she waited, the less reason she felt for telling him. And the more delay, the more it would seem as if she had something to feel guilty about.

William hadn't even noticed that it was not his own umbrella he took from the stand on that rainy morning. At least, he didn't seem to notice the difference.

"You look very white!" Deverell was striding toward her, frowning. "Good God, woman, you're ready to faint. You never have much color, even on a good day, now you're positively ghost-like."

Clutching the ink to her bosom, she blurted stupidly, "Mrs. Blewett said that you do not possess an umbrella."

He stopped two steps away and looked puzzled.

232

"That's nothing to get upset about. Or is that a sin in your opinion?"

"I just thought...you ought to have one. It always rains in England you know. One thing we can be sure of. About the weather."

"The weather?" He squinted. "That's it?"

"I'll put the ink in the—" She moved to pass him and he put his hands on her arms to hold her still. How ironic that *he* should be the one to stop *her* moving.

"I hope you have been more impressed by my son Storm, than you were by Damon."

Her mind was lost elsewhere, but she struggled to make sense of what he said. "Mr. Storm Deverell is a pleasant fellow," she managed, her voice barely above a whisper. "Yes, I like him."

"Good. There is one of my cubs who meets with your approval then. I have not been a complete failure as a father in your eyes."

He still held her arms, warming her with his touch, but not helping her pulse to find a steadier beat. "I did not *dislike* young master Damon," she said, speaking clearer. "It would be unfair to form any firm opinion, for he is still growing into his character. A boy inside a man as yet. Storm is more comfortable in his skin and it shows."

She looked up and found him studying her in that thorough, merciless way. It wasn't like her to wilt, but it was a good thing his hands were so firm, for his strength seemed to be the only reason she was upright at that moment.

Oh, the rain! The horrid rain. Pounding hard at his windows, it had taken her back to the last morning with William and that rush of guilt because she had, days before, received a visit— alone— with her stepbrother and not told her husband. A foolish thing. Why not tell William? Why should Christopher's visit have put her so out of herself?

Because the two men were not friends. They had quarreled, because William thought Christopher ought to sell her father's house and divide the profits equally to be fair. Olivia had not wanted that confrontation, but it was a subject that made her husband very cross and he refused to leave it alone. Christopher had told William it was none of his business. Thus the two men in her life were at odds and an unexpected visit from her stepbrother while her husband was absent could be nothing but awkward.

The glimmer of a silver umbrella handle...

"Storm tells me he invited you to dine at the farm whenever you are free."

Again Olivia dragged her mind out of that dark tunnel and back to the present. "Yes...yes, he did."

"Then you should go. Don't disappoint him."

"But I—"

"You need an evening off. Despite what you say, I think I *have* worked you too hard and it's taking a toll. Look how pale you are!"

"Mr. Deverell, I told you I wish you would give me more to do. I am not, by any means, worked too hard and I—."

"Go tomorrow evening— I insist— and dine with my son. If the rain has stopped by then."

He would bruise her arms if he didn't let her go. No man had ever looked at her the way he did on that rainy afternoon. *And* she was wearing her spectacles, but he still looked at her with hunger in his gaze.

Christopher always laughed at her in spectacles and said she looked like The Old Lacemaker in a painting by Nicolaes Maes.

Her mind was spinning and could not settle. The rain throwing itself at his window had put her on edge, her senses in a turmoil. She didn't know whether to weep or be angry. This too was not like her.

Now Deverell was trying to be rid of her for an evening. Was he tired of her company and in need of something more exciting? She thought of those mainland "hussies" Jameson used to bring over for him on the rowboat, according to Mrs. Blewett.

Anxiety and confusion made her voice sharp. "If you wish for me to dine with your son, I will, sir. After all, I must follow your commands while I'm a resident of this island. As you said when—"

"It's not about me." He let go of her arms abruptly and turned to walk back to his desk. "Storm likes your company and he's been waiting for you to go. It will be a pleasant evening for you, away from," he waved his hand through the air, "all this."

She swallowed hard and smoothed both hands over her bodice, but it did not calm her heartbeat. When he had touched her tonight, she had not wanted him to let her go again. Instead she wanted to lean against him and let his strength envelope her.

"My son will cheer you up, put some color back in those cheeks. In fact, you should make it a regular appointment to dine over there, a few times a week. Why not? I'm sure you're bored wretched with only my company every evening."

As he was with hers? Yes, he wanted rid of her, so he could entertain one of his lovers, perhaps. Or a whole gaggle of lovers, she thought, chagrinned. It was not only Mrs. Blewett's gossip she had to go on, was it? He'd boasted about his "urges" as a red-blooded male, and in his memoirs he held nothing back, so she knew what he thought of females and their place in the world. In his world, especially.

I told her I wasn't safe to be around. Never had been and never would be. I warned her that I was not the sort to fall in love. I'm not made that way.

So she ignored the fierce pain where she'd just bitten the inside of her cheek, and said firmly, "Very well, I shall go across to the farm tomorrow evening."

"Excellent." He still had his back to her and was arranging papers on his desk. "I'll tell Jameson and he can drive you over in the cart before the tide comes in."

"How will I get back again?"

"Jameson can row you back in the boat. Just arrange a time with him."

"It seems a shame to put Mr. Jameson to so much trouble."

Deverell shrugged his wide shoulders. "He's accustomed to it."

"I bet he is."

Her employer swiveled around to look at her. "I beg your pardon?"

She said nothing, inwardly kicking herself.

"I thought you said you don't gamble," he added, one eyebrow arched, a smug look on his face.

"It was a figure of speech," she snapped.

He swept her from head to toe with a slow, menacing gaze and then returned to his papers. "Stay as long as you like at the farm when you go. Storm will enjoy the company. There is no reason to rush back."

She wanted to throw something at him. Her fingers itched to reach for a weapon. It was ridiculous. She had never felt anger this raw.

But it was not only anger.

No man had ever held her so— physically or mentally— entranced. And perplexed. Olivia could still feel the imprint of his fingers around her upper arms. Like claw marks. Beautiful claw marks.

Perhaps an evening away from him *would* be a very good idea.

"While I'm gone, sir," she said sweetly, "you might consider writing to your daughter." He had been putting it off, ignoring her suggestion that he extend an olive branch. "If you have time."

Keeping his back to her, he made some noise that could mean anything.

"It might be a pleasant idea," she added, "with the Yuletide season upon us soon, don't you think?"

"Hmph. I don't celebrate. Never did."

"Well, if your daughter is as stubborn as you, I suppose this rift will never be mended. But you are the adult. It is surely up to you to lead the way and make a mature move toward peace. If that is the state you desire."

Now he turned to look at her again, scowling. "I thought you said, Mrs. Monday, that you know nothing about being a parent?"

"It was merely a suggestion, as your secretary. Should you need some way to pass the time, while I am gone tomorrow night." After all, why shouldn't she give him advice since he was always trying to give her commands and tell her how to dress?

His narrow-eyed, critical assessment scorched her

face. "I'm sure I'll manage. As I did before that pickled fool Chalke sent you to me. And as I must when you are gone again. Since you claim you can't stay with me. Or won't."

She swallowed. "Yes, I suppose so."

"Never let your happiness depend upon the company of another," he said, turning away again.

Ah, yes. Stand on one's own two feet. How ironic that his advice to her was so similar to dear William's. Olivia would have laughed, if she wasn't so close to tears.

* * * *

She ran to her room and lay on her narrow bed, fists clenched like those of a willful child. Although it made her sick, she forced herself to remember every second.

The Parsonage, West Lane, Upper Hollworth, near Chiswick
A quarter past ten o'clock in the morning
Monday, April 6th, 1841

Christopher was at the door when she opened it. The last person she expected. His hand, holding the silver swan neck of his umbrella, was poised to rap impatiently upon the door again.

"I began to think you were out," he exclaimed. As if it would be the height of stupidity if she was discovered anywhere other than wherever he thought she should be, exactly when he thought she should be there.

"I was not expecting guests." She panicked at the stains on her old apron. "I was cooking in the kitchen at the back of the house. I wish you had —"

But he swept by her and into the flagged passage, looking around with his usual sneering appraisal. "It occurred to me as I was passing, that I ought to call in. It has been sometime since I paid a visit. Where is Monday? Out it seems."

"William is at the church." She led him into the parlor, although there was no fire lit yet. Sooty paper was spread down on the hearth, as she'd been about to clean the grate when she remembered she still needed to peel the potatoes— which she had just begun when the doorbell rang. "I'm in the midst of spring cleaning. Please forgive the mess."

"You have no house maid?" he muttered, pulling off his gloves. "You might at least get some capable young girl from the orphanage."

"William doesn't like strangers about the parsonage and he thinks I should be able to manage by myself. It's not a big house."

Christopher gave a hollow laugh. "You mean he prefers to save money and won't hire anyone. He has a free slave at his disposal."

"I don't mind. I like to be busy."

He cast her a sour look and sat heavily, falling back into a chair by the cold hearth. "Of course you do. Good Lord, you look tired and worn. I cannot, in any sincerity, say that marriage suits you, Livy. It never did." He exhaled a short, harsh, smug laugh. "Well, I suppose this husband has lasted longer than the other two, at least."

She hoped he wouldn't stay long. If William came home early it would be uncomfortable. After the quarrel over her father's house, her husband never wanted to invite Christopher to dine with them and had been visibly relieved when the young man went north.

However, William was a man of routine. He was never early or late. It should be safe.

And what if he *did* come home and see Christopher there? She was doing nothing wrong to welcome her own stepbrother.

So why did it feel sinister?

The moment she saw him on her doorstep her heart sank, her pulse almost came to a dead halt. His sudden reappearance in her quiet life was like that of a black crow at her window, watching her with a beady eye.

"You are back then from Manchester," she managed finally, after searching for conversation. "I thought you liked it there and would stay. I thought you had found some good business there." Had *hoped* he would stay. But perhaps that was an unkind thought. Christopher had always been concerned for her wellbeing, especially since her father died. He could not help that he showed it in odd ways. She ought to be glad to see him.

"Good God no, the people there are barely civilized. The north is a miserable place."

"Oh, dear."

"But I do have some good news to cheer you." He announced proudly, "I have found a potential worthy bride. Miss Lucinda Braithwaite. Her father owns a successful mill, and she is his only child. His only heir. It could all turn out very well for me."

She was not surprised that he'd found a woman to marry. After all, he was effortlessly handsome and could be charming if he wished to be. But it did make her smile inside that he had to find a "worthy" bride— as if he had so much more than his looks to offer. "I am very happy for you."

"Yes, well..." he brushed a hand over his knee, clearly pleased with his accomplishment, "you must meet her soon, when she comes to Chiswick. I shall invite you to luncheon one day."

She felt a little pang of sadness as she looked at him sitting there, talking about Lucinda, the woman he meant to marry. The young woman he thought would fit his perfect ideal of a bride. No doubt she was a flawless beauty, confident and shining. Like him.

Olivia had never forgotten how her first sight of him took her breath away. That first fleeting smile as they were introduced. He was the most handsome young man she had ever seen. Instantly she—not the sort of girl anyone noticed unless she did something shockingly bad— fell under his spell.

Perhaps, somewhere in her wicked heart, she had hoped her stepbrother would never marry. Once he did, he would never need her for anything ever again— even that little bit of use she had been to him, could never be again.

But that was selfish of her.

"I am glad you have found love, Christopher," she said with great warmth of feeling.

"Love? Sakes, one does not marry for love, Livy. It will be a most advantageous match for me financially and socially. You see, that's where you always went adrift. Not that you can possibly claim to love that tight-fisted, bore, William Monday, anymore than you *loved* the drunken buffoon who couldn't pass up a wager, or the penniless old dandy who didn't chew his food properly and choked on that fish bone."

She folded her hands before her and said softly, "William is a good husband, very kind."

"And look how he makes you live." He waved his gloves around, gesturing at the damp walls and chipped furniture. "In a state of grim poverty that grinds you down like an old nag kept too long at the plow. Clearly he has no more liking for you than he would have for a housekeeper. You never married to get anything for yourself."

"I am content. He is a good man who can teach and guide—"

"You will never see sense, I know. You never did, Livy. Stubborn as an ox." He got up out of the chair and laughed, patting her cheek with his cool hand. "'Tis a jolly good thing you have me to look after you. Well, we all have our own reasons for marrying. I have mine and you had yours. But I daresay you'll be back again one day, my burden."

When he left she was so distracted and angry that she wandered around the house for some time before she continued cleaning the grate with a great deal of violent scrubbing. And so she forgot the potatoes that day, leading to William's indigestion later when they were not properly cooked in time for luncheon. She didn't even notice that Christopher left his umbrella behind.

Two days later her third husband was dead.

* * * *

She was bad luck for men, that much was certain.

Freddy —sweet Freddy— undone by a fall from a broken curricle that should never have been raced.

Allardyce, who choked on a fishbone at the same tavern in which he had dined in solitary splendor every Saturday for his entire adult life. A habit he had not broken when they married, much to Olivia's gladness, for it gave her a precious evening alone once a week.

And finally, William, falling from a rotted bridge, dragged under by his vestments and with no one to help him.

No, there could be no more husbands for her.

Like Deverell, she wasn't safe to be around.

Chapter Twenty-One

When he began winning at cards and dice, the other fishermen thought it was sheer luck. But then it happened too often and they became suspicious. They didn't believe him when he told them how he remembered numbers, how he read the probability and made calculations in his mind.

How could he, a boy who barely knew words, be so astute with numbers? No, he must be cheating. So they challenged him, accused him, threatened him with repercussions.

The boy did not shy away from winning, and he learned to protect himself — and his winnings—with his fists. Or with anything else he had nearby. He was labeled as a boy with a bad temper, but in his eyes he was only protecting what was his. That included his strange talent.

A rumor went around on the fishing boats that the feral boy had escaped the gallows. For some that was enough to give him a wide berth. Others looked to bully and belittle the boy.

It was a rough, harsh world, but then it had never been anything else for him. So he grew, like a hardy weed between cracks in a stone path. Not welcome, but too determined and stubborn to be eradicated.

The young man didn't seek friendships, for he had learned to trust no one.

But he was fascinated by women. Not girls. Women. And he went after what he wanted. As he grew up, they eventually stopped running away from him. He didn't know why they suddenly sought him out— it seemed to happen almost overnight— but he didn't care. He made the most of it.

Just as he knew a man had to eat whenever he had the opportunity, he felt the same way about women.

* * * *

Olivia had sent a note over with Mrs. Blewett to accept Storm's invitation to dinner, so he was well prepared, the long table already set and a large pot of stew and dumplings— made by the chuckling lady herself no doubt— kept warm over the fire.

It was a cold, windy evening with rain hovering in the air, but the farmhouse walls were sturdy and squat, built of thick stone to protect the inhabitants from those harsh storms that sometimes blew over the headland. Tonight inside it was cheery, the main focus being an enormous chimneypiece from which the blast of fire warmed the entire house.

"My father finally released you from servitude for one night then?" Storm exclaimed, dashing forward to take her coat and bonnet. "I began to think he would never give you up."

She tried to smile, even as she imagined True Deverell back on his island, preparing to greet a boat full of eager lovers. "He was most insistent that I come. I think he wanted me out of the way."

Storm laughed carelessly. "Probably. That sounds very much like father."

And all hope fell out of her. Feeling no such inclination to laugh, Olivia's struggling smile soon died away completely.

"You look damn cold, Mrs. Monday. Here... take a bench by the fire."

The journey by horse and cart across the causeway had been icy-cold indeed. It had also been fast and bumpy. Jameson wanted to get back to the island while he could still walk across, because he had to leave the horse at the farm. There was nowhere to stable horses on the island itself. Now she was, in effect, stranded here until the tide came full in and he could row across to fetch her. The handy man could have stayed with her at the farm, but, of course, he was needed to row some other woman back and forth, was he not?

She didn't have to be told the details to know what was going on. Even his son didn't try to hide it.

"It must feel odd to be away from the constant pounding of the waves," said Storm, pouring her a glass of something clear and very fragrant.

"I suppose so." She did feel a little giddy and uncontrolled. Like one of Deverell's paper bullets shot out of his slingshot, whirling through the air, wondering where she would land. Perhaps she was already accustomed to life confined to that small island. The sea air was in her veins now. How odd it was to think she'd never even seen it— in real life— until she came there. She had lived on a river, which was different. Quite different. Her knowledge of the sea came from books and paintings. Thoroughly different to being able to touch and smell and hear.

The sea was something that no one could control. Man had to learn how to live by the tides; no one had control of it.

Like Deverell.

Olivia had thought her fortress well-equipped to face the siege against its walls, but she sadly over-estimated her defenses. Now that she was away from True Deverell for one evening, at his own insistence, she realized how much she had fallen under his spell.

"Drink up!" Storm pointed at the glass in her hand. "It's some of my own recipe. Made by my own fair hands."

She took a sip and her eyes watered.

"Goodness."

He chuckled. "Some wines creep on you. This one runs you to ground and slaps you in the face." With one foot, he kicked a stool closer to her and dropped his backside to the seat. His casualness was very like his father, of course. As was his desire to see her inebriated.

Stop thinking about him. Stop seeing him in everything. Stop wishing he was there.

Damn the man. He sent her away, so he could enjoy an uninterrupted evening of sinful pleasure. Without her. Olivia wasn't certain which part of that bothered her more.

She licked her lips. "I like it. At least, I think I will. When my taste buds have recovered." Again she tried to smile, but found her lips too heavy.

Storm Deverell's blue eyes perused her with great warmth and he told her again how pleased he was that she accepted his invitation. "It can be a lonely life on this farm."

"I'm sure there are many other young ladies you could invite to dine." At the harvest dance, and on their trip to Truro market, Olivia had seen the local girls gazing at him wistfully. No, if he spent an evening alone it was by choice, so she found it mystifying that his father thought he should try and match-make for his son by using her. Of all people.

"How has my father been treating you? Well, I hope?"

Aargh! She didn't want to talk about *him*. "I have no complaint." Olivia wished she did. She ought to have plenty.

"He isn't working you too hard? He can be a terrible task master."

"Not at all." Another sip of blistering heat from that little glass of clear liquid.

"I wondered how father would manage," said Storm. "He hasn't had a woman around every day for a long time. Perhaps never." He got up to check the stew in the pot. "But you must know all about his marriage to Lady Charlotte by now. How they were seldom under the same roof."

"I know a little," she replied cautiously. "But they were under the same roof often enough to have three children."

"That much is true. Although I have my doubts about Rush— the youngest boy."

"Doubts?"

Storm winced and then shrugged, "I suppose it does no harm to tell you. Father must have decided you're trustworthy or he would have sent you home by now."

"Tell me what?"

"Lady Charlotte was not exactly a faithful wife, particularly in the last years of their marriage."

"Your father knew?"

"I'm sure he did. She was not discreet. Had she hidden her affairs better he might not have divorced her. Since they led separate lives anyway, he could have let things continue as they were. But she embarrassed him publically one time too many and when her behavior began to effect the children— when they were old enough to know what was going on— that was when he decided to put an end to it."

Olivia listened to all this, quite certain there must have been infidelity on both sides. Storm, faithful to his father, would never say that. He would prefer to think his father blameless. Or as close to blameless as he could be.

"Not that his brats out of Lady Charlotte have ever recognized how he tried to save them from her," Storm added. "His daughter, Raven, has caused him endless trouble. He was never very comfortable raising a girl. Didn't know how to treat her. As for Ransom, he idolizes his mother. You know, of course, that he shot at father." He drank an entire glass of his own recipe in one gulp and then smacked his lips. "Fortunately he didn't hit any of the important parts. As far as we know. "

"As...as far as you know?"

"Well, Ransom was in his cups at the time. He doesn't know what he shot at. Fool boy."

Olivia was amazed at how easily he spoke of his father being shot. Even True had mentioned the incident as if it was another practical joke. She could not comprehend ever wanting to shoot her own father, but she had to admit shooting at teasing, infuriating Deverell would be a different matter.

"Why did he shoot his father?"

"Ah..." Storm dug a poker into the fire. "Ransom has always had a bee in his bonnet. Felt ignored. I suppose that was one way to get father's attention."

"I see." Olivia had heard a rumor that the shooting happened over a woman, but she kept that to herself.

"Ransom also wanted to punish father for whatever sins he thinks have been perpetrated against his mother. All of it false, of course. As children we fashioned ourselves swords and helmets, pretending we were knights of Camelot. Ransom was always valiant Sir Galahad. I believe he never shed the idea and still sees himself the same way. As father says, it

249

makes him an easy mark for ladies with a sad story to tell and an abundance of clever tears to spend."

"And which Knight of the Round Table were you?"

"Sir Gawain, of course! Rough around the edges, but the true and rightful heir of Camelot. Fiercely loyal to his king and family, compassionate defender of the poor. And maidens." He laughed.

"So that makes Mr. Deverell King Arthur?"

"The mysterious boy, taken into hiding by Merlin for his own safety, raised in obscurity until he pulled the sword from the stone and became a great king. It is father's favorite story. Naturally."

She was amused by Storm's eagerness to paint his father in such a golden light. King Arthur, indeed! It was touching. But Storm was not disingenuous. He was honest, warm-hearted and spared no time for fools. So whatever he said about his father, she knew that he, at least, must believe it.

"When Lady Charlotte left the first time, Ransom was not quite two, but she was willing to abandon him. Didn't want the boy. She had no motherly instinct."

"But Mrs. Blewett said—"

"Yes, the general gossip is that he wouldn't let her take the child. Truth was, he told her she'd get no money from him if she left. Charlotte didn't think he meant it. When she discovered that he did— and she ought to have known by then that my father always means what he says— she had to come back. It was nothing to do with love for her son. My father cared for those children more than she ever did. And he only wanted her around for their sakes. He made that clear to her."

"Why doesn't he say that? Why not tell people like Mrs. Blewett the truth?"

He sighed heavily. "Folk believe what they want to believe about my father and he always had this infuriating belief that he doesn't ever need to explain himself, or apologize for what he is. He's held on to a lot about his life, mostly to protect the children from being hurt, I suppose."

"But now he means to tell everything in his memoirs."

"He thinks they're all old enough to hear it. He wouldn't tell it all for anyone except them."

Yes, Olivia had noted True's fondness for his children. It was in the way he spoke of them, the pride in his eyes, even when he would deny it. "Them? But you are one too."

"I suppose I am." He laughed and jerked one shoulder upward, almost shyly. "I often forget. Seems like me on father's side and them on the other."

"Perhaps because you're the eldest and he was so young when you were born. Really only a boy himself."

"Or because I'm a bastard?" He laughed easily over the word, but his eyes were too blue. Olivia had never known that "too blue" was possible until she looked into his gaze that night.

Blue could be something other than calm and summery. God help any woman who tried to tame that. "He does not discriminate between his sons born out of, or in, wedlock."

"He may not. But the world doesn't follow his rules." He looked away for a moment and she suspected he was calming his temper. "You do a lot of that, do you?"

"A lot of what?"

"Thinking about the meaning of things. Searching for causes?" He chuckled as if nothing ever troubled him, but she was not fooled. "With those big questioning eyes you must be driving father to distraction."

"I'm sure he finds me tiresome company occasionally."

"But I believe you're doing him some benefit, Mrs. Monday."

"Why?"

"He's been in a much better mood lately."

"Gracious, what is he usually like? I'd hate to see him in a worse mood."

"You're a good influence. He calls you an eye of tranquility. It's a novelty for him."

"A novelty?" she scoffed. "Then it will soon pass."

"No doubt," he replied breezily. "Women don't stay around for long. His attention invariably wanders to the next pretty new thing."

She took a braver sip of the burning liquid in her glass and tried not to show any effect. A little homemade wine would not get the better of her.

"That's why my father likes the solitude of Roscarrock. A woman has to be pretty damned determined to get there if she wants him and most concede defeat after a while. There's only so much they can put up with and even the money isn't enough inducement for some." He leapt to his feet. "Now that stew had better be ready, I don't want to keep you away from him too long."

Olivia moved to a seat at the table, hungry again. Her appetite had seldom been as lusty as it was since she arrived in Cornwall. Must be the sea air.

"Why doesn't you father celebrate Christmas?" she asked.

Her host thought about it for a moment and then replied, "I don't think he knows how."

It might have been be the saddest thing she'd ever heard, but she refused to let it pluck at her heart strings. The man was rolling around in his bed with a handful of light skirts at that very moment. He did what he wanted all the time, and was despicably smug about it. He made all the commands and followed none himself.

It was Christmas every day for a man like Deverell. The boy who came from nowhere to rule as king of his own island.

"Would you like another?" Storm held out the jug of wine.

She nodded. "Yes. Thank you."

Why not? Perhaps it was time she let her hair down a little. Who cared? Who was there to disapprove?

* * * *

Sweating after the exertions of his evening, True tucked in his shirt, returned to his desk and wrote a hurried letter. He signed it, blotted it, folded the paper and sealed it with wax. There it was done. May she now be bloody satisfied. He poured himself a large glass of brandy in some hopes of assuaging his thirst.

How quiet the damnable house was without Olivia, he thought suddenly. She'd been gone a few hours. It felt like days.

Strange. He'd never missed a woman's company before. Usually he felt great truth in the saying "familiarity breeds contempt". He was glad to see the back of most women after a brief while, although, in the case of Olivia Monday, there had been no physical intimacy beyond a few kisses. Theirs was a connection of a different kind. There was always something new to discover about her and he was still unfolding all her layers.

Poor woman had looked "all in" yesterday. He hoped her evening with his son would return her spark.

Something stung the back of his hand. Ah, a scratch. Bleeding now, a brilliant red drop falling to the sealed letter on his desk.

* * * *

Jameson was late with the boat. When they finally spied his lantern swaying in the wind, Storm exclaimed, "I thought they'd forgotten you."

"As did I," she replied, grim.

It had begun to rain again and all the warmth of the farmhouse had long since left Olivia's limbs. She huddled beside her host on his cart, waiting under the semi-shelter of a gnarled tree branch that overhung the narrow, muddy path.

"Well, good evening, Mrs. Monday, and thank you for sharing the time with me." Storm jumped down and reached up to help her. "Come again, anytime you need escape."

The next time your father wants rid of me, you mean, she thought icily. "I shall. Thank you. It has been most pleasant."

She walked down to the beach, one hand holding on to her old bonnet to save it from the slanted gusts of rain. Jameson waded to shore in tall boots and an oilskin coat, dragging the little rowboat behind him.

"My apologies for being late, Mrs.," he gasped out, rain shining on his big face.

"That's quite alright," she replied tightly. "I'm sure you were busy fetching and carrying for Mr. Deverell."

"Yes, Mrs."

Another who didn't even try to deny it.

Olivia stepped into the boat and sat with her hands in her lap while Jameson tugged the little vessel back out into the sea. Once she was bobbing afloat, he too climbed in, the boat rocking violently.

"What a night to be out," he exclaimed, shouting against the wind and rain as he hauled on the oars.

"It was your master's idea."

"Aye."

"You must be exhausted with all the rowing tonight."

"Aye, Mrs. Been a fair bit of to and fro for the master while you were gone."

"He keeps you hard at work at all hours, it seems."

"The master keeps 'imself busy too. Been going 'ard at it in the bedroom since you left."

She stared, rain getting into her mouth until she had the wits to close it. While she'd convinced herself of this fact already, hearing it in such plain terms made her sick to her stomach. The wild pitch and yaw of the little boat didn't help matters.

Yet again she told herself it was none of her business what he did. Or with whom he did it. She was getting too fond, too close, letting her eyes and heart see and feel things that weren't there. Begun to hope he might feel some affection for her. It was the same mistake other women, including his wife, had made.

After that last comment, Jameson saved his breath, putting his all into the task of rowing them back to the island.

Olivia looked over her shoulder toward the shore and saw the lantern on Storm's cart slowly disappearing. She closed her eyes and sighed, her shoulders sagging. That warm, cozy farm seemed far away already, and here she was being knocked about on a choppy sea, blinded by rain, going back to her strange existence on "Devil's Hell".

On a night like this it lived up to the name the locals had coined.

And its wicked dictator had the cheek to suggest she might one day be "in charge" there. As if she had any power over him. Or that much desire for revolution.

She gripped the sides of the boat and scowled up at the rugged silhouette of Roscarrock, almost invisible against the churning darkness of the sky, but just traced by a slender flicker of moonlight.

It would serve that scoundrel right if she *did* stage a coup.

Then she'd make him follow a few of her commands. She'd take that riding crop out of his hands and use it in a manner that might surprise him.

Hmm. She felt better already.

But the closer the little boat drew to the steps at the base of the rocky island, the hotter her blood boiled.

Chapter Twenty-Two

He heard her in the hall as he sprawled in a chair by the parlor fire with his brandy. True was tucked down so far that she wouldn't see his head if she looked through the open door.

"I suppose your master is still abed. So he won't require me tonight."

"Oh no, Mrs. You go on up to your own bed and get some rest."

"I'm sorry you had to come out in the rain to fetch me, Mr. Jameson."

"That's alright, Mrs. You can't predict the weather."

True heard the clank of a lamp handle and then the handyman's shuffling steps leaving the hall. He waited, expecting to hear the stairs creak as she went up to bed, but all was silent.

The air shifted and he sniffed. Her scent. Unmistakable.

She must have entered the parlor. Probably because there was still a low fire in the grate and the amber glow drew her into the room. If he hadn't drunk so much brandy, he would have thought to get up and shut the parlor door before she came in, but after his busy evening he had melted into the warm embrace of that chair and felt no inclination to get up.

Until he smelled her fragrance he was relaxed, but now he went very tense, hand curved tightly around his brandy glass. How long had she been gone? Must have been six hours at least, he thought grumpily. Surely it was after midnight and she was still gallivanting about. For once he wished he had a clock to prove it.

Perhaps it was the brandy's fault, but he was starting to feel...angry. Bitter. Jealous? Why the hell was he jealous?

It was his idea for Olivia to dine with his son, and he'd even told her to stay as long as she liked, but she was so damned conscientious about what was proper, he'd expected her to be gone just a few hours. Not all bloody night. He'd entrusted her to Storm's hands for an evening. Had that been a mistake? It did not feel like such a good deed as he'd expected. And why the blazes was he handing her over to that boy who couldn't seem to get her for himself? Storm certainly wasn't putting that much effort into it. Did he expect his father to do the hard work for him, tie her up like a present and deliver her for Christmas?

True began to feel quite indignant about the entire thing. He had spoiled his cubs. Well, that ended tonight. From now on they could hunt their own mates.

Storm had all his limbs functioning. Storm had youth on his side. Let him fight for the woman if he wanted her. True had done enough.

There she was, drifting into his side vision around the winged side of the chair. Soaking wet, dripping all over the place. She went directly to the fire and grabbed a poker to stir it up.

"So you finally decided to come back to me." His words bit at her scent as it drifted by.

She spun around, jumping a few inches, the poker swinging in her hand. Her face went white and she stepped back, almost stumbling over the fender.

"Thought you might have decided to stay at the farm in this weather," he added.

Olivia straightened up, clutching the poker like a

weapon. "And I thought *you'd* still be abed."

Still? What was that supposed to mean? Was she slurring her words? Surely not. Olivia Monday did not drink to excess. She could barely finish one glass of wine in an evening.

Her fiery gaze, like a beautiful dragonfly, flew over his rumpled, messy, undone attire and then landed lightly, tentatively on the bandage wrapped around his cut hand. "Seems you had quite a wild evening, sir."

"I did. And you? Did my son entertain you?"

"He did."

"Was he a perfect, courteous gentleman?" he demanded through gritted teeth.

"Yes. Surprisingly. For a son of yours."

He laughed lazily. "I see your opinionated tongue is in fine fettle this evening." What had *he* done to offend *her?* "I'd better not give you any more evenings off, if this is how you return to me."

"But how else will you manage your affairs with women while I am here underfoot?"He sat forward, elbows on his thighs. "If I cared about that, why would I invite you to use the room adjoining my own?" He watched the spark in her eyes burning brightly. "If I wanted the company of other women, why would your presence bother me? This is my empire here at Roscarrock, and I do as I please."

"Yes, you certainly do." She faced him boldly, just as she did on the night of her arrival, impressing him with her pluck. "For a man born a foundling with nothing — not even a name— it didn't take you long to cast humility aside and grow comfortable with great wealth. Now you act like one of those privileged aristocrats you purport to despise."

This was perhaps more wounding than any other insult she might have used. "And how, exactly, do I act like them?"

"Treating other folk like your minions! Not caring for instance that poor Jameson has been out all night in this rain, fetching and carrying for you and your *urges*!"

"Jim Jameson is paid very well for his services. I don't hear him complaining."

"Ah yes, as I am paid also and therefore I am not entitled to complain and question. I must turn a blind eye."

"A blind eye to what? I have hidden nothing from you."

"Until tonight. For some reason you thought it necessary to go through this charade to be rid of me for one evening."

"*Charade*?" True was having a hard time following. Bloody women! He should have sent her home that first morning. Should have known she'd eventually show her claws too.

"Money solves all your problems. Money keeps people quiet and on your side. Money pays off an unhappy schoolmaster for a broken curricle. Money brought your wife back to you time and time again. If she only wanted you for your money, whose fault was that? Apparently that was the only thing you were willing to give her! Money moves folk around at your disposal like...like chess pieces! Money, money, money." She pointed the ash-tipped poker at him for emphasis with each repetition of the word. "And now it brings you hussies too. Jameson rows them across to Camelot for you. How many can you get per pound?"

"Hussies?" He squinted at her. "Camelot? Are you drunk, Olivia?"

"Most assuredly not." She squared her shoulders but tipped slightly to her left.

He set down his brandy glass, suddenly aware of how volatile this conversation had become. In the hands of two people trying to keep their distance, but who had drunk too much, it could be dangerous.

"Don't come near me," she exclaimed, gripping the poker in both hands and swiping it in an arc, like a sword.

It might have made him smile if he wasn't so rattled himself that evening, besieged by new thoughts, ideas and feelings. "Put the poker down, Olivia."

"No."

He pushed up out of the chair. "Go on then. Strike me with it. I knew it wouldn't take you long to raise a weapon against me."

She hiccupped. "I shall." But her swaying became more pronounced and her eyes turned glassy.

"I don't approve of your behavior tonight, Olivia."

"And I don't approve of yours!"

"However I, being your employer, have an advantage. I can send you home to Chiswick tomorrow."

"Good." She dropped the poker, almost on his foot. "Suits me! Because I refuse to be one of your devoted, blind minions worshiping at the altar of money. Putting up with...everything...just because of the fee you're paying me. I'll do without it. I'll manage. Just pay me what you owe me for the time already spent and I'll leave. Sooner that than let you torture me for your own amusement."

Now he knew she had definitely drunk too much at the farmhouse, or she would never have spoken about her need of money.

"When have I tortured you?" he exclaimed, scratching his head. He thought he'd treated her well. He'd been on his best behavior. Well, most of the time. "You said yourself that I've treated you with prodigious care, madam. I believe that was the phrase you used." He watched her expression and noted the trembling lower lip. Her temper was hot tonight, but so was his. "Or is that not what you wanted? Perhaps you object to being treated so well, because you don't want to like me at all."

"Don't be ridic..ridiculous."

"Would you rather I treat you with a firmer hand, Mrs. Monday? Have I disappointed you by not living up to my reputation? If that's the case, we can remedy the matter at once."

Her lashes fluttered, her cheeks flushed. She raised both hands to her head as if it ached. "Ugh! You...you are impossible."

"Funny, that's what women always say when they know they've lost an argument." He paused. "And a wager."

She closed her hands into fists and they dropped to her sides. "What wager?"

"I told you the night you came that you'd soon flee back to Chiswick."

"It was never a wager. I refused to gamble with you."

"But I proved myself right, didn't I?"

* * * *

Olivia knew she'd gone too far, but with everything fermenting in her mind that night— helped along by Storm Deverell's dreadful wine— then coming back to find her employer in a shirt hanging out of his breeches and dampened by patches of sweat, was more than she could bear. He was laughing at her, enjoying the sight of her like this. She was sure the only reason he pried into her feelings was to know where to wound her. He used his money to draw folk into his web and then kept them tangled there, cunningly tying them into knots, making them another plaything, another devotee.

Now he gleefully celebrated the fact that he'd got her in this state of confusion.

He stood before her in a state of half-undress, his hair untidy, his hand clearly wounded from his erotic adventures— he'd warned her that he enjoyed rough sport. When he moved closer she could even smell the lingering whisper of perfume. It was not too sweet and floral, but soft and fresh. Very similar to the kind she distilled herself, so she knew it was a woman's perfume.

He had made love to someone who smelled like her— insult added to injury.

But no he had not made love. He didn't believe in "love". What he had done was called something else entirely.

Should that be a comfort to her?

Oh, she didn't know anymore. She didn't know anything. Her head ached with trying to hold everything inside, trying not to show what she felt and thought. Her stomach twisted as if she was still on that little boat being tossed about.

"Good evening, Mr. Deverell," she said stiffly, reclaiming some of her usual composure.

"Going to pack your trunk then?" He stood in her way, feet planted solidly apart.

She put her chin up. "Are you dismissing me from my post?"

"Perhaps. Haven't decided what to do with you. Yet." He picked up the poker to set it back on its hook by the fire, and while his back was turned she made her escape, hurrying out of the parlor.

Fancy thinking he looked at *her* with anything other than pity and bemusement. He teased her, took wicked pleasure in making her blush, but that was all it was. A game, like one of his wagers. Women, for him, were merely entertainment and in his mind he separated *that* from any sort of emotion. As the cook had said, it was exercise for him, like riding his horse and swimming in the sea.

He had told her plainly that he didn't believe in love.

Olivia's feet picked up speed across the hall and then up the stairs. Tonight she didn't pause to look at his faceless portrait. She wanted to get to her room and collapse on her bed. To think about nothing else until she woke tomorrow with a sober head.

She turned the door handle to her bedchamber and walked in.

And stopped dead.

Somehow she'd gone to the wrong room.

No. She checked. This was her bedchamber.

The fire was roaring. A hearth rug had been placed over the stone slab before it and a thick satin cushion had been added to the comfortable arm chair where she often sat to read. At the window new drapes of thick velvet had been hung to keep out the drafts, and the walls were insulated likewise by two colorful, rich tapestries. The bed was no longer the narrow, lumpy thing upon which she'd laid her head before; it was a large four-poster covered with a thick quilt and far more pillows than any one woman with only one head could possibly need. The table beside the bed had been swapped for a larger cabinet with extra books lined up on a shelf behind leaded glass doors. Her perfume bottle had apparently been spilled and set back, with a crack in it. There were three new oil lamps and a large, brightly colored rug that must be almost brand new— not a single worn patch of threads in sight. And it looked soft. Exquisitely soft.

So soft she dare not walk on it.

Or dare she?

Stumbling against the doorframe, Olivia quickly unlaced her wet boots, slipped out of them and ventured cautiously, in her stockinged feet, onto the luxurious carpet.

Only something wicked could feel this good. She wriggled her toes into the deep pile and then looked anxiously over at the mantle. William was still there, still watching over her in his silhouette.

He ought to be admonishing her tonight, but he was silent.

She went to the mantle and took his picture in both hands. "Oh, William. I fear I've let you down. I drank too much and made a fool of myself. I let my terrible, lurid imagination run away with me. I spoke silly thoughts aloud and made an embarrassing display of emotion."

"No, you didn't. You spoke your honest thoughts to me. At last." Deverell was standing in her

265

bedchamber doorway, one shoulder propped against the frame. "Finally you let it all out. Everything that was festering inside you and held back behind those tight lips."

"I didn't hear you follow me," she said, quickly blinking back the shameful tears that had threatened.

"Caught you talking to yourself again, didn't I?"

"No." She sniffed. "I was talking to William." She turned the frame to show him and he came into the room. Although she knew she should try to stop him, tell him to leave her alone, she also knew it would be futile. Besides, she didn't want to. "What have you done to my chamber?"

"Since you wouldn't come to my former wife's room, I thought I'd better bring the room to you. It took us most of the evening. Jameson and I."

The facts slowly formed shape in her mind, piece by piece falling together. This is what had exhausted him then. This is what Jameson had been fetching and carrying for him— all this furniture from the other wing of the house! *The master keeps 'imself busy too. Been going 'ard at it in the bedroom since you left.*

Abruptly a bubble of laughter shot out of her. She raised William's picture to hide her mouth, but Deverell snatched the frame from her hand, turned it over and studied the silhouette. "That's him, eh? The Kindly Parson."

"Yes." A rush of relief almost lifted her aloft.

"His forehead's a little long, isn't it?"

"Full of wisdom," she exclaimed proudly. "He was a deep thinker."

"Huh. What would he think of you coming here?"

"He always said a person should go where they

are most needed. A person should find their purpose."

"Well then, I suppose he was right, in this case." He set William's silhouette back on the mantle, cracked his knuckles and cleared his throat. "I do need you. Very much."

"Oh." She gripped the back of the chair by her hip. No one had ever said such a thing to her before, but he was good at it— shocking her with sudden, unexpected compliments.

"As a secretary," he added.

Of course. He lifted her up only to drop her back to earth again. "Yes. That's... why I came."

"And why you have stayed this long, despite my behavior and myriad faults?"

"That's a little more complicated, Mr. Deverell. I'm not sure I—"

He moved closer. "Call me True."

"I...I can't."

"Why not?" he demanded, chin thrust forward. "You said plenty to me tonight, but you can't call me by my name?"

"I said things I shouldn't. And no one is without fault."

He raised his eyebrows and swayed back on his heels. "Is that an apology, Olivia?"

"I leapt to conclusions about why you wanted me gone tonight. I am sorry for that."

Slowly he nodded. "And I'm sorry I sent you off to spend an evening with my son. I should have known he'd charm the drawers off you."

She sputtered, "He did no such thing."

"Plied you with strong drink. Put ideas in your head. Sent you back her to rail at me and threaten me

267

with a hot poker—"

"He did nothing of the sort." She felt the anger leaving her, pushed out by the waves of warm gladness.

True looked at the mantle again. "What's this?" He tipped his head toward the small, unframed painting.

"Can't you tell, sir, with your infamous talents of perception?" Taking it from the mantle she looked at it for a moment and then handed it to him. "Tell me what you think it is, if you're so clever." She would test him, she thought. Let him show off and impress her if he could.

He held it in both hands, considering the painting solemnly. "It's an amateur work, by someone with a heavy hand and not much artistic skill, although he thinks he has plenty. A picture of a childhood home, drawn by an impatient man who had no appreciation for its real beauty. "

"You're so sure the artist was a man?"

"Yes." He handed it back to her. "His name is Christopher."

"How...how do you know?"

With a sudden laugh he pointed to the back of the picture, where the black initials C.C. had been daubed in one corner. "You told me your stepbrother's name so it was not hard to put the pieces together. See." He tapped his brow. "It's all up here. Not magic."

Chagrinned, she ran a finger over the letters and then said, "But how did you know all the rest of it? The childhood home, for instance?"

"Because there is a child's swing hanging from the branch of the tree and you already told me your stepbrother is not married, so he has no children yet. It was a calculated guess that this is the house in which he—or you— grew up. But he does not look at the house with fondness. He has covered the walls in a messy proliferation of color, blobs of paint with no definition, no pattern, no care. Here, you see, the color of the leaves where there are any suggests late autumn. So how could there truly be so many bright and blossoming flowers growing up the walls of the house? They were not there, but he thought flowers would make the picture prettier. He did not see how the old stone of the walls, the crooked, chipped shutters at the windows and the winding path have a beauty of their own, without the unnecessary embellishment of a fictional overabundance of flowers."

"And his impatience?"

"Look at the strokes of paint. No time was taken with detail. I suspect he grew tired of the project when it did not come along the way he wanted, so he finished it in haste. Probably would have thrown it away in a fit of temper."

"Yes." Amazed she looked at him. "Yes, he did. I saved it from being burned in the fire." Slowly she set the picture back on the mantle. "I suppose now I must agree and say you are very clever. Very perceptive."

Deverell was quiet, just watching her.

"I had better sleep," she muttered.

"You stayed out late tonight."

"You told me to."

He looked down at the fancy carpet. "I also told Storm he ought to marry you."

Olivia gave in to a half yawn, half chuckle, and

shook her head.

He looked up again, his eyes suddenly uncertain. Boyish.

She walked around him, away from the temptation she felt to touch his face. To kiss him on the lips.

"Mr. Deverell, as you know, I was married three times before. While it was mostly pleasant, the experience did not impress me with a great sense of urgency to do it a fourth time. I did not come here to get another husband." The idea of another man dead because of her was unthinkable.

"You don't like my son?"

"I like Mr. Storm Deverell very much. He is amusing, easy company. But I am not going to marry him, and I doubt very much he would want me to."

"He needs a wife. It's time he—"

"Your son is enjoying his life just the way it is for now. And I can't say I blame him. He is happy and free to do just as he pleases."

"He's twenty eight!"

"Forgive me, sir, for being blunt, but when you were that age you didn't even want the wife you had." She paused, wrapping one arm around the nearest bed post, trying to appear less intoxicated than she felt. Trying to push away her desires. Something about his rumpled attire was shockingly alluring. But then he was equally handsome when he dressed neatly— as he did on the night of the harvest dance. And when he wore nothing at all.

She's doing it again. Someone ought to stop her.

Her palms were damp with sweat, but her mouth was dry.

He finally spoke again. "I suppose you're right. I

shouldn't meddle in romance since I know nothing about it."

"Precisely. Stick to cards and dice."

For another long moment they stared, gazes locked across the short distance.

Olivia leaned her back against the bed post for the room had begun to reel. "Now, if we might be done with the subject, I think I'll go to my bed. Good night, sir."

He hovered there. "You're staying then. With me."

"Is that another one of your commands?"

Deverell walked up to her, put his hands on her waist, tugged her away from the bed post and kissed her.

She was on fire, could hear the flames crackling through her body, catching on the tips of her hair. His hands slid upward to her back and held her close, forcing her against his torso, crushing her in his strength. She didn't want it to end, to go back to standing on her own feet. But she must.

When he released her she wilted against the carved bed post.

"Yes," he said. "I command you. I came up here to tell you that. I decorated this room to make you stay. So tomorrow you will write to your stepbrother and tell him you expect to stay longer. I don't care what reason you give him. But you will stay."

"I'm not your slave. I'll never be—"

"One of my money-blinded minions?"

She nodded.

"But you *are* here for the money."

"That is why I came, sir, but it's not entirely the reason why I've stayed," she confessed reluctantly.

"And that is what makes it 'complicated'? Because you daren't admit you enjoy the company of a man like me? That you want to be with me."

"I'm not afraid of you."

He looked puzzled, leaned closer again and touched her lower lip with his finger. "That's not what I said, Olivia."

Oh, she knew what he'd said, but she was not *that* intoxicated. She still had some wits about her and was regaining still more as the minutes passed. The tip of his finger ran slowly, painstakingly over her lips, down over her chin and followed the curve of her arching neck...down to the first button of her gown. "You showed me your fire tonight, Olivia. One evening you should let me show you mine. If you truly are fearless, as you claim."

He had slipped the button free, leaving a little patch of skin just below the indent at the base of her throat. She was breathing hard, suddenly powerless to move.

Until she closed her eyelids when his mouth touched her flesh.

His warm lips caressed her flesh, and then a little of his unshaven cheek scraped over it as he pressed in closer, nuzzling the side of her neck, breathing her in. "You say you don't want another husband. So perhaps you need a lover this time. Is that why you came to me? You planned to seduce me."

She shivered, clutched at the carved wood behind her. His hands reached around and covered hers, holding them to the bed post.

"No, sir," she groaned.

"Call me True," he whispered in her ear, his tongue flicking out to dampen her earlobe, toying with the dangling pearl.

"I...no...I can't."

His grip tightened on her hands so she could not get free. Even if she wanted to.

Meanwhile his greedy mouth traveled back to the buttons down the bodice of her gown and began to ease them open, one by one. She knew he would hear and feel how hard her heart was beating. A strange sort of elation had flooded her body and a little voice, smoky and rich, whispered in her head, *Now he notices you. Now he looks twice at Olivia Westcott.*

He would never step over her again.

He soon had four buttons undone, showing supreme mastery of his tongue and lips. Now a partial vee of skin was exposed, including the upper swell of both breasts and the valley between.

"Call me True," he repeated tersely.

"No."

He kissed the lace edge of her chemise and slid his tongue between the curves of her bosom where they rose up over the corset. Her skin reacted with goose bumps, which only heightened the effect when he licked across it again.

"Call me True."

"So much for your attempt at being a gentleman," she managed. "At behaving yourself."

"Call me True and then I'll be good. I'll be very...very... good."

He caught a little skin between his teeth and sucked gently. Olivia pressed her thighs together, swallowing a moan of sheer need. He sucked harder. Enough to drive a startled whimper out of her mouth. "I don't believe you."

"That's not *nice*, Olivia. I've always been honest

273

with you. Always been straightforward."

His tongue swept down, determinedly pushing the wet lace chemise aside, sliding further under her corset.

Catching her breath on a gasp, she closed her eyes. "Very well then...*True*. Tell me why you're doing this. What do you want from me?"

A soft chuckle blew against her neck. "I want you to come to bed with me, Olivia."

Her heart could not find a rhythm. She kept her eyes closed. "And... then what?"

"I don't know. What would you like? Some jewelry? Some new gowns. Definitely some new walking boots."

Olivia let her eyes drift open as he kissed her chin. "Your son said you've never lived this long with the same woman under your roof. That you always get bored and look for the next new, pretty thing."

He lifted his lips from her skin. "Why should a man stagnate? Why should a woman? Change is the essence of life."

Now she met his gaze steadily, despite her intemperate state. Perhaps the drink was wearing off. Or else it made her see everything with stark clarity. She was bold, ready to challenge this frustrating man who thought he could not love. "In my opinion, sir, you fear getting old, so you keep moving in the hope of preventing time from catching up with you."

He stared, eyes full of hot sparks.

"But you're going to die one day, just like everyone else," she added. "It's a certainty."

"Well, aren't you a cheerful one. I suppose you know all about that with your record of dead husbands."

"Yes, I have been unlucky. But at least I tried to find love. In the short time we have to live, the greatest gift we can give or receive is love."

He lowered his lips to hers, but they barely touched— just the slightest caress as he spoke. "Even better than a priceless pair of diamond earrings that once belonged to Marie Antoinette, while she still had her head attached? They can be yours, if you want them."

"What on earth would I want with diamond earrings?"

"I'll fetch them from my vault in London."

"Don't be foolish. *I don't want diamonds!*"

His tongue swept over her cheek. "Then what? I can give you anything, Olivia."

"Not what I want." She shivered and knew he would feel it, would know what he did to her. With her breasts pushed against his chest as he pinned her to the bed post, she was helpless, a sacrificial offering left there by the villagers to appease their pagan beast of a god.

"Tell me what you want," he whispered.

So he could mock her? "You know very well. And it is not in your power to give it to me, because it's something that cannot be bought. Not with all your *rotten gains.*"

"That's the wine talking." He kissed his way back down the side of her neck. "No sober woman would turn down my offer."

"If I were sober, True Deverell, I wouldn't let you do this. I wouldn't be this weak!"

"Good god, woman, I don't believe it's in your nature to be weak, even when my son has tried to pickle you in his wine. If anything, it's brought out the

275

fiery taste of you. The real Olivia."

He kissed her again, deeply, tongue plunging into her mouth. She felt her toes lifting off the plush carpet, his hard body pressed to hers, his fingers holding her wrists in that firm man-made cuff behind the bed post. Finally his lips released her. His eyes had turned smoky and she felt a fine mist of his heat dampening her body, under her gown.

Now was the moment to stop him.

Instead, she said nothing as he bent his head and kissed the little bit of lace chemisette over the peaked nipple he had so slyly teased out of hiding.

* * * *

"No sense of urgency to marry again, eh?" he murmured against her warm, soft, perfumed skin. "Must not have been so very *pleasant* after all, marriage with your kindly parson. Or the other two."

He felt her trembling as the tip of his tongue found the taut pink bud beneath her lace undergarments. "I won't discuss them with you," she ground out between apparently clenched teeth.

Her words ended on a hiccup and another gasp, as he drew her nipple between his lips.

True was close to the point when he knew he would not be able to pull away. His body was afire with need for this woman, but to take her now would not be fair. He wanted her eyes open and clear, he wanted her fully aware of each sensation he could give her, not partially numbed by that potion Storm optimistically called "wine".

So he backed away, slowly, reluctantly releasing her wrists. It took him every inch of self-control. Self-control he didn't know he had until then. Certainly it was something he'd never used to deny himself whatever he wanted.

The supposedly innocent target of his desire remained standing against the carved post, hands behind her back, eyes drowsy, cheeks washed with a faint blush. The sort of delicate tint he'd seen on antique china roses. His truculent secretary was temptingly beautiful and very evidently aroused tonight. That brown nipple he had teased, poked through the lace, eager and erect. Wanting more.

As he was himself.

Her gaze tracked downward to the very evident sign of his arousal. Her lips parted and he felt another raw surge of need pulse through his veins. Every muscle and tendon was tense, coiled to spring. "Come to bed with me," he said, his voice low, charged with desire. "Not tonight. But soon."

She did not reply, but licked her lips. He could hear her quickened breaths, his body attuned to every nerve and pulse within hers.

He had better leave that room now, while he still could. Slowly he walked backward, away from her. "Good evening then, Olivia. I will leave you to ponder my offer."

"An old pair of diamond earrings? You can have my answer now. No thank you."

Ah, there she was, regaining her senses. He smiled. Trust her to speak so disdainfully of the most beautiful jewelry that had ever been made. The finest pieces in his priceless collection. "You know all that I could give you, Olivia."

"And I know the limits of what you *would* give me."

He paused, one hand on the door. "Yes."

Her lower lip vanished beneath the upper. She nodded her head, still leaning against the carved Tudor-bedpost, making no move to close the buttons he'd chewed open.

With a deep breath inhaled, he walked out and closed her door behind him. Only then did he feel his blood calm.

It was no good. Tonight had proved he could not let her leave. He could not give her to his son either. Somehow he must come up with a way to make her stay. To keep her.

He'd even let her talk him into writing to his daughter and making a damned apology of sorts. Madness.

Absolute madness. But he felt like a young man again inside, where something else new was opening its shell and shaking itself, like a damp freshly hatched chick.

Chapter Twenty-Three

True poured her a cup of coffee. When he set it down on the desk before her, the slight chink caused Olivia to wince, one hand pressed to her brow. In the dreary winter's morning light through his window her face was the color of sour milk. No amount of pinching could put pink back in those cheeks, he mused.

"I shall have words with my son for giving you so much of that dreadful stuff he makes out of left over peapods and gooseberries. It ought to be a registered poison."

She groaned, wincing again. "Oh, it was not your son's fault." Her voice broke on a hoarse note. "I was perfectly aware of what I did last night. I take full responsibility of my own actions. No one and nothing else is to blame."

Once again she proved herself so unlike most women he'd known. It shouldn't really surprise him anymore.

"I won't even blame the wine," she added. "I'm afraid it was all me. Well, mostly me. The wine simply... assisted my tongue in its...unraveling."

Lowering to his own chair on the other side of the desk, True laughed gently. "That's remarkably honest for a woman, Olivia. One might even say, dangerously honest."

"Is it?" She took a careful sip of coffee. "Perhaps I'm still suffering the effects then."

"Perhaps." His fingers felt even more restless today, so he knitted them together and set his hands on the blotter, assuming his most business-like pose. Although it was damned difficult to be solemn when he was around this woman. "You do recall the conversation we had?"

"Yes. The earrings." Another sip of coffee. He sincerely hoped she remembered more than earrings, but before he could say anything, she continued, "I must turn down the offer, sir. I cannot think when I would have the occasion to wear something so costly and luxurious."

He frowned. "With me, of course."

"With you?" Her cup rattled against her saucer as she set it down again.

"I believe you know full well what I offered you and it went beyond earrings."

"Yes, sir. I know." Her expression was earnest, but she hid her hands from him, setting them in her lap out of sight. "And I am cognizant of the honor. But you would be even more costly than the earrings."

True stared. "I'm not sure whether to be flattered by that or annoyed."

"I mean that you would cost me in other ways, sir."

"Stop calling me *sir* like that!" He bounced up out of his chair, abandoning his decision to be calm. "I would not ask you for anything."

"Yes you would."

"Well..." He waved a hand through the air impatiently and walked in a circle, "nothing more than exclusive rights to your body whenever I needed it."

Behind him she muttered dryly, "Now *I'm* not certain whether to be flattered or annoyed."

"Very well then, you make the rules. You say where and when."

"That is brave of you."

True came to a stop before his window and stared out at the windblown garden. It always amazed him how some plants grew and survived on that rocky island, but he supposed they were like him. Stubborn and determined, they did not require tender nurturing. The more resistance they felt, the hardier and tougher they became out of necessity.

"When I see something I want, Olivia," he warned her carefully, "I generally go after it until I get it. I don't give in. I don't lose."

There was a pause, then she replied, "And once you have it, the *thing* quickly loses its sense of novelty. There is always something new you must have."

"I haven't found anything that keeps my attention. Yet."

"You don't want to. If you did you might have to stop moving and then you'd get old."

Oh, this again? Apparently she wanted him in his grave already. Would probably dig it for him. He thought for a moment, hands behind his back. Then he spun around angrily, opened his desk drawer and took out a letter, which he tossed to her across the desk. "Here. This came for you today."

She looked at it, a faint frown marring her brow. "Why was it in your desk?"

"Because I didn't feel like giving it to you," he confessed sulkily and then turned away again, listening as she tore open the seal.

"It's only my stepbrother," she said.

"Hmph."

* * * *

She stared at the words penned in obvious anger

across the paper.

I have heard a most disturbing report about your situation in Cornwall and I am of a mind to come there at once and remove you from the place. I know now I should not have allowed you to go, had I been made fully aware of the disgraceful terms of your employment and that you would be living there with him quite alone...

This was a most ill-advised enterprise and it will cause this family much shame if you do not return home immediately...

Having read enough, she refolded the letter. The thought of Christopher arriving there to drag her home by the scruff of her neck— as if she was an errant child— might have amused her if not for her sad state of health that morning.

Besides, her stepbrother was quite correct in imagining her descent into infamy and he only knew the half of it.

"Well?" Deverell demanded, his back stiffly turned to her. "What news?"

She sighed. "He thinks I am on the road to hell."

Slowly he glanced over one shoulder. "You cannot leave yet. You promised."

How like a boy he was, she mused. A spoiled boy who expected to get his own way. Christopher was the same, but things had always been given to him, he did not really have to work for them or put in any effort. True Deverell was this way because he'd always had to fight, always had to get what he wanted for himself.

"Write to him," he demanded. "Tell him you're staying. Tell him I insist."

"We'll see. Later today perhaps, when my head stops spinning and my stomach likewise."

Relief warmed his expression as he turned fully to face her. "You know what you need for that sour headache, Olivia my sweet? Some fresh air."

She winced up at him.

"Trust me." He grinned. "With my reputation, I ought to know how to handle a woman with a sore head, don't you think?"

* * * *

"I'm not a very good rider," she exclaimed, warily eyeing his horse.

"That's alright, because I'll be in command. You just ride behind me. And hold on with all your might." He was already swinging himself up, even without a saddle.

The animal was huge, its coat black and shiny, muscles oozing with power; hooves the size of a child's head.

Deverell looked down at her from the stomping, snorting beast. "I thought you said you were never afraid?"

"It looked smaller from a distance."

"Isn't that the case with most objects?" He reached down one hand, fingers twitching impatiently. "I won't go too fast. Come on! Help her up, Jameson."

Rather than appear cowardly, she gathered her wits. Gripping his hand and his sleeve, she prepared to mount the beast. Jameson gave her a boost from behind and suddenly she was up there, clinging around Deverell's waist as if her life depended on it.

He didn't wait a moment longer, but turned the horse toward the beach and they were off.

So much for not going "too fast". That, of course, was a relative term.

The cold air whipped by her face, even when she took shelter by resting her cheek to his back. Her bonnet soon slid off her hair, unable to hold its place, the knot in her frayed ribbons being the only thing that kept it attached to Olivia. Every bone in her body shook and rattled. Sea foam sprayed up, wetting her stockings.

But after the first few moments she dared open her eyes and she saw the clouds tearing by— dark, bubbling clouds that came as heralds to a storm. Their beauty swept her breath away. Quite literally.

The sea was a mass of froth today, churning waves to match the sky above, all of it merging and swelling around them as they tore onward across the sand. Salt air filled her nostrils. The screech of the gulls echoed through her ears, made her heart beat faster. And the man sitting before her was warm, solid, just as powerful as his horse.

Would someone traveling in a passing carriage up on the cliff road look down and see them? They might think she'd been stolen away on a pirate's horse, she mused.

They would envy her.

Suddenly Olivia felt as if she was absorbed into the scene, part of the horse itself, a creature of nature, just as wild, free and beautiful.

Yes, beautiful. For the first time in her life.

And belonging there in the picture, wanted, not out of place or superfluous.

The nausea was gone, her headache eased as if

someone slowly turned a winch and unclenched her tight skull again.

It was a glorious day, after all.

And True Deverell admired her, lusted after her. Made no bones about what he wanted to do with her.

She ought to be appalled, but honestly, how could she be? How could any woman?

But it wasn't *any* woman he wanted. It was her, the girl who'd been told he would never look twice at her.

The horse thundered across the sand and through the water until it felt as if they were flying.

She squeezed her companion ever tighter, but not from anxiety— from the childish, wild joy that thudded through her. Olivia wanted to laugh into the wind, even with tears in her eyes.

This was what it felt like to be unfettered.

Now she knew why he liked to ride so much.

He was a man who did not believe in the need to explain himself or apologize, so this was his way of opening her eyes, making her see the world as he saw it. The best way he knew how and the only way he thought she would let him.

* * * *

They reached the far curve of the bay and here he slowed the horse to a canter, then a trot.

Olivia was silent, clinging to him, leaning against his back. Would she be angry with him now?

He wasn't sure whether the tight arms around him were a good or bad thing. They felt very good, but she could be about to rage at him and beat him about the head with her fists.

He hoped not. True wanted her to experience this just as he did. Wanted her to understand—

"Thank you," she gasped against his ear. "That was wonderful."

He felt a smile playing over his lips. An unusually shy, relieved smile, because he knew she didn't use words like "wonderful" unless she really meant it. She was a woman sparing with her praise, which made it all the more valuable. "Head still aching?"

"A little. But it is much better than it was."

"We can go back, if you want. Or we can ride on."

She didn't hesitate. "Oh, let's go on! What's around the next bay?"

"We're supposed to be working on my memoirs." Usually she was the one reminding *him* of that.

"We can work later," she whispered, hugging him tighter still, her chin resting on his shoulder. "You know what they say about all work and no play."

He laughed. "Hold tight then, my sweet."

"You shouldn't call me that."

"I am your employer and I shall call you whatever I want. Remember? My rules!"

"But we're not on your island right now. Your sovereignty is suspended out here."

"Aha." He turned his head and his lips almost touched her cheek. "That's why you want to stay out here longer, Olivia?"

"Yes."

"Call me True. Please. Even if it's only for today, just now, out here away from the island."

"Very well." It was barely more than a whisper, but it touched his lips with a soft breath finer than any caress he'd ever known. "True."

He urged his horse forward again and the beast launched into another gallop, happy to stretch its legs, tearing up the wet sand and scattering seagulls in all directions.

* * * *

Even when the rain started, she didn't care. Olivia wanted to go on riding. Just the two of them on a horse, as far as they could go, leaving everything else behind.

They could catch fish to eat, as he had done when he was a boy, she thought. They would manage together. Start life in a new world.

Like Adam and Eve.

But reality set in when the rain came down harder and colder. The dark clouds linked and dipped low, threatening to obscure daylight several hours before night was expected.

True steered his horse away from the sea, up a sandy path and along a coastal road to the coaching inn that she remembered from her journey to Roscarrock. It was a whitewashed building, low and squat with wide chimneys, a slate roof, and a painted sign announcing "The Fisherman's Rest" swinging wildly in the wind. Warm light shone at the little windows and steady noise from within suggested it was a busy place, perhaps because it was the only inn on the road before Truro.

He helped her down and handed his horse to a stable lad who seemed to know him well, greeted him by name.

"You must be hungry by now," he said, wiping wet hair back from her brow with surprisingly gentle fingers.

She was, in fact, ravenous and apparently her countenance told him that, because he laughed, grabbed her hand and tucked it under his arm— very firmly— then took her through the door of the inn.

He whispered from the corner of his mouth, "They have a splendid pasty here and that will replenish everything my son's brew stole from your blood yesterday."

"A better pasty than Mrs. Blewett's?" she whispered back.

"Yes. But don't you dare tell her I said that."

Instead of steering her through to the private dining room of the inn— a place for grander customers to be apart from the general rabble— he took her into the crowded public salon. Feeling the draft from the open door, a few folk looked up from their cards or dominos, and nodded respectfully when they saw Deverell. He didn't stop to converse with anyone. Instead he led her directly to a corner table by the window and ordered two pasties and some beef broth. The settles had high backs, affording a degree of privacy from the other customers. If not for the low rumble of conversation, she could have imagined they were quite alone.

Olivia hadn't realized how wet she was until she sat down and dripped all over the table. Her bonnet ribbons were stuck to her shoulders, her hair drooping down around her face.

"I must look a sight," she muttered.

"You do," he agreed placidly.

"Why thank you."

He grinned. "Were you fishing for a compliment?"

288

"Good lord, no. I am aware of my limitations. I am useful, not ornamental, as we both know."

"Now, now, Olivia," he shook a finger at her and put on a grave face. "That is not entirely honest. I may have considered you plain when first we met, but you know full well that my opinion of you has changed. I have, after all, asked you to come to bed with me."

"You have? I only recall the earrings."

"Then like most women you have a selective memory. And me asking you to be my lover is a compliment, whether you might think it is or not."

"Hush." She felt her face heat up, despite the cold rain that still dripped down her cheeks. "Someone might hear."

"So what?"

She stared.

"Why should I care if they know how much I desire you. They'd be more shocked if I didn't try to seduce you. And you'd be offended if I hadn't."

"You are incorrigible," she whispered. "Dratted man."

"Now that you're insulting me again, I know you must be feeling better than you were earlier this morning."

She sighed, falling back against the high wooden screen behind her in a relaxed manner Great Aunt Jane would never condone. "I am much improved."

He waited, brows high. "Thanks to me."

"Yes. Thank you...True."

A smile ripped quickly across his face. "I like my name on your lips."

"But when we get back I cannot call you that. Not before your other staff."

"When we are alone then."

"Perhaps.

"When we are alone then," he repeated firmly.

Fortunately the inn-keeper arrived with food at that moment, so she had no need to reply. Olivia watched as he ate his broth, and she marveled at how far she had come with him, feeling comfortable in his presence, joking with him as if it was the most natural thing in the world.

He who should not be mentioned.

True Deverell might be the wickedest sinner that ever disrupted a drawing room conversation, and be unfit for the term "gentleman" according to Great Aunt Jane, but he ate his broth like any other man. Spilled it too sometimes on his chin. And she very much appreciated the fact that he didn't hide his nature, but put it all out there. Take him or leave him, he didn't care. He was unafraid to be himself, say what he wanted, admit to his faults.

"Tell me, Olivia, now that you're finally being open and honest with me...what was your first thought when we met?"

Just like a self-conscious boy he kept wanting to know her impression of him. So strange and yet endearing in a man who must have been told, many times, by many women, how handsome he was.

"If you must know, I thought it was a very good thing that I didn't have to do your laundry."

"That's all?" he exclaimed.

"I've always been the practical sort."

He shot her a dark look. "Fibber."

"I beg your pardon?"

"If you were practical rather than romantic, you'd come to bed with me and take me for every penny—

which I'm more than willing to give you."

"That wouldn't make me practical. It would make me a—"

"Woman of business?" He smirked.

"Something like that."

"Damn you. Why must you be so proper? And why did I have to find a conscience last night while you were soused as a herring?"

For a while they were quiet, enjoying their luncheon. Olivia thought over her conversation with Storm last night and how he had tried so hard to give her the glowing image of his father as noble King Arthur. Both men, it seemed, had been pushing her at each other. Clearly Storm hadn't given up on his father's heart. Perhaps he saw something there that no one else did. And which True would ferociously deny.

"What now, Olivia the merciless?" he grumbled.

"Your son is very fond of you," she said, feeling a warm glow inside as she curled her fingers around a napkin and fought the temptation to wipe his chin for him.

"Good. He should be. I do a lot for that boy."

"He's not a boy, he's a man. And he's not fond of you just because of the things you've done for him, or what material things you give him. He loves you because you're his father and he looks up to you. He won't hear a word against you."

"Oh, tried to speak badly about me to my own son last night, did you?"

"No. I couldn't get a word in sideways. He was too eager to assure me of how wonderful you are."

"Hmph." He tore a lump off the end of her pasty and stuffed it into his own mouth, scattering crumbs across the small table.

"I don't believe you really know what love is, True Deverell. That's why you don't think you're capable of the emotion. Perhaps you feel it already and don't recognize it."

Now he slurped broth directly from the side of the bowl and burped, his eyes boring into her the entire time, looking for a reaction. Olivia knew he was being deliberately coarse, trying to remind her of his upbringing. Or lack of it. Using that misfortune, once again, as his excuse.

"You don't wish to discuss it," she muttered.

The bowl drained, he let it fall back to the table and wiped his mouth on his sleeve. "Exactly. Just as you don't like to tell me what you're thinking and feeling. Just as you don't care to tell me about your husbands. I have to tease it out of you, don't I?"

She shook her head, looking down at her hands in her lap. He wanted so much from her and yet he was willing to concede so little. Olivia would be the one to make all the changes, if she wanted to be with him.

Suddenly a woman bumped into their table and exclaimed, "Why, it *is* you, Mr. Deverell! It's been a while since we saw you here." She was pretty, pink-cheeked, plump and bosomy. Her fair hair, full of wispy curls, framed her face like petals.

"Ah... Sally. It has been a while, hasn't it?"

"Aye." The woman rolled her hip against the table edge and gave a low, lusty chuckle. "Not like you to be stuck up there on that chunk of rock all alone with no female company for so many months. I thought you was ill. Rumor had it that bullet hit something vital after all." And then, as if she had not noticed anyone else seated there until he gestured with a nod of his head, she finally turned and looked Olivia up and down. "Who's this then? Not a local girl."

"This, Sally, is Mrs. Olivia Monday. My secretary. Olivia, this is Miss Sally White."

"*Secretary?*"

Olivia stretched her fingers out, letting the napkin fall to her lap. "How do you do, Miss White."

Sally merely twitched her small nose and looked back at Deverell. "Well, you know where to find me, when those cold winter nights set in. Ol' Sally will warm you up again."

"Yes." True smiled. "I know."

The inn-keeper called for her and slowly she walked away, collecting empty tankards from another table and stopping to chat with a group of laughing, ruddy-faced men by the ale taps.

Olivia picked up her pasty and ate, filling her mouth before she might feel the urge to say anything. All that needed to be said in that regard had come out last night and she would gladly move on, away from the subject of his previous female attachments. She looked out of the window to watch horses being prepared for a fine carriage.

"No comment?" her companion asked gruffly, wiping his mouth on his sleeve.

She widened her eyes. "About what?"

"Women I've had? Women I've tumbled? I suppose you want to know if Sally's one of 'em."

"Why would it concern me?"

"It was one night I spent with her a few years back. With her and her sisters. Can't remember all their names. Four or five hearty lasses."

293

A piece of pastry went down the wrong way and made her cough.

He was so brutally honest, it was painful. But better that, she supposed, than have him try to deceive her. "I know all about the way you lead your life. You've made it clear to me."

It was also evident to her now that he would not change for anybody. Would she want him to? He was the same all the way through and one would always know what to expect. Born wild, making his own rules. Not only had he survived against the odds that way, but thrived. Why should he change? Especially when he thought it would make him weaker and vulnerable if he opened his heart to one woman.

She understood. They all had their own way of getting on with life, overcoming obstacles and who was to say that her method was better than his?

The awkwardness, the immoral propositions, the naughty sense of humor, his brusque, eccentric ways were all a part of what made *him*. And made him strangely attractive to her. Olivia wouldn't want the man to be anybody but who he truly was. She must simply decide where she fit in his life, whether she had a purpose there that went beyond the post she'd accepted.

Perhaps she was not only meant to help write his story, but to be a part of it too.

But before she could say any of that, Miss Sally White was back, this time with a message from someone who waited behind the paneled walls of the private dining room.

"One of the guests wants to see you, Mr. Deverell. If you can spare the time, she says."

"She?" He scowled.

"Aye." She glanced at Olivia and smirked. "Very fine lady. The one they say was once your lady wife."

Chapter Twenty-Four

Her name, he learned, was Lady Charlotte Rothsey. She reminded him of a porcelain statue, all frail, cool, smooth edges. And she walked in on the arm of Lord Henry Duquesne. A man whose face and name True had never forgotten. It was the man that interested him more than the woman. Why wouldn't it be thus, since this was supposedly his father?

Duquesne; a man with a bad temper, so it was said. A violent, cold-hearted man, spoiled and arrogant.

There was always a chance that he was not responsible for the feral boy who once ran wild on his own father's estate, but it was just as likely that he was. No one would ever know. Not even Henry Duquesne, who had probably fathered many bastards and cared what became of none.

He studied the man's face and saw how bloated it was, over-filled with pride and self-contentment. Duquesne paraded his fiancée about as if she was the prize-winning sow at a country fair and she, unknowing and uncaring, bathed in the attention, her lips ever wide in a silly, empty smile. But yes, she was a handsome woman, a thoroughbred— elegant and fashionable. She was the kind of woman other men fought after.

True made up his mind that he would have her. Just to get his vengeance on the Duquesne's. Let them raise a child of his without knowing.

Yet, in the end, he found that he could not let his own cub be left to their mercy. He was not as heartless as he thought he should be.

He was not his father's son, after all, but capable of deep feelings for a being not yet born. And he was fraught with doubts about his abilities to be a father. He did not know what to do with this emotion. Like any beast of the farmyard, what he did not know or understand cast suspicion in his mind and so he kept his distance from it.

* * * *

"What the hell are you doing here, Charlotte?"

Her bitter gaze— always looking for some reason to claim she'd been misused or slighted— traveled greedily over him as he walked up to her corner table. She was the only customer in the private room, sitting there like an empress, dining in solitary splendor. A sneer curled her lip lazily upward. "Since you refuse to answer my letters, I was on my way to pay you a visit. Imagine my surprise when I heard you were here, in the public salon. To my relief I shan't have to take the barbarous trip out onto that island in this foul weather. I can handle my business here and now."

"I'm busy, Charlotte. If you have any matter to discuss regarding the children, you know how to—"

"I didn't realize I'd be intruding on a pleasant tete a tete, but I'm sure your companion can wait a half hour. She has nowhere else to go, does she?"

His shock at suddenly seeing her again was now joined by a fast rising temper, and considerable suspicion. Perhaps it *would* be a good thing to deal with her now, rather than have her come out to Roscarrock.

"What could possibly be so important that you came all this way?" He knew she hated Cornwall and would avoid the place unless she saw some opportunity to twist a knife in his gut.

Now she invited him to sit at her table, but he refused.

"Just get on with it," he snapped, impatient for pleasanter company.

"Very well. My father will pay for Raven's wedding and I suggest you don't interfere. He wants to hold it in Edinburgh and Raven is in agreement."

True suddenly had a toothache. He pressed on the troubled spot with the tip of his tongue.

"And Raven doesn't want you at the wedding. You're an embarrassment to her."

Her words were like a punch to his stomach, forcing him back into a chair on the opposite side of her round table.

Charlotte continued without even looking at him, helping herself to broth from the china tureen on the table before her. "You will, no doubt, be tiresome about it, but I've told my father to proceed with the plan as he sees fit. We would like a spring wedding. I thought I'd better come in person and tell you. It is, apparently, beyond your capabilities to write a civil letter and I realize you may not even bother reading anything I send."

He realized how shrill she was. Surely he'd noticed it before, but somehow tonight it was worse than he remembered it. Now, of course, he was accustomed to a gentler voice at his table— someone with a warmer, richer timbre, and, more often than not, a hint of wry amusement in her tone. Charlotte had no sense of humor. When she laughed it was because she had succeeded in making someone uncomfortable. It was generally amusing to no one else.

True had been rubbing his knuckles on his thigh so hard he feared he might wear a hole in the corduroy riding breeches. He had to find something to do with his hands because whenever she dangled his children about like bait, his fingers always wanted to squeeze around her neck.

"If my daughter is to marry, I will pay for it," he

muttered. "It is my responsibility. Nothing to do with Lord Rothsey." He would never agree to a wedding in Scotland, so far away. On Rothsey's turf.

"But plans are already underway." She waved a hand carelessly, making the candle flames dance like yellow butterflies.

"Then you'd better stop them, hadn't you?"

She scowled hard. "Raven wants to marry in Edinburgh."

"When I see her at Christmas, she can tell me that herself."

"Christmas?"

"I have written to invite my daughter and her young man to Roscarrock for the Yuletide season."

His former wife sputtered in shock. "You don't even celebrate."

"This year, I shall."

"Raven won't come here."

"That's up to her."

Charlotte's cheeks looked very thin tonight, and there were new lines at the corner of her mouth. When she forgot herself and allowed her brow to wrinkle, the creases were deeper than he recalled. No doubt he had a few more lines on his face too. Olivia would be sure to point them out for him, he mused. "I can't think what you plan to achieve by inviting them here," Charlotte grumbled. "If you mean to try dissuading her against marriage—"

"I don't mean to dissuade her against anything."

"Then why?" she exclaimed. "What good will it do if she comes here?"

"Whatever she decides about this marriage, I would like to make peace with my daughter."

"Make. Peace? Make. *Peace*?" She howled with

laughter, tipping her head back. "You? You wouldn't know how. You settle quarrels with your fists or your money. I doubt that's changed."

"You haven't known me for a long time. In fact never. Not properly. We weren't interested in learning about each other."

"Just as you never bothered to learn anything about Raven. Never had time for her. She's just another irritating woman in your eyes. And she knows not to trust you. I've given her good warning not to."

He pressed his tongue against the toothache again, and made it worse. Good. "I'm sure you have. And I've allowed that folly to continue because of my own bull-headed stupidity."

"I don't follow."

"You are right, Charlotte, when you say I know little about my own daughter. As I promised her in my letter, I will amend that when she comes back. Fortunately it's not too late for me to grow up and be an adult. A proper father."

She swallowed, fingers to the pearl choker around her slender throat, almost as if she could feel his hands there, squeezing. "Raven won't come here," she repeated flatly.

"We'll see. By the way, you're not invited for Christmas." He would get that clear immediately.

"Heavens I wouldn't want to be. I have plans in London. I'm on my way there now."

He nodded briskly, glad of it.

Now she tapped her fork to her plate, watching him with a thoughtful gleam in her eye. "So ... that funny-looking girl in the ugly grey dress...where did you find *her*?"

"Her name is Olivia Monday."

"She looks very young."

"She's not as young as she looks."

"And dour."

He said nothing to that.

"What's she doing here? Surely you're not sleeping with her. She's not your sort."

"That's none of your business. And since when have you known anything about *my sort*?"

"No need to be defensive," she sneered. "I was merely trying to make conversation."

True considered her powdered, rouged face and those stiff curls placed artfully against her brow. Conversation? Highly unlikely. "If that's all..." He got up, eager to leave the room and that stale air tainted by her presence.

But she stopped him. "Wait."

Ah, his former wife hadn't come so far out of her way just to rub his face in the Earl's plans for Raven.

Did she want money again? Likely. But she didn't usually take this long to ask for it.

"These memoirs you're writing," she said. "You had better not slander me in them, or I'll sue."

So that was it. "Who told you?" He didn't think any of her children knew about his memoirs and Chalke was sworn to secrecy. Damon, Justify and Storm would have nothing to do with her, of course.

If a python could smile, it would look just like that, he thought. "I'm warning you. Say one bad word about me in this True Story of yours and I'll take you for every last penny."

"You've already tried that, Charlotte."

"Yes, but you keep getting richer, while I get poorer."

"Then I suggest you curb your expensive habits.

301

Or find a way to earn money yourself. Stop waiting for it to fall into your lap."

"A *lady* doesn't work for money," she exclaimed.

"And you father cannot support you?"

"My father does his best."

He was amused to hear that. The Earl of Rothsey was notoriously tight-fisted with his coin and Charlotte had always complained about her father's failure to spoil her. It was probably one of the reasons why she ran after True all those years ago— mud in the eye for the pompous skinflint earl, and also, of course, she had stuck her claws into an abundant vein of riches. A very generous vein.

"It's getting late," he muttered. "You must excuse me. I need to get back to Roscarrock." She dabbed her napkin against those perfectly bowed, poisonous lips. "There is one more thing before you go."

He sighed. "What?"

She tittered in a girlish manner that had always made him cringe, even when she *was* a girl. "You don't know anything about that woman, do you? Has she pulled the wool over your eyes too?"

"If you refer to Olivia Monday, yes I do. I know she is nothing like you. Thankfully."

That only partially curbed her foolish noises. "But you don't know the truth about her." She slithered upward from her chair. "Three times a widow, I'm told. And yet she's only young. Don't you wonder whether it was misfortune, carelessness... or something else?"

"What the hell do you —"

"And she's desperately in love with her own stepbrother. Has moped after him for years, since she was sixteen. That's why she came here to heal her broken heart, because he's about to marry another woman and she cannot bear to see it. Has she told you that?"

Somehow he kept his temper and his countenance.

Charlotte moved closer, laughing. "Do be careful with her. You might not escape another attempt on your life. Even cats have a limit, and she's proven herself adept in the art of snuffing out inconvenient men. Just thought I should warn you. For old time's sake."

"Then let me return the favor, Charlotte, and warn you likewise. Stay away from her, and from me and from Roscarrock."

His former wife had sat to resume her dinner, but could not resist adding, "I received an interesting letter all about your mysterious new secretary, from her stepbrother who is most concerned about what might be going on between you."

True felt his fury mounting. "If he is worried for his stepsister, perhaps he should express his fears to me directly."

She laughed. "I'm not sure that she is the one for whom he fears."

* * * *

Olivia waited in her seat, as instructed by her employer. She would have preferred to wait outside in the fresh air, but rain was falling harder now and, of course, she had no umbrella. No, she would stay and be composed, as if her heart was not racing. As if it did not matter that he was with his former wife in the private dining room of the inn. His former wife. To

303

Olivia it didn't feel very "former" at that moment.

It must be some matter regarding their children, she thought. That would always be the one thing that they shared. As True had said, the children were her link to his money, even now. It was also the one way his former wife knew how to get his attention, because of his affection for those children. They were his one weakness, and it was more than an instinctual bond, whether he wanted to believe it or not.

He had married the most glamorous woman of the season twenty-three years ago— or thereabouts. True Deverell had seen her, wanted her and stolen her away from her fiancé, who may or may not have been his own father. He got what he wanted on that occasion, just as he boasted he always did. But it had bitten him in the behind when he found out that beauty was only skin deep.

Far from the first man to learn that lesson, she thought glumly.

She dreaded and yet yearned for a sight of Lady Charlotte— morbidly curious to know if she was as beautiful as rumor had it.

A terrible, hollow ache had started in her chest.

Half of her pasty sat untouched on the plate for she had no appetite now.

As she looked out of the window again and watched windblown lines of gray rain streaking across the inn yard, a woman passed her view, moving swiftly from the door of the building toward that fancy carriage. A young man in livery escorted her with his head bent against the rain.

Olivia stared, quite sure it must be the lady herself. Who else would be so well dressed in that place? There could not be two fine ladies dining at

The Fisherman's Rest on this bumpy road so far from civilization. It had to be Lady Charlotte.

The woman was tall, slender, her hands sunk into a huge fox-fur muff, her hair topped by an extravagant bonnet trimmed in the same reddish-brown fur. She was every bit as stunning to look at as Olivia had imagined, every inch as beautiful as a "diamond of the first water" should be. It was easy to see how she was once the debutante of the season, with a half dozen suitors trailing after her.

Lady Charlotte was laughing and through the warped glass of the very old, crooked window her face was grotesquely distorted for a moment. It sent chills down Olivia's spine.

A bitter frost seemed suddenly to cling to everything in the place, as if the fire had gone out and all the lamps too. Where before it had been warm and cheerful in that busy room— sanctuary from the dismal weather— it was now gloomy, menacing, unwelcoming. Olivia thought she could even hear ice crystals cracking over the wallpaper and freezing the wicks inside the oil lamps.

Where was Deverell? What kept him?

Perhaps he'd forgotten about her, she mused darkly. It was easily done, of course.

If he came back, she would shout at him for leaving her alone in this place. It was improper. What was she supposed to do there all alone? People were looking at her and whispering.

So what, as True would say.

So what?

It was so easy for him to say, because he had not been raised to worry about what other people thought or said. To him it was all a game, the object to stay alive and amass wealth. A heart was just another muscle to him; it kept his blood pumping around his body. That was its only purpose, as far as he was concerned.

Yet, whatever he claimed of having no capacity to care, he had shown that he did. That he could. Worrying about her drafty room, her comfort.

Yes, he had many faults— as most people did— and she couldn't change them even if she wanted to. Which she did not.

Now she had fallen in love with the wretched, impossible man. It was a silly, besotted sort of love, not at all sensible and mature. Quite shameful for a woman who should know better.

What would he say if she told him that?

So what.

That is precisely what he would say, if she relented and confessed her feelings.

She had fallen in love with him and there was not even a working clock there to help mark the occasion. Even the pocket watch that once belonged to her father had gone missing, leaving her without that familiar comfort too.

Now she was terrified; for the first time in her life Olivia could admit to herself that she was afraid.

Chapter Twenty-Five

Looking out at the rain again, she watched that fine carriage pulling out of the yard, splashing through puddles. Two unfortunate fellows hung off the back, like half-drowned rats clinging to a raft. Lady Charlotte apparently didn't care about the comfort of her servants.

When she heard someone slipping into the opposite settle, she expected True's return. But it was another man. This one had a broad, ruddy face, bristling brows and mean eyes the color of muddy water. He sneered at her, making a motion toward the brim of his hat with stubby, thick fingers, but never lifting it from his brow.

"Well, missy, you're a pretty, dainty thing," he growled through pointy teeth, his lips agleam with grease. When he leaned across the table she smelled bacon on his breath, onions and ale. "What are you doing with the likes o' Deverell, eh?"

She quickly drew her hands from the table into her lap.

"Don't be shy," he said, winking. "What's your name then? We ought to get to know each other. I'm Joseph. Friends call me Joe. And so can you, missy."

"I don't think Mr. Deverell would like you sitting in his seat." She recognized the man from the last stretch of her coach journey to Roscarrock several months ago. He was the man who had sat opposite her and stared rudely the entire time. Just as he did now.

"Deverell's not the possessive, greedy type, so they tell me. Wasn't selfish with his wife, to be sure. He'd share a little of his good fortune with Joe."

Abruptly he thrust one of his hands beneath the table and grasped her knee. "I watched you when you came in, that hair pulled loose by the wind. Caught my eye you did with your head held high, acting like a lady. But you needn't pretend to be all proud and prissy with Joe. You're his new bed-warmer up at Roscarrock, ain't you?"

"Get away from me at once." She jerked her knee aside, but he reached further under the table with surprising speed and trapped her hands where they were clasped together. His fingers were strong, his grip cruel and tight. The size of his one clammy claw completely overwhelmed the knot of her two joined hands.

"You stay there, missy." With a tug he pulled her hands toward him, bruising her arms on the table edge. "Spare a bit of lovin' for Joe."

As he dragged her hands between his legs, she freed her fingers far enough to administer a sharp, hard pinch. And she did not immediately let go, but twisted with the force of an angry crab claw. He yelped, releasing her, needing his hand to cover his wounded body part.

"You little *bitch*," he spat.

"Yes, and like any good bitch, I bite."

Olivia slipped out of her seat and walked out into the rain. Footsteps followed quickly after her, but when she turned to confront her assailant, this time it *was* Deverell.

"Where are you off to?" he demanded as he stepped through the door behind her. "I told you to wait there at the table."

Above them the sign creaked and groaned, buffeted about by violent gusts of wind. "Under the circumstances it seemed wiser to wait outside."

"Why? What do you mean?"

She shook her head, tempted to laugh as she remembered the startled, pained face of "Joe" when she twisted his seed bag in her fingers. "It doesn't matter now."

"Someone approached you?" Deverell exclaimed, eyes flaring with swift suspicion.

"A woman sitting alone in a tavern is subject to that sort of attention no doubt. You could not be oblivious to the possibility."

"How *dare* anyone approach a woman in my company?" A very dark look came over his face, a deep rage such as she'd never seen on those features.

"I was not in your company at the time."

"But they must have seen you were with me." His lips strained over his teeth.

"Quite. I'm afraid that gave them cause to think me a woman of loose morals."

Before she could remind him that she had managed the incident perfectly well without his assistance, he took her arm and led her back inside, demanding that she identify the miscreant. She refused, but even without her help it was not difficult to spot leering Joe, who still nursed his injury and now— since he thought it was safe to do so— loudly complained to anyone who would listen.

"I believe what they say about her now," he grumbled. "Every word. I shouldn't be a bit surprised if she did 'er 'usbands in. Every one o' the buggers!"

Olivia looked on in some mortification and anxiety. So that was what they were all thinking when they looked at her. They, like Inspector O'Grady, thought there was something more deliberate than a curse in her past. She could not get away from the gossip, even here.

Her stomach churned with renewed nausea.

Deverell walked up to the other man and tapped him on one burly shoulder. She wanted to turn away and leave again, but her feet would not move. Faces turned to watch and the tavern noise drained away like the last drip of wine from a jug. The would-be molester paled, eyes drawn into tight slits, shoulders rounded.

If anyone at The Fisherman's Rest that afternoon expected thrown fists, they were destined to be disappointed, however.

The villain was calmly brought over to Olivia and commanded, in a cool tone, to beg for her forgiveness.

On his knees.

One might have heard the proverbial pin drop.

Despite the large man's earlier bluster, he was remarkably cowed by True Deverell, whose unruffled demeanor held just as much menace as a pointed pistol. Olivia had already felt the aura that surrounded her employer, of course— something like the warning posture of a wild dog ready to protect to the death. And people knew he did not live by the rules, so in that sense he was unpredictable.

"Tell this lady you were mistaken in your assumptions about her."

Slightly appalled, she watched while the big man— yes, bigger in stature even than True— reluctantly complied, struggling down onto his stiff knees and muttering under his breath.

"I was mistaken, ma'am," he grumbled. "I'm sorry."

"That's better. I would make you kiss her shoes, but you are unfit to touch her." Then he cast a slow look around the tavern and said, "Mrs. Monday is a respectable lady I have employed as my secretary. For those of you who are curious, I asked her to be my mistress and she's not in the least interested. She is, therefore, deserving of your admiration, not your scorn. Next time you see her, remember that."

He held the door open, bowed his head and waited for her to walk through it. Somehow she managed to do so without laughing at all the shocked faces they left behind.

This was his idea of making the situation better?

As he helped her up onto his horse behind him again, he said, "See, fear is more powerful than that love you talk about."

She put her arms around his waist. "I don't fear you. I would never fear you."

But he didn't hear her for she spoke very quietly and the horse's hooves drowned her out.

True turned his face to look over his shoulder. "By the way, what I told you about Sally White and her sisters was a lie. I never shared a bed with her. Don't even know if she has sisters. I told you that to shock you, or get some reaction. I might have known it wouldn't make a dent in your armor."

Astonished, she did not reply. Why this? It was not necessary for him to tell her that, yet he did. He conceded defeat in that low voice, contrite and warm. Self-effacing.

He went, just like that, from striking fear into the heart of a great, stupid bulk of man, to lifting his palms to her in confession.

She wanted to ask about his wife, but could not

find the words.

"Are you ready to work this evening, Olivia?"

"Yes." No hesitation. She would be ready to help him whenever he needed it. For as long as he needed her. Gripping his waist tightly again for the ride home, she closed her eyes against the cold air, until all she saw and felt was the glow that seemed to surround True— and her too, when she was in his presence. The dreadful rumors and Christopher's angry letter were unimportant, cast aside.

She had seen his wife, who was indeed beautiful and everything Olivia was not. But it was over and he returned to her.

No one could do or say anything to hurt her anymore.

Even the rain had ceased to trouble her and she felt like a young girl again, as she was when she loved to walk out in it and did not care how wet it made her. Before she had any bad memories of death to cloud the simple pleasure.

She had sand in her hair and under her fingernails, yet she didn't care. He had the same.

The air was new, shining with expectation. Like a barrel of rainwater, it hovered, stretching at the brink, waiting for one more drop to fall and make it overflow.

* * * *

He knew better than to believe his wife.

Or he should.

But as they rode home to Roscarrock, he thought back over Olivia's little deceptions— beginning with the fact that her spectacles were merely glass.

He had seen her in the hall one afternoon, handing Sims a book. "I hear you are fond of reading. I thought you might like this."

Still and impervious as a stone monument the butler had stared down at the little woman and her offering.

"It's a very good book. Don't worry, it's not a silly romance. It's a history book. I think you'll find it fascinating." She paused. "You don't have to thank me."

Finally the butler accepted it from her hand. "I suppose I can peruse it, when I have some spare time."

"Yes, and I would love to discuss it with you in the future."

"You have an interest in history?"

She nodded eagerly. "And I understand you can tell me all about Roscarrock castle. Mr. Deverell did try, but you, I am told, are the expert."

"I...have some knowledge of the local area, madam."

"Then I would be intrigued to hear it, whenever you have the time. I know how busy you are."

Thus she succeeded in thawing a little of the chill from his butler's expression. It would take more than one book to befriend Sims, but the foundations were laid now on common ground.

At that time True had wondered why she cared to make the effort. What was she up to in his house? Helping his cook, flattering his butler, kissing his handyman...

He did not know what to make of it.

"Father," Storm had laughed, "you and I simply have to get accustomed to the idea of a woman with no ulterior motive. Not a bad one, anyway."

But the seeds of doubt were planted, and suddenly there was a sinister color to everything she did.

He'd known from the beginning that there was much more to her story than she would tell him. A woman who insisted on hiding herself behind pretend spectacles and deliberately unflattering gowns was clearly trouble. Over time, taken in by her wide eyes and reluctant smiles, he'd let her become too important in his life.

True had a great deal to think about.

* * * *

When they got back to the castle, she suggested making hot chocolate in the kitchen to chase the damp chill away. He was rather quiet, she noticed. It was unusual for him.

"Mrs. Blewett has been busy making mince pies," she said, to break the strained silence. "She's excited, I think, that the young Deverells will be home soon. You must be too."

"Must I?"

"And they will be looking forward to seeing their father, no doubt."

"Hmph. My children won't care if I'm here or not, as long as Mrs. Blewett feeds them well and the beds are aired." When he looked at her, his eyes were very dark, two rain clouds ready to break. "My family is very different to your own, Olivia. As you will see."

"In what way?"

His reply was a curt, "You'll see."

Oh, his wife. Whatever she had told him it had

put him in a bleak mood.

She put her hands behind her back. "I have no family left except my stepbrother."

"But you are close."

"I suppose so."

"You've known each other a long time."

"Twelve years."

"And now he's getting married...I believe you said."

"Yes." Olivia wondered at this sudden interest in Christopher. But not for long.

"Is that why you left Chiswick?"

There was no point in denying it had some part in her leaving her home. "There were certain reasons connected to that," she said carefully. "As I told you, I wanted to be of use, to find a purpose, not to be a burden on my relatives."

"On Christopher. You said he is your only relative now."

"Well, yes."

"You are fond of him."

"Of course. As a brother."

"As a brother. But he is not your blood brother."

"No."

There was a pause and then he snapped. "You look flushed."

"Because this is strange questioning and I do not know what has prompted it."

He shook his head, scattering raindrops from his hair. "You don't?"

She pulled her shawl tighter around her shoulders. "If there is something you wish to ask about Christopher, please do so."

"Are you in love with him?"

"In... love?" Olivia gasped. "Of course not." It was too ridiculous to comprehend.

"But you kept that picture he painted. You write to him with an excessive use of curls in your handwriting—"

"I am fond of him as a sister should be and so I write to him. Is that troubling to you?"

He was grinding his jaw, staring at her. "I do not know what troubles me the most about you and the things you don't tell me."

She waited a moment to see if he was teasing her again, but the anger did not fade and his face did not soften. It made no sense to her that he should bring this up now. "For all your much-vaunted talents of perception, sir, you failed this time. You know nothing about love, of course, so you could have no idea what the signs might be, but I can assure you that one letter and a painting, kept because of the subject matter, do not constitute a grand love affair."

"Now I am sir again?"

"Yes. While you question me as if I have committed some crime, I shall call you *sir*." The words flowed out now on a flood, her voice getting louder with every syllable. "I could call you many worse things after you left me unescorted in a tavern for half an hour or more, while you met with your wife in a private room. And I wonder if you knew she would be there all along and that you went to meet her, which means it was not merely a pleasant ride we took together after all. But I have not asked anything about it because I am being ladylike and composed and keeping my chin up, trying not to care, because you would say *so what*, and tease me. And no I am not in the mood to help you write your memoirs tonight,

316

I changed my mind."

Anxious for something to do with her hands, she poured out the hot chocolate.

"Would you like some or not?" she shouted at him in the same cross tone.

After a pause, he corrected her quietly, "*Former* wife. I met my former wife. And I told you before that you may ask me any question. I will always give you an answer."

Still holding the chocolate pot, she said, "Then what did she talk to you about? What did she want that has changed your mood?"

"We talked of my daughter Raven. We talked of the memoirs, about which she had somehow heard. And we talked," he paused, "about you."

"What about me?"

She had never seen him as still as he was now, hands at his sides, feet planted solidly, shoulder-width apart. "It seems your stepbrother wrote to Charlotte."

"He did *what*?"

"In some attempt to win himself an ally and get you sent back to Chiswick perhaps? He thinks you ran away because you're in love with him."

How dare he? She was speechless.

"Oh, and he enlightened Charlotte as to the matter of your three husbands and what you might have done to them."

It was so like Christopher to imagine her in love with him. His vanity knew no bounds. She supposed he wanted her back under his thumb again, had realized how much she did for him. To get her back he had decided to spread those terrible rumors about her three husbands. Did he imagine that would send her scurrying back with her tail between her legs?

"I see." She finished pouring the chocolate. "And do you believe me capable of murdering men?"

His eyes narrowed. "I don't know what you might be capable of. You don't show me your true self. You—madam—hide!"

"I certainly do not!"

"The only time you let the sparks out of your tinder box was last night and then you attacked me with a poker."

If he was joking again it had gone too far in her opinion. She slammed the pot of chocolate down, picked up her cup and walked out of the kitchen with her chin higher than it had ever been.

"Olivia," he called after her, "I command that you come back here to work. I have not yet dismissed you for the evening."

He was promptly ignored. Probably a new experience for him, she mused.

* * * *

Her letter to Christopher written, blotted and sealed before she could change her mind, Olivia sat for a long while before the mirror that Deverell had moved into her room with all the other silly luxuries. She'd never been one to study her face much in the past, for she knew its failings all too well and staring at them wouldn't change anything.

But tonight she looked at her reflection with newly awakened eyes and with the knowledge of True Deverell's attraction to her.

What did he see when he looked at her?

Whatever it was, no one else had ever seen it.

Twenty years ago, on the death of her mother,

her father had received a visit —the one and only visit since his marriage—from Olivia's grandmother. The fine lady had come to witness her "ungrateful" daughter laid out in a coffin, as if she needed proof of death. But just before she left the house, she turned that icy regard upon the grandchild she'd never before seen.

"Well, she's a plain creature, dreadfully thin. What are you feeding her?" As if Olivia was a dog or a horse being examined.

Her father had responded quietly, with only a faint hint of indignation, "Olivia has a hearty appetite and she is in good health. She also has a quick mind for study."

"Tsk, tsk! She looks sadly inadequate to me. Sadly inadequate!"

She heard her father draw a breath, swallowing whatever reply he might have given.

"What a disappointment," the lady continued, tapping her walking cane on the hall tiles. "But what else could be expected of such a union. We must make the best of it." She stooped just an inch or so toward the little girl at whom she glowered with disdain, and said, "Your mother married for love, child. See where it got her. May her premature end in this damp, miserable little nowhere house be a lesson to you."

With that she'd swept out into the rain, to where her ivory-wigged coachman helped her up into a very fine barouche box, and there ended the grandmother's interest in Olivia.

Sadly inadequate.

But the face looking back at her in the mirror tonight was not unattractive. It was heart-shaped, calm, the features well spaced, skin clear and slightly tinted with a flush of healthy pink. Her posture, thanks to Great Aunt Jane's ceaseless nagging, was excellent.

Slowly she reached up and unpinned her braid, letting the thick rope fall over her shoulder.

He wanted to see her True Self? So be it.

Chapter Twenty Six

He was undressing in his bedchamber when there was a soft tap on his door. Definitely wasn't Sims. He tied the belt of his dressing gown and opened the door.

"Olivia!"

She was in her nightgown and a woolen shawl, her hair in a braid over one shoulder, the end of it tied with pale blue ribbon. The woman who had haunted his dreams for the past few months looked very young and innocent. "Can I come in?"

Suddenly he was tongue-tied, for possibly the first time in his life.

"Well? If you're not too fearful for your life."

He stepped aside and she walked in, looking around with wide eyes. He still remained with the door open, not certain what she was about, until she said, "You can close it now." It could have been reference to his mouth, as well.

"Olivia. What are you doing?"

"I thought it would be obvious, especially to a man with deep powers of perception. I've come to finish you off since that is, apparently, what I do with the men I encounter."

He stared at her as she dropped her shawl to the bed and then slowly began to step out of her nightgown. "And how, exactly, do you plan to finish me off?"

"I'm coming to bed with you, just as you asked, Mr. Deverell."

"I see you are in the mood to gamble tonight," he murmured, watching the linen of her nightgown slip slowly down over her breasts, her waist, her hips.

321

"You're... taking a risk."

"A risk?"

"With a man like me it's always a risk, Olivia." The words choked out of him.

"It is good of you to advise me." She walked up to where he stood, rigid in more ways than one, and reached for the knotted belt of his dressing gown. "But are you not taking a risk too, in light of my reputation? I set the rules tonight. I'm in charge."

Excitement flared inside him. "Are you indeed?"

"If you want me, I am in charge."

She wasn't the first to try it, of course. But she was the first who might actually succeed. True didn't know whether to feel pleased or terrified. He nodded, not quite trusting himself to answer.

Her skin was pale, smooth, shimmering slightly in the candlelight. He thought of the time when he spied on her in the scullery, washing her hair. The hunger had begun right there and then, and there was no turning back from it. She was the fox and he the hunter. It was instinct.

"First rule," she said. "This will be one night only."

He stayed silent, grinding his teeth. Fine, if she thought once would be enough for her. They'd see, wouldn't they? Just like his ungrateful offspring, she thought she knew what she wanted and wouldn't be told.

"I know you like to overindulge in everything," she added wryly. "So I must set some limits." With both hands she slid the robe from his shoulders and he let it fall. Instantly her gaze lowered, trailing down his chest.

Limits, eh? He saw her eyes flame with desire

and then darken as her pupils expanded. She bit her lips so hard he was surprised not to see blood.

"Second...second rule. You will...you will be certain to withdraw," she managed on a taut breath. "I don't want any mistakes."

Again he said nothing. Her hands moved downward, following the path of her sultry gaze.

"Third rule. We will never speak of it again after tonight. Not to anyone, nor to each other."

Interesting. Totally unfeasible. He would remind her about tonight, every chance he had. If he survived, of course. He grabbed her braid and began pulling it apart with impatient fingers, not even waiting to untie the ribbon first.

"Are you listening to me?" she exclaimed.

"Hmm."

The silk hair ribbon fell, her hair tumbling freely with his fingers tangled in it. He looked down at her. At her beautiful breasts— more abundant than he'd expected— her softly curved stomach and the triangle of tight, ebony curls below, hiding treasure.

"What happens if I break one of your rules?" he muttered, cupping her breasts and then sliding his hands down her body.

"Then I'll have to punish you, shan't I?"

"And how, precisely, would you do that?"

"You'll find out."

Her eyes were bright, fearless, daring him to flaunt her blessed rules. Well, there would be a few things she'd find out tonight, too.

True moved his hand between her thighs and she exhaled a small gasp. "Are you in a hurry?"

"Yes, I damn well am." After these past few months of yearning for her, he had no intention of taking his time.

She was silky soft, warm, fragrant. And all his at last. His to discover fully.

"Now get on my bed and prepare yourself to take some... dictation."

Her hands caressed his manhood, exploring him in return. He felt her chuckling. "I haven't got my writing materials," she muttered coyly.

"Don't worry about that, Olivia, I have a large pen of my own, as you see, and plenty of ink."

* * * *

Olivia was, of course, no innocent maiden when she went to his chamber that night and stood naked before him, but, in many ways she was naive. In her life she'd seen three men naked before— and one of those by accident.

Freddy Ollerenshaw was very muscular, bore more than slight resemblance to a shire horse and had the grace and finesse to match. Allardyce had not been quite so well favored in that department and had preferred being administered to as if he was a naughty schoolboy and she his tutor. That was enough for him to reach his own satisfaction and if he ever gave any thought to his wife's pleasure it was not apparent.

William had never troubled her in the bedroom at all. He thought the "act of copulation" quite unnecessary and the only time she saw him undressed was when she walked into the kitchen one evening in search of an illicit midnight snack, and found him taking a bath with an extraordinarily lavish amount of soapy water and a small model of the H.M.S. Victory. She could only assume he had been in the water for quite some time as all his bits and pieces were terribly shriveled. The incident was enormously humiliating for them both and they never mentioned it again.

But now, here in her hands, was something unlike any of those. A man unlike any other. He was well made, hewn of rugged rock like this place he'd made a home. Savage too, heat blistering and surging through him as lava must once have run across the earth, forming new lands and wild, yet-to-be-tamed continents.

He hauled her up against his body, lifting her swiftly off her feet. And he kissed her while she struggled to wrap her legs around his waist, clinging on for dear life.

There was no doubt about what she was doing, no second thought.

Just this once she would have something she wanted on her terms.

She didn't want another husband— she was bad for them— and he didn't want another wife, for he was bad for them. But why shouldn't they have this fierce, delicious pleasure? A secret only they would share for the rest of their lives and she would cherish, even in her lonely future.

As they fell to his bed, she ran her hands over his shoulders, let her fingers trace the veins of his broad neck, marveled at the strength surging through his body, a vitality that seemed to belong to another time. Another species.

"I don't want to hurt you," he growled into her mouth.

"You cannot," she said, reaching urgently for him, her legs climbing his back. Nothing could hurt her again. She'd taken many blows and lived to tell the tale. Just like him.

He kissed her, one hand tangled in her hair, the other caressing between her thighs. "You've been yearning for me," he groaned. "All this time. As I've yearned for you."

"Yes."

Slowly he licked his way down her body and Olivia arched restlessly, her skin alive, hands trembling.

"I ought to punish you for making me wait so long." He very gently nibbled her inner thigh and she exhaled in a sharp gasp of shock. "But I can't."

"You can't?" she muttered dreamily.

"Because you're in charge tonight. The rules are yours."

And then his lips touched her so lightly, so intimately that she almost lifted off the bed.

He licked, stroked and kissed her with such care, seeming to know exactly where to touch her and how to adjust his rhythm. Olivia tried not to think of the other women upon whom he'd honed this skill. After all, she was now the one to benefit from his experience, was she not?

"You've been neglected, my sweet," he said.

She wasn't sure which part of her he was talking to, but she heartily agreed.

* * * *

When he entered her, he tried to be gentle, but he was close to boiling over. His need for her was too great. Their bodies melded slickly together at last, lifting and falling like the waves that crashed against the base of his island.

She ran her fingers through his hair, her legs wrapped around him, showing her own urgency.

"True," she moaned softly, "don't hold back."

Oh, he wouldn't, and he didn't.

If she thought she wanted all of it, then it was hers. He filled her, buried himself deeply in that tight warmth, and she keened under him, her glorious hair spread across his pillow like the thickest, richest, most extravagant blanket he could buy.

Except he could not buy it. She'd made that clear.

According to what his wife had told him about her past, he was taking a heavy risk with this woman. But he didn't care. He was a gambler. Besides, what could she do to him?

* * * *

This was like nothing she'd ever known, or even imagined. His heat surrounded her, consumed her like a wildfire through dry forest.

She rolled him over and sat astride, feeling bold and greedy.

It was her turn to grab his wrists and hold them over his head. The muscles flexed, tendons tightened— a look of surprise passed over his face— but he did not resist for long. Then *she* kissed *him*, eating at his mouth as if it was her last meal. He had teased her once that he was in danger of letting her take charge of him.

Tonight that would come true.

"Where is your razor?" she whispered directly into his ear.

"My what?" He stiffened.

Olivia stifled a chuckle. "Don't worry, I'm not going to cut anything off. Unless you displease me."

He told her it was on the washstand.

"Stay there," she commanded. "Don't move."

To her astonishment he obeyed.

She fetched the razor and cut her hair ribbon into two parts, which she used to bind his wrists to the bedposts.

"Olivia? My sweet, is this necessary?"

Her reply was an unequivocal "Yes." She'd had plenty of time to think about it.

Now she kissed his brows, his eyelids, the tip of his nose, his chin. She kissed every part of him — even those she'd never yet had the chance to thoroughly explore on a man—until his breathing grew shallow and he bucked his hips at her. Then she lay over him and tickled his nipples with her tongue, listening to the low groan rumble through his chest, like the purr of a very large, very hungry cat.

"Olivia!"

But she continued her wicked feast, taking delight in her position of power and in this opportunity of discovery. She heard the ribbons stretching as he fought his bindings, heard the threads popping. She could not keep him her prisoner for long; indeed, she was shocked he let her get away with it as long as he did, for she knew it wouldn't take much effort on his part to sever those ribbons.

Finally she sat astride him again, teasing him with her body, exploring herself while he watched, and learning as much about her own capabilities as she did about her lover.

Her lover.

The word excited her further still. She trembled,

blood rushing through her veins in a tumult of pleasure

His eyes glimmered up at her, the silver half hidden beneath black lashes as he tried to resist the temptation of all that she offered. This feeling of power, she suspected, could become addictive.

Her heart beating hard and fast, she held out her hand for his tongue and he almost bit her fingers off. He strained forward, growling, his muscles taut.

"I must touch you."

When she released his wrists, his hands went immediately to her waist. His manhood penetrated again with one thrust and then he gripped her thighs, squeezing hard.

"If you want me to keep that second rule, Olivia," he managed breathlessly, "don't chance your luck."

She tipped her head back, letting her hair fall over them both. That, it seemed, was the final straw. He roughly grasped hold of her bottom, desperately urging her to slow down, but she rode him rapidly to that first fence and with only seconds to spare she stayed in her saddle.

Suddenly he held her waist and his eyes smoldered smokily up at her. "You *do* gamble, Olivia. You fibbed."

In that moment his fingertips pressed into her skin, seemingly to prevent her from rising, but then he relented and Olivia escaped her wild ride— and potential unwed motherhood— in the same blink of an eye.

* * * *

Holding her close, he reveled in the sweet scent

of her hair and ran his fingers down her spine, his senses sharply attuned to hers. Feeling every breath as she took it. Never before had he lain like this with a woman. Not like this.

For the first time in his life he had trusted another human being, putting his body into her hands completely.

The possible murderess of three men.

He had to admit, the risk added an extra layer of heat to his pleasure.

In the past he was detached, but this time he could not be. He knew her too well, had lived with her and laughed with her. It was not merely a flame of sexual desire that might, at any moment, be snuffed out by a draft. This thing between them was a bonfire, tall and deep. The sort of fire that burned even on a rainy winter's day. And there would always be a glow somewhere within it, sparks and embers never extinguished.

When he was a boy, running wild through the fields, True used to annoy the local hunt by distracting the hounds to get them off the scent of a fox. Another reason for the old squire to curse his name. Now he wanted to save *this* wily fox from whatever hunted her. If he could. If she'd let him.

But there was a difference between keeping a person safe and keeping them trapped. There were men who didn't understand the difference— women too.

She had made a rule: one night only.

The best way for that rule to be broken was by her own will. He could not show her the way, for she was too strong, too clever, and she would resist any attempt to capture her. Let her find her own way to the answer, for then she could be sure. He, in the meantime, must be patient with her, as he tried to be with his offspring. Patient.

Somehow.

He nestled her closer, his legs tangled with hers, his arms tightly cocooning her to his chest.

"Tomorrow we will not speak of this," she murmured.

When he gave no reply, she tipped her head back to look at him. "Mr. Deverell? I said, tomorrow—"

"*True*, for pity's sake."

She sighed. "True, tomorrow we will not mention this."

Still he said nothing.

"*True*!"

"Yes, my sweet?"

"Answer me, damn you."

"But it wasn't a question. How could I answer it? It was a command that I must simply follow. You, Olivia the merciless, are in charge."

Glancing down at her, he saw she was frowning slightly, unsure. "Yes. I am. Don't forget."

"May I kiss you?"

She swallowed, considering his lips for a moment. "Very well."

So he did, lingering gently and deeply, as she'd never been kissed before. And as she never would be kissed again, until she cast her foolish rules aside.

Chapter Twenty-Seven

The next day she was back before him as if nothing had happened, her hair bound in that braid and knotted at the nape of her neck, her frock was another grey monstrosity. But he didn't see it anymore. He saw the woman within it. The woman who had bound him in silk ropes and tormented his nipples.

She must have seen his face change when he looked at her. As much as he tried to hide his thoughts the way she did, it was impossible.

"I do hope we can get on with our work," she said sharply. "Now that...other... distraction has been removed."

Removed? She made their lovemaking sound like an inconvenient extra limb that had to be amputated.

Lovemaking.

Never in his forty odd years had he ever called it that. Why the hell was he starting with that nonsense now?

He rubbed his lower lip and examined her small, prim face. There was definitely a twinkle in her eye that had not been there before. She sat quickly, all business. But he knew she had written again to her stepbrother— faithful Sims had informed him of a letter. He supposed he'd have to wait to find out what was in it and whether she'd told the impertinent fellow that she meant to stay longer than six months.

True reached into his desk drawer and took out the two halves of a blue silk ribbon. "I believe these are yours." He set them on the blotter, laying each one out carefully in a straight line.

She licked her lips. "Ah, yes." But as she moved to snatch them up, he laid his own hand over the ribbons. "I very much enjoyed our...distraction."

"I'm glad."

"Did you?"

Looking down, she hid her eyes. "Yes."

"It was *nice*, was it?"

With a heavy sigh, she exclaimed, "Perhaps you forgot the third rule."

He huffed, raised his hand and allowed her to reclaim the ribbons.

"Now, may we get on?"

* * * *

Of course, she'd known he wouldn't make it easy for her. But Olivia had not been prepared for the onslaught that came from within, joining in his effort to leave her a shattered wreck.

It must be faced; a taste of him had not been enough to quell her appetite.

Having experienced the comfort of drifting off in his arms just once, she could no longer get a full night's contented sleep in her own bed. The pores of her skin awoke when he was near, even if she merely heard his voice approaching, or the sound of his whistling— the Sailor's Hornpipe, of all unlikely things.

Despite this, she kept to her rule. There was nothing else to be done with a man who claimed he could not love.

If the other staff noticed a shift in the air, they made no mention of it. With the young Deverells all due home soon there was not much time to waste, in any case, and Olivia was pleased to help prepare the other bedrooms, glad to absorb herself in practical matters when she was not needed in his library.

But always he was in the back of her mind, galloping through it without a care for the mess he left behind.

She had cause before to suspect he entered her room occasionally without informing her— for instance the time he returned the money to her reticule. But she soon knew it for sure when she came back from a chilly walk along the sand and found a new pair of boots waiting for her by the fire in her bed chamber. There was no note of explanation, just the boots.

Naturally he wouldn't leave a note, she mused. As Storm had told her, the master of the house didn't think it necessary to explain himself.

In return, the next time she went to Truro with his son, she used the money her employer had slipped into her purse to purchase the stubborn fellow the one thing she knew he didn't have. An umbrella.

She left it in his room while he was out one morning, and she couldn't resist tying a blue ribbon around the leather handle.

That evening, as they worked together on his memoirs, True was clearly not concentrating. He paced the room, poked the fire, rearranged his desk, opened and closed the window...until finally she suggested gently, "Perhaps we should come back to this tomorrow?"

He rounded on her at once. "Why did you buy me that umbrella?"

Taken aback by his cross tone, she sat for a moment in silence.

"What is the meaning of it?" he demanded, jaw thrust out, arms folded.

"It was a gift," Olivia replied eventually, fingers clasping the pleats of her skirt. "It is customary to exchange gifts in the Yuletide season."

"A gift? Why? What for?" He looked at her hands.

She squinted, not certain if he was teasing. He did not seem to be. "Has no one ever given you a gift before?"

He squared his shoulders. "Not that I can recall."

Olivia got up and moved toward him. "You bought me a gift and I wanted to return the gesture, by finding something for you ...something you would never think to get for yourself. That's all." Her heartbeat slowed. Perhaps the addition of the blue ribbon had confused him. She should not have done that. "It is the season to exchange gifts, after all," she added with a spurt of enthusiasm.

True still eyed her with suspicion. "Is it usual for a woman to buy a gift for a man? In your world?"

"If ...she...if he...if there is...some..." Olivia could not finish. Torn between wishing she'd never thought of buying him an umbrella, and then feeling sadness for him that he did not know how to receive a gift because no one had ever given him anything before, she was moved beyond speech.

Turning swiftly she went back to her seat. Let him make of that gift whatever he would. There was too much in her heart right then to look at him, let alone defend her actions.

Very slowly he walked up to her chair. "Olivia."

Her eyes were too heavy to lift and she very much feared there might be tears, which would never do.

Chin up, Mrs. Ollerenshaw!
But today she could not do it. She was lost.

* * * *

Since she would not raise her eyes to his, True got down on his knees before her. When he placed his hand on her knee, she finally lifted her lashes. Her eyes were huge tonight and now there was nothing to obscure his admiration of their rich color.

"Every night, when you go to your bed in that drafty wing, and I go to mine at the other end of the house, I think about you. The taste of you. The softness of your skin under my hands. The scent of lavender in your hair. The sound of that little purr in the back of your throat when you're aroused—"

"Stop it. You shouldn't talk like that. It was a rule, remember?"

"Do you think of me, Olivia? Tell me honestly." He raised his hand to cup her cheek and then stroked a finger across to touch her lashes. "At night, alone in your bed? Or am I the only one who suffers?"

She blinked, her lashes fluttering like feathery soft moth wings against his fingertips. "I suffer too. In ways you could never imagine, despite your talent for tall tales."

"Tell me then. Tell me what you think about, Olivia."

Her lips rolled inward and he thought she would not answer. He expected to be reminded that they were at work and she should be writing. But instead she said, "I think of your eyes— the way they look at me and melt my skin. The way you smile when you

336

think you've just got away with a saucy comment. Your hands...holding me so firmly...as if they would never let me go. Your thighs...."

Apparently she couldn't go on, shaking her head.

"Olivia! I am intrigued!" he exclaimed huskily. "My thighs? What about my thighs?"

She turned her face away.

He clasped her hands tightly. "Tell me! Don't leave me to wonder what naughtiness you're thinking about my thighs."

"We're not supposed to talk of it. We agreed!"

"I didn't agree," he exclaimed. "And if you really wanted me to forget, my darling Olivia, you would not leave a gift in my room with a blue silk ribbon attached to remind me."

He was right, she thought, chagrinned.

A sudden sharp tap on the door startled them both.

"Sir," Sims called through the door, "Masters Rush and Bryn have just arrived."

The chaos of his youngest sons racing through the corridors, dragging their trunks and wrestling with each other, could already be heard echoing around the house, shaking the foundations. Even Bryn— a mute— managed to make plenty of noise without the use of his voice.

Olivia jerked her hands away and stood, turning her back to where he knelt. True wanted to laugh loudly, picturing how it would have looked if Sims opened the door just then. But there was no time to talk further. The young Deverells had descended upon their private idyll.

* * * *

The boys were full of energy, just like their father, busy from the moment they fell out of bed, until they moment they fell back into it at the end of the day. For Olivia it was tiring, yet at least she was more accustomed by then to the odd hours and the boisterous activity. Thank goodness she'd had some practice with their father prior to their arrival.

Rush — despite Storm's suspicions about his parental origins— was a miniature version of True, a jester who did not usually look where he was going. Bryn, the adopted boy, was calmer, steadier. Being a mute, he communicated with gestures that the other boy understood much faster than anyone else. Bryn had a kind face, Olivia thought, and he looked up to True as his savior, a man who could do no wrong, but a distant, awe-inspiring figure.

"Bryn is a little fearful of you," she said to True one morning.

"Me?"

"You have suggested that you would prefer to be feared than loved. Is that the case with your children too?"

He did not have a ready answer for that and grew thoughtful. But she dare not think she was finally getting through his stubborn defenses. Not yet.

"When Mrs. Monday and I are at work in my library," he warned the boys, "we must not be bothered and you will make no noise outside the room. Am I clear?"

"Yes, sir," the little soldiers chorused.

"And if Mrs. Monday asks you to do something for her, you will obey at once. Am I clear?"

"Yes, sir!"

But it was not all commands and salutes. Olivia

watched him on the sands one morning with the boys, exploring rock pools for treasure, hunting mussels and cockles, the three of them darting about and foraging like curlews. It was cold, but they did not come in for hours.

Damon arrived a few days later, bringing a letter from his brother, Justify, who was still at sea and would not be home until the spring. The eldest legitimate son, Ransom, was to remain in London at the club and True had promised to visit him in the new year.

"You are fortunate that not all my sons are home at once," he whispered in her ear as he poured her a glass of wine at dinner. "You would be quite outnumbered."

She was not the only female guest for long however.

On Christmas Eve, in the midst of a glistening snowfall, his daughter Raven arrived at Roscarrock. But she did not arrive quite as they'd expected.

Chapter Twenty-Eight

"Get off me, you filthy wretch!" She shoved the other bundled figure away from her as they entered the house. A whirl of snowflakes followed them into the hall, before Sims had the chance to close the door against the brutal wind.

"Raven!" True strode to greet her, recognizing the voice, if not the shapeless, windblown mass from which it emerged. "Why did you not send word? I would have arranged—"

"The damnable mail coach lost a wheel," she hissed, tugging off the hood of her scarlet cape. Ah, there she was.

"And the brat would have spent the night in a ditch," the other figure muttered, "if not for me. Not that I got any thanks."

True raised his lamp and recognized the other cold, wet face. Particularly those angry eyes. "Josiah Restarick, isn't it? What are you doing with my daughter?"

"I happened by just after the accident. Yon lass was the only passenger left and the coachman had disappeared. Stubborn missy would have frozen her arse off out there."

"I would have managed perfectly well," she shouted, struggling out of her hastily assembled layers. "I took clothes from my trunk to put them on. I was in no danger from the cold."

"Then I should have left you there, ungrateful—" He caught True's eye and swallowed whatever he meant to say.

Trying to make sense of all this, True put his hands around his daughter's face to warm her cheeks.

She resisted, but only to make a show of it. He could see in her eyes that she had been afraid and now she was relieved to be in the warm again. Not that she would admit it, naturally. "You traveled alone from Edinburgh? What of your fiancé?"

"He didn't want to come," she spat. "Lost his gumption when we got to Bath and decided he would visit his pompous uncle for the Yuletide season instead. We quarreled and I came on alone in the mail coach."

It was nothing unexpected for his daughter, although he knew such independent behavior would be frowned upon in general. He was furious, however, with the fiancé who left her to make her own way into the West Country. Already he didn't like the fellow. Good thing he wasn't there. "Well, fortunately you got here in one piece."

"I told the coachman to go for help on one of the horses. The blithering idiot didn't know what to do. I've never encountered such a slack-jawed, incompetent fool the entire course of my life."

Joss Restarick snorted. "He was wise enough not to come back again and left you there to shift for yourself. As I should have done."

"Are you still talking, you horrid person? You haven't shut up the whole way here. I wish you had left me there too. The ditch was quieter."

It became evident that young Restarick had practically dragged her onto his boat and across to the island. The stubborn girl would have stayed in the ditch all night, unless someone she deemed more "worthy" came along and rescued her.

"Well, *I'm* very glad he didn't leave you there," said True. "You should thank him, Raven, remember your manners."

She glowered fiercely. "Why would I waste good manners on a filthy rotten Restarick? You always say there's not a good one among them. Horse-thieves and cheats, you said."

His daughter had a point, he supposed.

Joss saved him from further argument by spitting at her feet, growling, "Jumped up hussy," and then walking out, pushing Sims aside and ignoring True's suggestion that he stay for a glass of brandy.

"I had to leave the rest of my things behind," Raven complained with a yawn. "Jameson can go back and fetch them tomorrow."

"Can he, indeed? Must I remind you that I am the master of this house and I give the commands? That much has not changed since you left, daughter dear."

She wrinkled her nose. "I'm not staying long. I only came because you sent me a letter, which you have never done in the entire course of my life."

He rolled his eyes. "You're seventeen, Raven. The course of your life has not been that long. And if you careen through life without a care for your personal safety, or who you insult, it probably won't continue very much longer."

"If I was a boy you wouldn't say that."

"No. If you were a boy I would have cuffed you round the ear."

* * * *

Everything about her was lush, extravagant, as if True Deverell's overindulgent nature had taken on human form in the shape of his daughter. From her long, languid eyelashes to her wide, bee-stung lips, she was the definition of excess. She moved with an unhurried pace that was accidentally graceful, like that of a sailboat cast adrift without a captain and crew, boldly continuing on its way.

"You came here to help him write his memoirs?" she demanded of Olivia in a slow drawl. "How awful."

"Awful?"

"That you have to earn money. I intend to marry for it."

"I see."

"Are you shocked that I admit it?"

No, she mused, *having lived with your father all these months nothing can shock me.* "I think it is rather sad, but no I am not shocked by that. You are honest, at least, about your motives." She must have got that disturbingly forthright trait from her father.

"Why is it sad? I shall be rich and happy."

"Rich does not always follow happy, Miss Deverell. I wish you well, and hope you find everything you want in one place, but it is never certain. We never know how life will turn out."

True had been eavesdropping, for he came over to where the two women sat and said, "You should pay heed to Mrs. Monday, Raven. She can tell you about love— something she believes in still. I, of course, am not equipped to give you those lessons, but she will. She knows all about it." Smug, he walked away.

Raven stared at her as if she might be unhinged. "Do you really believe in love?"

"Of course. Someone must."

She blinked slowly, heaved a bosomy sigh and

fell back into the corner of the settee. "Mother told me that love makes people stupid. She told me not to waste my time looking for love."

Olivia smiled. "I was told that too, once. Well, not in so many words, but with a look— an expression on my father's face."

"I suppose because you're so dowdy and plain."

"I suppose so." Glancing across the drawing room she caught True's eye just as he sipped his brandy. He was amused and... something else. She quickly changed the subject. "Your fiancé means to stay in Bath until you return?"

"Oh good lord, yes. He's too terrified of papa to come here. I must say, traveling across the country with a fellow certainly opens one's eyes to their failings."

"I'm sure it does."

"I didn't realize he was such a plum pudding. I have never, in the course of my life, known a man who changes his breeches so many times in one day." Then Raven added suddenly, "My father never wanted to celebrate Christmas before. Is that your doing?"

At that moment Damon, who declared himself bored, entreated her to play for them at the pianoforte and so she had an excuse to get up. "I really couldn't say, Miss Deverell, although I would like to think I had a positive influence on your father while I was here."

"But you're not leaving yet?"

"No." She looked over at her employer, who was now in deep and earnest conversation with Storm. "Not yet. I'll stay as long as I'm needed."

She prayed no one would hear the wistfulness in

her voice.

* * * *

On Christmas Day, Olivia went down to the kitchens with knitted gifts for the other members of staff—gloves for Jameson, a bookmark for Sims and a long scarf for Mrs. B.

"This has turned out to be a very good Christmas indeed," exclaimed the cook, her cheeks already crimson from an early glass of sherry— probably one that should have gone into the trifle.

"I hope we have many more of them," said Sims with his usual somber tone, despite the sherry.

But Olivia could commit to nothing of that sort. Who knew what would be happening next year, or where she might be, she thought with a pensive sigh.

The day was very pleasant. It was good to see True surrounded by at least most of his children, and especially heartwarming to know that she had played a part in helping him to reunite with his only daughter. Raven was a handful and no mistake, but it was not too late for the two of them to make peace. They had both made an effort, showed themselves willing— True by writing a letter he would never otherwise have penned, and Raven by leaving her fiancé and traveling into bad weather just to be there for her father.

Olivia, having been blamed by True as the "instigator of this Christmas business", was called upon to show them the games she had learned in childhood during the celebrations in her own house. The young Deverells repaid the favor by teaching her a fast game of cards. It was very loud, occasionally violent, and there were quite a few curse words thrown back and forth, but she had to admit she had never had such a lively Christmas day.

While they were all involved in a noisy game of spillikins that afternoon, True took her to one side and asked her if she would have a word with Raven about her clothing.

"She does, as you see, tend toward the bright and gaudy and...well, she is much more...rounded...and full... in certain parts... than she was. I mean to say, she's not a little girl anymore. It doesn't....it isn't...quite..."

Tenderly amused by this fumbling for words, she smiled warmly up at him. "You mean she's a little too curvaceous for a low cut gown of that nature."

"Yes." He looked relieved. "You can say it much better than me." Then he shook his head. "I fear her mother is a bad influence."

Not wanting to step on anybody's toes, Olivia approached the subject with great care, suggesting to Raven that a lace tuck might help retain some ladylike modesty.

"And why should I take advice from you?" came the retort. "You dress like a blind nun."

"Well, I'm sure I—"

"I suppose my father sent you to tell me this."

"I don't think—"

"I'll wear one of those silly lace tucks, Mrs. Olivia Monday, on one condition."

Olivia eyed the girl cautiously.

"You let me take your dress in hand!"

"My dress?"

"That's right." Raven's eyes sparked with excitement and she laughed huskily. "For dinner tonight, I'll dress you and you can dress me."

So she reluctantly pulled out her best gown— the one she had never expected to wear here— and Raven got to work "improving" it with some silk flowers from her own frocks. She also insisted on dressing Olivia's hair. In return she allowed Olivia to sew a lace tuck into one of her own gowns and remove some of the bows. Raven was forced to admit that she looked, "Not too dreadful" when she assessed her appearance in the mirror.

"It is actually quite nice to have you here, Mrs. Olivia Monday," the girl exclaimed. "You're very quiet and don't bother anybody, but you're also jolly useful when needed."

"I do try to be."

"I can see why father likes you so much."

"Does he indeed?"

"More than anyone. I can see it in the way he looks at you. Despite the sad dress. As mother says, there is no accounting for taste."

Her face hot, Olivia busied herself putting everything back in her sewing box. And then accidentally sticking her finger with a needle.

"If I didn't know him incapable," Raven added, "I'd think he was in love."

They both laughed.

Foolish girl was only seventeen! What did *she* know about men?

Watching Raven parade about before the mirror, smoothing hands over her abundant bosom and flashing a brilliant, confident and mischievous smile, Olivia decided it was probably best not to answer that, even in her mind.

* * * *

At dinner that evening, True could not take his
eyes from Olivia. For once she wore a color other
than ditch water. Her gown was dark burgundy velvet,
a little old-fashioned, but spruced up with some silk
ribbon roses at the shoulder. Her brown hair was
worn high in softened coils, decorated with more silk
blossoms— white, so they looked like hopeful
snowdrops peeping out of spring earth. He
recognized his daughter's handiwork and saw that
Olivia had succeeded in taming some of Raven's
fashion sense too.

"Thank you," he said, taking his secretary's hand
and kissing her fingers.

"Whatever for?"

"For bringing Christmas to Roscarrock."

She shook her head. "I didn't. It was here all the
time. You just didn't see it."

Her eyes shone as she chatted with Storm and his
other children. And whenever she glanced his way he
felt showered in warmth, as if caught out in a sweet
spring rain shower. Looking around his table, True
felt proud and blessed.

Oh, no. Was he getting old?

He ran a quick hand over his torso. No, all was
firm as it should be.

When his children had retired to bed, he went to
her chamber door and knocked. After a slight delay
she opened it, still in her pretty gown, but with her
hair loose, a brush in one hand.

"I wanted to wish you a Merry Christmas," he
whispered. "Properly."

She smiled. "Merry Christmas, True."

He reached into his waistcoat and took out a small parcel. "Here," he muttered awkwardly, holding it out toward her, wishing he had more finesse when it came to gestures like these.

"But...you already gave me a gift. My boots."

"This is something else."

With trembling fingers she opened the paper and found her father's watch, polished clean and nestled there like a big, plump silver coin.

"I got it fixed for you," he explained, scratching the back of his neck. "I saw how important it was for you to know the time. Though I've no idea why. "

When she looked up at him her eyes were misty and huge, two pools overflowing.

"I suppose now you'll keep looking at it, waiting for our time together to pass and—"

She grabbed him by the cravat and pulled him into her room.

Chapter Twenty-Nine

Strange how she knew, even with so few
experiences to compare in her own life, that the way
he touched her could not be like any other man's
caress. He explored her as a wolf would examine its
mate, employing all his senses, relishing her slowly to
make no mistakes. To imprint himself upon her.

"Do you believe me guilty of murder?" she asked.

"No," he said, this time without hesitation or
teasing. "I have trusted my secrets to you, my life to
you, and my children to you. I know you are
innocent."

He spoke steadily, firmly. Her heart filled with
his words and his trust. It lifted her above everything.

"You must be the only soul on earth who is sure
of that," she whispered. Sometimes she wasn't even
sure herself. Inspector O'Grady could be very
persuasive.

Pulling her into his arms again, he kissed her. "I
ought to be the only one whose opinion matters to
you."

"You are arrogant, True Deverell, and bold. And
impulsive." She touched his forehead, ran her
fingertips over his eyebrows, over his lashes, down
the sharp edge of his sculpted cheek, past a small scar,
to his lips. A long time ago she had imagined his
mouth and what it would feel like to kiss it. To kiss
the scandalous man she'd read about in the
newspaper. Now she knew. "But I cannot resist you."

"I know," he replied proudly. "You've broken
your first rule, Olivia— tsk, tsk!"

"There are no rules on this island."

"Hmm. Let's see...we've broken the rule about

only once. We've broken the rule about not mentioning *it*." His eyes glittered. "What shall we do about that other rule?"

"Oh, no. Do not even consider it. I cannot be an unwed mother. I would be ruined forever." She reached up to squeeze his chin. "And one would think you have more than enough children to manage."

Suddenly he became solemn. "I ought to marry you, Olivia."

That was an odd way of putting it, she mused. "Why? Do tell. What possible reason could you have for thinking that?"

"Because you are a respectable lady. And you need me."

It took her breath away for a moment. "No."

He had trapped her fingers between his lips, but he released them to speak again, "Why not?"

"Because marriage has not been good for either of us."

"I can protect you from the rumors."

She scoffed at that. "Out of the frying pan and into the fire."

"Marry me," he said again.

"No."

"I'll give you time to think of it, at least let me—"

"No." For his sake she couldn't risk it. Three good men dead already. Where would it end? "I do not want to marry you. Good lord, you would send me mad."

He flinched as if her refusal had finally stabbed through his hard skin.

Olivia stroked the dark hair back from his forehead. "You keep that portrait above the stairs as a reminder never to wed again. You don't want another wife, and I did not come here to find another husband."

Light from the one candle yet burning made little stars under his lashes. They danced, simmered and played, before they died away as he slowly closed his eyes.

Was he sleeping? She couldn't tell. He didn't snore.

Nestling closer to his chest, she listened to his thrusting heartbeat and eventually that rhythm put her to sleep.

When Olivia woke the next day he was gone from her bed. At breakfast she learned that he had left for London on business and to see Ransom. He left no note for her. Was he angry at her refusal?

One of them had to be sensible. Surely he understood.

"He said you're to wait here and be ready to work again when he returns," said Raven. "You're not to go anywhere, and we're to make certain you don't."

The man probably thought nothing of dashing off without an explanation. He didn't care about manners and could come and go on a whim.

How long would he procrastinate this time, she wondered glumly. The man simply would not stand still. But why should he, when he expected everyone else to stand still for him?

* * * *

Several cold days blew by and the younger boys returned to school.

"Will you be here when we come home again?" Rush wanted to know.

"If there is still work to be done, yes. As long as your father needs me to help write his story."

"He'll probably never let you go then. How can he until his story is finished, and he's still living it? Doesn't make sense."

Having said this the boy immediately spun around on his heels and chased after Jameson across the causeway, yelling for Bryn to make haste.

Damon stayed a little longer and then he too left. Only Storm and Raven then remained and she listened at dinner as the half-siblings teased and tormented each other. There was a sweetness about the relationship. With almost a full decade between them in age, Storm took his role as big brother very seriously, and Raven often acted nonchalant or brazenly disobedient, but if Storm mentioned that a certain ribbon didn't suit her bonnet, the next time that particular headwear made an appearance it was altered with something he liked better. No one, not even Storm, would dare point that out to her.

"I'm glad that common Sally White isn't still hanging about," Raven remarked one day. "Or is she?"

"None of your business, child."

"You ought to find a nice girl and settle down."

"Why would I want a nice girl?" he replied with a grin. "The naughty ones are more fun."

"I bet Mrs. Monday wouldn't agree."

Olivia realized they were both looking at her, waiting for a response. She put down her sewing. "I think whether it's naughty or nice, love is the most important thing."

* * * *

"Well, Livy, you seem intent on causing another scandal. Have you taken leave of your senses?"

There had been no warning. Sims had not even come to find her yet, so when she walked into the parlor in search of a book she'd left there, Olivia thought the room would be empty. Christopher was the very last person she would ever expect to see standing by the fire. It took her a moment to believe her eyes.

"Do you have any idea how your cavorting about here with this man will affect my courtship of Miss Lucinda Braithwaite? Her family is most upset about the association. It is a degrading connection for any respectable person."

How out of place he looked there! It was all wrong and she wanted rid of him quickly. He was far from Chiswick. Why? So many things sped through her mind.

He must have received her last letter, in which she expressed her desire to stay longer in Cornwall.

"I cannot imagine what you mean, Christopher," she replied, terse. "What are you doing here?"

His eyes widened slightly— almost imperceptibly. "Did you think I would not hear what has been going on? When I received your missive informing me of an intent to remain here beyond six months, I could scarce believe my eyes. You must come home with me at once, and end this shameful business, before it is too freely spread about and you are ruined forever."

"I'm afraid that is impossible. I agreed to stay and I—"

"You have been riding around with him in public, cavorting in taverns. I knew it was a mistake when I learned of this post, but that drunkard Chalke arranged it in such a manner that I had no chance to stop you. I was not informed of the circumstances— that you would be here with him, alone for most of the time."

"But you always told me I would be safe from a man like True Deverell. What could he see in me?"

"There is no time to waste discussing this now, Livy. You had better pack your trunk immediately and we can get back to the mainland before the tide comes in."

There was no doubt in his tone, or his countenance. He expected her to do exactly as he said, which was amusing because she never had and she was not about to start doing so.

"I'm not leaving him, Christopher."

After all, she'd waited a long time to come in search of Deverell, the wicked man of her even more wicked dreams.

"You are a horrid, unseemly child with a dark and devious imagination, Olivia Westcott. I cannot think what will become of you."

"I shall marry Mr. True Deverell, shan't I? People say he's not fit for polite society either. But he's rich as Croesus and I hear he knows his way under a woman's petticoats."

It had been a childish wish, spoken aloud eighteen years ago and never forgotten. And now she knew it was the real reason that brought her there to Roscarrock castle. Somewhere in her mind she had thought to make him fall in love with her. Ten-year-old Olivia and thrice widowed Mrs. Monday were not very different to each other, after all. Since she'd lived there with him it seemed as if very little time had passed. If anything, it was being reversed.

Suddenly her eyes were opened and she realized why she had gone there. Unwilling to admit what she wanted, she had tried telling herself that she came for the money and the measure of independence it would give her. But most of all, in truth, she had gone there to appease her lurid curiosity, and for him. For the man himself.

She had not, however, expected him to propose marriage. It didn't seem possible, too much of a fairytale, and she didn't believe in those. Not for her. So she had turned him down, lost her gumption.

"Pack your things at once," Christopher barked at her irritably. "We must leave immediately. The quicker we get back to Chiswick the better. Do you think I have nothing more important to do than chase about the country after you? We will catch the mail coach to London this afternoon."

London. That was where True had gone, to his club and to his son. He might not be back for weeks, his work on the memoirs stalled again for now.

He'll probably never let you go then. How can he, until his story is finished? And he's still living it?

Was this why he delayed so much? Because he feared coming to the end of his story, thought that if he finished it then his life too would end? In many ways he did think and act like a boy, and it seemed feasible that Rush, his fourteen year-old son, would understand him better than anyone.

But she had something to tell Deverell. Something that couldn't wait another eighteen years.

"Very well," she said to Christopher. But as she rang for Sims, she looked down at her stepbrother's side and finally her eyes saw and registered what he had in his right hand.

356

* * * *

"The name is O'Grady, sir, Inspector O'Grady of the London Metropolitan Police."

True was in his office at Deverell's when the tall, spare fellow in the grubby greatcoat came to find him.

"I understand you recently hired a lady by the name of Olivia Monday to work for you, sir."

"I did." Bloody woman wouldn't marry him. He still couldn't get over it. She was the only woman he'd ever asked— Charlotte had demanded he marry her, so there was no proposal in that case. Olivia was the only woman for whom he had these strange, unnamed feelings.

Had he gone about it all wrong with her? Was there something else he should have said? She had given one of her funny little snorts when he said he ought to marry her. Perhaps that wasn't the correct way to say it.

"If I might have a word, sir. There are things you ought to know about that lady."

He sighed, his mind forced back to less pleasant thoughts. "Say what you will." Although he knew already, of course, thanks to Charlotte.

But he let the detective speak and he listened, curious to hear the story unedited by his wife's spite.

"Captain Ollerenshaw was killed when his racing phaeton overturned. His young wife wasn't there at the time, but her stepbrother tells me that she did encourage her husband's wild ways and thought them amusing entertainment. Then the second husband choked on a fishbone in his pie, although the cook at the tavern where he ate every Saturday swore she took great care to remove the bones. Funny thing was, Sir Allardyce Pemberton always dined alone at the tavern, but on that night he must have had a companion for there were two ale-rings on the table where he was found— one smaller than the other. And one of the serving girls thought she saw someone with him, although she couldn't say who it was. Or if it was a lady. None of this would have raised an eyebrow, if not for the demise of a third husband. But I'm putting the pieces together and keeping an eye on that woman before she does away with another innocent man."

"What could have been her motive? She has not gained financially from their deaths, obviously."

"No, sir, but not all murderers need a motive beyond their own sick and twisted pleasure. Walk a mile in my shoes and you'd learn that. I'd advise you to take great care in your dealings with the woman. Who knows what she will do next, sir. She's hiding something, mark my words. I have made it my mission, Mr. Deverell, to bring that woman to justice, before she strikes again."

O'Grady seemed certain and resolved upon his course, but True refused to believe any of it. Olivia Monday may be a woman with an impish gleam in her eye from time to time, and an eagerness to hide her natural beauty, but she was not capable of murder.

"I thought I should warn you, sir, of the risk you take while she is under your roof."He smiled slowly. "Look around you. I'm no stranger to risk, Inspector O'Grady. I built my fortune on it. Don't worry on my account."

"And don't you be fooled, sir. The woman may have donned the garb of a wallflower, but she has a sly talent for distracting men."

That part was accurate, he mused.

"She took off a little girl's finger once," the detective muttered gravely. "Shut it inside a pianoforte, so 'tis said. Always had a bloodthirsty way about her, even from childhood."

"Is that so?"

"Found her cleaning the floor the day her last husband was killed. Just as calm as you please, scrubbing the flagstones."

"Yes, that sounds like the lady. She does have a dreary practical side, orderly to the point of obsession."

But the Inspector didn't crack a smile. "The wound against the side of Parson Monday's head was sizeable, sir," O'Grady told him. "And in my opinion, whatever that coroner said, that nasty hole in his skull wasn't caused by a fall against a bit of rotting, wood bridge."

* * * *

"Christopher, you found your umbrella," she exclaimed, breath rushing out of her, one hand to her breast.

He was holding the silver swan head in his gloved hand and frowning at her. "My umbrella, for pity's sake? What about it?"

Olivia saw again her husband take that very same umbrella from the stand by the front door, in a hurry to get to church on his last day alive.

Afraid to point it out to William, she had said nothing, fearing what he would think of her when she confessed that Christopher had been to visit two days before and that she had not told him about it. Guilt overcame her and she let him walk out of the house carrying the wrong umbrella. It was not only the last time she saw her husband alive; it was also the last time she'd seen that fancy silver swan's head. Until today.

When she watched them fish William's body out of the river, there was no sign of any umbrella with his body. Later she had supposed it sank to the riverbed or was taken away by the police. It was an ugly, vulgar thing and she was glad not to see it again.

But there it was, in the hands of its owner. As if it had never been anywhere else.

"What is the matter with you?" Christopher snapped.

"I thought you lost that umbrella."

He sniffed. "Certainly not. I take more care of my belongings than you do. You never had any appreciation for the finer things. Now, make haste. I understand we can catch the mail coach at The Fisherman's Rest this afternoon."

Sims did not come in answer to the bell, but Storm did. When he learned they were leaving he immediately protested, reminding Olivia that his father expected her there when he returned. She panicked then for she didn't want to make any trouble for the residents of Roscarrock and she could see that Storm was determined to keep her there, as his father had no doubt instructed. He stood guard over her like a sheepdog. But, not certain of what her stepbrother might do, she knew he had to be removed quickly from Roscarrock.

"I am sorry, Mr. Deverell," she said, clasping her hands behind her back, "but a family emergency calls me back to Chiswick and I must go." Her mind was hard at work unraveling the ropes that had blinded her for years, gagged her and held her down.

Christopher.

Always there, popping up to smugly point out her shortcomings, not even feigning commiseration each time she lost a husband. Christopher complaining she was his future burden and yet making plans to keep her nearby, being angry each time she left. Now he came all this way to fetch her home again under the spurious excuse of his fiancée's family being appalled by the connection.

Christopher.

"Father won't like this," Storm muttered.

"I shall return as soon as I can," she said, conjuring a final smile. "Please don't fret. Give my love to little Arthur."

* * * *

The club was busy that evening and he felt that old stirring of the blood again as he walked between the tables, greeting familiar faces, breathing in the rich scent of money. Deverell's was doing well with Ransom at the helm. Better, perhaps, than he'd expected. He should have given the boy more credit.

It was pride he felt, he supposed, when he thought of his sons' successes. Was it love too, as Olivia would insist?

That Olivia— a woman who had known such bad luck and was hounded by rumor— should still believe in love was incredible.

Ransom wanted to know what Inspector O'Grady had wanted.

"He tried to make me agree with him about a

lady of my acquaintance. Sadly I could not do so. It seems I know her better than he does."

"What lady?" Ransom frowned. "The one mother told me about? The black widow you hired?"

Of course, Charlotte wasted no time spreading the vile gossip once she got back to London.

"You should be careful with that woman, father. She's killed three men already."

Amusing counsel coming from a son who, two years ago, shot him in the shoulder.

"Ransom," he replied steadily, "Have you not learned by now that rumors are exactly that? Only that. Never believe until you know it for yourself. As a Deverell you ought to know that better than anybody. Always get the true story."

His son looked skeptical. "Perhaps, in this woman's case, you don't want to believe the gossip."

"Well, when you meet her, I'll let you decide for yourself." He smiled archly. "Hopefully you're a better at judging women and their motives these days."

"Women!" Ransom's lip jerked in disdain, his handsome face stern. "As you used to say, father, the wretched creatures are always underfoot, waiting to trip a man." Then he added with a knowing look. "I hope you still heed your own advice."

"Worry not about me, son." He clapped the boy on his wide shoulder. "I've had twenty or so years more than you. You're just beginning to learn that women aren't all bubbies and soft parts. I've known that a long time."

His son's eyes were wary. "What's changed about you, father? There's something new."

"I'm...maturing. Like a fine brandy."

"Mother says you're writing your memoirs." He

folded his arms. "Are you ill?"

"Me? Ill? Never." In fact, he'd seldom felt better. What did the doctors know anyway? "I'm writing my story for you. For all of you, but mostly I suppose for you." He laughed. "You're the one who prompted me into action when you put that bullet through me."

Ransom's face turned gray and he uncrossed his clenched arms. "I didn't mean to—"

"Oh, yes you did. We all make mistakes, son. We all act on impulses we will later regret. I realized then that I'd foolishly kept a great deal from my sons, thinking it would protect them. But I was wrong. Ignorance is not bliss. Every child needs to know the truth of where they came from and what they are. I hope my story will help you understand some of the choices I made— even the mistakes."

For a long moment his son studied his face, then he said, "I've never heard you admit to a single error before."

"See? I *am* maturing."

* * * *

When Lady Charlotte's first son was laid in his arms, he did not know what to do or feel or say. This tiny, squealing creature was made by him. He was responsible for it.

Overwhelmed, he wanted to pass it back to the midwife, but she had already returned to his wife's chamber and shut the door. So he took the babe to the light of a window and examined it carefully to be sure it had all its parts. The eyes were dark, like Charlotte's, and they stared up at him, slowly opening wider as the wrinkled mouth continued making noise of a terrible, ear-piercing tenor.

Well, he had brought this being to life. It was up to him

363

now to teach the child how to live. *Fortunately he knew something about survival.*

But he could not coddle the child when it cried. *That he could not do, for he had no knowledge of how.*

As if the babe knew this, it's wailing petered out. *Man and boy studied each other.*

"I'll do what I can," True muttered gruffly. "I make no promises."

It was all new to him. To them both.

The babe raised a fist toward his face and shook it.

"Just like your mother," he sighed.

It was some time before he realized it was trying to reach his nose, not blacken his eye.

They would be at similar cross purposes for many years to come.

Chapter Thirty

They took the mail coach to Launceston, but learned it would be impossible to travel farther that evening. Christopher grumbled at having to pay for a room at the inn and, to save himself a few pennies, he rented a small chamber for one, sneaking Olivia in behind the busy landlord's back.

"You have gone to great expense to fetch me home," she muttered sarcastically. "Was it really so urgent?"

"Yes. I don't suppose you have given a thought to my engagement. I am only weeks away from the wedding, and I cannot afford to have your behavior spoiling things for me."

"*Me*, spoil things for *you*?" The paradox was lost on him, however.

A servant brought them supper, but Olivia had no appetite. She watched as her stepbrother fussed with his hat and gloves. The umbrella leaned against the arm of his chair, that thick silver neck and beak gleaming in the firelight. She remembered those beady little eyes made of jet. There was only one now. The other must have become dislodged and lost somehow. Perhaps from a hearty blow against...

She closed her eyes, scrambling to pull herself back from this edge of suspicion.

Surely not. It couldn't be. Why would he do such a thing? What had Christopher to gain from killing her husband? The two men did not like each other, but it was no more than a clash of personalities. Nothing more than that.

It was simply her dark imagination at work again and that was all.

Taking a deep breath, she opened her eyes and said, "I suppose you and Lucinda will require a bigger house when you are married. For all those children you plan."

Christopher looked annoyed. "I suppose so. Eventually." He poured ale from a large jug, and the foamy amber liquid splashed up the side of his tankard like waves at the base of Roscarrock island. A little pang of homesickness shyly made itself felt, as if it didn't feel fully entitled. She had only lived there four months, but yes it was home to her now.

And her stepbrother had dragged her away from it, intent on moving her about like a chess piece, ordering the path of her life the way he always did. Or tried.

"Perhaps you have got that out of your veins now, Livy, and you see the error of an impulsive choice."

The news of Freddy Ollerenshaw's death had come to her from Christopher's lips, moments after the tragedy occurred. He had even known the details of the wager that enticed poor, reckless Freddy into that unstable phaeton. Knew it before anyone.

When Sir Allardyce died, Christopher, in his usual superior fashion, had commented that he never entered that particular tavern as it was full of "low company", inferring that he was shocked Sir Allardyce would patronize the place— that it was, perhaps, inevitable, such a terrible event should happen there. Yet, some weeks later, a barmaid cleaning tables outside the same tavern had seemed to recognize Christopher as they passed on their way to market. She had called him by another name, however, and so it was easy for her stepbrother to dismiss the incident as a case of mistaken identity. Olivia had put it out of her mind.

And then there was William and that swan-head umbrella.

Carefully she said, "We should sell my father's house now then. And divide the profits equally."

Christopher's head snapped up so violently she thought his neck would break. He cursed. "This again? Just like that skinflint Monday, always grinding on the same matter."

He looked frayed, she thought. Usually so handsome and well put-together, her stepbrother was decidedly worse for wear this evening, his boots not so shiny. There was a little smudge of dirt on his high collar and stubble on his chin.

"William only wanted what was best for me," she said.

"Best for him, you mean. He wanted to get his hands on that money."

She shook her head. "I think it's time you and I sold the house, collected what we are both due, and went our separate ways." Her father's house, as much as she once loved it, had begun to feel like a millstone around her neck, keeping her tied to Christopher.

He glared through bloodshot eyes. "Is that what you think?" he sneered. "Well, you're wrong. You'll stay with me, as it is supposed to be."

"I beg your pardon?"

"I haven't gone through all this just to let you slip through my fingers at the last damned minute!"

Olivia's mind fought to make sense of his cold words. "Last minute? I don't understand."

"Of course you don't. You're a bloody stupid woman."

There was silence then, while her stepbrother ate

greedily and she sat frozen in anger. Eventually she had to speak. There was no holding anything back now. True Deverell had taught her that it wasn't always wise to hide her thoughts and feelings. That sometimes things simply had to be said before it was too late.

"I remember the morning William died," she said.

Christopher continued his supper, not looking up.

"I remember he had your umbrella in his hand when he left the house. That one." She pointed to where the swan-neck rested against his chair.

Her stepbrother huffed and licked his fingers.

"You had left it there when you visited on Monday. I saw him take it in error, but he was so distracted and eager to get to the church, I don't think he realized it was yours."

"What on earth are you getting at, Livy?"

She took another breath of courage. "When they found William in the lake, the umbrella wasn't with him. Which means that you took it back from him that morning. Somehow. Between the time that he left the house and the time his drowned body was discovered."

Christopher drank his ale, leaned back in the groaning chair and laughed tersely. "So you think I killed him?"

She said nothing. Her palms, pressed together in her lap, were sticky with perspiration.

Suddenly he got up. She had never seen him move so quickly. The slap was hard enough that it almost knocked her sideways out of her chair.

She gasped and gripped her smarting cheek.

Tears sprang up to glaze her sight.

"It wasn't *my* fault," he hissed down upon her head. "The fellow should not have picked another quarrel with me that day. I had endured my fill of his grasping!"

Olivia choked on a sob, swallowed it down. She didn't want to look up at him and let him see her tears, so she kept her hand to her face.

"I was on my way back to the parsonage that morning to collect my umbrella," he continued, now walking around her chair. "When I saw him on the bridge, he confronted me about the blasted house again. I merely wanted my umbrella. We struggled over it and he was struck about the head. Then he fell into the water and began to sink. I had my umbrella, so I walked on. Why should I help him? He did nothing for me but try to take away what was rightfully mine."

He was struck about the head. As if it was not Christopher who wielded the weapon that struck. As if he was perfectly innocent of any crime.

"You have nothing and no one who cares about you, except me." Her stepbrother returned to his chair. "Now I do not wish to discuss the matter again. It was an accident for which he was as much to blame as I. Are you not hungry? We have a long journey ahead of us, so you may as well eat."

She was in the company of a mad man. Her cheek throbbed. "You can have the house, Christopher," she managed on a hoarse breath. "Let me go back to Roscarrock."

"No. Certainly not. Why should I be satisfied with the house when there is so much more to be had? Did you think I could let another man come along again and get in my way?"

Olivia had no idea what he meant. He was suffering some sort of delusion, that much was clear. And he was dangerous.

* * * *

Abraham Chalke was a small, bent man with two bushes of white hair sprouting above his prominent ears. His nose was broad and flat, his eyes two stale raisins peering out from behind smeared spectacles. His gait was like that of a crab, due in part to his wide curved legs which could not, as the saying went, stop a pig in a passage. All things considered, there were few men less prepossessing in appearance than poor Abraham Chalke. But he was valued for his trustworthiness, loyalty and honesty. There was not a bad bone in the man's broken body and his only vice was port.

True Deverell had known Chalke a great many years and entrusted countless secrets to his care. If the fellow was not so ancient and had a less shaky hand, he could have taken on the task of penning True's memoirs himself and that was the original plan. Until Chalke wearily suggested he wasn't up to it.

"I'll find you a secretary," he had warbled. "I believe I know just the person."

Despite his enthusiasm it had taken a considerable amount of time to find someone for the post.

"Why did you send her to me?" True demanded, seated across from the old solicitor. "You knew what you were doing, I have no doubt. You're a cunning old crab, Chalke." At first the man feigned innocence, but True persisted. "I mean to know. If you want to keep me as a client, old man, you will tell me why you sent Olivia Monday into my lair, knowing what she would do to me."

Chalke snuffled with laughter and shook his head. "It was quite by chance."

"Chance? You wanted to get her away from the stepbrother, is that it? Because she was in love with him? Or he with her?"

"Oh no," finally Chalke confessed, "it was nothing like that. It was much worse."

"*Worse*?" He didn't know how it could be worse than Olivia falling for another man. She wasn't the sort to fall lightly.

"I suspected Christopher Chesterfield of unpleasant intentions— and deeds— but I had no proof and so I thought it best for Olivia to be out of his reach, as far as I could put her. The lady's father, you see, was a dear friend and he had begged me to look after his only daughter. I considered it my responsibility."

True leaned forward, every muscle and tendon now on alert, ready to spring into action. "She was in danger? In what way?"

The old man groaned deeply and steepled his gnarled fingers to his lips. "I was sworn to secrecy. My colleague, Westcott, wanted no one to find out, for he feared his daughter would become the target of fortune hunters. He did not even want Olivia to know."

"Know what, for pity's sake!" he cried.

"That when Olivia celebrates her thirtieth birthday she will inherit her maternal grandmother's estate and considerable fortune."

True felt his world falling away, everything he'd

previously imagined about Olivia suddenly lost to his grasp. "And she...she knows nothing of it?"

"Nothing. It was her father's decision that it be kept from her. He didn't want it to cloud her judgment or change her in any way. His daughter was his whole world. He told me once, over a bottle of very good port, that Olivia wanted to marry for love. He worried that her grandmother's money would change things for her, make her prey to men with unworthy intentions. So he decided not to tell her about the inheritance that would come her way."

"Did she know her grandmother was wealthy?"

"It is possible she knew something of it, but Olivia's maternal grandmother had disowned her daughter for marrying against her wishes. Marrying *for love*, was frowned upon by that bitter, rich old lady and she refused to accept the union of her daughter with a humble solicitor. She only saw her grandchild once, just before her daughter's funeral. But when she herself died only a few years later she left her estate, in its entirety, to Olivia."

Slowly True let the pieces settle. Money. Yes, he knew how it changed people. It was more often a curse than a blessing. "But what has this to do with her stepbrother?"

Chalke sniffed nervously and eyed his port decanter. "I came to suspect that my dear friend had, in a moment perhaps of starry-eyed lust, mentioned the inheritance to his second wife, who then informed her son. They were very close— the mother and son. Almost, it must be said, uncomfortably so. At least, that is the impression I formed. And Christopher Chesterfield has something in his manner that I do not trust. He is almost... *too* charming." The old man laughed dourly. "I suppose it takes an ugly, despised creature like me to see through such a disguise." He reached for the port and poured it. "Master Chesterfield has expensive tastes and no real inclination to find employment. I daresay, had he known about Olivia's inheritance before his mother married her father, he would have scooped her up as a bride. But once they were stepsiblings he could not, of course, marry her. Instead, he had to hope she would remain unwed, leaving herself and her future fortune under his purview.

When Olivia married the first time, I hoped she would be safe, but that was over before it had hardly begun. Then the second...well, by then my suspicions about Master Chesterfield had grown. He was always most eager to have his stepsister back again, always making plans for her future, as if he had some right to do so. I did not like it. I tried to warn Westcott, but he could not see through his stepson's artful ways. I was quite sure that Master Chesterfield, knowing all about the inheritance, planned to keep Olivia under his roof, to collect her fortune once it came to her on her thirtieth birthday. Each husband, naturally, had to be disposed of, but the determined woman kept finding another." He chuckled and sipped his port. "After William Monday, I saw I would have to step in and get her away."

"So you sent her to me."

"Who else could keep her safe? I had a feeling she would put you in your place too."

True shook his head. "You're an old scoundrel."

"Yes," he readily agreed, smacking his lips. "And you are a younger one. Which is why we get along so well."

"That, and the constant supply of port I deliver to you." He looked at the old fellow and felt exceedingly grateful that Olivia had been sent to Roscarrock. He couldn't even be angry about the reason being kept from him. After all, he might have looked at her with different eyes, if he knew the truth from the beginning. Yes, her father had been right about that. Olivia would be prey to fortune hunters if her situation was generally known. And she, being a wide-eyed believer in love, might easily be drawn in by an unscrupulous rogue.

"Now, of course," said Chalke, reading his mind in his usual cunning fashion, "you can't marry her, or I'll know you're doing it for the money."

He sniffed. "For your information, I already asked— thinking her a penniless, difficult wench— and she refused me." Ah, it hurt to admit that.

Chalke's eyes became bright. "Has she really? Goodness!"

"And once she has money, she definitely won't want *me*. Bloody woman. I've nothing to give her, nothing to offer."

"True."

"What?" he snapped.

Chalke laughed. "I was agreeing with you."

"Pah!" He crossed his arms angrily.

"That's what becomes of giving yourself such a silly name."

"There is nothing *silly* about it."

"Suit yourself. Nicholas Alejandro Duquesne."

True leaned across the desk again and said with lethal politeness, "You tell another soul that name and I'll never send you another bottle of that very good port you enjoy at my expense."

Chapter Thirty-One

They got as far as Exeter the next day. Again Christopher refused to pay full price for the only available room at the coaching inn, and Olivia was smuggled up the stairs like a hunted woman. Or a prostitute.

She suspected her stepbrother had some experience of cheating inn-keepers and smuggling women into rooms. He was certainly a natural at it.

While he slept in his chair that night, overcome by ale and weariness, Olivia took her chance. Christopher had always underestimated her— and women in general. She went through his pockets for coin and then left the inn to find a man with a private chaise for hire. There was no point to going back toward Roscarrock, she realized, for that is where Christopher would expect her to go. Instead she would travel onward to London.

"I can pay half your fee now," she told the coachman, "and my husband will pay the rest when you get me there safely."

It was a very good thing she wore her tidy, expensive new boots, for the man looked her up and down, no doubt deciding whether she could be trusted to come up with all the money. To her immense relief, she passed inspection.

"I'll get the horses ready, Madam," he said. "You wait here."

Olivia bounced on her heels, rubbed her hands together and looked around nervously, anxious to be on the road again before Christopher woke and found her gone.

It was still dark out, but lanterns by the inn door

cast a bronze light over the front of the building and rush torches along the stable wall lit the fat puddles of the yard, making them glisten and sparkle where fresh rain drops peppered the surface. She blew out a cloud of white breath and watched it evaporate.

She wanted to shout, *Oh, do hurry*! But she held her patience and her composure. This was no time to bring attention to herself.

Several private carriages were being readied for departure across the yard, horses hooves scraping at the cobbles, eager to be off. As she watched them a figure suddenly stumbled out through the door of the inn. Lantern-light shone on his golden hair and then on his white face, as he stared directly at her.

Olivia backed up against the stable wall, her heart racing, blood pumping. Should she make a run for it? Where to? She was trapped.

He seemed to know this too, for he laughed nastily and lurched toward her. Of course he had his umbrella in hand— wasn't likely to leave that behind again, she thought darkly.

But as he moved forward he jerked to an abrupt halt. Something was caught...the point of his umbrella was stuck in the iron grate over the drain, into which rainwater ran from the cobbled yard.

She heard him curse.

The more he struggled, the faster his umbrella became stuck in the grate.

He didn't see the coach and four heading his way and apparently the driver was distracted, or in too much hurry to notice the man wrestling with his umbrella.

Just as Christopher pulled free and stepped out, the horses were upon him.

He was plowed over, first by hooves and then by wheels that bumped and churned his head into the cobbles. It happened in the blink of an eye, the sound a sickening crunch she would probably never forget. Somebody screamed, but it wasn't Olivia.

The crumpled figure lay still under the wheels as the coachman drew his vessel to a halt. Folk came running and a voice called out for a doctor, but anyone could see it was too late. Rivulets of scarlet blood ran between the cobbles and with it went the life of the man under the wheels.

"Poor gentleman was traveling all alone," she heard a woman exclaim. "Such a charming, handsome gentleman too! Such a tragedy!"

Oh yes, indeed it was. She'd suffered several of those in her life. Really, by now she shouldn't even bat an eyelid. Olivia turned, stepped up into the private chaise, and as Mrs. Arthur King, traveled onward to London.

Christopher should have traveled by railway, she mused, for she'd heard it was a safer mode of transportation.

* * * *

True went to Inspector O'Grady.

"I know you have your opinion already set, and I am merely a lucky gambler in your eyes— a bastard who came from nothing— but I can tell you that Olivia Westcott is not to blame for these murders."

"And you'll tell me who is?" O'Grady replied sardonically. "It's been years since she started murdering good men. You didn't know her back then."

"But I've known her since. And I came out of it unscathed."

"That's all well and good. I expect she pulled the lace over your eyes too."

"She doesn't like lace."

The detective looked sorrowful. "I regret, sir, if you've fallen under her spell too. But you're not the first."

Fallen under her spell. Oh, yes.

He was in love with her. Deeply and irrevocably in that painful state of love.

Damn her. And Chalke

Now he knew "love" was possible, which meant he had to pay twenty-five bottles of vintage port to Abraham Chalke. It was a wager they'd had. The only wager True Deverell ever lost.

"You may wish to inquire about a Master Christopher Chesterfield," he told the Inspector.

"The stepbrother?"

"Yes. I believe, if you bother to question a solicitor by the name of Abraham Chalke, he might tell you where you've been going wrong with your investigation. He has some confidential information regarding Chesterfield's possible motive. If he is reluctant to share it, just tell him I sent you. Oh, and tell him he won't have to worry about Mrs. Monday's safety any longer. That's up to me now."

* * * *

The moment he received Storm's rushed message, True set out toward the west country, hoping to find her on his route. She was in trouble and he could not bear to think of what might happen to her in Chesterfield's hands, but he took a sprig of comfort from the wording of her message, "*Give little Arthur my love.*"

Hope shining amid the darkness, like those ribbon snowdrops in her hair.

At a coaching inn somewhere between London and Exeter, he heard a woman complaining about the slush and her new boots. He would know that voice anywhere. And there she was.

True ran across to save her — and her boots— with his new umbrella.

She looked up, startled, pale but for a bruise on her cheek. "Oh, there you are."

"Where else would I be?" *Damn you, woman, I don't know where I am with you. From the first moment I was lost.* But he kept a civil tongue in his head and tried not to stare at her lips.

"Well, you did leave me behind."

He wanted to kiss her, so very badly. In front of the coachman who had just helped her down. "I had business to tend. You knew that."

"But you are supposed to be polite and say goodbye to a person when you're leaving them behind."

"Why should I? I was coming back again, woman."

She shook her head. "You have a lot to learn."

"And you can teach me." True carefully touched a finger below her bruise. "What's this?"

"The past," she said firmly.

Anger flexed its claws within. "Where's Chesterfield?"

Olivia blinked. "I don't know who you mean, dear. Oh, I almost forgot, you owe the coachman half the fee. And," she tugged on his sleeve, "your name is Mr. Arthur King. Don't look at me like that. It's not the first time you've used a false name, is it?"

He had to laugh at her prim expression. "I've missed you."

She smiled. "And I you. Let's hurry home."

"Home?"

"To Roscarrock, of course."

True dare not yet believe that she was staying forever. They'd have to take it one day at a time. He didn't want her to feel trapped.

As he helped her up into his own carriage, she said, "You ought to marry me, you know."

Jumping up behind her and closing the carriage door, he wasn't certain he'd heard her correctly. He fell back into his seat and she immediately moved across to sit beside him, wide eyes regarding him earnestly. "Because you need me."

He thought for a minute, his pulse speeding recklessly. "You turned me down, Olivia the Merciless."

"Well, yes." She reached up and tapped on the carriage roof as a signal to the driver. "But ladies do change their minds occasionally. It's a well known fact."

The horses set off, the carriage bouncing and rumbling back toward Cornwall.

True took her hand and kissed it. "I think we should wait."

She scowled. "For what?"

"For two years. When you turn thirty, I'll ask you again. You may decide by then, that you don't want me."

"Why, for pity's sake?"

"Your situation might be different. You might have met some other man who—"

She leaned over and kissed him.

The carriage went over a bump that bounced her right into his lap. And he held her tightly, keeping her safe, as he always would.

"In the meantime, it will be up to me to court you properly."

She laughed. "Good lord, do you know how?"

"No. You'll have to teach me, Olivia." He kissed her chin and her ear and then made his way down the side of her neck. "I'll be a very good pupil. Very diligent. Very determined."

* * * *

He had not asked her anything more about the bruise, or about Christopher, and for that she was grateful. Instinctively he knew when to let a matter drop, when it would cause more pain to discuss it. Most men would not understand that, but True Deverell was not "most men".

Of course, there were other ways to fill their time on that journey home.

It was January the twelfth in the year 1843. A Thursday and, according to her father's mended watch, it was just after half past three in the afternoon.

He was wearing a very fine coat, butter soft under her fingers and he smelled of spice, tobacco and warm leather. His eyes, mercurial in color and temperament, swept over her like a rain shower, cleansing and magical.

And that was the moment when True Deverell finally said, "I love you."

* * * *

Two Months later...

"My love, we're never going to finish your memoirs, if this is how things continue," she muttered as they lay together by the fire in his library, both naked and wrapped in a fleece-lined blanket. "We have written precisely six sentences tonight."

But True was too busy counting the colors in her hair, until, in his corner vision he spied her hand, on the end of that long, elegant arm, crawling out of the fleece in search of her father's watch.Again.

He reached over and caught her fingers, bringing them to his lips. "I'm beginning to wish I never got that damn thing fixed for you. What was I thinking?"

She chuckled. "It's a good thing you did, for that was when I knew for sure that I was in love with you, sir."

"Sir? Back to that again are we?"

"It seems only proper. I am your employee still. Since you refuse to marry me yet."

He licked her palm. "There's no haste, Olivia sweetheart. I want you to be sure. But I'm not going anywhere. I know what I want."

She moved her head against the fleece to look up at him. "Are you afraid I want you for your money?"

True shook his head.

"Well, I *am* after your money," she said with a smile. "I don't want to be poor. I'm not a fool.'"

He grinned. "Mercenary. So much for love."

"I love you too, of course. How could I not? You are wickedly irresistible."

As he looked down at his very special secretary, True realized she was the most beautiful woman he had ever known. She was utterly unaware of it, and a good thing too. Wouldn't want her getting too bold and taking advantage of his hapless state. But at that moment he simply wanted to show her how much he loved her, and thus he proceeded to do so, kissing his way slowly down her body.

"We have all the time in the world to finish my story. All the time in the world."

Because he had a great deal more of life yet to live after all.

ABOUT THE AUTHOR

Jayne Fresina sprouted up in England, the youngest in a family of four daughters. Entertained by her father's colorful tales of growing up in the countryside, and surrounded by opinionated sisters - all with far more exciting lives than hers - she's always had inspiration for her beleaguered heroes and unstoppable heroines.

Website at:www.jaynefresina.com